# A Man After God's Own Heart

## By Dan Cater

PRESS

Nancy,

Psalm 46:10
"Be still, and know
that I am God."

Rest in His undying, unchanging
love for you!

Happy reading,

Dan Carter

*This book is dedicated to my mother, the real Joyce.*
*You never gave up on me.*

*December 12<sup>th</sup>, 2003-*
   *If I could write the story of my life*
   *And have it all come true,*
   *I'd think about it for a little while*
   *Then hand the pen to You.*

# 1.

I am going to tell you a story that you probably aren't going to believe. Whether or not you believe that it actually happened isn't up to me. What's up to me is that the story is told.

This is a story about my brother. His full name is David Jeremiah Sullah, but everybody calls him Dave. I say "calls" as if he were still alive; although Dave has passed on, he is always on my mind. At times I wish that he was here, but then I remember that Dave is in a much better place...I just really miss my little brother.

*June 2ⁿᵈ, 2002-*
*We in Christ carry within ourselves a large task to*
*fulfill God's will that is, in retrospect to the whole, a very*
*small piece of the puzzle; but a very, very important one,*
*nonetheless.*

# 2.

When I was seven years old, our father left us. Dave was only five at the time, and he didn't really know what was happening. Mom explained to us that Dad had to leave for a while, but that he would visit us every weekend. After about two weeks, though, Dad stopped coming over. Dave was heartbroken. I, on the other hand, was glad to never see the man again. Of course I missed having a father; but I sure didn't miss *him*. You see, I was old enough to notice the bruises on Mom's face and on her arms. I was also old enough to know that she was covering for Dad when she said that she fell, or that she just banged her arm on the counter.

After Dad disappeared, Dave took out everything on Mom. He blamed her for the fact that Dad had left, and seemingly every time that they got in an argument, Dave would shout, "I hate you! I'm going to live with Dad!"

I stuck up for Mom whenever they got in these arguments, which lasted pretty much from when Dave was seven all the way up to his late teens. You see, Mom ran a pretty tight ship - we weren't allowed to stay out late, to hang out with people that Mom didn't approve of, or to leave the house without permission. Dave, being the rebel that he was, always seemed to want to do the things that he knew weren't allowed.

One time, when Dave was fourteen, he asked Mom if he could go to a sleepover at a friend's house. I had just gotten home from baseball practice, and as I opened the front door, I heard Dave yelling through his tears…"You never let me do *anything*! I *hate* you!"

I slammed the door shut and tossed my cleats down , as I stepped into the small kitchen where my brother and Mom were. Dave was standing rigid as a pole right next to Mom, with his fists clenched and tears streaming down his face. Mom was leaning over the kitchen counter by a sink full of dirty dishes, seemingly staring off into space with a sad look on her face. She looked exhausted; worn out…she looked twenty years older than she really was.

"What's going on?" I asked harshly, as I furrowed my eyebrows down at Dave.

I went to step in-between them and he exclaimed, "This has nothing to do with you! Why do you always get in the way? You're not my father!"

Before I could respond, Dave ran off to his room and slammed the door, hard enough to rattle the family photographs that hung up in the living room.

I put my hand on Mom's shoulder and said, "Are you okay?"

She shook her head and took off her glasses. I could tell that she was trying to keep it all in; trying to be strong. But after a moment, she pulled me tightly to her and wept as we hugged. Her body was shaking as she said through her sobs, "I can't take it, Jonny! I just can't take it anymore!"

"What'd he say?" I asked through clenched teeth, staring down the hall where Dave's room was.

Mom was too hysterical to answer at first. I took her to the dining room and we sat down at the table. She wiped her face with some tissue, blew her nose, and patted down her unruly curly blonde hair.

"What'd he say?" I repeated after Mom had gained some composure.

"Oh, he wants to go to his friend's house to spend the night - that boy, Eric. I know his parents, and they don't supervise their kids."

Muffled pounding from Dave's room began to resound through the walls of our small ranch house. He was throwing his typical temper tantrum. I bit my lower lip and started to get up but Mom stopped me, saying, "Just leave him alone."

"Why do you let him do this to you?" I asked her, with bitterness in my voice. "Why don't you just let him do whatever he wants and get him out of your hair?"

Mom had been staring at the oak dining table with a melancholy look on her face; but after I said that, she quickly looked right into my eyes and without hesitation responded, "Because I love him, Jonny!"

*February 12th, 2001-*
   *He calls me "David." When He speaks to me with love, He calls me David. When He is rebuking me, He calls me David. To love is to rebuke; He always calls me David.*

# 3.

A few days after Dave turned sixteen, I told him that Dad had physically abused Mom. Mom didn't want to tell him, but I was sick of Dave always sticking up for the guy.

It was on a sunny summer afternoon, a few weeks before I would go off to college. Dave and I were outside tossing the football around in the backyard…

"Go deep!" Dave yelled with a large smile on his face. He slapped the pigskin with his hand, and waited until I was far enough away, so that he could show me how far he could throw.

I ran until I was almost in the neighbor's yard, which was about fifty yards away from where Dave was. When he saw that I had stopped, and probably figured that I thought there was no way that he could throw the ball that far, Dave launched the ball high into the sky. I had to run a few steps up, but still, it was a very good throw for someone his age.

"Let's see if *you* can throw it that far!" Dave cheerfully called out.

I couldn't let my little brother show me up. With a grin on my face I yelled, "You'd better back up!"

"Yeah, right!" Dave hollered back.

I reached back and tossed the ball as hard as I could. It actually hurt my arm a little bit. The football flew through the air, and Dave caught it almost exactly where he stood.

"Alright," I said as I jogged towards my brother. "I'm tired. We'll play again later."

"Aw, what are you, an old man or something?" Dave said with a smirk on his face. He flipped the ball in the air a few times and then sat down next to me on the soft green grass.

"So, are you excited about college?" he asked.

"Sure," I responded with a nod. "It's gonna be fun."

Dave started to pick bits of grass from the ground and casually tossed them into a slight breeze that was blowing. His face became somber as he looked at me and said, "It's gonna suck not having you around."

"You'll get over it." I said, giving Dave a little punch on his shoulder.

"No, I'm serious. When you leave, it's just gonna be me and Mom."

"So?" I asked, squinting my eyes a little. "What's so bad about that?"

Dave sighed and lay down on his back. He stared straight up into the sky as he said, "I love Mom. You know that, right?"

"Yeah." I answered apprehensively, unsure of where Dave was going with this.

Dave sighed deeply again, then said, "Well, don't you wish that she never divorced Dad? I mean, you're the only father figure that I've got...and now you're leaving. I know that Ma and Dad had problems, but why did she have to just kick him out like that?"

Dave lay still on the grass with his hands folded on his stomach, waiting for a response.

I pulled my knees up to my chest and wrapped my arms around them. After thinking about what I should say, I decided that Dave needed to know the truth. I looked right at him, trying to make eye contact, but he just stared at the clouds overhead.

"Mom never told you this, but I'm going to." I paused for a moment, knowing that just saying it would bring tears to my eyes. "Dad used to beat Mom."

My prediction proved true. Tears began to brew in my eyes, and I had to swallow a large lump in my throat before going on.

"I guess you weren't old enough to realize it. She never told me, but I knew. Just to be sure, one day I asked her . I said something like, 'Tell me the truth, Mom: Did Dad used to hit you?' I guess she never thought that I had known that, because she looked at me with, like, a look of shock on her face. She said, 'How did you know that?' I told her that I remembered seeing bruises on her. She said that he had, and asked me if you knew about it. I told her no, I didn't think so, and she said that it was probably best that you didn't know."

Dave hadn't moved an inch while I was speaking, but after I had finished, he sat up and looked at me with a grim expression on his face.

"What a freakin' prick!" Dave said slowly, certainly shocked by this. "Dad...hit Mom? Are you sure?"

I nodded my head as Dave sat Indian-style with his mouth half opened. He cocked his head to the side, obviously stunned.

"She...she never told me that." A tear slowly trickled down Dave's cheeks, and I had to look away; otherwise, I was sure to break out in tears.

"I guess she was trying to protect you," I said in a weak voice. I didn't want to cry in front of my brother. For some reason, I thought that it would be "unmanly."

Dave got up and began walking towards the house.

"Where are you going?" I asked as I stood up.

"I'll be right back- if Mom asks, tell her I went to the store."

He ran inside and got the keys to his Ford Escort that I had handed down to him for his birthday. I wouldn't be needing a car for college, so Mom and I thought that it would be good to let him have it.

Dave quickly hopped into the rusty old Ford and screeched out of the driveway. After I saw the way he was driving, I became concerned for his safety. I wasn't sure if he had flipped his lid or not.

I waited outside until he came back, which was only a few minutes later. I was still in the back lawn, and I started to walk towards the Escort. The driver's side door flew open, and Dave stepped out. He had in his hands a bunch of long stemmed purple tulips - Mom's favorite. Dave looked at me and nodded, then shut the door and walked into the house. As soon as he was inside, I fell on my knees and sobbed like a little child. I was so proud of my brother!

We had a good talk that night before we went to sleep. I told Dave that Mom loves him, and that he better start treating her right, and listening to what she said. He said, "I know. You're right. You're absolutely right; I'll try my best."

*October 14th, 2003-*
*The night is so quiet that I can't even hear the crickets chirping. The sky is so black that the stars give off no light. Time stands still, yet I see it speeding away. Why am I here? What am I to You? What are Your plans for me? For my job? For my talents? For my love life? For my faith in You? When will I hear Your voice? When will You appear to me? When will You quiet my shouts, and set my soul at ease? How can I follow You when I can't see how You lead? I know these things will pass- but when, Lord? I know that You see their end, and that time for You is of no importance - but for me it is! I know Your thoughts are higher than mine, so how will I ever know them? How can I follow Your ways? When will I be able to say with no doubt that "This is what the Lord wants," and "This is what God has said to me"?*

The righteous cry out, and the Lord hears them; He delivers them from all their troubles.
-Psalm 34:17

*Hear me, Lord; as undeserving as I am, yet I trust in Your promises to love me, to lead me, to never leave me.*

I call on the Lord in my distress, and He answers me.
-Psalm 120:1

*When, Lord? When will I hear Your voice? Don't I come to You for answers? Don't I call on You for help? I pray, Lord: show Yourself to me and in me so that my distress turns to praise!*

Why are you downcast, O my soul? Why so disturbed within me? Put your hope in God, for I will yet praise him, my Savior and my God.

-Psalm 42:5

Amen.

# 4.

Dave loved the outdoors. When we were little kids, Mom used to take us camping along with our Aunt Sheila to Lakeside Park. Lakeside is a fairly large camping ground, nestled snugly in the woods in the town of Oeshida, a fifteen-minute drive from home.

We went there every summer for ten years. We fished in the lake, rode our bikes around the trails, played table tennis, and roasted marshmallows at night. Now that Dave is gone, I truly cherish these memories as if they were gold. One summer in particular has a very special place in my heart that I will never forget...

We had just finished putting up the tents in our campsite. Mom's and Aunt Sheila's to the right of the fire pit that was in the center of our site, and a smaller tent for Dave and I on the left.

"I'm going for a ride!" Dave shouted out as he hopped on his mountain bike and pedaled out onto the paved road.

Mom popped her head out of the tent and yelled,

"You keep your helmet on, Davey! And watch out for cars!"

"I know!" Dave responded, seemingly annoyed about Mom's concern.

Dave always wanted to do things without anybody's help. He would get irritated when someone would try to tell him how to do something. Even something simple like Mom saying 'Watch out for cars' would cause Dave to get angry. His attitude was 'I can do it by myself- leave me alone.'

Dave was only twelve years old at the time, so Mom walked up to me as I was laying out my sleeping bag in the tent and said, "Dave just went out on his bike. I'd like it if you followed him, just to be sure that he's safe."

I rolled my eyes and sighed. I was always checking up on my brother in one way or another. Whether it was at school or at home, it seemed like my life was centered on following Dave wherever he went.

"Do I have to?" I pleaded to Mom. "I want to go down to the Rec. Hall and play horseshoes."

"You can do that later," Mom said sternly. "Besides, you can't play horseshoes by yourself. Find your brother and you can play with him."

Mom disappeared from the tent, and I quickly followed after her.

"I was supposed to meet Ben there at two o'clock!" I cried out to Mom as she walked over to the car. Ben was a good friend of mine who was also at Lakeside that week. We had planned earlier to meet up at the Recreation Hall and spend the day together.

Mom turned around with her hands on her hips - a sure sign that she had had enough. She was wearing a purple tank top with flowers sewed in the middle, a shirt that Dave and I had gotten her for Easter that year. I remember that because, now that I'm older, I realize how ridiculous that shirt looked. We had bought it for probably five dollars, and it showed. There were loose strings hanging down almost anywhere you looked, one of the flowers had almost completely fallen off, leaving little strands of white string showing, and the shirt was probably two sizes too big for her. But Mom wore that shirt because Dave and I had given it to her. That's all that she cared about.

"I said, go and find your brother."

Aunt Sheila came out from the tent with a smile on her face. She was Mom's younger sister of five years; Dave and I would think of her later as our "cool" aunt. She came up to me, while putting her long brown hair into a ponytail and said, "Oh, go and get your brother, Jon! Your mother and I will finish setting everything up so that when you get back we can roast some marshmallows and tell some ghost stories!" Her eyes opened wide with anticipation as she said this. I really think that she was just as excited about marshmallows and fires and ghost stories as I was.

"Okay," I said with a grin. I couldn't help but smile along with Aunt Sheila. It was contagious.

I got my bike from behind the tent and walked it out to the road.

"I love you!" Mom called out as she watched me put on my helmet and climb on the bike.

"I love you." I answered her, loud enough for her to hear, but still pretty quiet. I was at that age where it wasn't cool to proclaim your love for anything; especially your mother. If any boys happened to be around, they would be sure to cry out, "Momma's boy!" as I rode by.

As I pedaled away, I heard Aunt Sheila cry out in a painfully loud, mocking voice, "I love you, Jonathon Sullah! Come back and give Momma a kiss!"

I lifted my butt from the seat and pedaled away as fast as I could.

Although Dave was nowhere in sight, I knew where he would be. The year before we had found a secluded clearing in the woods by the lake. There was a fallen tree that we had rested against after swimming. As we were leaning against the tree, two deer came out from the woods and strolled towards the lake. Dave's eyes lit up and he said, "Look! Jon, do you see that? Look at them deer!"

The deer drank some water, and again Dave exclaimed, "They're drinking from the lake! Isn't that cool?"

I didn't share Dave's enthusiasm. To me, it was a real simple thing. But Dave loved it. Every day after that until we left, Dave went back to that spot in hopes of seeing the deer again.

I rode along the loop and out onto the main road of the campground which led out towards the lake. I passed by the Rec. Hall and thought about forgetting about Dave and going to see Ben. I stopped pedaling and sighed as I saw all the kids playing on the playground. I was so mad at my brother for making me miss my time with Ben, and I was determined to let him know.

Now that I had seen all the kids having fun, I was more perturbed than ever at Dave. I quickly pedaled towards the lake, in hopes of finding him promptly and making him come to the Rec. Hall with me.

I reached the lake, got off my bike, and walked it. There was no path there, only grass, so it made riding a bike difficult. The spot where I was sure I would find Dave was about a hundred yards away, and I hastily made my way towards it.

I walked alongside the woods until I came to the small clearing. Sure enough, I saw Dave sitting on the collapsed tree; but something was wrong. He had his head bowed, and his shoulders were quivering. I let my bike fall on its side as I unbuckled my helmet and hurried over to him.

Dave saw me coming and turned his back to me. By now, it was obvious that he was crying.

"Dave!" I said worriedly as I went around the tree and looked at him. "What's wrong? What happened?"

Dave was sobbing very softly. He looked up at me with a red face full of tears.

"I...I had an accident," he said shamefacedly.

At first I didn't know what he was talking about. I glanced over at his bike which was on its kickstand next to the tree, and saw that it wasn't banged up.

"Are you hurt?" I asked.

"No," Dave responded as he wiped some snot from his nose. "Not that kind of accident!"

Then I saw what he meant. There was orangish brown excrement sticking to Dave's legs and on his socks.

"Oh!" I exclaimed, not really knowing what to say. I felt so bad for him. He was so humiliated that he couldn't even look at me.

I cleared my throat and said, "It's okay, Dave. Let's go back to camp and you can change into some different clothes. Then we'll go play at the Rec. Hall and you'll forget all about it."

"No way!" Dave cried out. "There's no way I'm going back! Aunt Sheila will laugh at me and tell everybody what happened!"

She would have, too. Not that Aunt Sheila was mean or anything, but she would have never let Dave live that one down.

"Okay," I said, trying to think about what to do. I folded my arms across my chest and tapped my foot on the soft ground. All of a sudden it came to me.

"I've got it! I'll go back to camp and tell Mom that we're going swimming. I'll grab our trunks and towels, then bring them back here. You can take the shorts and socks that you have on now and wash them out in the lake. How about that?"

Dave stopped crying and looked at me.

"Yeah," he said. "That'd be good."

"Alright," I said with a smile. "Don't worry, I'll be right back."

I stepped out of the clearing and picked up my bike. As I was walking away, Dave feebly called out, "Hey, Jon?"

I turned around and replied, "Yeah?"

"You...you sure that you ain't gonna say anything?"

I grinned at Dave and answered, "I'm sure."

"You promise?"

"I promise."

After a slight pause he softly said, "Thanks."

Just before I was out of earshot, Dave screamed out, "Hey, Jon! Don't forget some underwear!"

With a huge smile on my face, I yelled back, "I won't!"

Seeing my brother sitting helplessly on that tree made me love him more than I ever had before. I was proud to be able to help him, and proud that I had kept my promise to him and never told anyone about the incident. (Until now, that is!) You don't mind, do you Dave? I didn't think so.

*September 12ᵗʰ 2002-*
*I see my Jesus; the only One Who loves me.*
*I see my sins adding scars to His body.*
*I see me whipping Him, as my soul cries out:*
*'Stop! Stop it!!'*
*But I do not listen.*
*I continue to whip He Who loves me.*

# 5.

Dave got into drugs real bad when he turned sixteen. It's difficult for me to remember those years. When I came home from college for holidays and breaks, it was like someone had taken over my brother's body.

Dave would go through these terrible mood swings. One minute he would be smiling and upbeat, then all of a sudden he'd act nasty and say mean things.

Late one night when I was a freshman in college, Mom called me. I was studying for an English exam when my phone rang. As soon as I heard Mom's voice, I knew that something was terribly wrong…

"Hello?" I said, wondering who would be calling me this late.

"Jonny…"

I immediately stood up from my bed. Mom was crying profusely on the other end, so hard that it seemed like she couldn't breathe.

"Mom, what's wrong?" I asked, terrified. All that I could think was that *someone had died. I stood frozen in my room, eyes bulging, waiting for her response.*

Intense sobbing, though, was all that I heard.

"Mom, you're scaring me." I said anxiously. "What's going on?"

"Davey...oh, my little boy! Dave's missing! No one knows where he went!" Mom had to catch her breath, and then after blowing her nose, she continued.

"He went to work today, and, and I went there to get some groceries, but he wasn't there."

More heart-wrenching sobs came through the phone before she could go on.

"So I waited, and I waited, and I got so mad...Then finally I saw him pull up, and I rushed over to his car, and he had two of his friends in there, and...and they were all smoking pot! So his friends saw me, and they got out of Davey's car and walked away."

By now Mom had stopped crying, but her voice was so weak and shaky. I was still standing, gritting my teeth, infuriated with Dave. I was thinking, 'If only he could hear her! If only he knew how much pain he causes Mom! Then maybe he'd stop!'

"I didn't know what to say to him; I mean, I suspected that he was on drugs, but I didn't know for sure! So I just said that he was grounded, and as soon as he got home I was taking away his car keys, and he was going to rehab."

"You know what he said to me, Jonny?"

"What?" I asked through tightly clinched teeth; I knew that this was going to be bad.

Mom started crying softly again as she said, "He…he said, 'I'm never coming home. Take a good look. This is the last time that you'll see me.' "

Mom stopped crying again, and said real quietly, "Then he looked at me with this…this mean look on his face and he said, 'I hate you. I've always hated you!' "

At this, Mom broke down into uncontrollable wailing. I bit down on my bottom lip so hard that I soon tasted blood.

"That's not true, and you know it," I said after a moment, with tears of my own trickling down my face.

"What happened to my little boy?" Mom cried through the telephone. "Lord God, protect my child!"

"Where is he now?" I asked, ready to go knock some serious sense into him.

Mom took a deep breath, and responded in a calm tone, "I don't know where he is, Jonny. His boss from the grocery store called me about an hour ago. He said that Dave apparently stole almost a hundred dollars from his cash drawer and disappeared. He never came back from his bathroom break, so they went out to the parking lot, and his car wasn't there, and…Jon, I just don't know what to do! I've called all of his friends that I know about, I've driven all around town…"

"I'm coming home," I said, sitting back down on my bed and putting my sneakers on.

"No, you can't come home. That's not why I called you. Your Aunt Sheila is on her way over. You stay there."

"Mom," I said with conviction, "I'm coming home."

"You don't have a car, Jonny. Besides, you can't miss all your classes."

"I'll borrow my friend's car. And I only have one class tomorrow. I'll e-mail my professor and tell him that I have a family emergency."

Mom sighed and said, "You're a good boy, Jon. If you can get a car, just make sure that you drive safely. Don't be speeding or anything."

"Okay, Mom. I love you. Don't worry about Dave, we'll find him."

"I love you, too."

I lived in a suite with two other guys. As I opened my door, I saw them both sitting on the couch in the living room that we all shared. They were playing Madden on the big screen television that my roommate, Eric, had brought from home.

"Eric," I said while throwing on my winter coat. "I need to go home real quick. Can I borrow your car?"

They paused the game and turned their heads towards me. Eric, a tall, skinny redhead with some pretty bad acne, raised his eyebrows and said, "Is everything alright?"

"No, it's not," I answered him. "My brother robbed a store, and my mother is freaking out. I really need to borrow your car."

"Geez, he robbed a store? What, with a gun or something?" Larry, my other roommate, asked.

"I'll tell you about it later, Lar. How 'bout it, Eric? Can you help me out?"

"Sure," Eric said, reaching into his jeans pocket. "Just be careful, okay?"

I nodded as he threw the keys at me.

"Thanks," I said, and turned towards the door.

"When're you gonna be back?" Eric called out just as I twisted the knob.

I turned around and answered him, "As soon as I find my brother."

*October 21*<sup>st</sup>*, 2000-*
    *God's love:*
    *It's like a child falling down and skinning his knee. He*
    *cries in pain and shouts for his mother. The mother*
    *feels deep sorrow for her child, and wants to comfort*
    *him. Even though the mother didn't cause her child to*
    *fall; he did that on his own. But still, she falls down at*
    *his side and holds him in her arms. The boy's whim-*
    *pering subsides when he is in the arms of someone who*
    *loves him.*

# 6.

November 1<sup>st</sup>, 1998; the day that Dave came so close to death...

I jumped into Eric's Dodge Neon and started it up. Usually it would only take me about twenty minutes to drive home from college, but it was "blizzarding up a storm" outside, as my grandfather would say.

I had to wait for a little while to let the car warm up. As I shivered in the cold, I closed my eyes and said a quick prayer.

By the time that I had opened my eyes, the car was defrosted and warm. I backed it out and headed home.

The ride back to Auburn, Pennsylvania was probably the longest forty minutes of my life. I didn't dare drive over thirty miles an hour because of the snow and because of the fact that I was driving a borrowed car. If it had been my car, I suppose that I wouldn't have cared about the snow - I would have driven sixty miles an hour; and probably into a ditch.

The initial shock that I had received upon hearing about Dave had vanished, and now all that was left was fear. I couldn't help but imagine the worst. I let it sink into my mind and have its way with me. I began thinking awful things like,

'You will never see your brother again...'

And,

'You think that you know Dave? He is evil, beyond help! Why care for him? What kind of person does these things to his family? Why waste your time on him?'

These thoughts were terrifying me. Along with that, the snow was coming down so fast that I could hardly see. It felt like any moment now I was going to lose it, crash into a tree, and then Mom would have two missing sons.

Just then, as my hands were shaking on the steering wheel and my face was tense in trepidation, a warm, peaceful feeling came into my heart. I took a deep breath as my hands relaxed on the wheel, and a verse from the Bible literally resounded through my head:

"Whatever is true, whatever is noble, whatever is right, whatever is pure, whatever is lovely, whatever is admirable-if anything is excellent or praiseworthy- think about such things."

I drove the rest of the way home repeating the verse over and over in my mind.

At about midnight, I pulled into our driveway. Aunt Sheila's blue Cavalier was already there.

I walked up the wooden steps and opened the front door. Stamping the snow from my sneakers, I called out, "Hello? Mom?"

But the house seemed empty. I walked through the kitchen and down the hallway, where Mom's room was. The light was on, but there was nobody there.

"Hello?"

I went back down the narrow hallway, wondering where Mom and Aunt Sheila were. After checking all the rooms, I went back to the front of the house, where the door leading downstairs was. Walking down the stairs, I opened another door that led into the basement, where Dave's room was.

I opened Dave's door and found Mom and Aunt Sheila. They were kneeling by Dave's bed with their heads bowed.

Aunt Sheila was praying out loud, and she kept her eyes closed and continued praying, although I was certain that she had heard me come into the room.

Mom looked up with a face stained with tears. She motioned for me to come over, and I knelt down beside her, as she put her arm around me and wept.

Aunt Sheila was speaking in a cool, calm manner. I guess that she had to be that way, since Mom was so frantic.

"Lord God, You know where Dave is. You see him, even though we can't. Lead him home, Father God. Lead him safely home to us. Keep evil far away from him, Lord; protect Your child throughout the night. We trust in You, Lord."

"Yes, Lord!" Mom weakly affirmed through her tears.

"We trust You to watch over Dave. We trust that You will guide him back into our arms. Let him know, Heavenly Father, that he will be accepted back with love, no matter what he has done. Give to Dave Your love, Father. Guide him back into Your arms. Sovereign Lord, You have everything under control. May Your peace fill Joyce's heart. The peace that passes all understanding, Lord Jesus; let it fall upon my sister."

We sat in silence for a minute, eyes closed and heads bowed. Then Mom choked out some words in an obviously strained voice, "Lord Jesus...You said that when two or more gather in Your Name, there You are. Lord, I know that You are here. I feel Your presence, and that is all that is sustaining me right now. Father..."

Mom began crying so hard that she shook, and I thought that she wouldn't be able to go on. I didn't realize, though, that these tears were tears of joy.

"Father, thank You! Thank you for being here with me, Lord! Thank you for bringing me Sheila and Jonny! Lord, bring me back my son! Bring Davey home! Let him feel Your love, and he will never walk away again!"

I couldn't hold it in any longer, and I wasn't peeking, but I don't think that Aunt Sheila could, either. I hugged Mom so tight and burst out in tears. Aunt Sheila wrapped her arms around us both, and the three of us stayed like that almost throughout the whole night.

*May 16th, 2002-*
*What evil that lurks around at night,*
*No longer do I have of any fright,*
*Nor add my sins to Satan's delight,*
*But rather, walk within the light.*
*There where Beauty came into sight,*
*And I fought for Her with all my might,*
*And saw that 'Beauty is Truth' is right,*
*And found that Truth is worth the fight.*

# 7.

I woke up upstairs on the couch after a night of tossing and turning. I was lucky if I got half an hour of sleep.

Mom and Aunt Sheila were already up. I'm not sure if they had even gone to sleep at all...

I smelled coffee brewing, so I got up and walked into the kitchen. As I was pouring myself a cup, Aunt Sheila came into the adjacent dining room. Her long brown hair was in complete disarray, as if she had just been in a hurricane.

"Good morning, Jon," she said with a half-hearted smile.

"Morning," I replied with a yawn.

"Did ya get any sleep last night?"

"A little," I said as I took a sip from the coffee. "Where's Mom?"

"She's in the shower. We're going to go to Dave's school in a few minutes. Do you want to come along?"

"Sure," I said, nodding my head. "But I doubt that Dave'll be there."

It was six in the morning, and if I remembered correctly, school began at six-thirty. Auburn High School was a very small school, and rumors ran rampant within. I knew that everybody there would be talking about Dave.

"You think someone at school knows where Dave is?" I asked as I sat down with my aunt at the dining room table.

"I sure hope so," she said, shaking her head. "Otherwise, I don't know how we'll be able to find your brother."

Aunt Sheila squinted her eyes at me and asked, "Do you know any of Dave's friends?"

"Yeah," I said. "I know a few that were on our baseball team."

"Good," she said. "Maybe you should go in and talk with them. They'll probably feel okay telling you where Dave is, as compared to your mother and I. Just look at me!" she said with a smile. "I look like a train wreck! People'll think I'm a zombie or something!"

"Oh, you look fine!" I said, returning her smile. "But yeah, I'll go in and talk with some kids. They'll tell me what they know."

A little while later, Mom came out of the shower. Her skin was pale white, her eyes wide opened, mixed with a look of fear and hope. She had on a purple turtleneck sweater, the one that Dave had given her last year for her birthday.

We climbed into Aunt Sheila's Cavalier and headed toward the school. It had stopped snowing, but the temperature outside had fallen to about twenty degrees. During the ten minute ride, Mom told me to make sure that I found out where Dave was. She said that someone there had to know.

As we pulled into the school's parking lot, Mom turned around to me and said,

"Be persistent, Jonny. As soon as you find out where Dave is, come right back, okay?"

"Okay, Mom." I gave her a reassuring smile and added, "Don't worry. I love you."

"I love you, too."

I stepped out of the warm car and into the freezing cold. The busses were just arriving and dropping the students off. I walked briskly past them and went into the foyer of Auburn High. There I stood, blowing warm air into my hands, waiting for a familiar face to walk by.

Mobs of kids were moving about all around me. I saw some laughing, some were whispering into each other's ears, some smiled at me as they passed by, and some didn't even notice that I was there.

I began to notice that there were hardly any "older" kids around. I hadn't recognized one single face so far.

Finally, Paul Sebastian, a kid that I had played baseball with, came through the front doors with two pretty girls. I took a couple of steps towards him and said, "Hey, Paul."

Paul took off his black wool hat and nodded at me. He looked at the two girls and said, "I'll meet you in Homeroom."

The girls walked away, and I went with Paul over to a corner.

"What's up, Jon?" Paul said. The look in his eyes told me that he knew why I was there.

"My brother's missing, Paul," I said, cutting right to the chase. "You know anything about that?"

Paul set his backpack on the carpeted floor and nodded.

"Yeah, I do. He called me last night, looking for a place to stay."

"He did?" My eyes lit up in anticipation. "So what'd you say?"

Paul shrugged his shoulders and responded, "This was like, at almost midnight. My parents were sleeping, and I was just going to bed. I asked him what the hell was going on, and he told that he was in some trouble and needed some place to spend the night. He, uh..."

Paul looked hesitantly into my eyes, and I said, "Just tell me, man."

"Your brother must've been tripping, like, hard core."

"Why do you say that?" I asked, as a warm uneasiness spread throughout my stomach.

"Well, I told him that I couldn't really help him out, and he said that he had some acid. He told me that he'd give me some if he could come over. But I had to tell him no. My parents would've freaked out on me, that's for sure. Dave was, well...I don't know, he was just actin' really weird. He was definitely tripping."

"Where was he calling from?" I asked, trying to stay as calm as possible while feeling terribly despondent.

"I don't know," Paul said, furrowing his eyebrows. "Sorry, man."

I sighed and crossed my arms over my chest.

"So you have no idea where my brother is?"

I stared Paul down, wondering if he would hold any information from me. He slowly shook his head, then raised his eyebrows and said, "Well, he did ask me for Brian's number. Maybe he knows."

"Brian who?"

"Brian Dollenbeck. You probably don't know him."

"Is he here yet?" I asked, ready to go meet the kid.

"Naw," Paul responded with a grin. "Brian doesn't go to school. He dropped out last year."

"Great," I said in frustration. I thought for a second, then said, "Where does this kid live?"

I ran out to Aunt Sheila's car and hopped in the back seat. She and Mom both turned around towards me as Mom asked, "Where's Davey?"

"I think I know," I replied with optimism. "One of his friends told me that he's probably at this Brian kid's house. It's just a block away, on Lincoln Street."

Mom looked at Aunt Sheila with expectation and said, "Let's go."

We came to the two-story, light blue house that Paul had described to me and pulled into the short driveway. Dave's Escort was the lone car parked in front of the house.

All three of us jumped out of the car at the same time and ran up to the door. Mom tried to open it, but it was locked. She pounded on the door with tightly clenched fists, as Aunt Sheila repeatedly rang the doorbell.

After almost a minute, the door opened. A very sleepy-looking, plump teenager with short, curly black hair glared at us and said, "What the hell do you want?"

"Where's Dave?" Mom asked sharply.

"Who the hell are you?"

"We're his family, young man," Aunt Sheila answered sternly. "Dave's in trouble, and if you don't want the cops after you, too, you better go get him."

Brian huffed at Aunt Sheila and turned his back on us. He took a few steps into the house and yelled, "Dave! Hey, Dave!"

Mom opened the door and let herself in, as Aunt Sheila and I followed along. Brian turned towards us and exclaimed, "Hey! No one said that you could come in here!"

I couldn't stand the way this disrespectful kid was talking to them, and I was already upset and sleep deprived. Needless to say, Brian was asking for it. I marched right up to him, got right in his face and said, "My mother is looking for her son!" I took a deep breath through gritted teeth, seriously wanting to knock this kid in the jaw. "Don't talk to her like that," I said, pointing my finger right in front of Brian's eye. "Now, where's Dave?"

"Damn, man! Calm down!" Brian said as he backed away. "I just freakin' woke up! He's on the couch."

We followed Brian into a spacious, nicely furnished room with a large entertainment center. There was a leather wraparound couch with blankets tossed on the floor - but no Dave.

"Where is he?" Mom asked, darting around the room, as if Dave had concealed himself in a dark corner.

"I don't know!" Brian answered, in obvious confusion. "He was here when I went to bed. Maybe he left already."

"No, his car is still in the driveway," Aunt Sheila said, staring down Brian. "Did he run off when he heard the pounding at the door?"

"I don't know! I was sleeping upstairs; Dave was on the couch last time I saw."

Mom started going all about the house, from room to room, shouting, "David! Dave, where are you?!"

Brian rubbed his eyes and pleaded, "Aw; man! Can you please ask her to be quiet?"

I gave him an icy glare and shook my head 'no'.

"Where else would he be?" Aunt Sheila asked Brian. "Where could he have gone?"

"I have no freakin' clue, okay? I don't know."

My attention was drawn to the sliding glass doors next to the entertainment center. As I walked towards them, I saw footprints in the thick snow that coated the ground outside.

*August 8<sup>th</sup>, 2002-*

*Will I pass on tonight? I don't know, God knows. Will I
live to be a hundred? I don't know, God knows. God knows,
and He knows that I trust in Him.*

# 8.

I slid the door open as the cold winter air came upon me.
I stepped out into the ankle deep snow and saw that the
footprints led out to some woods not far from the house. I
noticed then that the footprints were just that; prints made
with bare feet, not shoes.

I ran past Brian's small back lawn and into some dense
foliage. From there on in, I couldn't see any more footprints.
I called out, "Dave? Dave, where are you?"

I frantically looked around, while inching my way
through the trees. As I was about twenty yards in, I saw a
horrible sight(one that I have not yet been able to forget).
There was a large pile of snow by a tall oak tree. Underneath
it was Dave. His feet, which were purplish-black, stuck out
from one end. His head was laid to the side, and his face was
gray. Dave's eyes were closed. I was sure that he was dead.

"Dave!" I cried out, as I frantically began shoveling
away the snow with my hands. I tried to pick him up, but he
was too heavy.

"MOM!" I screamed with tears in my eyes. "MOM!"

Dave's body was ice cold. I tried to check for a pulse, but I felt no heartbeat.

The trees around me began to rustle, and Aunt Sheila appeared with Mom close behind her. As soon as they saw Dave's lifeless body, they fell on their knees beside him.

"Davey!" Mom cried out in terror, as she laid over him and began rubbing his cheeks. "Lord Jesus, no! Don't let him die! Lord don't let him die!"

Aunt Sheila had a look of horror on her face. Her mouth hung open and the look in her eyes made it seem like she was far, far away.

"We gotta get him inside!" I said, putting my hands on Mom's shoulders.

Brian came through the trees behind us just then and said, "What's going on?"

"Here, grab a hold of his legs!" I demanded urgently. "Help me bring him inside!"

As Brian saw Dave, a stunned look came upon his face and he said, "What the hell? What's he doin' out here?"

"Damn it, just grab his legs!" I cried out in frustration.

I took Dave under the arms, as Brian lifted him by his legs. We carried him out of the woods and laid him down on the leather couch.

"Get a bunch of blankets; all the blankets that you've got!"

Brian went running upstairs, as Mom buried her head on Dave's chest. She was absolutely panic-stricken.

Aunt Sheila had come back to her senses, and she quickly got on the phone and called 911.

"We just found my nephew outside. His whole body is purple. He needs an ambulance right away…"

We sat in the waiting room of the hospital for half an hour, praying and crying. Finally, a short man with neatly combed black hair came walking up to us.

"Are you David Sullah's mother?" he asked, looking at Aunt Sheila.

"I am." Mom answered weakly, looking hopefully up at the man.

He smiled and said, "My name is Doctor Cosgrove, ma'am. Your son is going to be just fine."

At this Mom broke out into tears. She stood up and embraced the doctor, saying, "Praise the Lord! Oh, thank you!"

Mom sat back down between Aunt Sheila and I as we all held hands. Doctor Cosgrove took a chair and, sitting with us, said, "Dave is a very lucky young man. When you got him here, his body temperature was a mere thirty degrees Celsius, and his heart beat was less than twenty beats per minute." He took a deep sigh, then continued.

"Now, he was too cold for us to inject him with some warm I.V., so we placed him in a heated humidified oxygen room, which slowly brought up his body temperature. We got him up to almost normal body heat now, but he's going to have to stay in the room for at least a couple of hours. Luckily, Dave didn't slip into a coma, so as far as we can tell, there will be no brain damage."

Mom squeezed my hand really tight as tears streamed down her face. Unable to speak, she just nodded her head.

"Can we see him?" I asked.

"Not just yet. He is awake and alert, but we need to keep him as still as possible, as his body temperature rises. Just hang on, and try to relax for now, okay?"

"Yes, thank you so much," Aunt Sheila replied.

Doctor Cosgrove smiled as he stood up and gave Mom a nod.

"Everything's going to be just fine, ma'am. Don't worry."

*January 3ʳᵈ, 2001-*

*Think of our troubles as rain clouds. While we are in pain, we see their blackness and think, 'How ugly! Why would You create such a thing, Lord? I do not understand!' But after the trouble passes, as it always does, we see the rain clouds in a new perspective; in a new 'light', if you will. We see that the rain clouds bring rain; it falls down and brings life. These 'troubles' give birth to new beginnings- new grass, new plants, pretty flowers. These things, if used wisely, bring us closer to the Lord.*

*I see the puffy white clouds that used to be dark, loathsome times in my life. I see the good that they gave life to, and I say, "Father, forgive my foolishness. Yes, it is true what I have known all along- You are the Lord, and You love me so. I am humiliated by my former outbursts of Your wrongdoing and uncaring. You truly care more for me more than I can comprehend. The ugly clouds have given me life, and after their troubles pass, they become beautiful."*

*Always praise the Lord. It is right to praise Him in times of good, but it is also easy. It is just as right to praise Him in times of trouble - this, though, is not easy. I will not lie and say, 'Yes, I always praise the Lord. I never question His ways.'*

*Truthfully, I question what He does many times- but each time I do, I am filled with deep humility when He shows me His deep, unending love for me. He is the Lord. He is slow to anger, and quick to love. Receive His love and honor Him. Do what He calls you to do, and you will be blessed. Praise Him forever, and try so very hard to keep in mind that dark clouds bring beautiful, renewed life.*

# 9.

Dave was released from the hospital the next day. I didn't get to see him, because I had to go back to college. Mom told me to just keep him in my prayers and do my best at school. She e-mailed me a day after I had gotten back and said that Dave would be starting rehab in a week. I wrote Mom back and told her to be sure to fill me in on everything.

Dave was in a program with other teens addicted to drugs. It just so happened that one of them was his ex-girlfriend, Susie Blanchard. Dave had gone out with her for the whole year that I was a senior in high school.

One night when I was still in high school, I had fallen asleep on the couch while watching ESPN. I awoke as the door leading uptairs from the basement creaked open…

The light to the kitchen flickered on as I rubbed my eyes and looked at the time on the VCR. It was one a.m. I yawned and sat up on the couch, stretching my arms.

"Dave?" I called out in a whisper, as to not wake up Mom. "'S that you?"

Dave came through the kitchen while hurriedly throwing on his sneakers.

"Yeah. What're you doing up?"

I sleepily shook my head and answered, "I musta fallen asleep watching TV."

"I gotta go," Dave said, seemingly out of breath. "Don't tell Mom, okay?"

"Gotta go?" I repeated as I squinted my eyes. "Gotta go where?"

Now that I was slightly awake, I saw how panicky Dave looked. His eyes were bulging out, and he was white as a ghost.

"Something's wrong with Susie; I really can't talk now. I'll tell you later, okay?"

Before I could respond, Dave was out the door. I got up from the couch and looked out the window, just in time to see him sprint down the driveway. It was pouring rain outside, so hard that it sounded like pellets were hitting the side of the house.

I sat back down on the couch, wondering what was so important that Dave had to leave the house at one in the morning. Dave had looked so distraught that it made me worried. I decided to get in my car and go after him.

As quietly as possible, I went into my room and grabbed a coat and a winter hat. Mom's room was just down the hall from mine, so I had to tiptoe around and make sure that I didn't clumsily knock something over in my drowsiness.

Finally, I made my way out of the house. As I stepped outside, the rain instantaneously dowsed me from head to toe. I ran to the Escort and quickly hopped in. I was glad to be out of the rain, but I knew that Dave had to be absolutely drenched by now. I started the car, and not waiting for it to warm up, I drove onto the road.

Susie lived in the heart of town, about five or six miles away. I expected that by now, Dave should be nearing the end of our street. From there he would have to turn left to go into town, which would take at least ten minutes, even for a kid as fast as Dave.

I drove slowly down our road, anticipating seeing Dave at any moment. But I soon came to the stop sign at the end of the road without passing him.

'That's impossible!' I thought to myself. 'There's no way that he could have made it this far by now!'

I sat at the stop sign for a minute, thinking of what to do. All of a sudden, it hit me: Dave must have taken the short cut.

The short cut to Susie's house was the railroad tracks that intersected our road and led into town. These tracks were unsafe by day, and even worse at night. It wasn't because of the trains. It was rare to see a train on these tracks. They were dangerous because of the people that lived on them.

The railroad tracks cut through a dense forest, and at night, you couldn't see anything ten feet ahead of you. As I sat in my car with the rain slamming down, I remembered the stories that I had heard about the tracks, and I was filled with fear for my brother.

There were devil-worshipers who either lived on the tracks or went there at night. They would find stray cats and dogs, or whatever they could get their hands on, and mutilate their bodies. At first I was sure that this was just another of many tall tales that flew about the town of Auburn; until this 'tall tale' made the six o'clock news.

People in town had been calling the police, insisting that they heard strange, screeching noises coming from the nearby woods. At first the cops had disregarded their complaints, saying that it was probably just some wildlife animals, mating or prowling for food. But after receiving so many calls, they decided that it would be best to at least check it out.

So one morning, a couple of cops were sent out to walk along the tracks and see if they saw anything out of the ordinary. As they were walking along, one of them noticed something very out of the ordinary. Nailed on a large maple tree, in the shape of an upside-down cross, they saw mangled animal body parts. Heads, limbs, torsos, all torn from the body. And the most sickening thing was on the base of the tree - animal entrails nailed on to form the number '666'.

The police eventually chopped the tree down, but they never found out who had done it. Some of my friends who live in town swear that they still hear animals shrieking sometimes at night.

Dave wasn't scared of anything. I was sure that he had taken those tracks to get to Susie's. All I could do was bow my head, say a prayer for his safety, and drive back home.

I got back home and changed into some dry clothes. The TV was still on, and I decided to watch it, hoping that it would take my mind off worrying about Dave. It wasn't until about an hour or so later that I thought to myself, 'You idiot! You could've gone to Susie's and picked Dave up there!'

So I threw my jacket back on, and was putting on my sneakers when the front door opened. Dave came in, shivering and red in the face.

"Hey," he nonchalantly said, as if he were just getting home from school.

I shook my head in amazement at him and said, "What's going on? Why did you have to go to Susie's at one in the morning?"

"We're gonna wake up Mom," Dave said, as he slipped off his sneakers. "Come down to my room with me."

I followed Dave downstairs, and, after he had changed, he opened the door for me to come in. He sat down on his bed, clearly exhausted.

"Did you take the tracks?" I asked him as I sat down beside him.

"Yeah. Why?"

"Because, I drove out trying to find you, but you were nowhere around. I figured you must've ran down the tracks." I looked him straight in the eyes and said, "Promise me that you'll never go down them again. I was worried out of my mind, man."

Dave nodded as he bowed his head and responded, "Yeah, I know that it was pretty stupid; but I just had to get to Susie as fast as I could."

"Why?" I asked, wondering what was so important for my brother to run in the rain on a dangerous path to see his girlfriend at one in the morning.

Dave sighed and bit his lower lip, seemingly contemplating on whether or not he should tell me.

"Susie's had some tough times lately, man," Dave said as he stared up at the ceiling of his tiny room.

"Whad dya mean, 'tough times'?"

Dave leaned back with his elbows on the bed and replied, "I don't know, it's just…a bunch of stuff. She thinks her step dad hates her, and they're always fighting about stupid stuff. Her older sister calls her crap like 'Moo-Moo Sue', so much that now Susie thinks she's fat. Lately she's always saying how fat she is, and how ugly she is. She really believes it, I think."

This was strange to me, because Susie was a knockout. She was around five foot seven, with long blond hair, a very pretty face and a curvaceous body. She was, without a doubt, the cutest girl in my brother's grade.

Dave blew some warm air into his hands and rubbed them together before continuing.

"Lately she's just been so down on herself. She called me tonight, and…"

I saw that Dave was getting choked up. His eyes began to get misty, and he nervously began picking at his fingernails.

"She called me, and she was crying. She said something like, 'I just called to say I love you, and goodbye.'

"And I said, 'What do you mean, 'goodbye'?'"

A tear trickled down Dave's face. He wiped it away quickly, probably hoping that I hadn't seen it.

"She said that she had a razor blade in her hand, and that she was gonna slice her wrists, then lay down by her parents' door."

Dave's lips began to quiver, as he did his best to keep it all in. I looked at him sympathetically, trying to non-verbally tell him that it was okay to cry.

"She was serious, too," Dave said, looking at me with watery eyes. "She would have done it. So I told her to just wait, and I'd be over in a few minutes. She said by then it'd be too late. Her voice, man!"

Dave shook his head and cleared his throat. He had seemed to regain some composure.

"Her voice was what scared me. It wasn't Susie. She seemed so...I don't know, it was like she just didn't care about anything anymore. I told her, and I was pretty much screaming at this point, that if she really loved me, she'd wait for me to come over. So she said okay, and I made her promise."

"What'd you do when you got there?" I asked.

"I don't know; nothin', really," Dave replied humbly, as he shrugged his shoulders and stared at the blue carpet. "We just talked, you know. She needs someone that'll show her love, I guess. She doesn't really get that from her family, so I'm the one that has to do it."

I slowly nodded my head, suddenly feeling very tired. Now that I knew that Dave was okay, it was time for bed. Before I left, I asked, "Is she gonna be alright? I mean, does Susie need professional help or something?"

Dave shook his head and said, "No, I don't think so. We talked for a while, and at the end I could tell that she felt really good."

I stood up and smiled at my brother and said, "You're a good kid, bro. Now get some sleep, okay?"

He returned my smile and replied, "Don't worry; I'll be asleep as soon as my head hits the pillow."

*March 13th, 2003-*

*If I think, 'I'm so smart, and have learned so much that there's nothing more for me to learn', first of all, I'm an idiot. Secondly, I will learn nothing more.*

# 10.

Before going further into Dave's troubled years, I think it's necessary to share with you how devoted to God he was as a child. As soon as Dave learned how to read, he would always choose to sit down and read some Bible picture books that Mom had bought for me when I was his age. His favorites were David killing the giant, Goliath and Daniel in the lion's den.

Most kids his age were watching TV and making mud pies and snowmen. Not Dave. He would read the children's books, then ask Mom things like,

"How did God shut the lion's mouths?", and

"Why did Delilah want to cut off Samson's hair?"

The Bible intrigued Dave; he wanted to spend his time reading from it, and spend more time asking questions about it.

Mom has told me this story about Dave so many times that I can picture it in my mind...

Mom is sitting on the sofa, reading her morning devotion. The passage for that particular day was from the gospel of John, chapter six, verses twenty-eight and twenty-nine:

'Then they asked him, "What must we do to do the works God requires?"

Jesus answered, "The work of God is this: to believe in the one He has sent."

As she was meditating on the verses, Dave, who was five at the time, walked into the living room in his pajamas.

"Hey, Davey!" Mom said with a smile as she sat her devotional book down and held out her arms. "You're up early today!"

Dave gave Mom a hug and sat down by her. He played with the zipper of his blue pajama suit as he said, "I've been thinkin'...I want Jesus in my heart, but...how does He get in there?"

Mom couldn't answer at first, because immediately she became choked up, and tears of joy fell from her eyes.

"Oh, Davey!" she said weakly, as she hugged him and gave him a kiss on the head. "All you have to do is ask Jesus, and He will come into your heart. You have to tell Him that you believe in Him, and that you believe that He died on the cross so that you can go to Heaven."

Dave looked up at Mom with a puzzled expression on his face.

"That's it?" he asked.

"Um-hmm. Do you want to ask Him into your heart right now?"

"Yes," Dave answered confidently.

"Okay. Let's close our eyes and bow our heads, and you repeat what I say, okay?"

"No," Dave said, shaking his head. "I want to do it all by myself."

"Well, honey...do you know what to say?"

"No, but...can't you write it down for me?"

Mom tried to persuade Dave that it'd be easier, (and more reassuring for her) if he would just repeat what Mom would tell him to say. But Dave was adamant about doing it by himself. So finally, Mom gave in and wrote down a prayer for Dave to say on a piece of notebook paper that she still has to this day.

Dave looked over the paper quickly and then ran outside with it. Mom followed after him, and watched as Dave walked over to a large oak tree. This was Dave's favorite tree. It had plenty of branches sprouting all around, making it easy to climb. Dave put the paper in his mouth, as he climbed up to a broad branch about ten feet up. He sat down with a leg on each side of the limb and bowed his head.

Mom looked at the breath-taking sight with elation and thanks to the Lord in her heart. Her son was asking the Lord into his life, something that she had prayed that he'd do even before Dave was born. Not only that, but Dave was in his favorite tree, in his pajamas, with a beautiful sunrise as the backdrop. There was a beauty in all that that Mom could see, but couldn't quite explain.

In her heart, Mom said, 'Praise You, Lord Jesus! Praise Your holy Name! Bless Davey by coming into his heart this very minute, and stay with him always! Lord, I don't know what to say…You are just so good! Praise You, Father, and thank You for my boys!'

By the time that Dave had climbed down from the tree, Mom's face was saturated with tears. He walked up to Mom shyly and said, "I want to say my prayer in front of you; just to make sure that I did it right."

Mom faintly responded, "Okay."

She knelt down on the moist grass and closed her eyes as Dave said his prayer.

"Jesus Christ, I believe that You are God. I believe that You came from Heaven and died on the cross, and I believe that You rose again. I do some bad things sometimes, and I know that only You can forgive me. I pray that You come into my heart, and that when I do bad things, I will ask You to forgive me, and I will do my best not to do them anymore. Now that You're in my heart, I pray that I live how You want me to live, and I pray that You will always be the most important thing in my life. Amen."

After Dave read that to Mom, he eagerly looked up at her and asked, "Did I do it right? Is Jesus in my heart?"

"Yes!" Mom cried out, as she embraced him. "Yes, Davey, Jesus is in your heart! You don't know how good that makes me feel!"

As Dave hugged her back, he said, "I do know, Mom, because I feel it, too!"

*November 25, 2002-*
  *"I must decrease, He must increase..."*
  *How true that is! I pray for humility, and I know that as I receive it, a part of me is dying. My natural instincts of 'I can do it alone' would never allow this to happen. I pray for wisdom, and I know that as I receive it, a part of me is dying. I begin to realize things that were always there, but had remained unknown to me. Have I taught myself? No! Every nature of my being rejects the grueling process of humility. My wisdom says that I am wise, and need no further teaching.*
  *But the Spirit of God says otherwise. He says that His foolishness is far greater than my most intelligent thought. He says that pride leads to destruction. He tells the Truth. He is Truth, and He reveals this to me because He is Love.*
  *This is humility and wisdom tied together: saying, "I realize that I have certain abilities, and that these abilities are gifts from God, not something that I have given to myself. Also, I will use these gifts from God to glorify the Lord." - Humility and wisdom.*

# 11.

D ave was a popular kid his entire life. He always had a good number of friends from Kindergarten until adulthood. But Dave didn't use his popularity to look down on others who weren't 'cool'. In fact, I remember him doing the exact opposite.

Dave started the sixth grade when he was twelve years old. I was in the eighth grade, and we were both in the same building. I'd see Dave in the hallways from time to time, horsing around with his friends or nervously talking with girls. (At that age, girls went from "disgusting" to "beautiful" in the eyes of boys.)

I was going to the drinking fountain one day before the bell rang. The fountain was by the bathroom, right next to the sixth graders' lockers...

I stooped down to get a drink, and as I did, I heard someone say from behind me, "Man, you smell like B.O., new kid! You're gonna have to get a locker outside or somethin'!"

I turned around and saw four kids in a semi-circle. They were laughing at the boy, and they were surrounding him while he was trying to get into his locker. He was wearing an old jeans jacket and red sweatpants that looked as if they were his grandfather's childhood clothes. The jacket was stained with dirt and oil, and the sweatpants had tears and holes around the knees.

The kid looked like he was trying to pretend that he wasn't being taunted. He didn't give the other boys a glance. He just kept twisting the combination lock, trying to open his locker.

"That's a nice perm you got there," chuckled a lanky boy, as he flicked a lock of the kid's brown curly hair with his finger. "Looks like you and my mom go to the same salon!"

All the boys laughed, and their laughter drew a crowd, as more and more insults were hurled at the new kid.

I felt bad for the kid, but what was I going to do? If I stuck up for him, then everybody would think that I was a loser. Sure, I was a little older than everyone there, but age wasn't important, popularity was. So I just leaned against the wall and laughed along with everybody else.

All of a sudden, I saw my brother cutting through the pack of kids. He made his way to the front where the kid with curly brown hair was still trying to get into his locker. Everyone became quiet, waiting for what Dave was going to say to him.

"Ya havin' trouble with your locker?"

The kid, with his head still bowed in humiliation, nodded slowly.

"What's your combo?"

He showed Dave the slip of paper with the combination written on it. Dave took a look at it, turned the lock to the correct numbers, then pulled up hard on the handle. The locker opened, and Dave said, "Sometimes you just gotta tug up real hard. These things are a little rusty, ya know."

"Hey Dave," a short boy who was in the middle of the crowd, called out. "How can you stand so close to him without dying from the smell?"

Dave shrugged his shoulders as he looked at the new kid and replied, "He smells fine to me."

After that, the bell rang, and the mass of kids dispersed. I slipped away, not wanting Dave to see that I had been there. The way that he handled that situation impressed me, and at the same time made me feel like dirt for not doing the same thing.

Every now and then, I would see Dave walking around the halls with the kid. Over time, I also saw that Dave's friends, the very ones who were making fun of him at first, had accepted him into their clique.

I later found out that the boy's name was Eddie Bauhmer.

*April 2ⁿᵈ, 2003-*

*People say I'm different; I say everybody is. No two people are exactly the same. So who isn't different? And what's 'normal'? Who is this Average Joe that everybody seems to accept as the norm? Is it normal to be comfortable in crowds, having mindless chit-chat about school and 'What's your major?' as if you sincerely care? Is it normal to base conversations and life around sports? Is it normal to wear designer clothes and drive a clean car? Is it weird to prefer solitude at times? Is it weird to be silent instead of blabbing off at the mouth? Normal? Is that really a word to describe people? I don't think so, but if I'm wrong, I don't care. You might not see it my way, and you know why? Because we're different. I don't think that I'm 'normal', and I don't think that you are, either. We're just different, that's all.*

# 12.

Almost every guy in our family loves to hunt. When deer season rolls around, my uncles and cousins leave the city life for a few days and come down to Auburn, where there is plenty of woods in our back yard. The younger boys will push the deer out to where we are set up in the tree stand, as we wait patiently for a buck.

It's sort of a family tradition. We all work together, doing our own part. Whenever a deer is killed, no matter who shot it, we all claim it as our own.

I started pushing deer for my uncles when I was fifteen, and now it's my younger cousin's turn to push out the deer for us. I've always enjoyed these times, regardless of what my job was. Of course, it was better when we came home with a buck or two; but even if we returned empty-handed, I still enjoyed the time out in the woods.

Dave sort of broke the custom. When November arrived in his fifteenth year, he decided that he wasn't going hunting with the rest of us. My uncles jokingly kidded him about being a 'tree hugger,' and they tried to persuade Dave to come along, but he stayed firm in his resolve.

My Uncle Stan, a witty, muscular man who is a die-hard hunter/fisher asked me as we were going out that year...

"So what's wrong with your brother? Does he think there's something wrong with hunting?"

I gave it some consideration as we trudged out into the woods, then answered, "Nah, I don't think so. I mean, he likes animals and stuff, but I don't think that he objects to hunting. It's probably just something that he doesn't want to do."

After a long, cold day of not seeing even one deer, we made our way back to the house. As we broke out of the frozen woods, I saw Dave up in his favorite tree, not too far away from the house. He was too far up for any of my uncles or cousins to notice him, though. They were too busy talking about a better strategy that they would use tomorrow.

"I'll be in in a minute," I told them, as they set their guns in the garage and went inside the house to warm up. Mom always had coffee and donuts waiting for us, and even though I was cold and hungry, I wanted to talk with Dave.

I walked over to his tree and looked up at him. He was sitting contently on a lofty limb with his back against the shaft of the tree.

"Nothin', huh?" he said with a grin.

"Nope," I replied. "We didn't see one damn deer."

"Oh well; there's always tomorrow, right?"

"Yup."

I slid my hands in the pocket of my warm Carhart and said,

"Uncle Stan asked me if you think there's somethin' wrong with hunting deer."

"Did he?" Dave said with a smile.

I paused a moment then asked, "Do ya?"

Dave sighed as he looked out to the woods and responded, "Truthfully, I did for a while. You remember those deer that we saw that one day when we were camping?"

"Yeah."

"Well, I used to think, 'Why would anybody want to kill deer?' I'd a been pissed if someone shot them deer that we saw. There was just somethin' about the way that they drank from the water. It was like...I don't know, it just gave me a good feeling.

"But then I started thinking about all those deer that run out into the road, and cause accidents and stuff. If someone had shot them deer, then there wouldn't be so many car crashes and people dyin' and stuff.

"So, I guess it works both ways. Sometimes it's good that deer live, and sometimes it's better if they die."

I stared at my brother, as he seemed lost in his thoughts, as he gazed at the woods. I was as equally as transfixed with him as he was with the forest. I mean, the kid was only fifteen years old, and he had just blown me away with his maturity.

"That's a good way to look at it, Dave," I said, nodding my head in agreement. "You should come on in now, it's freezing out here."

Dave cupped his hands and blew in them, never turning from his gaze as he replied, "I'm coming. I just wanna see the sunset first."

*October 10ᵗʰ, 2002-*

*The very thought that 'I am a good person, so when I die I will go to Heaven' is nothing but damnation within itself. Who is a 'good person'? Not one of us. Not you, not I; not one. We cannot by our own deeds save ourselves from Hell, which is what we all deserve. Buddha cannot save us from Hell, Joseph Smith cannot save us, traveling to Mecca cannot save us; we cannot save us.*

*The only human whom ever lived that can save us is Jesus Christ, and by Him, His Father, the Lord Almighty. Saying to another person something like, 'Oh, you're a Buddhist?' or 'Oh, you're a Mormon? Well, that's okay, as long as you believe in a higher power, I'm sure that God will allow you into Heaven,' will only further that person's descent into Hell.*

*We cannot be saved by conforming what the Gospel says into wishful thinking, and the Gospel says:* "I am the way, the truth, and the life. No one comes to my Father but by Me."

*Jesus is the only way. It is the truth - unbendable, unbreakable, forever- the truth. And the truth shall set you free. The fear of the Lord, which we all must feel, is ever presently profound in this statement: If you do not acknowledge Jesus as your Lord and Savior Who died for you and took upon Himself the sins of the world, you will spend eternity in Hell.*

*If you love them, don't sugarcoat the truth; let them know.*

# 13.

A lot of bad things happened to Dave after he turned sixteen, and I believe this is what started them all: About two weeks following his sixteenth birthday, his best friend died in a plane crash.

Billy Anderson had been Dave's closest friend ever since they met in second grade. We took him camping with us one year, and he was over at the house nearly every summer day.

I liked Billy. Even though he was extremely hyper, and at times would never stop talking, I usually would enjoy his presence. Sometimes during the summer, a bunch of my friends would come over to play football in our back lawn. Whenever Dave and Billy or any other of Dave's friends were around, they'd always be invited to play.

Dave and Billy loved to go fishing, and sometimes I went with them, even though fishing wasn't my thing. Billy never fished in the same spot for over ten minutes. Dave and I would cast out and sit there the whole day, patiently waiting for a bite. Billy, however, just couldn't sit still. He'd start out right next to us, talk our ears off for a bit, then reel his line in and run off ten yards away. By the time that we had been fishing for half an hour, Billy would usually be nowhere in sight; but we'd still hear him!

"Dave! Hey, Dave!"

Billy came running towards us from around the bend in the river. With one hand he kept his baseball cap on his head from flying off, and in his other hand was his Zebco fishing pole. His red t-shirt and overalls were completely soaked.

"You'll never believe it!" he said with a wild grin on his face. "I had a bass on my pole this big!"

Billy tucked the fishing pole in his armpit as he showed us about a five foot space between his outstretched hands.

"Oh yeah?" I said, indulging him. "What happened to it?"

"That's what I was about to say," Billy responded as his eyes grew wide with excitement. "There I was, just standin' by the edge, when all of a sudden, a fish grabs hold of my line and yanks me in the river!"

"What?!" Dave said with a grin. "It did not!"

"Uh-huh!" Billy insisted. "Swear to God it did! So, it was pulling me along, and I started climbing up the fishin' line toward it."

I had to turn away to keep from breaking out in laughter. As I was composing myself, Billy went on.

"It had me probably 'bout ten feet under the water, and it was only goin' deeper, so I knew that I had to get to it and knock it out before it dragged me too far down."

"Why didn't you just let go of the pole?" Dave interjected.

"Will you just let me finish?"

"Alright, sorry. Go on." Dave said with a grin as he cast out his line.

"So anyway, there I was, probably ten feet under the water. I finally got close enough so I could see it, and man, this thing was huge! So I reach out for it, and I catch 'm by his tail. He turns around at me, and he gave me this real mean face, like he was all pissed off that I had his tail."

I was imagining all this in my mind, and the more vivid my imagination became, the harder it was not to laugh out loud.

"So I shake his tail real hard to, you know, to try an' get him all dizzy and stuff, and that's when he slipped out of my fingers and snapped the line."

"No kidding?" Dave said in an obvious tone of disbelief.

Billy didn't pick up on that, though.

"Oh, yeah." He put his hands on his hips and shook his head. "That was without a doubt the biggest fish I've ever seen! It was a monster!"

We knew that he was just making up the story, but we didn't let him know that. Billy put a new hook on his line and grabbed a few worms, then ran back to the spot where he had supposedly hooked the five foot bass. As he disappeared around the bend, Dave and I smiled at each other, shook our heads, and cast out into the river.

Billy died when the airplane he was on had difficulties in the takeoff and crashed, less than a minute after it had left the ground. Dave was absolutely devastated. He wouldn't come out of his room for three days for anything except using the bathroom.

When Mom or I tried to talk with him, he'd just turn around in his bed and say,    "Leave me alone."

Dave wouldn't even speak with Susie when she called or came over.

Mom thought that it would be good for Dave to go to the funeral, so three days after the crash she and I went into Dave's room to try and persuade him to get out of bed.

I stood in the open doorway as Mom knelt by Dave's bed. Dave was wrapped up in his blankets, and I saw a bleakness in his eyes that scared me.

"Davey, honey." Mom said tenderly as she ran her hand through his soft blond hair. "Don't you want to get up so you can go to Billy's funeral? Jonny and I will go with you."

Dave didn't respond. In fact, he didn't move an inch. He just stared desolately at a spot in the wall.

"Honey, I called Billy's aunt, and she said that the funeral is today at three. It's almost noon now. Don't you want to get up and take a shower, so you'll be ready?"

"I'm not going," Dave responded weakly.

"Why not, Davey? I think Billy would want you to be there."

"That's true, Dave." I agreed. "I'm sure that he would like you to be there."

Dave's eyes squinted as a look of pain came on his face. Tears began falling from his eyes as he opened his mouth wide and exclaimed, "Do you know where Billy is?! He's in Hell!"

Dave threw back his head and covered his face with his hands as heartbroken sobs pierced through the air.

I quickly stepped up to the bed beside Mom as she reached out and grabbed Dave's hand, saying, "Davey! Why would you think that?"

His exclamation had shocked me. I wasn't sure what to say or do, so I just sat on the bed and put my hand on his shoulder, simply to let him know that I was there.

"Because," he cried out through intense sobs, "Billy wasn't a Christian!"

Mom stood dead still for a moment. It was obvious that she didn't know what to say. She bowed her head and closed her eyes, and, still holding onto Dave's hand, she prayed,

"Heavenly Father, Billy was taken from this earth at a young age. We pray, Lord, that if You weren't in his heart, that You take into account the fact that this child was so young. You alone know, Lord, that had Billy been allowed to live longer, he may or may not have accepted You into his life. We know that You are a good and just Lord. We know this even in times of despair. Lord, comfort Dave. May he feel Your presence."

Mom reached out and picked Dave up in her arms, as I put my arms around them both. Mom's prayer didn't seem to have any effect on Dave. He was still crying as hard as he had been before. As I looked at Mom, I saw an indescribable expression of anguish on her face that I was surely reflecting myself. I think we all painfully knew where Billy probably was.

We all ended up going to Billy's and his parents' funeral later on that day. It was probably the most sorrowful experience of my life up until that point. Dave didn't say a word the whole time. He just sat in a chair with his head slightly bowed, and his eyes looked like he was far, far away. As I stared at the three coffins, Dave's shout echoed again and again in my mind:

"Do you know where Billy is?! He's in Hell!"

Soon after that, Dave turned away from God, and towards marijuana.

*August 22nd, 2002-*
> *Drugs once controlled me,*
> *But by God's grace,*
> *That is the past,*
> *And only the past.*
> *Forgotten; not remembered.*

# 14.

I don't like recalling this time in Dave's life and mine. Truthfully, I wanted to exclude it from this book. The memories are heart wrenching, and as I sat down to write this chapter, I became almost too depressed to go on.

I stared at the computer screen for a long time, thinking to myself,

'Do I really want to do this?'

The answer came easily; 'No way'!

Discouraged and sad, I went outside for a breath of fresh air. I sat down on my front steps and sincerely thought about why I was writing about my brother Dave. The first thing that came to mind was because I miss him. I could tell right away that although that was true, it wasn't the main reason.

'Then why?' I thought to myself. 'God, why?'

When I had first been inspired to write this book, I knew that it was God telling me to do so. It felt right, and I trusted in Him to guide me, chapter by chapter, word by word.

As I sat there alone in the quiet summer afternoon, God spoke to my heart.

'Do you write only when it makes you feel good? That's quite selfish, Jonathon. Will you quit now, when things get tough? Or will you live up to your word, and trust in Me?'

I literally jumped up and went back inside. Sitting down at the computer, I bowed my head, said a prayer, and began typing.

My college buddy dropped me off at home on Thanksgiving Day. He lived in the next town over, which was only a ten minute drive away. I hopped out of the car, grabbed my suitcase, and told him to have a happy Thanksgiving. As he pulled out of the driveway, I stood in the garage, wondering how happy mine would be.

Dave was not getting better. In her e-mails to me, Mom said that he was failing his drug tests, and his counselor was threatening to release him from the rehab program if he continued to use marijuana.

I took a deep breath and stepped into my house.

"Hello?" I called out as I sat my suitcase on the linoleum kitchen floor.

A pot was overflowing with boiling water on the stove, and the sink was turned on full blast. There was a large plastic bowl of peeled potatoes sitting under the spout, and water was splashing off from it and spraying all around.

I quickly turned off the stove, grabbed some potholders from the cupboard, and moved the pot off the burner. Then I turned the faucet to off and started to soak up the water on the counter with a towel. Before I got too far, though, the smoke rising from the boiling pot caused the smoke alarm to go off. I threw the towel down and took the battery out from the alarm to stop the shrieking beeps.

I heard Mom's door open, and her fast paced footsteps sounded down the hallway. She came running into the kitchen, her blond hair in complete disarray. When she saw me, she put her palm on her chest and inhaled deeply.

"Oh, Jonny!" she said as came over to me and gave me a big hug. "When did you get home?"

"Just now," I replied. "What's going on in here?"

As we let go from our embrace, I noticed how miserable Mom looked. First of all, she wasn't smiling; and Mom was always smiling, especially when we hadn't seen each other for a while. She stood a little hunched over, as if she was carrying a bag of bricks on her back.

"Oh, darn it!" Mom exclaimed in dismay as she surveyed the kitchen. She went over to the stovetop and looked into the pan. "My corn! Oh! It's ruined!"

She put her hands over her face and shook her head.

"Don't cry, Mom" I said, putting my hands on her shoulders. "It'll be al-"

"The turkey!" she shouted, cutting me off. She bent down to open up the oven door, and as she did, thick, gray smoke came pouring out. She frantically started waving it away from her, crying out, "Oh no! Oh, no!"

After most of the smoke had cleared, Mom saw that the turkey was burnt to a crisp. She fell on her knees in front of the stove and began crying hysterically. It took some persistent convincing, but I finally got her to come into the living room and sit down on the couch with me. At first, she just leaned on my shoulder and wept. Mom wasn't one to cry over spilled milk, so I knew that this had to do with much more than a ruined turkey.

"What happened?" I asked Mom as her cries began to subside.

"I've been working on Thanksgiving dinner since one o'clock in the morning," she said through her tears. "I wanted everything to be so perfect...and now it's all ruined!"

"Shhh, it's okay," I said gently, patting her back.

"I was so happy that you were coming home..." Mom said feebly as she buried her face in her hands.

I didn't know what to say: I had never seen Mom so distraught. She wiped the tears from her face and said, "I had the turkey in the oven, and the corn was on the stove...I went to lay down, and I must have fallen asleep. All that work, and now..."

Her shoulders began to shake as she bowed her head and whimpered, "I can't take it, Jonny! I just don't know what to do! Your brother is worrying me half to death; I can't sleep at night, I can't think straight at work...I just..."

She trailed off and ran a hand through her hair. Her eyes squinted in pain, as tears again fell from her eyes.

"It'll be okay," I said. I felt an uneasiness in my heart that told me I doubted those words. "Dave will get better, and don't worry about the dinner. I'm just happy to be home with you. Okay?"

I put my arm around her as she leaned on me. She was still crying too hard to respond verbally, but she nodded her head and gave me a half-hearted smile.

After a few minutes passed by, I told Mom to go lay down and try to rest while I cleaned up the kitchen. She refused, saying that she wouldn't be able to sleep now. So together we salvaged what we could, basically a few ears of corn and the potatoes and a few scraps of turkey.

I found some burgers in the freezer and was cooking them on the stove as I saw Dave, two of our uncles, and our cousin, Bernie, through the kitchen window. They were coming out of the woods and towards the house.

"So Dave went hunting this time, huh?" I said to Mom, while flipping the burgers over.

"Yeah. I was pretty surprised. He didn't go out yesterday, but for some reason he wanted to go today."

Uncle Stan came through the door first. He stomped off some mud from his boots and smiled at me as he said, "Hey, Jonny-boy! How're you doing?"

"Good," I replied, setting down the spatula to shake his hand. "Did you get anything?"

He pressed his lips together in a look of shame, then said, "No; but you'll have to ask your Uncle Frank why."

He peered at the stove with a questioning look on his face and asked, "What're you cooking burgers for?"

"I burnt the turkey," Mom answered shortly, while mashing potatoes at the sink.

Uncle Stan laughed, certainly sensing that Mom felt bad about it.

"That's okay, Joycey," he said, walking over to her and kissing the top of her head. "I'll eat whatever you put in front of me."

My Uncle Frank walked into the kitchen then, calling out over his shoulder, "Make sure those guns are unloaded before you clean 'em."

"I know, Dad!" Bernie retorted from inside the garage.

My Uncle Frank was a short, stern man with a thick black beard and mustache. He lived with my Aunt Harriet and their son, Bernie, in the city of Allensdale, a two-hour drive from our house. Uncle Frank was a no-nonsense type of guy; pretty much the exact opposite of Uncle Stan.

"Hello, Jon," he said, giving me a nod. "How's college treating ya?"

I sighed and said, "So far, so good."

"Good," he said, taking off his boots. "Make sure you keep up with your schoolwork. You miss one assignment, and you're lost for the rest of the semester."

"I will. So, Uncle Stan said to ask you why you guys didn't get a deer?"

Uncle Frank shook his head as he looked at his brother and said, "Oh yeah?"

Uncle Stan was standing by Mom with a huge grin on his face.

"Go ahead, Frankie; tell him," he said.

Uncle Frank put his hands in his coat pocket as he looked at me and said, "Okay; I'll tell you what happened. Me and Stan were in our tree stands, you know, the ones overlooking the old corn field?"

I nodded my head, and he continued.

"Well, all of a sudden, out pops this huge buck; I mean, it was at least a ten-pointer. He's about fifty or so yards away, so I slowly bring my rifle up, and I get him in my sights. I look over at your uncle, and he's motioning for me to wait. Mind you, I could have dropped him dead right there, and I should have. But no, I have to do everything that Stan says."

Uncle Stan let out one of his trademark laughs; a high-pitched "Haaaaa-ha-haaaaa!"

Hearing that always made me smile, but I had to try not to now, because Uncle Frank was obviously a little peeved.

"Slowly but surely, the buck starts walking towards us. It eventually got so close that I could see the moistness of his nose without using my scope. When he got about twenty yards away, I looked over at Stan, and he gave me the nod to go ahead and take the deer down."

Uncle Frank bowed his head and sighed, seemingly not wanting to go on.

"Now, you have to remember the fact that I had been sitting down on the stand for hours."

Uncle Stan started chuckling again, and this time I didn't feel bad about laughing because even Uncle Frank was smiling now.

"I had to stand up, because there was a limb in the way of my shot. Again, if I had just shot the deer when he had first came through the woods, we'd be cleaning and gutting him right now.

"Anyway, as I went to stand up, my leg was asleep and I fell out of the tree."

Uncle Stan started laughing hysterically, as Mom put her hand over her mouth to cover her smile and said, "Oh my goodness! Are you okay?"

It was good to see Mom laughing; even if it was at the expense of Uncle Frank. Seeing her smile made me feel like everything was normal.

"Yeah; no thanks to your little brother! I fell around ten feet down, and as I looked up to him in his stand, he's bent over backwards laughing!"

"You should have seen yourself!" Uncle Stan cried out through tears of laughter. "You were wobbling all around, trying to keep your balance, and then, kurflunk! You fell down like a ton of bricks!"

We all laughed as Uncle Stan did an impression of Uncle Frank with his arms flapping up and down, as if he were trying to fly.

Our laughter was cut short as Dave came in from the garage. He didn't even say hi to me. He just quickly opened the door leading downstairs and called out, "I'll be right up!"

Both of my uncle's faces turned from cheerful to solemn in an instant.

Uncle Stan folded his arms across his chest as he looked at Mom and said, "Joyce, I-"

"Guns are clean, Dad," Bernie interrupted, as he came through the front door. "Hey, Jon."

"What's up, Bern?"

Bernie was a smart, good-looking kid. Unlike his father, he was tall for his age, and like his father, he was very intelligent. Although he was only fourteen, Uncle Frank had allowed him to go hunting this year, something Bernie had wanted to do ever since he could walk.

"You didn't clean all those guns already," Uncle Frank said.

"Yeah, I did!" Bernie insisted, as he wiped the grease from his hands onto his bright orange hunting coat.

"Go back and clean them again," Uncle Frank said sternly.

Bernie threw back his head and said, "Aw, Dad! Do I have to?"

Uncle Frank cocked his head a little and gave Bernie the "Do-what-you're-told" look. Bernie slumped his shoulders and retreated back into the garage.

"What were you going to say?" Mom asked Uncle Stan, as the front door slammed close.

Uncle Stan cleared his throat and replied, "Frank and I think that Dave was getting high while he was supposed to be pushing the deer to us; in fact, we're sure that he was."

"Oh, no..." Mom said weakly, as a look of sorrow came onto her face. Just a minute ago, she had been laughing and smiling and, well, acting how she normally did. Now, though, as the wrinkles appeared on her disheartened face, she seemed like a whole different person.

"Bernie told me that Dave went off by himself and wouldn't let him follow along," Uncle Frank explained. "I specifically told those boys that they were to stay together at all times. When we met up to come back, Dave's eyes were bloodshot and he didn't say a word the entire walk back. It was obvious that he was stoned; he seemed paranoid when he saw me looking into his eyes. I'm sorry, Joyce, but Stan and I thought that it was best to tell you."

Mom bowed her head and put her hands on the kitchen counter, as if she needed the support to keep from falling. I had had enough.

"That's it," I said, handing the spatula to Uncle Stan. "Can you finish the burgers? I'm going to talk with him."

Uncle Stan nodded approvingly as he rubbed Mom's back. I opened the door that led to the basement and dashed down the stairs. Before I got all the way down, I heard Uncle Frank say,"Why are we cooking burgers?"

*January 11ᵗʰ, 2001-*

*In our balanced state on Earth, half of our body is
covered in a dark shadow while the other half is brightly lit.
At times the shadow overtakes us, and we reform so that the
light comes back into existence. At other times, we see that
the light is so plentiful that we allow a little darkness to
settle in, thinking that it's okay since we have so much light.
But the little darkness spreads, and the cycle continues.
Lest we need no such balance. Lest we grow so much as
to love the light and hate the darkness. Then by not seeing
the darkness, we see no need to let any of it in, and hold so
fast to the light that is Jesus Christ. We see that we see the
light- not because of the contrast that the darkness supplies
to it, but because of the light itself. Then there is no need
for the darkness when we recognize the light as it is: pure
and without shadow.*

# 15.

D ave's bedroom door was shut, so I gave it a good pound
to let Dave know that I meant business.

"Hold on!" he called out. "I'm getting' changed!"

I leaned up against the wall and began to nervously tap
my foot on the carpet. I was so mad at Dave for what he was
doing to Mom. She never did anything but love him, and this
is how he was repaying her!

As I waited for Dave to open the door, I thought about what I was going to say to him.

'Should I grab him by the shoulders and shake him, and tell him he better stop doing drugs and wasting away his life?'

'Should I yell at him and point my finger in his face and let him know how terrible he's making Mom feel?'

Anger was all that I felt. I pictured Mom upstairs, anguishing over Dave. Her plans for a happy Thanksgiving ruined, not because of the charred turkey, but because of Dave's selfish drug use.

I bit my lower lip and thought, 'Man, I'm going to give it to him. I'm going to really let him have it.'

Even though I wanted to scream at Dave and tell him how awful he was behaving, something inside of me told me that that wasn't right. Verses from the Bible began to flow through my mind. (Truthfully, I can't recall them now. I think that they were mainly Proverbs, such as, 'A gentle answer turns away wrath' and many words that Christ spoke about being kind and caring. I'm not sure now, but at the time, they were clear as crystal).

An overwhelming sense of peace came over me at the precise moment that Dave opened the door.

"Hey, Jon!" he said. "Good to see ya!"

I smiled at him and said, "You, too. You look a lot better than last time I saw you."

"Oh yeah," Dave said gravely. "Mom told me that you came home from college when I...well, you know."

I shut the door behind me as Dave sat on his bed. He had pictures of our family and of nature pinned up all over the walls. There was dirty laundry and books scattered all about the floor, and his walk-in closet was overflowing with more clothes and sports equipment.

I leaned up against the wall with my hands in my pockets and replied, "No, actually, I don't know. What happened to you that night?"

Dave nonchalantly shrugged his shoulders as he stared down at his feet and said, "I don't know...a bunch of stuff happened. Didn't Mom tell you?"

"Well, she told me that she caught you smoking pot, and that you stole money from work and ran off somewhere. Besides that, all I know is that we found you in a pile of snow at your friend's house."

Dave slowly nodded his head as he gazed blankly towards the floor. It was obvious that he didn't want to talk about it, but I wouldn't let that stop me. I cleared a spot on the floor and rested myself against the corner of the wall.

"What happened, Dave? How'd you end up outside, almost freezing yourself to death?"

Dave sighed deeply as he looked up at the ceiling. He leaned back on his elbows and began playing with his fingernails as he replied, "Okay. So Ma caught me smoking or whatever, and she was all like, 'I'm gonna take your car away, and you're grounded, and datta datta dat...' So I was all pissed off and I know that it was stupid and everything, but I stole some money and took off. Then I called my buddy from a pay phone and told him that I needed some acid."

Dave glanced at me quickly to see what my reaction was. I just nodded my head, even though I was scared by the fact that Dave had tried LSD.

"So I met him at his house, and bought some acid and I took it right away. I wasn't thinking straight- I had no idea of what I was gonna do and no idea where I was going. I thought that maybe the acid would just, you know, make me forget about everything. I told him what was going on, and asked if I could spend the night, but he said no way. I called a bunch of my friends until finally one said that it'd be okay for me to spend the night."

"Brian." I said, feeling the need to say something.

"Yeah, Brian. So anyway, by the time I got to his house, I was tripping pretty hard. I gave him some acid, and we laughed and had fun for a while."

Dave looked up and squinted his eyes, saying, "The last thing I remember, Brian went upstairs and I was all alone. I think I started to freak out a little, so I ran outside...I don't really know why. Maybe I was getting claustrophobic or something."

Dave shook his head in apparent shame as he concluded, "I ran to the woods, and...I thought that I was gonna die. So I laid down by a tree, and I..."

His eyes got misty and his bottom lip began to quiver.

"I,uh...I said a prayer to God, and told Him how sorry I was, and...I asked Him to take care of Mom..."

Dave sat up and put a hand over his eyes as his whole body began to shake. He whimpered high-pitched sobs as tears began to pour down his face.

I hastily got up and sat down on the bed next to him. I wasn't sure what to say, so I just put my hand on his shoulder as I bowed my head and prayed to God.

'What do I do, Lord? What do I say? Lord, be with me. Be with us.'

"Do you know how much Mom loves you?" I softly asked Dave as he began wiping the tears from his face.

"Yes," he muttered weakly.

"You know that she wants what's best for you, and, well, what you're doing now is killing her."

Dave wiped some snot from his nose and sniffed. He nodded his head in agreement with a painful look of remorse on his face.

"I mean, the rehab that she's got you in isn't cheap, Dave. But Mom doesn't care about that. She'd spend all the money she has if it'd make you get better. I love you, too. You're my brother, and I'll always love you. If I didn't, I wouldn't be here. I want to see you get better. I want my brother back. The guy who's always happy. The unselfish kid who's always more concerned about everyone else. The guy-"

Dave cut me off as he threw his arms around me and squeezed me tight.

"I want him back, too!" he said through his tears.

We stayed in the embrace for a while in silence, just holding onto each other. I smiled and thought to myself, 'Praise the Lord! Thank You!'

After a minute, Dave withdrew and wiped his face with his shirtsleeve. He looked at me and said, "Thanks, Jon. I needed that."

"No problem," I responded with a smile. "But don't thank me, thank God."

Dave nodded as he sniffed and ran a hand through his hair.

"I'm hungry. Are you ready to eat?"

"Yeah. Just give me a minute, okay? I'll be right up."

"Okay."

I left Dave's room and walked up the stairs. As I went through the kitchen, I saw Mom, Bernie, and my uncles sitting down at the dining room table. They were all holding hands, with their heads bowed in silent prayer. I stood motionless as the sight caused my heart to burn with a soothing warmth. I knew who they were praying for, and I knew that God had already answered their prayer. Immediately, I began to cry as I looked upon my family. In that simple picture, I saw their unconditional love for my brother and the sovereignty and the profound love of God.

I pulled out a chair that was in between Mom and Uncle Stan. They looked up at me and saw that I was crying.

"Jonny, what's wrong?" Mom asked as everybody opened their eyes and stared at me.

I shook my head and smiled as I responded, "Nothing's wrong, Mom. God has heard your prayers."

Before I could explain, Dave came up and saw us sitting at the table. He lifted his hands and showed us a sandwich bag with marijuana in it and a metal pipe.

"I'm done with this," he said assuredly. "I want it out of my life, and I'm sorry for all the pain I caused you."

With that, Dave opened the door under the sink and stuffed both the bag and the pipe deep into the trashcan. He stood in the kitchen, teary-eyed with his hands in his pockets.

Mom jumped out of her seat and ran to Dave, giving him a big hug as they both exploded in tears. After giving them a few seconds, one by one we all left our seats and joined in the embrace.

It was, so far as I can remember, my happiest Thanksgiving ever.

*September 30th, 2002-*
  *Everything means something. Nothing happens by chance. God created the universe, and as I think Albert Einstein said, "God doesn't play dice." We are so slow to see it at times, and so quick to disregard it as mere coincidence. I tell you, 'coincidence' is not in the vocabulary of God.*

# 16.

The next time that I saw Dave was at Christmas. We had been keeping in touch in e-mails, though, and he told me that Susie and him were back together. She was in rehab, because her Mom had found marijuana in her room, and threatened that Susie either got some help or she'd kick her out of the house.

Dave was happy. He had not used any drugs since Thanksgiving, and he had his girlfriend back, whom he absolutely adored. I'm not sure why Dave and Susie broke up in the first place. He never told me. I'm almost certain that she called it off, however. They separated in the summer, and for days Dave moped around the house, not playing outside or hardly saying a word. He was heartbroken.

In one of his e-mails to me, Dave wrote that 'This is a blessing from God; the devil was trying to destroy me, but God used it and worked it out for the good.'

Mom was her old, jovial self again, as well. She wrote me that things were going well; Dave was making good progress in the rehab program, and she was delighted that he and Susie were back together. Mom always liked her.

I received an e-mail from her a few days before coming home for Christmas break in which she said,'I have my boy back! Like the prodigal son, he has returned home. Can't wait to see you; praise God for my boys!'

I wrote her back, 'Can't wait to see you, too.. Praise God for our Mom!'

Although Mom was small and frail in stature, she was like a mighty warrior on the inside. I often wondered how Dave would have turned out if it hadn't been for her. She never gave up on him; not once. Mom was a godly influence on Dave and I. The importance of that could not be over-emphasized. She suffered words that wounded her, and trials that would have brought any other single woman down. Mom has been repeatedly healed by the hand of God; not by psychiatrists or psychologists, but by the Great Healer Himself, the One, the Only, the Lord Jesus Christ.

That's what Christmas is all about, the birth of our Lord. It's not about Santa, it's not about presents. It's not about the Christmas tree, or getting time off from work. Of course, presents and decorations are good, but not if they deter you from the real meaning of Christmas. Thankfully, that never happened in our family.

When we were kids, Mom would wake Dave and me up on Christmas and take us into her bedroom, away from the presents and the tree. She'd read us the story of Jesus' birth, and we'd say a prayer of thanks before we ransacked through our gifts.

We've done the same thing every year, and for us, Christmas has not lost its meaning...

I was sleeping in my old bedroom on Christmas morning when Mom came in and began singing,

"Rise and shine, and give God the glory, glory! Rise and shine, and give God the glory, glory! Rise and shine and, give God the glory, glory, children of the Lord!"

She sang that old song to us nearly every day of our childhood. Mom did not have a good voice, to say the least. I used to secretly think that she sang just to annoy us enough, so that we got out of bed in a hurry!

"I'm up, Ma. I'm up," I said a little grumpily, as I stretched my arms over my head.

"What, don't you like my singing?" she asked in a cheerful voice.

I smiled at her and responded, "No, Mom; I love your singing."

She returned my smile and said, "You never were a good liar. Come on into the bedroom. Davey's waiting for us."

I followed Mom down the hallway and into her room. Dave was sitting on her bed, wearing a faded white T-shirt and an old pair of blue jeans.

"Merry Christmas," he said with a tired look on his face.

"Merry Christmas," I repeated as Mom and I sat down on the bed with him.

Dave was holding his Bible in his lap, and as he flipped through the pages he said to me, "Mom's letting me read this year. You don't mind, do ya?"

"Not at all," I said.

Dave read the story of Jesus' birth as recorded in the book of Luke.

"But Mary treasured up all these things and pondered them in her heart. The shepherds returned, glorifying and praising God for all the things they had heard and seen, which were just as they had been told."

Dave shut the Bible as we all bowed our heads and held hands. After taking a deep breath, he said, "Lord, we thank You for Your Son. We thank You for the miracle of His birth.

We thank You, Lord, for the most precious gift ever given to man; Yourself."

"Yes, Lord," Mom whispered in agreement.

"We cannot forget to thank You, Lord, for His death and resurrection. He died for our sins, and He rose again and went to You, so that when we die, He will take us to You. Lord Jesus, You are with our Father. You accomplished His will, and glorified His Name. We thank You, Jesus, for loving us so much. We thank You for sending us the Holy Spirit, Who keeps us on the right path. May we always remember You, Lord, and be ever thankful for what You did and Who You are.

"Happy birthday, Jesus. May this day remind us always of how much God loves us, and like You, may we also live our lives as God has willed us to. In the Name of the Father, and of the Son, and of the Holy Spirit, Amen."

"Amen," Mom and I said together.

After that, we all went into the living room and sat down with some coffee. Our modestly decorated Christmas tree stood in the corner, and Mom started handing out the presents.

Dave said that he wanted nothing but books for Christmas. He had so many already that I had to ask him to write down the ones that he wanted. On the top of his list were Bunyan's Pilgrim's Progress and C.S. Lewis' Mere Christianity and The Screwtape Letters. Mom had read to us The Chronicles of Narnia when Dave and I were young, and ever since then he has loved anything written by Lewis.

As Dave opened my presents to him, he smiled and said sarcastically, "Hey, whad dya know? How'd you guess?"

I shrugged my shoulders and grinned at him as I said, "I had a hunch."

Dave didn't have a job, so he couldn't really buy any presents. The manager at the grocery store had actually told Dave that he was welcome to come back to work, but Dave was too ashamed to go back. So I really didn't expect a gift from him. I was surprised when he reached around the side of the sofa and handed me a horribly wrapped present.

Dave could never wrap anything. It looked like he just tore several pieces of wrapping paper and stuck them on the gift, and then used a whole roll of tape to keep it altogether!

"What's this?" I asked as I set my mug down and reached for the present.

"Nothin' much," Dave said as he looked down at the carpet.

I began ripping open the package with some difficulty and said, "Man, Dave; how much tape did you use on this thing?"

Mom laughed and said, "You know that Davey wrapped it when it looks like that!"

I finally tore away all the paper, and my jaw dropped as I saw what Dave had made for me. It was a wood burning of Mary holding the baby Jesus in her arms, as she looked down at him with a smile. Above them were three angels with their arms spread up to Heaven. It was on a slab of wood that looked like it came right from a tree. You could see the rings on the wood, and there was bark covering the outside.

"This is beautiful," I said sincerely. "Did you *make* this?"

"Yeah," Dave answered humbly. "It's a wood burning. My rehab counselor told me that I should pick up a hobby, so I went to the art store and found this set. It has a metal pen that you plug into the wall, and when it gets hot enough, you burn pictures and stuff onto the wood."

"Let me see," Mom said with excitement as she sat down in between us. I handed it to her without taking my eyes off of it; it was profoundly beautiful.

The moment that she saw it, Mom covered her mouth and cried out, "*Davey!* This is awesome! How come you didn't show me this?"

"Because I didn't want to spoil the surprise," Dave said as he handed Mom another terribly wrapped present.

"I'm gonna cry," Mom said as she received the gift from Dave. "Am I gonna cry?"

"I don't know," Dave said with a chuckle.

As Mom ripped apart the paper, Dave said, "Hopefully I'll get better at this. I messed up so many times it's not funny. I just wanted it to be special, 'cause you guys have done so much for me and everything."

Mom pulled out another slab of wood and set it on her lap. It was coated with a light finish, and Dave had burned a poem on it. As Mom read it, her bottom lip puffed out, and she began to cry. I looked behind her at Dave, and saw that he was fighting back some tears himself. After she had read it, Mom shook her head and gave Dave a big hug, choking out the words, "I *love* it. Thank you, honey."

"Thank *you*." Dave replied.

"What is it?" I asked after they broke from their embrace.

Mom handed me the piece of wood and got up from the couch, saying, "I need some tissues."

I took the wood in my hands and looked down at it. It was an almost exact replica of the Virgin Mary smiling down upon Jesus that Dave had made for me, except written below the picture in beautifully written calligraphy was:

> *There is no other mother quite like you,*
> *And I thank God every day,*
> *That He gave me a mother just like you*
> *To help me along the way.*
> *Merry Christmas,*
> *Love Dave*

*October 27th, 2002-*

*What can a man learn from learning? Can he be taught love? No, it must be shown to him. Wisdom has brought with it confusion. I have been shown my inadequacies. Who am I? To You, my Lord; who am I? The weight in my head has caused me to bow it down. I am nothing without the love of God. Teach me, Lord, with Your faithful, enduring patience. Make Your heart be known to me. Your promise is resounding throughout my spirit… 'Seek and ye shall find…' I am knocking, Lord. I ask You by Your grace and mercy to open the door, that Your Name may be glorified. By Jesus, for Jesus, Amen.*

# 17.

Susie's Mom dropped her off at the house around eleven-thirty. She came in carrying a plastic grocery bag that looked like it was about to burst with presents. Her face was rosy red because of the cold and her blonde hair was pulled back in a ponytail.

Mom met Susie at the door with a big hug.

"Merry Christmas! You look so pretty, as always!"

Susie smiled shyly and said, "Thank you. Hey, Jon."

"How's it going, Susie?"

"Good, good. I can't complain. Where's your brother at?"

Susie flipped her ponytail out from under the white sweater that she had on and sat the bulging plastic bag down on the floor.

"He went down in his room when he saw your car pull up. I guess he's trying to avoid you," I responded with a grin.

"Don't say that!" Mom said as she hung Susie's coat in the closet.

"I was just kidding, Ma."

"Come on in the living room, Susie," Mom called out. "I got something for you."

We walked into the living room. Susie sat down next to Mom on the couch. I took the reclining chair and sat back in it.

Mom handed Susie a small package and said, "Now, if you don't like this, be sure to tell me. I won't feel bad. I kept the receipt just in case."

"Oh," Susie beamed as she took the gift. "You didn't have to do this, Mrs. Sullah."

"I *wanted* to," Mom said assuredly. "You're my little girl- well, you're *Davey's* little girl, but that means you're mine, too!"

Susie unwrapped her gift and opened the small black box inside.

"Oh my goodness!" she exclaimed with delight. "It's beautiful!"

"What is it?" I asked curiously.

Susie got up and showed me what Mom had gotten her. It was a gold ring with what looked like an emerald in the center.

"Wow," I said. "That's real nice."

Susie went back to Mom and gave her a hug.

"Thank you," she said. "I love it!"

"Oh, good!" Mom said with a big smile on her face. "I wasn't sure what to get you, but everybody likes jewelry, and that ring was just so pretty. A pretty ring for a pretty girl!"

"You're such a dork, Mom!" I said with a grin.

Mom looked at me quizzically and asked, "Why am I a dork?"

Before I could reply, the basement door squeaked open and Dave came into the living room. His hair was still sticking up all over the place, and he hadn't showered yet. Even though he looked quite unsightly to me, Susie didn't seem to mind at all. She jumped up from the couch, her face glowing, ran to Dave, and gave him a huge hug.

"Merry Christmas, Teddybear!"

Dave got an agitated look on his face and replied a little harshly, "Don't call me 'Teddybear'!"

"David!" Mom said sternly. "Is that any way to greet your sweetheart?"

Dave huffed and rolled his eyes up at the ceiling.

"Yeah, *Teddybear!*" I said with a giggle.

Dave socked me one in the shoulder before he and Susie sat down next to Mom.

"Knock it off, you two!" Mom said with a half-smile on her face. "Or Susie and I will go spend our Christmas with some *nice* boys."

Susie bent down and reached into the plastic bag, pulling out a long, thin box.

"This is for you, Mrs. Sullah," she said, handing the present to Mom.

"Oh, how nice!" Mom said with a wide smile. "You didn't have to get me anything!"

Mom opened Susie's gift, a hand-knitted red sweater. Mom held it up in the air as she gleefully exclaimed, "I *love* it! Did you do this yourself?"

Susie blushed and nodded her head.

"Thank you so much!" Mom said, as she gave her a big hug. "I'm going to put this on right now!"

Mom got up and went to her room as Susie gave Dave her presents. She got him a watch, a couple of CD's, a book entitled *Wild at Heart*, and a gift certificate to the mall. By the time that he had finished opening the gifts, Mom came back with her new sweater on.

"It fits perfectly!" she said with a joyous look on her face.

I was impressed. I didn't get to look at it real close before, but now that Mom had Susie's sweater on, I saw how good it was.

"That's really nice, Susie," I said honestly. "*Real* nice."

Dave rubbed Susie's back as a look of pride came on his face.

"What'd Susie get you?" Mom asked as she stood by the side of the couch.

"Oh, I got him a book he wanted, a watch, some music, and a gift certificate. He's *so* hard to buy for!"

"Well, I bet he loves everything you got him. Right, Dave?"

"Yeah," Dave answered as he nodded his head.

"So?" Mom asked as she put her hands on her hips. "What did you get for Susie?"

"*Ma!*" Dave said with slight annoyance. "You know that I don't have any money!"

"I would have lent you some money! Poor Susie!"

"That's okay, Mrs. Sullah. Dave already told me that he couldn't get me a present this year."

Mom and Dave smiled at each other as Dave got up and walked into the kitchen. When he came back, he had another awfully wrapped present in his hands.

Susie covered her mouth and laughed heartily as Dave placed it in her lap.

"What?" he said with a grin. "You've seen my wrapping before."

"I know," Susie said, almost in tears. "But this is the worst one I've *ever* seen!"

Mom started laughing as well, and said, "Wait Susie. Don't open it yet. I *have* to take a picture of this!"

Mom was notorious for her picture taking. She had about five disposable cameras on standby at all times, just in case something like this happened. She ran to her room and came back with her camera.

"Okay, Dave; stand by your *honnnneeeey!*" she said in a merry voice.

Dave shook his head and grinned as he and Susie stood in front of the couch. Susie held up the gift (which *was*, I must say, the most atrociously wrapped present that Dave had ever produced) and Mom took the picture.

"Wait!" she said, before they could sit down. "One more, just in case that one doesn't turn out."

Mom took one more picture, then sat the camera down on the coffee table. She had a grin on her face that seemingly stretched from ear to ear. It was so good to see her so happy.

Susie ripped open the wrapping paper, chuckling the whole time. She pulled out a large white, fluffy teddy bear holding a heart in its arms.

"Awww!" Susie exclaimed in joy as she squeezed the bear in her arms. "How *cute!*"

Dave smiled at her and said, "There's a note there, too."

"Where?"

"Taped behind the heart."

Susie turned the bear around and found the note that Dave had attached to it.

" 'Look in the refrigerator' ?"

"Go on, better do what it says."

With a puzzled look on her face, Susie got up and went into the kitchen. The door to the fridge opened, and Susie called out,     "Flowers! They're beautiful!"

She returned to the living room with a dozen long stemmed roses wrapped in fancy plastic.

"I love them!" Susie said as she sat by Dave. She placed the roses on the table and picked up the white bear as she kissed Dave on the cheek.

"You see? You *are* my Teddybear!"

At first Dave gave Susie a perturbed look, but that only lasted for a split-second. He flashed her a huge grin and planted a long kiss on her lips.

*June 1ˢᵗ, 2001-*

*I have become sick to my stomach because of worry.
I know that it is against what God says about worry, but
still, I do. What sense is there in hiding my sin? I worry that
God is trying to show me so much and it is all for nothing,
because I understand so little. I picture Him slapping His
forehead in disgust, thinking,* 'How can this kid be so
ignorant?'

*I worry that I am doing much to impress men and
hardly anything at all to enrich my life with Christ. I worry
that I am a hypocrite. As said before, God is showing me
much; but what am I doing with it? I'm learning some, but
for what? To say that I have learned? What's the point of
knowledge if it's not a part of my life?*

*I know what God has wanted me to know, and some-
times it seems that that's the end of it. It's like I have riches
in my head but my heart is blacker than before, because
now that there is good in my mind, my actions hide what is
stored up there. It's like God has given me so much, and I
say,* 'Well thanks, God. This is all very interesting and all,
and I appreciate it, but hey, Your instructions are too hard to
keep, so I'll just do what I want and take the easy way out,
thank you very much.'

*I feel like I'm taking advantage of God. I pray,* 'Lord,
let it not happen. Let me do Your will.' *So I feel better for a
time, but then I feel like I'm being lazy; manipulative.*

'Let God handle it, and I'll do whatever I want; then if I
sin, I'll say, "Hey; I *told* God to handle it; it's not *my* fault."

*My head is heav,y because I know so much and so little
at the same time. I need a Savior; His name is Jesus.*

*Lord, despite my faults, my evil thoughts, my hypocrisy, my manipulation; come quick and save me. Have I confessed my sins? You know I have, even though there are more. The pen would lose its ink if I continued. 'Blessed is the man who fears always.' I fear You, Lord- I fear You. I do not want to disappoint You, although You already know the outcome. Hear my prayer now, as You already have:*

*Forgive me for my sins, rebuke me so that I might discontinue them. Show me Your way so that I might follow You, and in the end may You look at me with the undying love in Your eyes and may You say,* 'Well done, good and faithful servant.'

*In the name of my Savior Jesus Christ,*
*Amen.*

# 18.

I n one of his journal entries, Dave wrote:
*'No one puts me down like I do.'*

My brother was always so hard on himself. Nothing that he did was ever good enough - for *him*, that is. In the latter part of his life, Dave learned that God *had* given him some great talents. He learned that it was a disgrace to God if he used what He had given him for His name's sake then said, *"It's not good enough."* That's *not* humility. That's kind of like saying the gifts that God has given you aren't satisfactory for you.

One day when I was a sophomore in college, I received a large manila envelope from Dave in the mail...

I went up to my dorm room on the second floor. Both my roommates were at class, so it was nice and quiet for a change. I sat on my bed and opened the envelope that I had gotten from the mailroom. There were a bunch of papers stapled together, and on the front page Dave had written:

*Hey Jon,*

*I know that you're busy with school and all, but if you get a second, please look over these poems and tell me what you think. When I first wrote them, I thought that they were pretty good, but the more I read them the more I think they suck and I should just throw them out. I haven't shown them to anyone else; not even Mom or Susie. They'd both tell me that they were good, even if they weren't. Please tell me the truth, either way. Hope all is going well, and that you're doing well in school. I know you are!*

*Your bro,*
*Dave*

I flipped through the pages, and figured that there were about ten poems in all. Dave had written each one by hand, which made it a little difficult to read because he wrote so sloppily. I turned to the first page and began reading.

'Oh, David'

*Livin' a life of silence*
*when all I want to do is shout.*
*Always afraid of somethin'*
*but I just can't figure it out.*
*Never quite fittin' in*
*wherever it is that I go.*
*Is this the story of my life,*
*to wander 'round the dark and cold?*

*"Well it's dark sometimes, David,*
*and the cold can freeze your bones.*

*Never once did I say*
*that it'd be a safe trip to your Home.*
*But oh, I love you, David,*
*and one day you will see*
*that the darkness and the cold were used*
*to bring you to the warmth and light of Me.*
*The darkness and the cold were used*
*to bring you to the warmth and light of Me."*

*Lord, I know You love me,*
*that I can plainly see.*
*But what about the things I do*
*that drive You away from me?*
*You know I love You, Jesus,*
*but I sometimes treat You second best.*
*What is there besides You?*
*Why can't I throw out the rest?*
*Sometimes, Lord, I just can't tell*
*if I am doing any good.*
*I always wonder if I'm walking*
*down the path that I should.*

*"Oh David, oh David!*
*Why do you talk this way?*
*When we were on the mountaintop,*
*didn't you hear what I did say?*
*Even though you're in the valley now,*
*My promises never die.*
*We are one together, son,*
*your pain is also Mine.*
*We are one together, son,*
*your pain is also Mine."*

*Lord, my Savior, Jesus Christ,*
*I want to live for You.*

*If that calls for hardships,*
*with You, I can walk them through.*
*Just never leave me, Jesus,*
*even when I push You away.*
*You have made a place in my heart,*
*and forever may You stay.*
*Lead me, guide me, Jesus,*
*correct me when I do wrong.*
*Lift my voice to our Father above,*
*and let Him hear my song.*

*"David, oh, dear David!*
*The Lord hears every word!*
*He hears the wind blow through the grass,*
*and the chirps of every bird.*
*How much more so the cries*
*of the righteous He will hear.*
*My son, I am your megaphone,*
*when you talk, keep Me near.*
*My son, I am your megaphone...*
*when you talk... keep Me... near."*

I was astounded - literally shocked. I read the poem over and over. It seemed to me like something a seasoned theologian might have penned; *not* a seventeen year old kid!

I read through the rest of Dave's poems, and they were all very good. None of them touched me the way the first one had, however; probably because it was so personal. Reading it made me feel for my brother in a way that I never had before.

The last sheet of paper in the stack was titled, 'Man's Best Friend'.

*Man's best friend is ever-faithful. If the man leaves his*
*house for a long period of time, his best friend will still*

*greet him warmly upon his return. He won't say, "How come you left me for so long?" or treat the man with contempt, but only celebrate with glee when he sees that the man has come back home.*

*Man's best friend is a good companion. He offers the man joy and comfort just by being there with him.*

*Man's best friend takes a scolding from the man, but never runs away.*

*Man's best friend chases away robbers and evildoers; he does not let them enter the man's house.*

*Man's best friend listens to the man, but doesn't always do what he is told.*

*Man's best friend has no problem with taking long walks through the dark woods with the man; he is fearless.*

*Man's best friend offers his love to the man, and expects the man's love in return.*

*Man's best friend will lead the blind across a busy intersection.*

*Man's best friend barks loudly at times, and whimpers softly at others.*

*Man's best friend is spelled with the letters 'd-o-g', but not in that order.*

*Man's best friend doesn't make messes on the rug.*

*Man's best friend doesn't bite the neighbor.*

*Man's best friend doesn't sniff rear ends!*

*Man's best friend cannot be trained by man to do evil.*

*Man's best friend understands us, even though we cannot always understand him.*

*Man will never again bury his best friend; he tried to once, but his best friend overcame death.*

*Man's best friend loves man so much that he offered himself as a sacrifice.*

*Greater love has no one than the love of man's best friend for man.*

*Man's best friend wants man to know that* God *is man's best friend.*

After reading that, I immediately picked up the phone and called home.

"Hello?"

Since going through puberty, my brother's voice had gone from squeaky and high-pitched to very deep and quite soothing to the ear.

"Dave. What's going on, man?"

"Oh, hey Jon. Not much."

He seemed depressed; his voice was so despondent.

"Are you okay?" I asked.

"Yeah," he answered in an unconvincing tone. "I guess I'm just having one of those days."

"Hmmm." I thought about whether or not I should ask him what was wrong, but Dave didn't really like to talk about his problems. I decided not to pry.

"I got the letters you sent me."

"Oh yeah? What'd you think?" Dave asked hesitantly.

"I gotta tell you, man; they are awesome. I can't believe that you actually wrote them!"

There was silence for a moment. Then Dave sighed and said, "Are you just saying that, or do you really mean it?"

"Dave, I'm serious," I replied firmly. "They're really good."

"Thanks," he said, as a little bit of cheer crept into his voice. "I don't know...it's hard for me to tell if anything I do is any good. It's like, I think it is at first, but then I start thinking that it was only wishful thinking. I don't know...it's tough."

I smiled and shook my head as I responded,

"Well, believe me, Dave; those poems are...I can't even explain it. They're just so insightful. I don't know how you do it, man. And that first one you wrote, "Oh, David"? I mean, I could tell that it was right from your heart. Did you actually hear God respond to you?"

"No." Dave replied with no hesitation. "Not audibly, at least. Do you wanna know what happened?"

"Yeah, of course." I replied eagerly.

"Alright. I was outside smoking a cigarette, and-"

"Whoa!" I interrupted. "Since when do you smoke cigarettes?"

"Mom didn't tell you?"

"No."

"Huh. I know that she's keeping it a secret from everybody else, but I figured that she'd a told you. I started smoking a few weeks ago. Don't give me a speech, okay?"

"Alright." I said, a little concerned.

"So anyway, I'm outside before school one day last week, and it's about five in the morning. I don't know if Mom told you this, but I joined the Youth Group at our church."

"Yeah, she did tell me that."

"I don't know - it's got me reading the Bible again; and not only reading it, but kind of meditating on what I read. I used to think that I knew every story in the Bible - well, the more I read, the more I find out that there's a lot in there that I haven't seen before.

"And a lot of times after I read...it's like I'm inspired to write. Stuff just flows from my pen.

"Well anyway, I'm outside, and I look up at the sky. It's still real dark and everything, and it's cold, and...I don't know - it's like I was staring right through everything and seeing God. Not like I saw Him; but I knew that He was looking right back at me. You know what I mean?"

"I think so, yeah."

"So I was staring up at the sky, and...I can't put it into words - I heard this voice in my head. But it wasn't like I was thinking it, 'cause it wasn't my voice. It was like I felt it through my whole body...it was saying, 'write'.

"And I kinda answered it with a question in my head. I thought, 'Write what?' But I didn't get any response. I couldn't deny that I heard it, so I went down to my room and opened my notebook. I sat there for a couple of minutes, just staring at the blank page, but I couldn't think of anything to write. Finally, I took the notebook outside and looked back up at the sky and said in my mind, 'Lord, what do You want me to write?'

"Right away, I began thinking of everything that I've been feeling lately....Just really alone, confused, and...just real bad. So I began writing it all down. After I wrote the first few lines or whatever, I felt God giving me His words.

"Does this sound weird to you?"

"Not at all," I said, listening intently to every word that Dave was saying.

"As I wrote what God was telling me..." Dave trailed off, and there was silence for a few seconds. Just as I was about to ask him if he was still there, his voice came back over the phone; but now he was in tears.

"He kept telling me, 'I love you, David, I love you!!' And that's all I heard!"

I had to swallow a large lump in my throat, as tears began to brew in my eyes. The way that Dave had said that; so emphatically through his tears...it was clearly evident to me that God had spoken to my brother.

He continued on in a strained voice.

"And I wrote that poem, not really even knowing what I had written! All I knew was God's love...God's love, even for me!"

Tears were now flowing down my cheeks as Dave wept on the other end. Before I could speak, I again had to swallow a large knot, then said, "God does love you, Dave. You know that, right?"

Dave sighed deeply, then answered, "Yeah, I know."

November 19th, 2000-

Temptations to a pilgrim given
(If he's obeyed the call from Heaven)
From ev'ry side attack his flesh.
They come, and then come back afresh
That they may overcome the man
And quite destroy him, if they can!
So, Pilgrim, guard against the wrong
And in thy mighty God be strong!
                    -John Bunyan, *Pilgrim's Progress*

*My Lord has set before me a path that leads to Him.*
*Guiding me along this path is my Lord. When I venture*
*from His way, which I shamefully admit happens more than*
*it ought, my Lord does not go about without me. He does*
*not leave me; for if He had even once, I would forever be*
*lost. No, He calls out for me. I hear His voice, and I see His*
*voice at times as well. Only then do I look around and see*
*that I am being led by one other than my Lord.*

*Being strengthened by His call, I rush back to the*
*clearness of the path where my Lord is waiting for me.*
*Faithfully, He accepts me as I'm on my knees. He picks me*
*up, and we travel together again.*

*Great is His mercy! Great is His love! Great is my*
*Lord!*

*I follow Him to the best of my knowledge, and as I*
*follow Him more, my knowledge increases. Praise the Lord*
*forever!!*

# 19.

In the year 2000, I met a lovely girl named Anne whom would later become my wife. In contrast, Susie broke up with Dave for the second and final time.

Mom was unsure why they split, and told me that Dave would not talk to her about it. She was worried about Dave, and said that he was more depressed than she had ever seen him.

I wrote Dave numerous letters, telling him that I was there for him if he needed to talk. He never wrote back.

Late one night, I was alone in my dorm room, studying for a test. As I sat on my bed going over my notes, I received an unexpected phone call...

"Hello?"

"Hello? Jon?"

"This is?" I said, not quite recognizing the voice on the other end.

"Hi, it's Susie."

"Hey," I said, wondering why she would be calling me. "What's going on?"

"I hope you don't mind," Susie said in a timid voice. "I got your number from your mom. I told her that I wanted to talk to you about Dave."

"Yeah? What about him?" I asked as I shut my notebook, puzzled and concerned at the same time.

Susie took a deep breath, then responded, "I didn't want to tell your mother, because she worries so much, but...I have to tell *somebody*."

Susie paused for a moment and left me in suspense.

"Tell somebody what?"

After another prolonged silence, she said, "Dave's back on drugs."

My heart sank, as I sat slack-jawed and stared at the wall. This was certainly dreadful news. I was in shock.

"Are you sure?" I asked softly, not wanting it to be true.

"Yes. He didn't tell me at first, but I could tell that he was back on pot. He was always in a nasty mood, and he'd say real mean things to me and your mom. I was hoping that I was wrong, but I knew that Dave wasn't acting like himself, and I know that marijuana makes you do that.

"I let it go for a while without saying anything, trying to ...pretend that it wasn't happening. But one day he said something to me...something that I won't repeat. We were walking to my house from school, and I said to him, 'What the hell is wrong with you? Are you using drugs again?'

"And Dave looked at me with this sorta blank expression on his face, and he said something like, 'Yeah, I'm smoking weed again, because pot doesn't bitch at me the way you do!'"

Susie's voice began to tremble, as she continued talking through her tears.

"Your brother never talked to me like that! I mean...oh! That wasn't him! That wasn't him, and it scares me!"

She began to weep profusely, unable to go on.

"It's okay, Susie," I said, trying to use my most comforting tone, while at the same time sick to my stomach.

"No, it's *not* okay!" she said adamantly through her sobs. "I can't stand it! I loved...I love Dave so much, that even after the way he treated me, which is like dirt, even after all that, and all the things that he said, I still wanted to be with him."

Susie sniffed and exhaled deeply. Her tears subsided, and she said, "But I told him, I said, 'You have to stop doing drugs.'

"He just laughed at me and said, 'What are you, my mother?'

"I told him I was serious. I said that I'd leave him if he wouldn't quit. I told him that he was acting like a jerk, and I wouldn't put up with it. Then he got really mad and started screaming at me, saying that if I really loved him I'd never leave him, no matter what. We got in a big fight, and at the end he said, 'Fine, get outta here, I don't want to see you ever again.'

"He looked at me with this cruel expression on his face and said, 'All this time I really thought that you loved me.'

"And that's it," Susie concluded, as her voice began to shake again. "That's the last thing Dave ever said to me."

I took a long breath and exhaled deeply.

*Why would Dave do this?* I thought. *He was doing so well, he seemed to have everything going for him...and now he's thrown it all away.*

A verse from the Book of Proverbs immediately came to mind; something about a dog returning to his vomit.

"Oh Susie," I said gently. "I'm so sorry. Why would Dave do this?"

"I don't know!" she cried out. "Everything was going so good! I was so happy...we were so happy! I don't know!"

I hated hearing Susie cry. It was heartbreaking.

"My Mom doesn't know about this?"

"No. I thought about telling her, but I just couldn't. I wouldn't be able to stand the look on her face."

"Are you gonna be okay? I mean, is there anything that I can do?"

"No, I don't think so," Susie replied tearfully. "I gotta go; just...I don't know. He's your brother. I thought maybe you could talk to him."

"I will," I said. "And thanks for telling me, Susie. I mean it. Try to keep your chin up; I'll be praying for you."

"Thank you," she said weakly, and then she hung up.

I sat on the bed with the phone in my lap, wondering if this was all really happening. Returning to drugs was the last thing that I expected Dave to do. Not after all he'd been through; not after all we've been through.

After several minutes of sitting motionless on my bed, I finally hung up the phone and began to think about what to do.

*Do I tell Mom? No, that is my last resort. First I have to talk with Dave.*

I looked at the clock. It was after midnight. I couldn't call home now. Mom would know that something was up. I closed my eyes and ran a hand through my hair. I knew with a sudden assurance what I had to do.

'Lord God, Father…You love us like no other. Your hands created us with tenderness, and You watch us live our lives with compassion for us in Your heart. There is no God but You, and I am thankful that You are Who You are.

*Lord, my brother is in desperate need of You, as we all are at all times. I pray, Lord, that You send down Your angels to protect him…that you grab Satan with Your mighty hand, and rip the evil mongrel away from Dave, and not permit him to ever return.*

*He needs you, Lord…he is blinded by darkness, by Satan himself. Only You can save him, Lord. Have mercy on Dave, the great mercy that You alone possess. Father, I am in anguish…tears of pain fall from my eyes. Tears that only You can wipe away…Lord, I trust in You. I trust in Your power, I trust in Your love…I trust that You have great empathy for Your lost sheep, that You will call them back to Your pasture.*

*Also, Lord, be with Susie. Heal her wounds, Lord. If she does not know you as her Lord and Savior, I pray she calls out to You in her distress. Show Yourself to her, Lord; let her see Your love for her, and may she love You in return.*

*Lord…my strength fails. I don't know what to do, or what to think. I am greatly discouraged…Lord God, lift up my spirits. Let me know that You have everything under control, and that You, oh Lord, are Love.*

*I ask all this in the most precious name of the Lord Jesus Christ,*

*Amen.'*

I sat there in silence, with my eyes still closed, not moving a muscle. I had never prayed like that before. Usually when I prayed, it was a quick 'Thank You' or an even quicker, 'I'm sorry, Lord.' This time, though, I felt connected with God in a way I never had before.

I slowly opened my eyes, half expecting that I would see the Lord Himself, or maybe an angel, sitting on my bed across from me. The prayer was that powerful; I knew that my words had been prompted by the Holy Spirit, and I truly felt His presence in the room.

It was then that I fell in love with prayer.

*June 20ᵗʰ, 2001-*

    *Lambs get lost sometimes. They wander off, thinking,
'It's okay for me to go there. I will be alright on my own for
a little while.' But after a time the lamb looks up and sees
that the flock is gone. He is all alone and scared. He finds
himself surrounded by darkness, with dense foliage in every
direction. He knows not which way to go.*

    *In distress, the lamb cries out to his shepherd, "Help
me! I have turned away and now am lost! Please, I need
you to come find me, because I don't know where I am!"*

    *The lamb hears a rustling to his right...is it a wolf? He
shrinks back in fear, assuming that this will be his demise.
But his thoughts disappear when he sees his beloved shepherd appear through the foliage. With no condemnation on
his face, the shepherd picks up the lamb into his arms as he
says,*

    *"You are mine, little one. I heard your voice, and I have
found you."*

    *The shepherd loves his sheep. He does not complain
about the scratches or bruises that he received while journeying through the foliage. He does not complain about
having to crawl through the muck and climb up tall hills.
He does not complain about what time was 'wasted' to
retrieve his lost sheep. He is only filled with joy, because he
loves his sheep.*

# 20.

I realize that the last two passages I used from Dave's journal pertain to the same subject, and I also realize that their message is probably all too familiar to you. So why do I include them both, back to back? Why did Dave write of this topic, not twice, but at least seventeen times altogether? Because sometimes we take God's grace for granted. Read that last sentence again.

Dave poured his heart out on numerous occasions in his journals regarding the grace of God. He knew that without this amazing grace, he would be a goner. God's grace is amazing. Where would we be without it? Where would you, dear reader, be without it?

Let's not ever lose our appreciation for the patience and love that God has for us. Remember it now as you read on about Dave, and remember it always as you live your life.

The day after I received Susie's dispiriting phone call, I sat in my room, thinking about what I should do. I wanted to talk with Dave, but every time I picked up the phone, I had to set it back down. I didn't know what to say to him, and was fearful about using the wrong words.

After much prayer, I decided to write him another letter. I got on my computer and sent my brother this simple note:

Hey, Dave. Haven't heard from you in a while. What, are you too busy to write to your brother?! Come on, man; just a quick 'hello', that's all. Let me know how you're doing. Take care, Jon.

Five days went by with no reply. I thought to myself, *'That's it, I can't take it anymore! I have to call him and tell him that I know about the drugs.'*

I picked up the phone and called home. To my surprise, Aunt Sheila answered.

"Hello?"

"Hello? Aunt Sheila?"

"Jon! Wow, that's weird; I was just about to call you."

"Oh yeah?" I asked apprehensively, sensing that something was amiss.

"Jon, I...are you sitting down? Maybe you should be sitting down."

"Why?" I asked urgently, as I sat straight up on my bed. "What's wrong?"

Aunt Sheila took a deep breath, then said, "Your mother and I weren't going to tell you at first. We thought that you had enough stress, just being in school, and that you didn't need any more...but you really should know.

"Jon, your brother took off last night, and he made it pretty clear that he isn't coming back."

I closed my eyes and solemnly shook my head and asked, "What do you mean, he took off?"

"Basically, Dave told your mother that he was sick of her controlling him, and that he was going to move in with one of his friends. At first she thought that Dave was just lashing out at her; she didn't think he was really gonna do it. But last night he came out of his room with a couple a garbage bags full of his stuff. Your mother was watching T.V. on the couch, and she said that he just looked at her and said, 'I'm leaving, and you can't stop me.'

"Well, she chased after him outside, but Dave got into a car that was waiting for him and left. I'm worried about him, but I'm even more worried about your mom."

Her voice became quiet as she whispered, "I've never seen her like this, Jon. She's been laying on her bed all day, not saying anything or even moving a muscle."

I felt a rage brewing inside of me. I could just picture Mom, laying down on her bed with a look of despondent submission on her face; her hands folded neatly on her lap, as she sorrowfully stared off into space. I knew Mom, and I knew that she was probably blaming herself for this. I was no longer concerned for Dave; I was *infuriated* with him.

"She called me earlier today," Aunt Sheila went on. "And it really scared me. Her voice was so...I can't describe it. She just kept repeating, 'Dave's gone...Dave's gone' in this eerie...*nonchalant* tone.

"I couldn't get her to tell me anything on the phone, so I rushed over here as quick as I could. It took a while, but she finally told me what happened. I guess Dave called after he left last night and told your mother where he was."

"Where?" I asked immediately. I stood up from my bed, as if I was going to run to where Dave was and bring him home.

"He's at a trailer park a mile or so down the road from your house. He gave your mom the number, but wouldn't tell her what trailer he was staying in."

"Did you call him yet?"

"Yeah, but no one answered. I probably left a dozen messages on the answering machine, though. Oh, the kid's name is Jeff. Do you know who that is?"

I thought for a moment, but I couldn't recall any "Jeff's" that Dave might know.

"No, I don't think so."

Aunt Sheila sighed and said, "What are we gonna do, Jon? I mean, legally, he has every right to leave the house. He's eighteen, so we can't call the cops or anything."

"Did Mom get a look at the car that Dave got in? Maybe you could drive around the trailer park and find it."

"Yeah, I thought about that, too. But you know how your mother is with cars. All she knows is that it was red."

I leaned forward with my fist under my chin as I thought.

"Okay," I said. "Give me the number, and I'll keep on calling until somebody answers. Tomorrow I only have one class, and then I'm done for the weekend. Would you be able to pick me up Friday in the afternoon and then take me back on Sunday?"

"Yes, I suppose so. Why? What are you thinking about doing?"

"I'm gonna find out where Dave is," I responded with assurance. "And I'm gonna talk to him; I'm gonna have a *long* talk with him."

"What do you think is the matter with him?" Aunt Sheila asked. "I know that he broke up with Susie, and that really upset him...but do you think there's something else?"

I knew what she was hinting at. She might as well have said, 'Is Dave using drugs again?' Although I knew the truth of the matter, I felt no need to add to hers and Mom's discouragement.

"It sure seems like it," I replied. "But try not to worry. We'll get Dave all straightened out. What about Mom? Are you going to stay with her?"

"Oh yeah. I wouldn't even think about leaving her alone right now."

I nodded my head and said, "Good. Thanks, Aunt Sheila. I don't know what we'd do without you. Do you think that Mom feels like talking?"

"Hold on, I'll ask her."

After a few seconds, Aunt Sheila whispered, "Looks like she's sleeping, Jon. I don't want to wake her, she's probably been up all night."

"That's okay," I said. "I'll call around noon tomorrow and see what a good time would be for you to come and get me. 'Til then, just take care of Mom. Let her know that I'm coming home, and tell her I love her."

"Okay, Jon. Will do."

I hung up the phone and immediately fell face down onto my pillow, screaming as loud as I could into it. By the time that I stopped, I was completely out of breath. I looked at the alarm clock on my nightstand. It was two-thirty eight, and I was late for class. I hurriedly threw on my jacket and rushed out the door.

I didn't learn one thing for the half-hour that my professor spoke. The only things that were on my mind were my mother and Dave.

*March 10ᵗʰ, 2002-*

*I looked up at the starry sky; at one star in particular, a very bright one. I prayed, "Lord, make Jesus as true in my heart as He is true. As He lives, may He live in my heart." As soon as I had said that, a cloud covered the star that I was gazing upon, and I became discouraged- but I did not look away. After a few seconds, the cloud passed, and I saw the star again, shining brightly. I thought to myself, 'No mere cloud can hide the glory of God! Though clouds come and go, His presence is always there!' I fell to my knees, and praised the Lord. Live on, Jesus. Live on.*

# 21.

I decided not to call the number that Aunt Sheila had given me. I didn't want Dave to know that I was coming.

Aunt Sheila picked me up at campus around three in the afternoon on Friday, with Mom riding along in the front seat. Not much was said on the trip home. Aunt Sheila tried for a while to make pleasant conversation about school and the weather, but it didn't last long. I can speak for all of us in saying that our hearts were far from cheerful; we were grief stricken.

We pulled into the driveway at four o'clock and parked the car in our garage.

"Are you hungry?" Mom asked me as we stepped into the house.

"Yeah, a little bit. What do you got?"

"Oh, I don't know," Mom said, as she opened the refrigerator and bent over to look inside. "There's some ham and some turkey- I could make you a sandwich."

"That's okay. I can get something for myself," I said, as I walked up next to Mom. "Why don't you sit down and relax?"

Aunt Sheila was right about how Mom was acting. I had never seen her like this before, either. Her sad face showed wrinkles that hadn't been noticeable before, and there was a blankness in her eyes. She walked away towards the living room, shoulders slumping, feet dragging, as if she barely had the strength to lift them.

Aunt Sheila solemnly watched as Mom disappeared around the corner. She set her car keys down on the kitchen counter, looked at me with one hand on her hip, and asked in a whisper, "So what are we gonna do?"

In a way, I was sort of proud of the fact that Aunt Sheila was asking me for advice. She had been a strong influence on me growing up, and I deeply respected her. She was there with Mom, cheering me on when I played baseball and basketball in High School. She was there on all of my birthdays, and for my graduation. She was there when I needed to talk with someone about things that I was too embarrassed to talk with Mom about; namely, girls. She was there to give me godly advice, and there when I needed a helping hand or a good laugh. She was always there.

I folded my arms across my chest as I leaned against the refrigerator and responded, "Well, I guess I'm going to go down to the trailer park...but I don't know how I'll find where Dave is. Maybe I'll just knock on every door that has a red car parked by it until I find him."

"Why don't you give Dave a call and ask him where he is? I bet he'll tell *you*."

I shook my head and answered, "No, I thought about that, and I think he might take off somewhere if he knows that I'm coming. I'd rather play it safe and catch him by surprise."

Aunt Sheila looked toward the living room with concern in her dark brown eyes. She then came up close to me and put her hands on my shoulders. When I was little, I knew that when Aunt Sheila got on her knees and laid her hands on my shoulders, she was letting me know that she was going to tell me something important. It hadn't lost its effect, even now that I was a good six inches taller than her.

"Your mother and I have been praying about this a lot, and I have to tell you something that I couldn't tell her."

She glanced to her left to make sure that Mom wasn't in earshot, then looked back into my eyes and continued.

"I've got a bad feeling about this, Jon...a real...*bad* feeling." Her bottom lip began to tremble, and she had to bite it down before going on.

"I think God's trying to tell me that Dave is in a load of trouble. I got this...this sinking feeling in my stomach when we prayed about him. It was so bad that I nearly threw up."

I nodded slowly at Aunt Sheila as I said, "I know what you mean. I have that same feeling."

Her eyes squinted as if she were in pain, and then she pulled me close and hugged me tightly. I gently caressed her long brown hair as she quietly wept in my arms.

"Jonny? Sheila?" Mom's barely audible voice called out from the living room. "Come in here, please."

We pulled apart from each other, as Aunt Sheila wiped her face dry. I rubbed her back and asked, "Are you alright?"

She nodded her head as she sniffed and replied, "Yeah, just give me a minute. I don't want her to see me crying."

After a couple of seconds, Aunt Sheila took a deep sigh and smiled at me.

"Okay," she said. "Let's go."

We walked into the living room and saw Mom sitting on the couch. She was holding a Bible in her lap and had her head bowed. When she lifted her head up, I was surprised to see a warm smile on her face.

"Sit down," she said, patting the cushion of the sofa.

We sat with her, me being in the middle of Mom and Aunt Sheila.

"I want to read you something that really touched my heart just now."

Mom didn't have her glasses on, so she had to hold the Bible real close to her eyes as she read.

"Matthew eleven, starting in verse twenty-two: 'Have faith in God,' Jesus answered. 'I tell you the truth, if anyone says to this mountain, "Go, throw yourself into the sea," and does not doubt in his heart but believes that what he says will happen, it will be done for him. Therefore I tell you, whatever you ask for in prayer, believe that you have received it, and it will be yours.'"

Mom closed her Bible and looked at me with a joyful countenance. Taking my hand, she said, "Let's pray."

I grabbed Aunt Sheila's hand as we all bowed our heads.

"Lord God," Mom started. "Like the song goes, 'how great Thou art'...You *are* great, Lord. When we feel nothing but despair, You come in and fill us with hope. When there is nothing but darkness around, You come in and show us light. All we need to do is look, Lord; and there you are.

"I feel Your love...and it has taken away my fear; in Your presence, dread flees, and hope flourishes. You alone can turn tragedy into triumph; and in You, oh God, we trust."

"Amen." I said, as Aunt Sheila squeezed my hand.

"Lord, we face a mountain; one that cannot be removed by us. But what is impossible for man is possible for God. How good it is to trust in You! How good it is to know that You care!

"Lord, by Your love, by Your grace, by Your power; take this mountain and toss it into the sea! My boy...my Davey... he needs You, Lord. You alone know what he needs. You have made Yourself known to us time and time again. Now Lord, we pray that You do the same for Dave. If he needs light, Lord, show him light. If he needs hope, Lord, show him hope. Whatever it is, we pray that You give him the goodness of You.

"As always, Lord, we pray in the name of our Savior. We pray in the name of the only Mediator between God and man. We pray in the name of the Lamb that was slaughtered for our sins. We pray in His name, with no fear in our hearts, because, although sometimes the world overcomes us, He has overcome the world. We pray in the name of Your blessed Son; our Lord and Savior, Jesus Christ."

"Amen."

"Amen."

I lifted my head and opened my eyes. We hugged each other, and I noticed that all three of our faces were the same. Tears poured down our cheeks, but these were not tears of sorrow. They were tears of joyful hope.

*August 14ᵗʰ, 2002-*

*As my eyes closed, I saw Jesus pick up a lamb who had trotted towards Him. A smile shown brightly on His face, as He held the lamb in His arms. After a while, the lamb began to kick and struggle, but Jesus would not let him go. His hooves struck the Lord in His face, but His gentle countenance never changed - it always held the expression of love and care. Finally, the lamb quieted, and rested in His arms. He looked up at Jesus with the same love that He looked down upon him with. The lamb licked His cheek and looked at Jesus with an expression on his face so power-fully emotional that it can't be expressed by mere words, but is best described as, "Thank You so much for not letting me go!"*

# 22.

After a light dinner, we sat around the table and discussed what I should say to Dave. The three of us agreed that it would be best for me to go alone, because Dave would probably feel more comfortable talking with me.

"I think that you should ask him why he left home right away - you know, don't beat around the bush," Aunt Sheila suggested, as Mom sat steaming mugs of coffee before us. "There must be something that's really bugging him, and I'm sure that deep down he wants to talk about it."

"I don't know," I said, shaking my head. "Dave likes to keep his problems to himself."

"He's right," Mom agreed, as she took her seat at the end of the table. "It usually takes a lot of convincing before Davey will open up."

We conversed about it for a while, but in the end decided that it would be best just to trust in the Holy Spirit to guide me, as Mom and Aunt Sheila sat at home and prayed.

Clarkson County trailer park was a three-mile drive down our street, in the opposite direction of the village of Auburn. After we said a quick prayer, I took Mom's 1997 Ford Taurus and headed down the road.

It was just after six p.m., and the sun was going down in the distance, creating a spectacular view in the sky. The whole way there I prayed that on my way back, Dave would be in the car with me.

I turned into the trailer park with no idea where I would go. It was a small park; maybe fifty yards across and a hundred long. There was the main road that ran straight to the back of the park, with smaller streets off shooting from the main strip. I decided to drive all the way to the back, then go down each side street on both sides of the main road.

As I reached the end of the main road, I took a left and drove slowly down the street. There were trailers lining both sides of the road, so close to each other that they were nearly touching. I thought to myself, *'Just how do I plan on finding Dave in all this?'*

I slowly drove down street after street, stopping the Taurus in front of every trailer that had a red car parked in its tiny driveway. Most of the time, I could assume whether or not the car was a teenager's or an adult's simply by the bumper stickers. A few had the 'I'm a proud parent of an honor student' attached to the rear of the car, and I knew that that wasn't the trailer I was looking for. Others had kid's toys or small bikes lying in the miniature front lawn.

When I saw a trailer with a red car that had no telltale signs either way, I wrote the street name and the address down. My plan was to go through the whole park, stake out all the possible trailers that Dave might be in, and then go back to each one until I found him.

I was halfway through the park when I came across a light-blue trailer near the end of the street. There was a red El Camino parked next to it with a bumper sticker that read, 'Bad cop; no donut.' Somehow I knew that this was the trailer I was looking for. I parked Mom's car on the side of the road and took a deep breath.

'God be with me,' I thought. 'This is it.'

The trailers all sat long ways facing the road. You could see through a wide window in the front, if a curtain didn't cover it. The lights were on in what looked like the living room of the blue trailer, and I saw some teens walking by the window. I walked up to the door and heard muffled music being played inside. There was no doorbell, so I knocked loud enough to be heard.

After a few seconds, the door opened and the music poured clearly into my ears. It was some funky sort of song; I thought maybe by the Grateful Dead.

A black haired kid who couldn't have been older than nineteen stood in the doorway with a confused look on his face and said, "Yeah?"

He was wearing a black T-shirt with a picture of a skate-boarder doing an Ollie on a half-pipe. He had on a green mesh trucker's hat with his hair puffing out from under it.

"I'm Jon Sullah, Dave's older brother. Is he here?"

The kid gave me a questioning look and said, "I don't live here, man. Let me ask around if anyone's seen him."

He shut the door in my face, and I waited on the cement steps. I put my ear to the door, but couldn't hear anything over the music. By the way that he had looked at me, I was sure that Dave was inside. I considered letting myself in and demanding to see my brother, but before I could, the door creaked back open, and out stepped Dave. He quickly shut the door behind him and stepped down onto the steps next to me.

Dave's hair was all messy, as if he hadn't showered all day. He had on a tie-dye shirt and faded blue jeans.

"Hey Jon. What's up?" he asked in an uneasy voice.

Dave kept his head slightly bowed, and he wouldn't look me in the eyes. His clothes reeked of pot, and his breath smelled like beer. He reached into his pocket for a pack of cigarettes and lit one as I thought of where to begin.

"So...you're living here now?"

"Yeah, for a little while, at least" he answered in a proud sort of tone.

"You mind if I ask why?" I said, while stuffing my hands in my pockets. It was getting a tad chilly outside, and I had forgotten my jacket.

He shrugged his shoulders and responded, "To get away from the house. I just need some time to...to just think about some stuff."

"Think about *what*?" I asked, raising an eyebrow at him. "What can you think about here that you can't at home?"

Dave exhaled some smoke and stared down at his feet.

"I don't know," he said. "You probably wouldn't understand."

"Try me."

Dave sighed then responded, "Okay. Mom's been treating me like a baby. She won't let me do anything. All I want to do is hang out with my friends, you know. What's so wrong with that?"

I looked into the window and saw kids walking around with beer in their hands. .

"Why do you think Mom doesn't want you hanging out with these people?"

"I don't know," Dave said in an agitated voice. "She doesn't even know them. She always says stuff like, 'I heard through a reliable source that so-and-so is a bad kid.' Then when I ask her who this 'reliable source' is, she won't tell me."

"So, this isn't really about you getting away to think about things. It's about you getting away from Mom."

"I guess," Dave said. He took a drag from his cigarette, as he looked me in the eyes for the first time during our conversation.

"How'd you know where I was?" he asked.

I smiled at him and replied, "You can't hide from me, bro. I have my ways of finding you."

Dave gave me a slight smile then said, "I guess so."

There were a few seconds of awkward silence. I looked down at the ground, unsure of what to say next. Very quickly I prayed,

*'Guide me, Holy Spirit.'*

I lifted my head and said tenderly, "I heard about you and Susie. I'm sorry, Dave."

He slowly nodded his head and said, "Yeah, it sucks, but what are you going to do, you know? What did Mom tell you?"

"She told me that you guys broke up, and she didn't know why…But later Susie called me, and she told me the reason."

Dave had been looking off to his left, but as I said that, his head snapped towards me, and his eyes opened wide.

"What? What'd she say?"

"She said that you're back on drugs," I replied coolly, while looking him right in his eyes.

Dave's jaw dropped as he turned his head and stared off to the side a little. We stood perfectly still for a few moments, as I waited for his response. He took one last drag from his cigarette, before flicking it out towards the road.

"I'm not 'back on' drugs," Dave said firmly as he looked at me. His eyes told a different story. They were bloodshot and glossy. "I mean…maybe I smoked a little pot or what-ever, but it's not like I'm smoking all the time. What…what exactly did Susie say to you?" Dave asked with a hint of frustration.

I cocked my head to the side and responded, " S h e said that you were using drugs again, and that you were treating her like crap. You were saying nasty things and not acting like yourself."

Dave huffed, as he rolled his eyes and bit his lower lip.

"She *would* say that! She blames everything on me, you know. Nothing's ever her fault. I can't believe it…after all the things I did for her."

He shook his head and said, "What a waste of my time."

"Listen to you!" I exclaimed as I took my hands out from my pockets and folded them across my chest. "You're talking about Susie; the girl that you were head over heels in love with! I know about the things you did for her; some of them, at least. You guys have been through a lot together, and now you talk like you hate her! What's wrong with you?"

Dave sneered at me and said, "What's *wrong* with me? What's wrong with me is that no one is letting me live my life! First Mom, then Susie, and now you! I don't need your help, but if I did, I'd ask for it, okay? So until then, just leave me the hell alone!"

With that, Dave turned his back on me and stormed into the trailer, slamming the door hard behind him.

I hung my head with regret for what had just happened. I wasn't trying to make Dave angry. I was trying to convict him of his ungodly behavior.

My heart felt like it had dropped down into my stomach. I had hoped to get my brother back; to bring back the Dave I knew. But it seemed as if I had just made matters worse.

I slowly began walking towards Mom's car, but before I reached it, I turned around. Dave and I had gotten into our fair share of arguments before, but they never lasted long, and they almost always ended with an apology and a hug. I half-expected to see the trailer door slowly open, and Dave walk out to say that he was sorry for yelling. If he had, I would have run up to him and given him a big hug. I would have said that I didn't mean to shout at him, and I would have told him I just loved him so much.

That's not what happened. What I saw was Dave staring at me through the window. At first I thought I saw sadness on his face. If I was right, or if I imagined it, I don't know. But I do know that as soon as he saw me look at him, he frowned and fiercely drew the curtains shut.

*December 16ᵗʰ, 2003-*

*Will the Lord excuse me for my outburst?*

*Confusion; doubt; utter darkness…why have you befriended me? Has my soul invited in such foulness? Yesterday and its joy are a million miles away; I wonder even if I had ever known it. I will borrow Paul's words, and make them my own:*

*"…we despaired even of life. Indeed, in our hearts we felt the sentence of death."*

*Where is the Lord? I cannot blame Him for anything, because I know that He is perfect and just. So how could I cry out against You? But Lord, how can I not?*

*I know that battles take place; but where will they take me? To the brink of insanity…or worse, beyond? Has my soul not cried out to You? Do You deafen Your ears to it?*

*Why, oh God, have You taken me to this place, this desolate wasteland? I don't know where I am, and I don't know why I'm here. I step to the left, and anxiety shakes my body with fear. I go a step forward, and confusion rips apart my mind. I feel as if my Lord has left me to wander alone in an unsafe territory.*

*Have I ventured so far off that Your promises no longer hold true? Not that I'm perfect; but haven't I been resiliently following You? I answer myself humbly that yes, by Your grace, oh God, I have been following You. So I must conclude that You have led me to this place; this horrid, grisly place that not even a man's worst enemy would wish upon him.*

*I pray, Lord, that if I'm wrong, and I'm here because of my sin, then let it be known to me. Open my eyes and convict me of my wrong, so that I might toss it aside and forever be rid of it.*

*But if You, oh God, have led me here, then here I will stay until You lead me elsewhere. For who follows the Lord into unknown territory, then leaves without Him, thinking to find his own way out? Not me, Lord, not me. Give to me strength to overcome, wisdom to chase away doubt, and faith to demolish fear. If I can survive in this land, where then could I not survive? It is only by Your grace and mercy, oh God, that I will ever venture through this terrible place. This place that stinks like the stench of rotted souls, where fear and horrible confusion are all that you see. But the Lord has fixated mine eyes upon Him; my heart, Lord, beats for Thee.*

*Now I will borrow Paul's words again, and know that they are also my own:*

*"But this happened so that we might not rely on ourselves but on God, who raises the dead."*

*Lord be with me. The Lord is with me.*

*Amen.*

# 22.

Wow!

That's all that I could think of the first time I read that in Dave's journal. Only in the Psalms have I seen a man's heart more dramatically poured out into words. Every time that I read that passage, the same word comes to mind - Wow!

In one way or another, I think that every Christian feels the way that Dave did on December 16th of 2003. Not all of us, though, have the gift that God gave Dave. If you haven't already read the above passage at least twice, I urge you to do so now.

It's important to remember that we will find ourselves in grave situations from time to time. It's also important to remember that Jesus is the "Wonderful Counselor" as well. Don't hold back your thoughts to Him; let Him know how you feel. (He knows already, anyway!!) But we must first ask Him for help.

I was in that "desolate wasteland" for a time, as well. Nothing made sense, because I felt as if my Lord had abandoned me...

My body was numb; not because it was cold outside, but because all emotion had seemingly escaped from me. I felt as if my insides had been scooped out and replaced with air.

I got into Mom's car and started driving out of the trailer park. As I turned onto the road, the emptiness inside began to fill up with terrible thoughts:

*'That's the last time that you will ever see your brother; Satan has him.'*

"No," I whispered aloud. But my voice was so weak, and the thoughts were so strong.

*'Yes; accept it. He has chosen his own path, and you cannot force him onto another one. There is nothing that you can do.'*

I pulled the car sharply over to the side of the road. Where were these thoughts coming from? My eyes bulged out in fear, as the vile churning in my stomach grew worse.

I took a deep breath and closed my eyes.

*'Oh, Lord,'*

I began. But as soon as I said it, I was counter-attacked.

*'Oh Lord? Ha! Why waste your time? God doesn't hear you. You have no faith. Look inside yourself...yes, good! There is nothing there!'*

My head snapped up, and I opened my eyes. My hands were shaking as they gripped the steering wheel tightly.

"God, who speaks?" I almost shouted through gritted teeth. I loosened my grip on the steering wheel and ran my hands through my hair, nearly pulling some out.

"Where are You, God?" I asked as I closed my eyes again. "Where were You when I was talking with Dave?"

I sat for a moment in silence, but no answer came. I felt an uncontrollable anger stirring in my heart.

"What? Are You silent? Won't You answer me?!"

I clenched my fists together on my lap, as if I was about to punch something.

"Fine! Thanks so much for Your help, God!" I yelled sarcastically, while looking up at the black sky. "It's good to know that I can count on You!"

I peeled away from the side of the road and sped towards home. I was pressing my teeth together so forcefully that it seemed like they would crack at any moment.

I sighed when my house came into view. Mom and Aunt Sheila were going to be heart-broken when I told them what happened. I slowed down and gradually pulled into the driveway. I didn't want them to hear that I was back, because I needed some time to compose myself.

I parked Mom's car in front of the garage and turned off the ignition. Reclining back in my seat, my eyes were drawn to the night sky.

*'You blew it, God.'* I thought with disappointment. *'What good is there in trusting You? We prayed our hearts out for Dave...I guess You just don't care.'*

As soon as I had expressed that thought, a voice that was not my own came into my head. It was tender and soft; completely unlike the voice that I had heard earlier. As surely as I live, it said,

*'I care, Jonny. I care more than you know.'*

My bottom lip quivered rapidly, as if a small earthquake was taking place within. I immediately closed my eyes in shame, as tears erupted from my sockets.

"I know You care, Lord!" I cried out through my sobs. "I *know* You care and I *love You!*"

I sat in Mom's car for a good five minutes, hanging my head in disgrace and gasping for breath in-between whimpers.

*September 12ᵗʰ, 2002-*
*Praise Him, and know that He is the Lord. His righ-
teousness overcomes me. My problems that seemed so everlasting are but mere remembrances of what used to be. He
is God, always and forever. He has made a home in me, so
that I will return to my home with Him. He is all-powerful,
and His love and grace and mercy endures beyond my
sufferings. He is God, and He is well worthy of our praise.*

# 23.

I shut the door behind me and walked through the kitchen and into the dining room, where Mom and Aunt Sheila were sitting at the table. My face must have been streaked with dry tears, because Mom immediately got up when she saw me.

"What's wrong, honey?" she asked with a worried expression on her face. "Were you crying?"

I shrugged my shoulders, just a little embarrassed, and answered, "A little, I guess."

Mom gently rubbed my shoulder and said, "Why? What happened?"

I took a deep sigh and replied, "Let's sit down, okay?"

"Did you find Dave?" Aunt Sheila asked, as Mom and I sat down with her at our oak finished table. She was sitting straight up in her chair, leaning slightly towards me. Her voice sounded so hopeful; I hated to give them bad news.

"Yeah, I found him, and we had a little talk."

Both sets of eyes were staring unblinkingly at me. But what should I tell them? Wouldn't the truth only crush their hope? But I had no choice. The fact of the matter was that I needed some encouragement, and I knew that the only way to receive it was to tell them the truth.

"I think that Dave's messed up on drugs again." As Mom's face dropped, I looked down, then slowly added, "Actually, I know he is."

"Are you sure?" Mom asked weakly. "I mean, how do you know?"

I looked up at Mom. Her face had turned pale, and her eyebrows were furrowed up. Her eyes were wide open with a look of pain and sorrow that came from deep within.

I wanted to take back what I had said. Seeing her hurt made me feel even worse than I already did.

I solemnly shook my head and responded, "I just know, Ma."

Mom put an elbow on the table and leaned the side of her head onto her hand.

"I knew it," she said sadly. "I didn't want to know it; I didn't want it to be true…but deep down, I knew that Davey was back on drugs. He just wasn't acting himself."

Mom began twirling a strand of her curly blonde hair with her finger, a sure sign that she was nervous.

Aunt Sheila pushed her seat out and walked over behind Mom. She looked at me forlornly, with her lips pressed tightly together and began patting Mom's back.

I let a few moments of silence pass by before I asked the question that was eating away at my heart.

"What I don't get is…why would God let this happen to Dave? We've been praying and praying and praying about it; and I…I don't know. I can't really describe how I'm feeling right now."

"A little angry?" Aunt Sheila said, nodding her head. It was really more of a declarative statement than it was a question.

"Well, yeah; I guess. I mean, I know that God really cares about our problems and everything...but a lot of the times, it's like I know it but I can't see it. Does that make sense?"

"Sure it does," Aunt Sheila said. "There are so many times in our lives that we just have to trust in God. What does it say, uh...?" She looked up at the ceiling in thought. I snuck a quick peep at Mom; her eyes seemed vacant as she stared down at the table.

Aunt Sheila looked back at me and said, "Oh. His ways are above our ways, and His thoughts are above our thoughts. We just have to remember, we have to know, that His thoughts of us are love."

I slowly nodded my head and pretended to be interested at staring at my fingers as I said, "I, uh...I got really mad at God after I talked with Dave. I said some things that I really shouldn't have. I blamed Him for not caring."

I glanced over and saw that both Mom and Aunt Sheila were paying close attention to what I was saying. I looked back at my hands and continued on in a strained voice.

"After that, I was just sitting in the driveway, and out of nowhere, this voice..."

My voice failed me, and I was unable to go on. I covered my face with my hands, as I wept uncontrollably. Mom leaned over and put her arm around my waist, holding me close. I felt Aunt Sheila's warm hands on my shoulders, and I was comforted.

After a few short moments, I continued.

"It said, 'I care, Jonny. I care more than you know.' And, I mean...I just *know* that it was God, and I just know that He cares!"

I took my hands from my face and sniffed a few times.

"But even after that," I said with shame, "I still...I still doubt that in a way. I feel like an idiot," I confessed while shaking my bowed head.

"No, you're not an idiot, honey." Mom said tenderly as she pulled her chair right next to mine. "We can know God's promises to us, and know that they are true, but if we don't see them right away, it's easy to become disheartened. More than once, I felt like God had forgotten about me...much more than once! And I gotta tell you, every time the Lord proved to me that He had everything under control, and that He hadn't forgotten about me for one second!"

"Let's keep that in mind right now," Aunt Sheila said. She put her right hand on Mom's shoulder while keeping her other hand on mine.

"Lord God," Aunt Sheila began. I reached out and grabbed Mom's hand as we all bowed our heads. "We believe in Your promises. Your promises to love us, and always be there for us. We admit, Lord, that we so easily find ourselves frustrated when what we hope for or what we pray for doesn't happen as soon as we'd like it to. We ask You to forgive us, and to give us great faith in You; that You have every aspect of our lives under control.

"Your thoughts of us are love, Lord. They are more than the sand on the beach; more than the stars in the sky. We thank You, Heavenly Father, that You love us so, and that You truly care. How good it is to know that You hear us, and that You have in mind for us Your good will.

"We pray, Father, that You watch over Dave. He is in a place where he should not be. He is doing things that he shouldn't be doing. Lord, only You can take him out. Open his eyes, Lord; let him see his sin, and may he fall on his knees and ask for forgiveness...In Your Word, it says, 'Humble thyself in the sight of the Lord, and He will lift you up.' Convict Dave, Lord; rebuke him, we pray.

"We trust in You, Lord. We trust that You hear our prayers, and that You will answer them, in Your perfect timing. We ask that Your comfort falls upon Joyce and Jonny. Fill them with assurance, Lord…Fill us with assurance…for faith to trust in You, and for wisdom to know that You are the Lord. Lead us by still waters…Restore our souls. In the precious name of our Lord Jesus Christ, Amen."

"Amen."

"Amen."

*November 15<sup>th</sup>, 2002-*

*When I pray, I know that the Lord hears me- not because of my well-worded sentences; if He heard only intelligent men, He would be deaf to my thoughts! No, the Lord hears my soul. He hears my passionate cries of desperation and praise.*

# 24.

About a month before my second year of college was over, I brought Anne home to meet Mom. We had been dating for four months, and I already knew that this was the woman that I would marry. Dave was supposed to meet us at the house, but he never showed.

I was worried about Mom. She was all alone with no one to talk to, no one to help with chores, no one for any comfort or support. I prayed for her every day, and I prayed for Dave as well.

We pulled into the driveway, and Anne parked her red Dodge Neon in front of the garage.

"You ready?" I asked her as I unbuckled my seatbelt.

She smiled at me and replied, "Yeah, but I'm a little nervous."

"Don't be," I said, leaning over to kiss her cheek. "My Mom is a sweetheart, and Dave is the nicest guy you'll ever meet. And you," I finished with a smile, "you are the prettiest, smartest, funniest girl in the world."

"Oh yeah, right!" Anne responded with a grin. "Okay, Mr. Charmer; let's go."

She might have thought that I was kidding, but I wasn't. Anne was one of those girls that everybody liked. She was the quintessential girl next door - long blonde hair, pretty face, great figure and smile; beautiful, yet approachable. Her hearty laugh could put a smile on the face of the gloomiest individual. She was so smart that she could talk your ear off on nearly any subject, and so constantly cheerful that you couldn't help but feel good whenever she was around.

I opened the front door for Anne as we walked inside the house.

"Hello?" I called out as we took off our sneakers.

"Hello!" Mom answered back happily from the living room. "Come on in here. I'm trying to warm up."

Mom had just bought a large heater that vented out hot air to replace the electric heat. She was standing in front of the heater in the corner of the living room, next to the sofa.

"Hi Mom!" I said, giving her a hug. "This is Anne."

"Hello there, Anne," Mom said with a big smile as she hugged her. "Aren't you so pretty? Here, sit down on the couch by the heat."

We took a seat and Mom asked, "Can I get you guys something to drink? Or are you hungry? I have some homemade meatloaf in the fridge."

"Naw, I'm fine," I said, leaning back and stretching my arms up over my head.

"How about you, Anne?"

"I'm fine, Mrs. Sullah, thanks."

"Are you sure?" Mom asked with a sort of hurt look on her face. "I made this nice meatloaf dinner with a whole bunch of mashed potatoes and peas. It'll just go spoiled if no one eats it."

"On second thought, I am a little hungry," Anne said. "Maybe I'll try some of that meatloaf."

"Oh good!" Mom exclaimed, her countenance changing to one of delight. "What about you, Jonny? I made it just for..."

The smile on her face vanished, and she bowed her head and stood still.

"Just for what?" I asked.

Mom looked at me and responded, "Well, I was going to say, 'Just for you'-meaning you and Anne, of course. But I cooked enough for four people."

"What, is Dave not coming?" I asked disappointedly.

Mom sighed as she folded her arms and replied, "I called him a little bit ago to ask him what time he'd be here, and he said that something came up so he couldn't make it." She shook her head with sadness in her eyes and said, "I asked him what was so important that he couldn't see his brother whom he hadn't seen in so long, but he just got mad at me for asking. He said to tell you that he said hello, and sorry he couldn't make it."

I took a deep breath and exhaled through my nostrils, turning my face to the side, so that Anne wouldn't see my disappointment. I had so wanted Dave to be there. Not only so that he could meet Anne, but so that he would be home. Mom had told me that Dave hadn't visited her since he left months ago. He had, at one point, called her nearly every day. That lasted for only a couple of weeks, however.

Mom warmed up the food, and we all sat down at the dinner table. I wasn't hungry at all, but I forced down as much as I could. After eating, we went back into the living room and sat and talked.

Mom and Anne got along perfectly. Their personalities were much the same, and the conversations flowed from childhood memories to the present. For the most part I just sat and listened as they got to know each other.

Anne was telling Mom about how she was studying to be a veterinarian when I interrupted to say, "I'll be right back."

"Where are you going?" Mom asked as I stood up from the couch.

"I…just gotta do something. I'll be back."

"Okay," Mom said with a puzzled expression on her face.

I went through the kitchen and down the stairs that led into the basement. Opening Dave's door, I stepped into his room. Besides the missing mattress and TV, everything was the same. Photos hung all about the walls, and books, dirty clothes and garbage literally covered the floor.

I closed the door and stood in the middle of the room. I had never really carefully looked at the pictures that Dave had tacked onto the wall, so I began to do so. I went all the way around his room, closely looking at every single photograph. There were pictures of the woods during winter and fall. Pictures of deer, birds, frogs, butterflies and dogs. Beautiful sunsets that made the sky seem like it was a masterpiece of art. Even though they were all stunning in their own way, what really got me were the family photos. They outnumbered the wildlife and nature pictures considerably. Pictures of our grandparents, who had since moved to sunny Florida, pictures of Dave with Susie, of our aunts and uncles, of me, Dave and Mom together. Some were taken at holidays, some were taken at birthdays, and some were taken for no reason in particular. But they all were the same in one way - everybody was smiling.

By the time that I had gazed around Dave's small room, I had wiped a fair amount of tears from my eyes. I missed him so much! I missed horsing around with him as a kid. I missed his individuality and his sense of humor. I missed…him; I missed the good kid that I knew he was. And my heart sank, as I thought about where he was now, and what he was probably doing.

I looked down at my feet and saw Dave's Bible. Its cover was worn with use, and bookmarks littered the pages from beginning to end.

I solemnly shook my head as I stared at it and said aloud, "Come home, Dave. Dear God, bring my brother home."

I had gone down there to pray for Dave, but the longer I stuck around, the more my insides seemed to melt in pain. I took one last look around and was about to leave, but before I did, I slowly got on one knee in front of Dave's box spring, which still lay on his bed frame.

I bowed my head to say a quick prayer, and as I did my cross necklace came out from under my T-shirt that I was wearing. It swung forward to back from my chest to Dave's bed. As I looked at the shiny gold cross, I got a strong notion to do something; so I did it. I unhooked the necklace from my neck and placed it under Dave's bed.

Bowing my head again, I said with strong conviction,

"In the name and by the grace of the Lord Jesus Christ, bring my brother Dave back home. Bring him home to You, dear Lord, and to us. God, hear me. Amen."

*February 11ᵗʰ, 2001-*

*There was once a man who loved God. Every day he prayed to the Lord. He gave Him thanks and asked Him for his daily bread. As time went by, the man became rich. He also fell in love and married a beautiful woman, and was very happy.*

*Things went well, a little too well. He stopped praising God, because he was too busy enjoying life. "What do I need?" he thought to himself. "I have all that I desire."*

*One day, his wife became sick and died. Soon after that, his business went under, and the man was bankrupt. He fell on his knees, looked up to Heaven with grief on his face and said, "Why, God? Why?" And the Lord answered him, "Because I missed talking with you."*

*God will do what it takes to bring you where you should be: on your knees before the Lord Almighty.*

# 25.

Much of what Dave wrote in his journals was from his own personal experiences. He had an ability to describe things so that everyone could understand. That means that sometimes he had to change some words around, or change the actual instances that inspired him to write; but the message would stay the same.

I am convinced that what he wrote above on February 11th of 2001 stems from an incident that occurred on May 1st, 2000...

Five days after I had brought Anne to meet Mom, I came to my dorm from class and set my books on my small computer desk. I sat on the bed and pulled my fleece off over my head.

It had been a busy day for me, four hours in a row of three different classes. Now I had about an hour of free time before I would have to go to the library and get some studying done for my finals.

I saw that the little red light was flashing on my phone, telling me that I had a message. I picked it up and dialed *11 to listen to it. A woman's robotic-sounding voice said, "You have two new messages. Message one:"

"Jon,"

It was Aunt Sheila.

"your mother is in the hospital. She collapsed at school; they think she had a heart attack. It's...three o'clock right now. I'll call you again when I know what's going on. Please pray for her!"

I sat barely breathing and motionless on the bed. Was this really happening? Mom was only forty-nine, and she was in great shape. Before I could do anything, the robotic voice came back through the phone.

"End of message. Message two:"

"Jon,"

Aunt Sheila again; this time even more panicky than before, and she was sobbing as she spoke.

"I'm at the hospital; Lehigh Memorial. You might want to come down here if you can...Joyce is in surgery...it's pretty serious. Call Dave if you can, and let him know. I tried calling him a million times, but his phone is busy. I hope you get this soon...I don't know what to do! I'll call you again, if I don't see you."

"End of message. To delete your messages, press one. To save them, press zero..."

I let the phone slip out of my hands and fall to the ground. My jaw hung down as I stared at the wall, which appeared to be getting blurrier...

My eyes snapped open. I was on my back, looking up at the ceiling. The phone was making that annoyingly loud beeping sound because it was off the hook.

I quickly sat up on my bed. My head was pounding, and my heart fluttered in my chest. It took me a moment to realize that I had passed out.

"Mom," I whispered out loud.

Looking at the clock, I saw that it was four-thirty. I had only been out for a short time. I stood up, feeling very dizzy and weak. I walked through my door and went out into the main room of the suite. It was dead quiet; all my roommates were gone.

I ran back to my room and picked up the phone. After clicking the button a few times, I got a dial tone and rang Anne's number.

"Be home," I said nervously. "Be home."

"Hello?"

"Anne, thank God. I need to borrow your car. Mom had a heart attack."

Anne had wanted to go with me, but I told her to stay put. She had a night class to go to, and truthfully, I wanted to be by myself. I didn't want to talk on the ride to the hospital at all. I wanted to cry my eyes out and pray my heart out, and I wanted to do it alone.

Anne gave me her cell phone and told me to call her as soon as I knew what was going on. As I neared Auburn, I thought of Dave. I didn't know his number, however, but I *did* know where he lived.

I sped down the road and into the trailer park. I wasn't sure if I would remember the street that his trailer was on, but fortunately, I found it right away.

I screeched the car to a halt and left it running as I jumped out of the driver's seat and marched towards the trailer. Dave and I hadn't spoken since the last time I was there. I had written him letters, and he wrote me back once or twice. But I felt like things had changed between us. It was almost as if he resented me in a way.

I wasn't going to let that stop me now, though. Whether or not he wanted to see me didn't bother me anymore. I threw open the trailer door without knocking and walked right inside.

To my left was a small living room. There were two teen-agers sitting on the couch, staring at me in alarm. One of them had a bong in his hands. Across from the couch, sitting on a yellow beanbag chair, was Dave.

"What the hell's going on?" Dave asked in a perturbed tone.

I waved a cloud of smoke that hung in front of my eyes and replied, "Mom's in the hospital. *That's* what's going on. They're doing surgery on her right now. Are you coming or not?"

I answered Dave much more sharply than I had intended to. At first I thought that he might tell me to get lost, but I was wrong. Dave's eyes opened wide as he hurriedly stood up from his chair.

"What's wrong with her?" Dave asked fearfully as we walked outside.

"She had a heart attack."

It was a ten-minute drive to Lehigh Memorial, and it was spent in almost complete silence. I could tell that Dave was stoned, but I think that the shock sobered him right up.

We reached the hospital at twenty after five in the afternoon. I ran inside to the front desk, with Dave right behind me. A nurse directed us up to the second floor waiting area where we found Aunt Sheila sitting alone in the small room. She was on her cell phone, but when she saw Dave and I practically running towards her, she flipped it shut and stood up, holding out her arms.

Aunt Sheila held me tight as I asked, "How's Mom?"

"I don't know," she replied, her mouth buried in my shoulder. "I don't know."

It certainly wasn't the assurance that I was hoping for. My heart dropped in my chest as I feared the worst.

After a few seconds, Aunt Sheila let go of me and embraced Dave. He had been quietly standing behind me with his head bowed and his hands in his pockets. It was as if he didn't expect a warm greeting from our aunt. Maybe he hadn't expected a greeting at all.

"Hello, Dave," Aunt Sheila said, as they hugged each other. Her voice was strained and weak, very uncharacteristic of her.

Dave's face looked almost cheerful in a way, as he rubbed Aunt Sheila's back and said, "It's good to see you. Well…not like *this*; but it's good to see you."

We all sat down next to each other in a row of padded aluminum chairs that lined the back wall of the otherwise empty waiting area. Aunt Sheila filled us in on what she knew.

Apparently, Mom had collapsed in her classroom at Stony Brooke Primary School, where she was a second grade teacher. This happened around two-thirty, just before school was let out. An ambulance rushed her to the hospital, and the school called Aunt Sheila, since she was the one Mom had put down as the person to call in case of an emergency.

When Aunt Sheila arrived at the hospital a little before three, one of the nurses informed her that Mom had had a heart attack, and she had to have an immediate surgery performed.

"How long is it supposed to take?" I asked.

Aunt Sheila shook her head and looked at me with watery eyes.

"I'm not sure," she replied. "I didn't even think to ask."

Not much was said as we sat and waited. I held Aunt Sheila's hand for a while, as Dave paced back and forth. From time to time I heard Aunt Sheila whispering things as she lowered her head. I could only make out the words that she stressed, some of them being: *Please God, heal,* and *in Jesus' name...*

I had almost forgotten the most important thing that I should be doing. So I joined Aunt Sheila and said some very heartfelt prayers.

One of the longest hours of my life slowly passed by. Aunt Sheila was sitting in between Dave and me when a tall, skinny man with brown hair came into the waiting area and walked towards us. He was wearing a light green smock accompanied by a pair of blue jeans.

Dave and I stood up as he approached, wide-eyed with anxiety.

"Hello," the man said in a rather high-pitched tone. "My name is Dr. Smiley. Are you relatives of Joyce Sullah?"

"Yeah," I answered faintly. "We're her sons, and this is her sister."

"Why don't you boys sit down?" Dr. Smiley suggested with a slight smile.

I literally fell down in the chair. I expected the doctor was going to tell us that our Mom had just died.

Dave didn't move a muscle. He stood as rigid as a pole in front of his chair, and without changing the blank expression on his face said, "Just say what you got to say."

Dr. Smiley nodded and cleared his throat. He put his hands behind his back and changed his gaze periodically to each of us as he explained.

"Joyce suffered a heart attack, because there were blocked coronary arteries that wouldn't allow blood to properly flow from her heart. After we found the clogged arteries, we hooked her up to a machine that continues to circulate her blood flow, so we could operate on her heart after we stopped its beating."

"Wait a minute," Dave sharply interrupted. "Is she alive, or...?"

"She *is* alive, yes," the doctor replied. I took a deep sigh of relief, as Aunt Sheila grabbed my hand and squeezed it tight.

"*But*,"

I didn't like that 'but'. My eyes stared unblinkingly at Dr. Smiley as he went on.

"Like I was saying, we had to stop her heart in order to operate on it. We successfully took a radial artery from Joyce's forearm and grafted it over the clogged artery.

"The operation was a complete success, and the grafted artery is in perfect working condition. But, we are having problems starting Joyce's heart."

Aunt Sheila let go of my hand and clutched at her chest, saying in a wretchedly despondent voice, "What does that mean? What do you mean, you can't start her heart?"

Dr. Smiley took our tearful aunt's hand as he explained.

"When we do these kinds of operations, we stop and start the heart with electrical impulses. Her heart stopped like it should have, but for the moment, we haven't been able to start it again. After a few tries, we had to stop so that Joyce's heart can have a chance to regain some strength. For now, she's still hooked up to the machine that's pumping her blood, and we have a machine that will breathe for her on standby if needed. We will try to start her heart again shortly, but if it doesn't work, there's a good chance that it will *never* work."

Tears flowed down from my face as I weakly asked, "So what...what does that mean?"

I was sure that I knew, but at the same time, I didn't *want* to know.

The doctor sighed and looked at me sorrowfully as he replied, "We can keep your mother on life support for a while, but if her heart doesn't start back up, we're going to have to pull the plug."

*'This is all a bad dream,'* I thought to myself. *'This isn't really happening.'*

I quickly glanced at Aunt Sheila and Dave. Their demeanor revealed that they were probably thinking the same thing.

"We'll keep on trying to shock Joyce's heart back to life, but besides that, we've done all that we can. It's in God's hands now."

Dr. Smiley slowly stood up and walked away.

Tears literally poured from my eyes and ran down my cheek, as I bowed my head and screamed silently. I felt Aunt Sheila's body shaking next to mine, and knew that she was doing the same.

As I was catching my breath between sobs, I heard Dave whispering something. I looked up and saw him, still standing in the same position, with a look of awe on his face. A single tear rolled down his right cheek, as he slowly repeated what the doctor had said.

"It's in...God's... hands."

"Dave?" I said with a sob.

But he didn't answer me. I looked at Aunt Sheila and saw that she had stopped crying and was staring at Dave as well. His eyebrows were raised high, and a look of utter remorse was clearly on his face.

Dave fell on his knees with his head on the floor and covered his face with his arms, crying like I had never seen anyone cry before. He wailed profusely, as every inch of his body seemed to quiver.

I rushed over to him and knelt by his side.

"Dave?"

Dave reached out and gently pushed me away. In doing so, he revealed his face to me. Although it was for only a short second or two, the image would be forever embedded into my memory.

Dave's eyes were squeezed shut so tightly that it appeared as if his eyeballs had sunk down somewhere in the back of his head. His face was beet-red, and his mouth was stretched so far open that it looked as if his jaw had become unhinged. Saliva poured down the side of his lips, as his tears added to the pool that lay under his face.

Aunt Sheila sat on the floor next to Dave, as I stared on in amazement. She laid her head down on his as she rubbed his back and said, "It's okay, Dave. It's okay."

After a few moments, Dave sat up on his knees and threw his arms around Aunt Sheila. She pressed her lips together with a mix of joy and pain on her face, as they cried together.

We sat on the floor for a good two or three minutes. I knelt in silence, as tears streamed down my cheeks. My mind was racing with thoughts, but my heart was warm, completely filled with love, as I took in the scene. My aunt and brother stayed tight in their embrace, as Dave choked out through his tears, "I forgot all about Him! And now... this is all my fault!"

An anguished expression appeared on Aunt Sheila's face as she tried to respond, but her emotion seemed not to allow her.

"Lord!" Dave cried out as his head turned up towards the ceiling. "I'm sorry! Lord, please...*forgive me!*"

I felt an inexpressible sense of overwhelming peace in the air about me, as Dr. Smiley came running into the room.

*August 14th, 2001-*

*This is very true:*

*I said, in a faint whisper through my tears, "Will You ever lift me up, Lord? After all that I have done; will You lift me up?"*

*A voice not my own answered me: 'Again, and again, and again...'*

*Tears came down twice as hard after that. My God is an awesome God!!!*

# 26.

D r. Smiley hurried to us with a huge smile on his face. He shook his head, as if he couldn't believe what he was about to say.

"Joyce's heart is beating again!"

I jumped up from the chair, wide-eyed and smiling, as a tingling sensation flowed through my body. Dave and Aunt Sheila looked up from the floor, as Aunt Sheila put her hand over her heart and exclaimed, "Oh, praise God!"

"Praise God *indeed!*" the doctor affirmed, nodding his head. "You see, Joyce's heart started on its own. When I returned to the operating room, my colleague, Dr. Reiner, was getting ready to administer the electric impulse to Joyce's heart. As he was standing over her, all of a sudden he looked at me and said, 'Come look at this.'

"I hurried over next to him and saw what he was looking at - a live, beating heart."

No one could say anything. We all just stared at the doctor in amazement as he continued.

"So we turned off the circulation machine, and right now we are working on sewing up the incisions that were made. It appears as if Joyce is going to be just fine. I have to get back now, but I just wanted to let you know myself."

Aunt Sheila stood up and lunged at Dr. Smiley, grabbing him in her arms and hugging him tightly. The good doctor smiled modestly as she said,

"God *bless* you! It's so good to see a man of faith in your profession! God bless you!"

"Thank you, ma'am," Dr. Smiley said, as they withdrew from their embrace. "He already has."

As the doctor walked away, I looked down at Dave, and saw that was kneeling motionless on the floor with his eyes closed. A smile began to slowly grow on his face that soon seemingly stretched from ear to ear.

After just a few seconds, Dave slowly began to sing, keeping his eyes closed while bowing his head slightly. I had heard Dave sing at church before, but his voice was too quiet for me to really hear. But as he sung in that waiting room, all else was quiet, and for the first time I heard how pleasant his voice was in song. It was deep, yet soft and tender.

"Amazing grace…"

As soon as he started, Aunt Sheila covered her mouth as new tears fell down her cheeks. We both looked on at Dave in silence as he sang.

"How sweet the sound, that saved a wretch like me! I once was lost, but now am found. Was blind, but now I see.

"Through many dangers, toils, and snares, I have already come! 'Twas grace that brought me safe thus far, and grace will lead me home."

Before he sang the final verse of the song, Dave's face lit up as he snapped open his eyes and looked up towards the ceiling with an indescribable expression of joy on his face. I immediately broke down in tears as his voice boomed:

"When we've been there ten thousand years, bright shining as the sun! We've no less days to sing God's praise than when we'd first begun!"

I can't accurately express how I felt, but if you've ever experienced God's presence, then you know what it was like for me. Aunt Sheila and I fell down next to Dave, and we all hugged each other so tight that I could barely breathe.

*September 3rd, 2000-*

*Does God give us pain? No. We learn in the Book of Job that it is Satan whom brings us ill will and hardships. God allows the devil to try us. Why? Because God will do whatever it takes to make us learn not to rely on ourselves. He will reveal to those who love Him our need of Him.*

*Think of the hardest time in your life. Now remember how God alone brought you through it. Do you recall looking up to Heaven with tears in your eyes and joy in your heart? Do you remember exclaiming, "My God; how great Thou art!"?*

*Servants and friends of God are allowed pain so that we can remember where our help comes from. He will take us through any trial, any pain, and He will show us His greatness so that we will give Him praise. I do not like pain, but I rejoice in the assurance of my faith in the Lord. He knows all, He cares for us, and He allows us opportunities to pour out our hearts to Him. Praise God!*

*But do I blame the devil for all my woes? No, certainly not. I, in my foolishness, have caused much pain to befall me and those that I love by the choices that I alone have made. God grants me the option of choices to make in my life; will I follow the goodness of the Lord, or will I succumb to Satan's evil? Sadly, and to my disgust, I have at times listened to the devil instead of my Father. What a putrid confession! It causes my body to shudder.*

*But I see, on looking back, that God had never departed from me. He is faithful beyond all comprehension. I know this, for if my Lord God had left me, I would be hell-bound with no hope.*

*But one day in the midst of terrible darkness I looked up, and what did I see? I saw my faithful friend, Yahweh, Lord God Almighty, smiling down upon me from above! God is there, in all things. Those that love Him will see this. How do I thank Thee, oh Lord? My life, take it! It is in good hands. My love, it is all Yours. Not that I first loved You; You have loved me forever, and for that I am forever thankful!!!*

# 27.

Mom made a complete recovery. She was in the ICU for two days, and then four days later she was released from the hospital. Mom had to take medication to block calcium from getting into her arteries and pain killers for six months, and she was out of school for the remainder of that school year; but other than that, she was her normal, healthy self.

Dave moved back home on May 2ⁿᵈ, and he graduated from high school with modest grades. Since Mom couldn't drive for almost a month after the operation, Dave took her to doctor's appointments and did the grocery shopping. They began to bond as mother and son in a way they never had before.

My brother rededicated his life to the Lord. Mom wrote me one day, just before I was finishing up my second year in college, that Dave had sold his TV and his video games and had bought a countless number of books from a local Christian bookstore. He did wood burnings and other works of art for our family and also sold some at the bookstore. I later found out that Dave adopted a deprived child through an organization called The Christian Children's Fund, although he did not tell anyone about this. He went with Mom to a Bible study that she had begun to attend soon after her heart attack, and later became the assistant leader in our church's Youth Group.

If this were a fairy tale, the story would end here. I would say, "And they all lived happily ever after…" Dear Christian, be persuaded: We *will* live happily ever after, but until our mortal end, the path we walk will have troubles of all kinds laying about.

Dave picked me up at college one day towards the end of May. I was happy to be halfway done with school, and looking forward to a few months of rest.

"Where's Mom?" I asked him as we tossed my suitcases into the trunk of the Escort.

Dave smiled and replied, "She's zonked out on medication. She was lying on her bed when I asked her if she was coming. She looked at me with her eyes half-opened and said something like, 'For-frohful-lika-trooful-do.'"

Dave chuckled to himself then said, "She was all smiling and everything, totally unaware that I was even there! I think she's taking too much of those pain killers," he added jokingly. .

"What about you?" I asked as we hopped into the car. "How are you doing on the drugs?"

Dave shrugged his shoulders as he started the engine and responded, "I haven't smoked pot since Mom's heart attack."

"Good."

I sensed a defensive tone in my brother's voice; a sure sign that he didn't want to talk about it.

I stared out the window as we pulled out of the campus and onto the road. The leaves on the trees were a brilliant green, due to a season of heavy rain. I rolled down the window and listened to the high-pitched chirp of the chickadee and the squawks of some blue jays.

I heard a lighter flick and turned to see Dave lighting up a cigarette.

He looked at me and said, "Yeah, I still smoke cigarettes, though."

"Hey, better that than pot," I replied.

We drove on in silence for a short while. Dave was acting a little antsy. He would bite his lower lip from time to time, and he seemed unable to keep his focus on the road. He'd glance at me, then quickly look out the side windows, then the rearview mirror, then he'd bite his fingernails and run his hand through his hair. It was obvious that something was on his mind.

"So...how're things at home?" I asked, trying to strike up a conversation.

"They're good," Dave responded contentedly. "Me and Mom have been hanging out a lot, you know, kinda making up for time lost. I got some money for graduation, and we've been going out to eat and stuff like that."

I nodded my head and said, "That's good."

Dave cocked his head and sighed, saying, "Yeah, I know...but...I don't know."

"What?"

He flicked his cigarette out the window and replied, "Well, it's weird; it's like...I've lost all my friends. When I told them I quit smoking, half of them didn't even believe me. They said stuff like, 'Oh, sure, I bet *that'll* last a long time!'

"I mean, all we did all day long was sit around and smoke pot. Now that I don't do that anymore, it's like I'm an outcast or something."

"So you still hang around these guys?"

"Not really. I did for a while, but I had to stop. I'd just sit around and watch them get high, the whole time with this really bad vibe that I shouldn't be there. So I stopped calling them, and they stopped calling me, and now...it's like I have no friends. It sucks, you know, it…I'm just so lonely all the time."

I paused to think about how I should respond. It wasn't often that Dave openly shared his feelings, so I knew that this was really bothering him. Before I could say anything, though, he continued.

"And I've been getting these…these real *bad* thoughts in my head, man. These real, just, like…*crazy* thoughts that I can't get rid of. As soon as I stopped smoking, I've been getting some hardcore migraines. I don't know if I'm thinking too much, or if I'm worrying about stuff too much…or if I'm not worrying *enough*…"

Dave sighed deeply and shook his head.

"It's just like…I can't explain it."

"What kind of 'crazy thoughts'?" I asked him uneasily.

"It's not what you think," Dave said as he looked at me with assurance. "I'm not like a nut-ball or anything."

"I know you're not," I replied with a slight laugh. "And I wasn't trying to suggest that. But what kind of thoughts have you been having?"

Dave kept his focus straight ahead on the road as he answered me.

"Just…thoughts that no one would want to have. And what gets me is I don't know *why* I'm having them. They'd come and go every now and then when I was smoking pot, and in the past I just thought that I was too stoned or something. But now that I'm sober, and I'm still having them… it's…it's just really scary sometimes."

I pressed my lips together and bowed my head a little as I thought of what to say. Now I knew why Dave had been acting so nervous. This was really eating him up inside.

"Have you prayed to God about it?"

"Oh yeah," Dave responded, nodding his head with raised eyebrows. "And sometimes the headaches go away, and the thoughts leave for a while…but before I know it, the headache's back, and my mind is, like…just *swarming* with these terrible thoughts again.

"So what I do is I go through the Bible, and I read a lot of the New Testament. Mostly about stuff Jesus said, and miracles He did. I read about promises God's made, and it really does give me a lot of comfort.

"I'm reading these books about Paul and all that he went through, and I just got done with this one book about Job, and how important it is to trust in God."

"That's awesome," I said sincerely.

"Yeah, but…it's like, after I put the books down, and I try to just sit there and relax…there comes the headaches again, and then the bad thoughts. I can't seem to get rid of them."

"Hmmm," I said, not really knowing how to reply. "Did you tell Mom about this?"

"No way!" Dave exclaimed as he looked at me with his eyebrows furrowed down. "And don't you, either. I've put her through enough already. You know Mom. This'd just make her worry like crazy."

"Alright, alright. But you gotta do *something*. You can't just keep everything to yourself, you know."

"I know," Dave responded calmly as he looked straight ahead. "And honestly, I feel better now that I've told you; even though I haven't told you everything. I don't know… maybe I should see a shrink or something. But I can't afford that crap, and I don't really trust them, anyway."

My eyes opened wide as a solution came to me.

"There's this lady that Mom knows who's a Christian counselor. Mom went to her a few times when you were, uh, when you had left the house. Did she tell you?"

"No," Dave replied curiously.

"I guess she's really good. Mom told me that she knows the Bible as good as any pastor, and that she really helped her out, emotionally, mentally, and spiritually."

"Oh yeah?" Dave said, gaining interest.

"Yeah. And I don't think you'll have to worry about money; Mom said that she wouldn't accept any from her."

"Then how does she make a living?"

"Her church pays her. She's from the United Methodist Church; you know, the one on Abby Street?"

"Yeah, I've seen it before. So...*anybody* can just go to her and get free appointments?"

"Well, usually only members from her church are supposed to be able to see her. But since Mom knows her, she had no problem helping her out. I bet it'll be the same for you."

Dave nodded his head, seemingly encouraged.

"Her name's Angie...something. I forget her last name. So? Whad do ya think?"

"Well, I'd have to ask Mom to talk to her, right?"

"Yeah. So?"

"*So*, then she'd know that something was wrong with me."

I put my hand on Dave's shoulder and smiled as I told him, "Believe me, Dave; she isn't going to worry about you. This Angie lady will be able to help you; I'm *sure* of it. What if you let this go, and you become crazy or something? *Then* Mom'd worry! Seriously, I'll talk to Mom, and make sure she knows that everything's alright; you just need someone you feel comfortable to talk to, that's all."

After a couple of seconds, Dave turned to me with a smile of his own and said, "Alright. Thanks, bro. Let's do it."

*January 6ᵗʰ, 2002-*
   *Lighthouses are buildings. If that were all that they were, they would be of little to no use. But someone has put a light inside, and this light is used to shine on troubled parts of the sea. It lets the ships sailing along see the danger ahead.*
   *We all have "lighthouses" in our lives, and like the song says, "I thank God for the lighthouse...if it wasn't for the lighthouse, this ship would be no more..."*

# 28.

Angie Ashbery is one of the lighthouses that God had graciously put in my brother's life.

I met Angie for the first time at Dave's funeral. She was a rather tall and pretty woman in her forties, with long, straight golden hair. She carried herself well and spoke with elegance, and had some very touching and comforting words to say on the day of the funeral.

I called Angie a few months after, and told her that I was beginning to write a story on the life of my brother. I explained to her that I was hoping to include in the book a chapter or two on how she had helped Dave out during a very trying time in his life...

"Ooh, I don't know," Angie responded. She always seemed very careful about her choice of words, as if she thought about each one before speaking. Angie would talk very slowly sometimes. But, even so, her sentences seemed to flow beautifully from the beginning to the end, and on to the next. "Your brother made it quite clear to me that he expected that our conversations would be held in utmost confidence. I really don't know if I'd feel comfortable divulging any information."

"I know exactly what you mean," I said as I sat down on the leather couch in our living room. Anne was outside walking Aslan, our golden retriever, so I had the house to myself. I put my feet up on the couch (something I couldn't get away with if Anne was around!) and laid down as I talked with Angie. "And I would never want to do anything that hurt Dave. But I know that whatever you guys talked about really helped him. He never had anything but good things to say about you."

I sighed and scratched my head, giving myself a moment to think of how I should put it. I prayed again for God to guide me, and He did.

"Angie, the night that Dave died, I went down in his room and I threw myself on his bed. I laid there facedown for about half an hour and cried continuously."

Just remembering that got me misty-eyed, and I had to choke back some tears.

"I felt, just…it was the absolute *worst* time in my life."

"Mhmm," Angie said sympathetically.

"I remember sitting up on his bed, and just hanging my head in this *terrible* grief. I didn't notice at first, because my eyes were all blurry with tears, but I soon saw that I was staring down at one of Dave's journals that was lying by his bed. So I picked it up and started to read it."

I shook my head as I recalled that moment, and then went on.

"I mean, I can't tell you how…just how *inspiring* and *insightful* Dave's words were. If you don't mind, I'd like to read to you one of his passages that I read that night."

"Sure, go right ahead." Angie replied with interest.

I opened one of Dave's journals that I had book marked beforehand. It had a maroon colored cover with three shiny crosses as its lone design. I cleared my throat and read:

"March 12th, 2004-

"It is not by our strength that we make it up the mountain - the mountain that tells us to give up, that we are too weak, that all hope is lost, that the climb will break us, and all will be for nothing. It is not by our strength that we are able to tread up this mountain; it is by the word of God whispering in our ears, 'Keep on going...just a little bit further...you can do it, because I am with you...remember My love for you, and go on...'

"That is what keeps us alive, what keeps us climbing; what takes us to the top, with our limbs numb with exhaustion, our stomachs groaning for food, our lips cracked with thirst. The motivation from the heart of God propels us over every obstacle, and we find that there is no mountain tall enough that can separate us from the love of God in Christ Jesus.

"Freedom from this world is good - but freedom will not taste as sweet until our tasks at hand are complete."

I waited for Angie's response, wondering if that had impacted her as much as it did me. After a moment, she said,

"Wow, Jon. That is very well said. It's as if I could *hear* Dave's emotions in his words. I think it's obvious that Dave was recalling a tough time, or maybe going through a tough time when he wrote that. And what he says is very true; if we rely on God, there's *nothing* that we can't do."

I smiled with joy at Angie's response. I had been questioning whether or not I esteemed Dave's writings so much just because he was my brother. But now that she had responded to this one with such evident praise, I was sure that it wasn't just me.

"And that's not even the half of it," I explained. "Dave has three journals, and they're all just completely *filled* with writings like that one. I immersed myself in them for the days following his death, and I can't tell you how much they helped me out.

"In one of Dave's journals he wrote: 'God has made the story of your life, and He has given you the ability to write it.' "

I paused for a couple of seconds to let that sink in.

"And that's what his journals are; the recordings of Dave's life. His ups, his downs, his prayers, his pleas…and written in absolutely amazing words. Before I had even finished reading the first journal, I had decided that I would use Dave's own words to write a tribute to him. At first, it was going to be something I would give our family to read; but the more that I thought and prayed about it, I became convinced that it was going to be for more than just my family's eyes.

"You see, I found pretty much right away that when I read some passages from Dave's journals, I was able to recall a time in his life that might have compelled him to write it. So I figured that I'd use one passage from his journal to start out each chapter of the book.

"The more I wrote, the more I realized that Dave's life really *is* a great story; one that I think every Christian could relate to, and that it might provide to them some hope or wisdom, or…there's just really *so many* things.

"I've been praying a lot about this, and I really am sure that this is something that God wants me to do. I wouldn't do it if I thought otherwise. I'm being led by God, and I…I feel really good about it. I don't know, I can't explain it any better.

"So, I was wondering…what do you think? I mean, how do you feel about telling me what you and Dave talked about?"

Angie took a deep breath and exhaled through her nostrils.

"Well, I don't know, Jon. I'm certainly going to have to spend some time in prayer about it."

"That's perfectly fine," I responded. "I wouldn't have it any other way."

I thanked Angie for her time and gave her my phone number, asking that she'd call me either way with her answer. I sat the phone down and prayed to God that His will be done.

About a week later, I was sitting in the den, correcting some tests from my fifth grade class. Anne came in the room and handed me our portable phone, saying, "It's Angie Ashbery."

"Hello?"

"Hi, Jon, it's Angie. Did I catch you at a bad time?"

"No," I said, turning in my swivel chair to smile at my wife as she left the room. I had been anticipating this moment for days. "Not at all."

"Well, I've been thinking about what you asked, and after a lot of prayer I concluded that even though this is something that I would normally never do, I've decided that God is telling me to do it. I will meet with you and share what Dave and I discussed."

My heart felt like it leaped for joy inside of me as I exclaimed, "Oh, praise God! Thank you, Angie, this means a lot to me."

After a brief discussion, we planned to meet the following Friday at her house.

*May 12th, 2002-*

*I'm on a large ship sailing to a beautiful land, and I cannot reach my destination alone. I need a navigator to guide me. I need a captain to keep things under control and give orders. I need rowers to speed me along. I need cooks to prepare food for the voyage. I need friends to keep me company. I need doctors to heal the sick. I need a cleaning crew to swab the deck and keep things tidy. Most importantly, I need the breath of God to blow the sails, pointing me in the right direction of the beautiful land.*

# 29.

I met with Angie on a warm spring day at around four in the afternoon. She invited me into her Victorian style house with a friendly smile, and we sat down at the dinner table. Mr. Belvedere, her portly Calico cat, rubbed against my legs as I sipped the hot coffee Angie had poured for me.

After a brief session of chitchat, we got down to business. Angie took me upstairs into an office where she held her meetings with the people she counseled. There were two tall bookcases on the left side of the room as you walked in, filled from top to bottom with all different sorts of literature. A futon rested against the opposite wall, facing a comfortable looking black leather chair.

There was a wood burning hung on an otherwise bare wall that I recognized right away. It was Jesus with a huge smile on his face, lifting a smiling baby up over his head.

"Dave made you that, didn't he?" I asked as I sat down on the futon, nodding towards the artwork.

Angie turned in her seat and smiled at it.

"Yes, your brother gave me that the last time he came here. He had such a talent!"

"That he did," I agreed.

Before she sat in her leather chair, Angie had pulled a large manila folder out from the desk that was in the corner of her room. She was a meticulous note taker, and began describing to me what she and Dave had talked about. I listened intently, and took some notes myself. Angie also had an extraordinary memory, and was able to recall things as if they happened yesterday.

After an hour and a half, Angie had told me all that she could. I was a little shocked about some things, but I had prepared myself beforehand.

After thanking her for her time, we hugged and I went home. I immediately went into the den, fell on my knees, and prayed for God to continue to guide me. It took a few days, but I finally decided what needed to be shared about Dave's meetings with Angie, and what needed to be left out.

Dave had several sessions with Angie over an almost eight month span, and I have collected some of them into these next three chapters. Keep in mind that since I wasn't there, some things I used my imagination for. But thanks to Angie's notes and her brilliant memory, the most important things that they talked about did not require my mind's eye.

Dave nervously sat down on the bright red futon. He lowered his head and began tapping his fingers on top of his knees. He was never that good at conversing with strangers, but this was going to be even harder than usual. Was he really going to tell his deepest thoughts and concerns to a woman that he had just met?

Angie sat across from Dave and crossed her legs. He stared at her pointy black shoes as she said, "I understand that this might be awkward for you, Dave, and that's normal. It's tough sometimes to share things with someone, but I want you to be as relaxed as possible. Know that what we say here is between you, me, and God. I'm here to help, and I want you to honestly say whatever is on your mind. Okay?"

Dave nodded his head and hesitantly responded, "Yeah."

After a few moments of silence, Dave lifted his head and looked at Angie. She had a notepad on her lap and a pen in her left hand, ready to write. He sighed and said, "First of all, I...well, I don't want you to take this the wrong way. I know that you're doing me a favor, and I appreciate it, but..."

"Go on," Angie said with an encouraging smile. Dave would soon get used to that smile; it almost seemed to be engraved on the kind woman's face. "Say whatever's on your mind, and don't hold back."

"Alright, I'll try."

Dave lowered his head again and began to twiddle his thumbs as he spoke.

"I feel like it's wrong to be seeing you. It's like...I'm trusting in someone besides God to help me through this."

That certainly wasn't the first time Angie had heard that. She leaned forward in her chair a bit as she responded, "Let me make this clear right away: I want you to trust me, but I *don't* want you to trust *in* me."

Dave picked up his head and gave Angie a questioning look as she explained.

"There *is* a difference. You can trust me, because I'm here to help you. I am a trained counselor with a degree, and I have nothing but the best intentions to help you through whatever problems you are facing.

also a Christian, like you; therefore, I believe that
that I may have has been given to me by the Lord. Let
k it down for you a little bit. Who led the Israelites
Egypt?"

"Moses."

"Mmhmm," Angie said with a nod. "And there are *many*
examples that I could use, but I'll use this one. We know that
Moses parted the sea; but was it by *Moses'* power that this
happened?"

Dave shook his head, seemingly becoming aware of what
Angie was saying.

"No, of course not. *God* told Moses what to do, Moses did
it, and *God* made it happen. You see, Dave, God has chosen
to let people do His work; not *always*, though. Many times
He does it Himself. And He certainly could do it without us;
but He graciously *allows* people to serve Him for His name's
sake. I think one of the reasons why is because we take great
pleasure in doing things for the Lord, and that's a *good* pleasure, because we are pleasing *Him*.

"God uses people throughout the Bible. He used Adam to
create Eve. He used Esther to save the Jews. He used Jonah
to prophesize to the Ninevites. He used Paul and the apostles
to preach the gospel, and to record what we now know as the
Bible."

Angie cocked her head and smiled at Dave as a thought
came to her.

"I think that I can pinpoint a direct answer to your
concern."

"I'm all ears," Dave said with a hopeful countenance.

"What do you know about Luke?"

Dave shifted weight in his seat and asked, "What; Luke
the gospel, or Luke himself?"

"Luke himself."

Dave's eyes drifted off as he began to think.

"Well," he said, "he wrote Luke, of course, and Acts. He was a physician...well, there's not much more that I know about *him*; I know what he *wrote*, but...what are you getting at?"

"Like you said," Angie began, "Luke was a physician. Why do you think that he followed Paul around so much?"

"Because Paul was *beaten* so much."

"That's right," Angie replied with a nod. "Paul must have thought it necessary to have Luke as his own personal traveling doctor. Does that mean that Paul had no faith in God? Of course not!" Angie chuckled as she answered herself. "Besides Jesus Himself, I don't know anyone in the Bible who had greater faith in the Lord besides Paul. I mean, he was beaten a countless amount of times, he was whipped unjustly, uh, he was stoned, he was falsely accused of being evil by the very people he was trying to save; and never once do we read that Paul cried out that God was mistreating him; never once do we read of Paul losing any faith."

"Well yeah, I get what you're saying," Dave interjected. "But..." he furrowed his eyebrows as he gave Angie a questioning look and asked, "Does it ever say anywhere in the Bible that *Luke* healed Paul? I mean, after he was stoned and dragged out of the city, they thought that he was dead. But it says that he just got up all of a sudden by himself. And also, after he was shipwrecked, he was bitten on his hand by a viper, and the people there just watched him, expecting him to fall dead at any minute."

Dave progressively spoke faster and faster. His enthusiasm seemed to provide him with energy.

"And I'm not sure whether or not Luke was there when Paul was stoned, but I *know* that he was there on the island of Malta when he was bitten by the snake. But Luke didn't do *anything* about it; and still, Paul was healed."

Dave sat back in the futon, waiting for Angie's response. She cocked her head and squinted her eyes a little as she slowly responded, "I don't believe that it actually comes out and says that Luke healed Paul. But Paul does call him the 'beloved physician', and he says in his last letter, Second Timothy, that Luke was the only one still with him. That would leave me to believe that Luke was there, not only for moral support, but for medical reasons as well.

"As we know, Paul had a thorn in his flesh that God would not remove. Paul says that it was there to keep him humble; perhaps this humility was there to remind Paul that he needed the help of others."

"Yeah, but that's only speculation," Dave declared. He shook his head and raised his eyebrows a bit as he said, "This just makes me so frustrated, and I don't mean to vent out at you, but...why can't God just make things more clear? Why can't He just come out and say it already, you know?

"It just seems like there're so many things that are hidden...so many things that I *want* to know. And the more I try to find a particular answer to something, I find instead more things that I know *nothing* about!"

Angie nodded her head and smiled as she replied, "Believe me, Dave, you're not alone. It truly is remarkably frustrating at times to try and understand the Bible. I've nearly lost my head on several occasions, because I just didn't have the proper insight or point of view to figure out exactly what God meant when He said this or that."

She leaned forward with her hands in her lap, giving Dave a big smile as she looked directly into his eyes.

"You know what got me through those times, and gets me through still today?"

"What?"

"God's promises. I study them; I memorize them...I *rely* on them. For what you're talking about, nothing else has brought me more encouragement than Jesus' own words: Matthew seven: seven, "*Seek*, and ye shall find."

"Jesus doesn't say, 'Just sit on your butt and all life's answers will come to you.' No; He says, '*Seek,* and you *will* find.'"

Angie leaned back in her chair, letting Dave think about that. He sat silently in thought for a few moments before saying, "I know that I'm disproving my own point here, but I gotta admit; and I never really thought about this 'til just now, but I *do* depend on other people for help. I've got in my room, like, four or five different books that are people's commentaries on the Bible. I used to think that if I just prayed hard enough or whatever, that God would kinda just open my eyes to things that made no sense to me. But the only thing that happened was I would get so frustrated that I'd slam my Bible shut and not read it for a while. So I bought those books, and they've really helped me out a lot.

"But I still don't get it. It's like…why is it like that? To go along with Matthew seven seven, '*Ask,* and you shall receive.' So if I ask for understanding, why doesn't God just *give* it to me? You know? Why do I *always* have to learn from someone else?"

Angie opened her mouth to respond, but Dave wasn't quite finished. He continued on in fast-paced words, "People are imperfect, so why would God choose to make me learn from them? Why can't He just tell me things Himself, so I would have, like, no doubt that what I'm being told is the truth?"

Angie cleared her throat as she continued to write on her yellow notepad.

"My, my," she said with a smile. "You just said a mouthful!"

She placed her pen on the pad and gave Dave a sympathetic look as she responded, "And I don't pretend to have all the answers, Dave. I certainly have my own theories on many issues, but like you said before, that's only speculation. You're asking a lot of good questions, and I feel for you, because I've asked many of them myself. There are some things that are left for God alone to know."

A sincere expression came on Angie's face as she asked, "Do you trust in God?"

"Yes, I do," Dave answered firmly.

"Good. Do you pray to Him?"

Dave chuckled slightly and replied, "Only about a million times a day!"

Angie rested her chin under her hand, her elbow on the arm of the chair.

"It's so important that we trust in God; that we know that He is perfect in all that He does."

Dave nodded his head in agreement as she went on.

"I urge you to pray to God, that He would reveal to you what is needed, and that you would trust in Him to do so. Take it one step at a time, Dave. Don't expect all the answers to come to you at once; and don't expect that all the answers *will* come to you.

"Fervently seek the Lord, and you will not be disappointed. Study His Word; not just one verse here, and one verse there. Study the Bible as a *whole*, and you will see things coming together in a way that I can't explain."

Dave took in everything that Angie had said, then responded, "I read the Bible everyday. When I wake up, I read one chapter from the Old Testament, and before I go to bed, I read one from the New. And I agree with you; things *are* coming together for me in a way that…well, I just *know* that God is in control."

Dave sighed as he looked up at the ceiling.

"And I have so much going on in my life that I need to talk about; I mean, I could go on for weeks. But I just wanna go back one more time to what I asked you about before.

"My Mom had a heart attack earlier this year. I don't know if you knew that?"

"Yes," Angie responded. "We've spoken about it."

Dave nervously itched the back of his neck and then continued, "Well, then I'm sure you know that her heart stopped, and the doctors couldn't start it back up."

Angie nodded.

Dave's eyes drifted off as he continued.

"I know that you probably already know this, but I was off doing my own thing at the time. I had left the house, I was doing, just...*bad* things. I knew that I was hurting Mom... that I was doing things I shouldn't be doing. I was living how *I* wanted to live, not how *God* wanted me to live...and I just didn't care."

Angie listened intently to what Dave was saying. Joyce had told her tidbits of information about Dave's departure from home before; but it was always more 'reliable', in a sense, when you heard it from the source itself.

"When that doctor came in, and...and he said that Mom's heart wouldn't start; well, I nearly lost it. But then he said something that I'll never forget. He said, 'It's in God's hands.' "

Dave bit his lower lip as his eyes began to glaze over.

"I think I repeated that, like, five times to myself. It all sort of came together for me right then in the waiting room. I had kicked God aside, I had worried my Mom to death... *literally*; and now God was punishing me."

Dave shook his head as he said, "I can't describe the feeling that I got. It's like...I *felt* God's love calling to me. Even after all the bad stuff I did. Man, I fell on my knees so fast that it felt like I cracked my kneecaps. But I didn't care about any *physical* pain; my *emotional* pain hurt worse than any injury I ever had."

Dave took a deep sigh as he looked up at Angie and said, "I really wish I could describe it better, but there's no way. I just *knew* that God was speaking to me...and that He loved me still. I was crying so hard that I could barely breathe, thinking about my selfishness and all the hurt I'd caused. As I was crying, I was praying…"

His eyes furrowed a bit as he looked up at the ceiling in thought.

"It's weird; in my mind I was just saying, 'I'm sorry, God, I'm sorry.' But in my heart I was saying much more than that.

"You know how Jesus is the mediator between God and Man?"

Angie nodded her head.

Dave grinned as he said with assurance, "Well, I just *know* that somehow, in some way, Jesus was speaking to God in a way that I never could. I was groaning and whining…but…"

Dave squinted an eye as he looked back at Angie and said, "It's like I felt what I was saying; even though it wasn't in words."

Angie was about to respond, but Dave chuckled and then said, "Whoa, I went *way* off track there! What I wanted to point out is this; *God* started Mom's heart back up, *not* the doctors."

"Yes," Angie responded quickly. "And this will go along with what I've been saying the whole time: Who unclogged your Mom's artery? Who stitched her back up and gave her medication to keep her blood flow normal?"

Dave sat still for a moment, then nodded his head slowly and replied, "The doctors."

"That's right. Sometimes God will do things entirely on His own, and sometimes He will use others. But *nothing* could be done without God. He gives different abilities to different people; to *help* them, not to *hurt* them. That's God's intention of how we are to use these gifts; to glorify Him and to support one another in love."

Dave was a stubborn old mule at times, but he mostly could admit when he was in the wrong.

"I feel much better now," he said with a smile. "You've persuaded me. I just didn't want to…well, in lack of better words, I didn't want to piss God off by trying to get help from someone other than Him."

Angie warmly smiled and responded firmly, "*Always* go to God first, Dave. Go to Him first, and know that sometimes He will lead you to people for the help that you need. But any good thing that you learn, or any problem that you overcome; know that it is *God alone* Who has taught you, and it is *God alone* Who has carried you through your trials."

**Amen!!!**

*January 16th, 2002-*

*Fight, warrior! The Lord is your God, and He holds you in His righteous hand! Good things He has in mind for you, and good things you will achieve, so long as you continue in His will!*

*What's this? You complain because of a scar that you have received due to fighting with the enemy? Gentle knight, take joy in your wound! The Lord has stopped its bleeding so that it will not kill you, but He has allowed the remembrance of the wound to show on your skin. It will tell you why you have received this battle scar, be it because of sin or because of faithfulness.*

*If it's because of sin, then you are reminded of the pain that was brought upon you for it. You are reminded that God forgave you because you asked Him to, and also, you see the consequences that come from disobeying the Lord. Let this scar remind you not to be wounded a second time.*

*If it's a wound brought about by faithfulness, then you will show it to your Father in Heaven, and He will award to you a tenfold of riches for each and every scar. Then all these scars will vanish, and you will receive for them also a crown upon your head.*

*Good knight, until that day, remember that you are in battle! Yes, you have strong armor that will repel any attack from the enemy - but you, in your foolishness, do not always wear it! You put on daily many pieces of armor, but sometimes you forget a piece or two, and that is where the enemy will strike!*

*Be wise and strong, good knight, and carry with you always the faith of God, the love of God, and the very word*

*of God Himself. Prepare yourself, and be aware of the
present danger that awaits you. Fight the good fight; finish
the race!*

# 30.

S in hurts. It hurts the sinner, and it hurts those closest to
him.

I knew how Dave's drug abuse had caused our family so
much pain; but I had no idea of how much pain that it had
brought to Dave.

As Angie told me about their second meeting together,
I remember feeling sick to my stomach. Even though Dave
has passed on, and is in pain no longer; still, hearing what he
had gone through caused my heart to sink.

It is hard for me to write about this; even now tears are
swelling in my eyes.

*Lord, give me strength! I can do all things through Christ,
Who strengthens me. I can do all things…*

Dave sat down on the futon, his head bowed low as he
tapped his feet. He pulled up the sleeves of his Pittsburgh
Steelers sweatshirt, as Angie took her seat in the leather
chair across from him.

She brushed some curly strands of bright yellow hair
away from her face and got ready to write in her notepad.
Dave rubbed the back of his neck and began to speak, never
changing his focus on the brown carpet below.

"I've, uh…had some real bad problems with drugs, as
I'm sure my mom has told you, and…and I think they're the
reason why I've been…just not feeling right lately."

Dave bit down on his lip, seemingly unsure of how to proceed. Angie sensed his uneasiness right away, and asked him in a soothing, almost cheerful tone, "What's making you 'not feel right'?"

Dave cleared his throat as he leaned back, still looking down at the floor.

"Well, it's just...I really feel weird about telling you. You're probably going to think that I'm a whacko or something."

Dave glanced up quickly to see Angie's reaction. She smiled warmly and replied, "You're not a whacko, Dave. Believe me; I've been around, and I've heard a lot. Don't be ashamed. Just tell me whatever it is, and then we can start to work it out together."

Dave sighed as he folded his hands in his lap, nervously rubbing his thumbs together.

"I smoked weed for a while, and I did some acid; and, at first, I really enjoyed it. I smoked, like, *all* day, *every*day; and that's pretty much *all* I did."

Dave's eyebrows furrowed down as he said, "But then I started getting some *real bad* thoughts and images in my head. Just these...violent, *weird* images. Every time that I got high it'd happen. If there were other people in the room, I'd end up having to leave, because I thought...I thought that I might hurt someone."

Dave closed his eyes and sat perfectly still, a mixed expression of distress and fear showing clearly on his countenance.

"Can you tell me what these images were like?" Angie asked softly.

Dave opened his eyes and shrugged.

"I don't know," he said. "It's kinda hard to explain. It's like...you know, I'd see a knife sitting on the table, and I'd think about..."

Dave's lips began to quiver, and tears trickled down his cheek. Angie got up from her chair and sat next to him on the futon. She put her arm around Dave and rubbed his back as he wept.

"Cry; let it all out," she whispered tenderly.

Dave's upper body was still shaking as he wailed through his tears, "I just can't *take* it anymore! I *hate* violence, and I don't know *why* I'm thinking all this crap! I wanna die! I don't want to live! I want to die!"

The anguished expression on Dave's face caused tears to stream down from Angie's eyes. She threw her other arm around Dave. He leaned towards her, his head resting just above her breast.

After a few moments, their tears subsided, and Dave leaned forward with his forehead resting in his hand.

"I don't know what to do," he said faintly.

Angie gently placed her hand on Dave's shoulder and asked, "Would you like some tissue?"

"No, I'm okay."

Angie returned to her chair, crossed her legs, and sat down. After clearing her throat, she said, "So...these images; they're of hurting people?"

Dave sniffed and slowly nodded his head.

"Have you quit smoking marijuana and taking acid altogether?"

"Yes."

"And these images...you still have them?"

"Well, yeah; not as frequently or anything; but they're still there."

"Umhmm." Angie jotted something down in her note-book, and then asked, "Tell me a little more about exactly what happens when you get the images in your mind. Are they triggered by something; like when you see a knife? And what goes through your mind when that happens?"

Dave sat quietly for a few seconds, breathing heavily, seemingly staring off into space, yet still gazing at the carpet. He ran a hand through his hair and slowly rubbed the top of his head as he answered, "Like I said, it would happen when I was stoned. And the thing was; I *knew* that it happened because of the weed, but I still couldn't stop smoking. I'd think, 'Maybe it won't happen this time; maybe I'll just get high, and that's it.' And it didn't *always* happen; but for the most part, it did."

"*What* happened?" Angie asked.

Dave sighed and puffed his cheeks as he breathed out.

"Well, I remember this one time; I think it's the first time that it happened. I was sitting at the kitchen table with three of my friends playing Euchre. And we were just smoking blunt after blunt after blunt, you know?"

"Actually," Angie interjected with half a grin on her face, "I *don't* know. What's a 'blunt'?"

"Oh; a blunt's when you take a cigar and cut it in half, take out all the tobacco, fill it with weed, roll it back up, and smoke it."

"Oh, okay. I'm sorry; go on."

Dave wiped his nose on the back of his hand and then continued.

"So, we were all just really high; I don't even think we were playing cards anymore, we were so stoned."

Dave's eyes trailed away, as if he were staring through the wall in front of him.

"And there was a pair of scissors sitting next to my friend; he used them to split the blunt open. All of a sudden...and I don't know why, but..."

Dave shook his head as he looked at Angie and said, "I don't even want to say it."

"You're going to have to, Dave," Angie said calmly, yet firmly. "It will only help you if you do."

Dave pressed his lips tightly together, then said, "Okay; I thought of…taking the scissors…and stabbing him in the forehead."

Dave sat dead still after saying that; his eyes stared blankly ahead, and it seemed as if he had stopped breathing.

"What happened after you thought that?" Angie asked after a couple of seconds.

"I just sat there," Dave replied. "I mean, I was just, like, in total shock. I remember thinking, 'Now why the hell would I think that?' I tried to play it off, and pretend like it never happened; but I couldn't. I just kept on thinking it…and I *imagined* it. I couldn't get it out of my mind; the more I tried, the more I thought about it.

"Then, one of my friends says, 'Holy S*h--!* Look at Sullah's face!' I said, 'What? What about it?' And they're all pointing at me and laughing, and one of them told me to go look in a mirror. So I go to the bathroom, and I see myself in the mirror; my face is just *completely* white as a ghost.

"I just stood there and stared at myself; it was like I was looking at someone I had never seen before. I remember…I remember thinking that I was going to freak out."

Dave stopped talking and slumped back in the futon. It was almost as if he had just done a rigorous workout and had completely used up all of his energy.

"What did you do then?" Angie asked, after she had scribbled something down in her notes.

Dave wiped some sweat from the palms of his hands onto his jeans and answered, "I knew that if I sat back down at the table…I don't know, something bad would happen. So I told my friends that I had to get some air. They looked at me all weird when I left; they knew that something was wrong."

Dave stared down at his hands, twiddling his thumbs as he went on. It was obvious to Angie that he was much less than comfortable in sharing this with her.

"It was getting dark outside," he continued. "And I had no idea where I was going. I eventually left the trailer park because...I don't know; I just had to be alone.

"There're some woods by the park, and I kinda wandered into them. I was thinking about just walking and walking until I was in another town or something. But it got pretty cold, and I didn't have a coat on or anything, so I eventually made my way back home."

"What happened when you got there?"

"Nothing, really. My friends were gone; it was just my roommate, Jeff, and me. He asked me where I was, and I just told him that I was out walking."

Dave sat silently, with his head stooped down, while Angie quickly looked over her notes. Then she looked up at Dave and asked in a solemn tone, "Do you ever think about hurting yourself, Dave?"

Dave lifted his head and looked Angie directly in her eyes as he replied, "I would never do that. I know at times, like...I really *feel* like I want to die, but I would never do that to myself."

Angie nodded her head, satisfied with Dave's response.

"And I would never hurt anybody else, either." He continued, "I think that's one of the reasons this is bothering me so much. I mean...it's the people that I love the most that I get these...these images about. It's so frustrating...I feel so *rotten* inside. It's like, I have no idea *why* I get these thoughts, you know?"

Angie slowly nodded her head as she squinted her eyes a little, thinking about what to say.

"When was the last time that you smoked pot?"

Dave looked up at the ceiling as he answered, "March first; the day that Mom had her heart attack."

"Okay, so that means that the marijuana should be out of your system by now." Angie scribbled something down on her pad and then asked, "Now, what's going on when you get these thoughts? Do they usually come at a certain time, or when you're doing something in particular?"

Dave shrugged and replied, "Not really. They just…come *whenever*, you know. I guess it's mostly when I'm just sitting on my bed not thinking about much; or when I'm trying to go to sleep."

"So, at nighttime?"

"Yeah, I guess. They're not as, like, *vivid* as they were when I was high…but I still…it's like I *feel* them coming, and I have to fight to keep my mind on something else."

"Mmhmmm," Angie said as she nodded. She quickly wrote in her notepad, then looked at Dave and said, "Tell me what you do before you go to bed. Is there some sort of a process that you usually follow before you go to sleep?"

"A *process*?" Dave asked, with a confused expression on his face.

"Yes. Like do you watch TV before bedtime, or read, or listen to music…?"

"Well, yeah. I think I told you before that I read a chapter from the Bible every day and night. And after that I always read from whatever book I'm on; usually right up until the point where I'm so tired that I can't read anymore."

"And then you fall right to sleep?"

Dave scratched the back of his neck and responded, "No, not really. I *think* that as soon as I turn off the lights, I'll just pass right out; I mean, that's how tired I am after I read. But it hardly ever happens. Usually, I just lay on my bed in the dark; you know, tossing and turning and stuff."

Angie rested her arms on the chair's armrest and asked, "What kind of books do you read?"

"Christian books," Dave replied in a proud sort of tone. He leaned forward slightly and said, "I've read Pilgrim's Progress; I read books by C.S. Lewis, Lee Strobel, uh, Charles Stanley, Jon MacArthur. I mean, I got, like, a *hundred* books that are all about God, and I really *love* reading them.

They've helped me so much…it's just, there's *so much* to learn, you know?"

"That there is!" Angie agreed with a smile. She flattened out a crease on her dress and then said, "You said that you have to fight to keep your mind on something else when these thoughts come, and that the thoughts usually come at night, when you're kind of just relaxing on your bed."

Dave nodded as Angie went on.

"What do you think of to counteract these thoughts?"

Dave pushed out his bottom lip as he thought for a moment, then responded, "It's usually, like, childish dreams, I guess. You know, like winning the World Series with a ninth-inning homer, or singing my favorite songs to a sold-out arena. And it works for a while; but after my imaginary game is over, or after the fifth encore…the thoughts come again."

"Hmmm," Angie said, as she leaned towards Dave in her chair. "Do you know the verse that says, 'Whatever is true, whatever is noble, whatever is right, whatever is pure, what-ever is lovely, whatever is admirable-if anything is excellent or praiseworthy-think about such things.' ?"

"Yeah," Dave replied as he looked down at the carpet. "I've heard that before."

"This is what I want you to do," Angie said. "First of all, it's *great* that you read the Bible every day, and that you're reading Christian literature; continue doing so. Now, after you are done reading, I want you to *meditate* on what you've read, especially chapters and verses from the Bible. Really *think* about them; don't just *read* them."

Dave looked up at Angie, nodding his head in agreement as she went on.

"Do that every night, and also during the day. And if, or *when*, these bad thoughts come, turn your mind right away towards God. Bring Him into your mind, your heart… anything that you possibly can. I *guarantee* you that if you do, these thoughts will have no power over you whatsoever. God is stronger than any evil; and He won't allow evil in His presence.

"There are many verses that I could quote to support that, but one of my favorite ones is from Psalm sixteen. David starts out by saying, 'Keep me safe, O God, for in You I take refuge.' Then in verses seven and eight, he says, 'I will praise the Lord, who counsels me; even at night my heart instructs me. I have set the Lord always before me. Because he is at my right hand, I will not be shaken'."

Angie paused for a few seconds, then said, "The thing is, Dave, to always have God on your mind; there is no better way to do that than by reading the Bible and praying. Really use those commentary books that you have to study His word. The closer that you are with God, the more you'll trust Him; the more you trust *in* Him to bring you through whatever difficulty you're having.

"Now, I'm not saying that the thoughts will automatically disappear, and I'm not saying that they *won't*, either. But use this experience to really lean on the Lord; ask Him for help, and trust in Him *with all* your heart. God will not let you down, Dave, and He is bigger than all our problems."

Angie noticed that Dave didn't appear to be too encouraged. He cocked his head to the side and down so much so that his left ear almost touched his shoulder. With a troubled look on his face, he said, "Yeah, and I *know* that, but…" He slowly shook his head as he looked up at Angie and said, "but sometimes these thoughts give me such a headache, and I'll say something like, 'God, take it away'…but He doesn't. I know He could if He wanted to, but *He doesn't*. And I know that it's not right, but it makes me feel like either He doesn't care, or He just *can't* take it all away."

Dave squinted his eyes at Angie, as a painful expression covered his face and asked, "I mean, *why* is that? If He *is* stronger than all of my problems, then why would He just let me suffer like this?"

Angie rested her chin on top of her right hand as she cleared her throat and asked, "Do you love God, Dave?"

Dave was clearly caught off guard by her question.

"Yeah," he replied, not sure of where Angie was going with this. Then he added with assurance, "More than anything else."

Angie smiled warmly and said, "Good. Then know this: He will work everything out for your good. It is God's *promise*." She leaned back in the chair and crossed her arms, still wearing her comforting smile as she said, "And God doesn't lie. It's times like these, when you're really feeling your worst, that you must *completely* depend on and trust in the Lord. You'll find that, after He brings you through this, which He will; you'll find yourself trusting in God for *all* things, and relying on Him always."

A slight grin appeared on the corners of Dave's lips as he nodded his head at Angie and said, "Wow; that's just really weird that you would put it like that."

Angie cocked her head to the side with an interested look. Dave explained.

"Just before I came here, I read a commentary by Charles Spurgeon on..." Dave glanced quickly up to the ceiling in thought, then returned his gaze to Angie. "I *think* that it was on Second Samuel, something. Uh, the verse he used was something like, 'Do as Thou hast said,' and Spurgeon was talking about knowing God's promises and asking Him to do them for us."

Angie nodded in agreement as Dave went on.

"And *last night*, I was reading from Second Corinthians; the chapter where Paul talks about the thorn in his flesh. You know, how Paul asked God, I think it was three times, to take the thorn away from him, but God wouldn't do it."

Angie raised her eyebrows as she grinned at Dave and said, "Wow, how fitting that is! I've always loved Spurgeon; he just had such *great* insight! I have learned a great deal from his writings. Just such a *beautiful* mind and a loving heart towards God!"

Angie spoke of Spurgeon as if she were remembering a dear old friend. Her eyes gazed off in the distance. A smile stretched across her face, making her look ten years younger.

After trailing off for just a few seconds, Angie turned her attention back to Dave and continued.

"And... I *believe* that it's Second Corinthians, chapter twelve where Paul speaks of the thorn; in fact..." Angie sat her notepad in her chair and went over to the tall wooden bookcase that sat against the wall. She took a worn Bible with a red leather cover from a shelf and handed it to Dave.

"Why don't you look that verse up, and read it out loud," she said. "I think it starts in verse seven."

As Angie took her seat, Dave leaned forward with the Bible in his lap. After flipping around a bit, he cleared his throat and read,

" 'To keep me from boasting because of these surpassingly great revelations, there was given to me a thorn in my flesh, a messenger of Satan, to torment me. Three times I pleaded with the Lord to take it away from me. But He said to me, "My grace is sufficient for you, for my power is made perfect in weakness." Therefore I will boast all the more gladly about my weaknesses, so that Christ's power may rest on me. That is why, for Christ's sake, I delight in weaknesses, in insults, in hardships, in persecutions, in difficulties. For when I am weak, then I am strong."

Dave gently shut the Bible as Angie exclaimed, "Now, does that shed light on your situation, or what?! Think about that, Dave; memorize those verses, and know that God has *everything* under control. He *has* a reason for everything that He does, and everything that He allows to happen."

Dave sat the Bible down next to him and replied in a hopeful tone,"And what I need to do is really read the Bible and understand."

"That's right!" Angie said enthusiastically. "There is nothing that *we need* in life that can't be found in the Bible." She stared confidently at Dave for a couple of seconds to let that sink in. "Whether it be God's promises, God's directions of how to live, or how to handle this or that; it's *all* in there."

Angie noticed a dramatic change in Dave's expression. When he had first come into her office, it was clear that Dave was on edge-- it seemed as if he were about to explode! But now, a peaceful look replaced the tortured one!

Just to be sure, Angie leaned forward with a sincere expression on her face and asked, "So, what do you think, Dave? Do you feel any better now, or do you think that after you leave here these thoughts might get the better of you?"

Dave opened his mouth to respond, but Angie interrupted him, saying, "Don't answer right away; give it a moment and think. And please, *please* don't be ashamed to tell the truth; there *is* no shame in that. If you need to talk more about it, then we'll talk more. If you need some other sort of help, then we'll get it for you.

"So take a minute and reflect; we've talked about battling the thoughts by thinking of God and His many wonders. We've also briefly covered *why* God *might* be allowing you to have these thoughts - so that in your weakness, you are made strong by going to and seeking after God.

"Think about it, and if you have *any* questions or concerns, certainly let me know."

They sat in silence. Dave bowed his head a little and stroked the stubbles on his chin. Angie was well aware of how people could be so enthused by hopeful emotions at one moment, but then let down all the more hard when a difficulty would emerge that they thought never would. Dave's response would let her know where he stood.

After about a minute, Dave looked up at Angie and said, "I feel a lot better; I really do. It's like; I can't really explain it, but…"

He again stared down at the carpet as Angie looked on with much interest.

"I don't know…I *know* that God does everything for a reason, and I know that He loves me, and I know that He wants me to trust in Him; I *do* trust in Him."

Dave looked back up at Angie as he continued.

"And I don't expect all my problems to just go away…" He smiled and chuckled as he added, "In fact, I'll probably have *more* problems the more that I live. But I do believe that God will use whatever I'm going through to my advantage, so that I'll trust more and more in Him."

Angie smiled affectionately at Dave as she nodded her head, saying, "That was a very intelligent response. I want you to know, Dave, that God will always be there for you; just continue learning of Him, praying for His will to be done, and earnestly and steadfastly seeking Him. He will not disappoint you, dear; He *will not* disappoint you."

Dave returned Angie's smile as she laid her notebook on the carpet and got up from her chair. Angie picked up her Bible and placed it in her lap as she sat by Dave on the futon.

"Let's end with a prayer."

They held hands, closed their eyes, and bowed their heads as Angie prayed, "Lord God; Heavenly Father; we thank You for being who You are. We thank You for Your faithfulness to us; for You gently guiding us along life's path; for Your all surpassing and wonderful love.

"Keep us always in Your sight, Lord, and remind us that You would never let anything befall us that we couldn't handle; and there is *nothing* that we can't handle, so long as we call on You.

"Lord, be with Dave, and let him know that You are with him. I pray, Lord, that as Dave studies the Bible, may You give him insight into the many wonders of Your word. May he grow in faith, and rely solely on You. Let him know, Lord, that any obstacle that he may face is no obstacle for You. Lord God, *fill* him with a desire for You, and make known to him Your promises. May the Holy Spirit remind Dave of Your Word, and may he call out to You in supplication and in praise.

"Lord God most Holy; protect Your children, for Your name's sake. May we glorify Your name, Heavenly Father, in all that we do. Keep us, Lord, in Thy hands.

"In the name of Jesus Christ, we pray: Amen."

"Amen."

*August 8th, 2002-*

*One must be quite cautious in dealing with the knowledge granted by God to him, lest it stain his soul and cause him destruction. But how could one turn a great gift of God into evil? Good question.*

*Take, for example, a musician. God has granted him his talent, and has also granted him the choice of how to use it. There are musicians out there who choose to sing praises to Satan and Satan's wickedness. Is that not evil? Of course it is!*

*Now back to knowledge. It is a certainty that one might suffer from it. A wise man can become a fool if he has no faith. His mind, expanding in knowledge, may ask increasingly advanced questions. And if the man's mind becomes perverted by pride because of his intelligence, he will find no answer to his inquiries. Even if the answer presents itself crystal-clear in front of his eyes, he will not see the truth. His heart is hardened; he thinks, 'If your answer is not my own, than you cannot be right.'*

*If pride takes over, the devil steps in; it is his ancient foothold. He will have the man using his knowledge to say, 'Aha! Here is a contradiction of the Lord! I have proved His falseness!' What a fool that man is! He puts his so-called intelligence on a pedestal, challenging others in debates. Although he is clearly in the wrong, he does not notice. He holds his head high, praising himself for his wisdom.*

*But what is man's wisdom? It is foolishness to the Lord! The man must counteract his growing knowledge with faith. He must humble himself in the sight of the Lord, calling for forgiveness and proclaiming to Him the fact that all is not attainable by wisdom alone, and that he does not have all the answers. Then he must whole-heartedly put his trust in God, and not in his own discernment of what is and what is not. Faith and wisdom must coexist; but faith must over-power wisdom.*

*Do not let sin corrupt you; it has many ways. Know the Bible, seek after the Lord with all your heart; and He will give you your heart's desire.*

# 31.

Instead of going straight to college after graduating from high school like most kids did, Dave elected to stay at home with Mom. He got a job as a waiter at a well-known "fine dining" restaurant and actually did quite well financially. Since he had no bills besides car insurance, Dave was able to save a lot of money.

It was at this time in his life that my brother became quite the night owl. He worked nights at the restaurant, and would usually get home at around midnight. Mom was the only other one in the house, and she would have been in bed hours before Dave returned. He truly cherished those quiet times. He would read, write, and do his artwork with no disturbances. Dave's collection of books grew rapidly, as did his "smarts."

At age nineteen, he became the assistant leader in our church's Youth Group. His appeal to the teens and his knowledge of Biblical doctrine so impressed our pastor that often times Dave was left alone to lead the meetings. Dave's wood burnings, paintings, and poems sold so fast at the Christian bookstore that there was always a demand for more.

I talked with my brother frequently over the phone, and told Dave how proud of him I was. His ever-humble response was always something like, "It's all God, Jon; He's just using me for His work."

This was a great time for me in my life. My brother had turned his life around from drugs to the Lord, Mom had fully recovered from her heart attack and was back on her feet, and Anne (for some reason) had agreed to marry me! Although Dave was still seeing Angie from time to time, he assured me that he had never been better.

All was well; or so it seemed. Something was eating away at my brother from the inside; something invisible, and therefore quite difficult to detect. Dave left it unchecked for such a long time that it slowly grew and grew until it finally overtook him.

This is what happened in one of Dave's last meetings with Angie...

Dave plopped down on the futon as Angie wiped some dust from her chair and took a seat. They had met with each other six times so far, and Dave had grown quite accustomed to sharing things with her. He seemed more relaxed and less hesitant to say exactly what was on his mind.

"I like your hair like that," Dave said as he sank back a little on the futon.

"You do? Thanks!" Angie replied with a smile, running a hand through her newly straight long blonde hair. "I've always wanted to get it straightened, but it was so curly that I didn't think I could. You don't think that it makes me look weird?"

"Not at all," Dave responded with a smile. "It makes you look..." Dave paused and cocked his head at Angie, trying to find the best way to put it. "Even *more* elegant."

Angie blushed a bit, opened her notepad on top of her crossed legs, and pretended to write in it as she said, "Okay;

I'm writing, 'Dave is attempting to flatter me; he must want something!'"

After a quick chuckle, Dave got right down to business. He squinted his eyes a little at Angie and asked, "Do you ever have any problems connecting the Old Testament with the New?"

Angie cocked her head to the side and said, "What do you mean?"

"Well, like…they just seem so *different* to me at times."

Angie leaned back in the chair, legs still crossed, and said, "Give me an example."

Dave sighed and looked off to the side at nothing in particular. After a moment of thought, he said, "Okay. In the Old Testament God says that if someone was caught committing adultery, both the man and the woman were to be killed. That was a *law*; a law from *God.*"

Angie nodded slowly as Dave continued.

"But in the New Testament, when the woman who had been caught committing adultery was brought to Jesus, He basically told them, 'Hey; you're not perfect either, buddy. Let her go.'

"So…what's the deal with that? I mean, I know that Jesus died for all our sins…but He hadn't yet at that time. Does that mean that God's laws were null and void even *before* Jesus died?"

Angie opened her mouth to respond, but Dave cut back in.

"And if they *were*, which doesn't make sense…I mean, *why* would God make them in the first place? I really almost don't want to say this, but…wasn't Jesus going against what God said *must* happen to those who break the Law?"

Angie jumped right in, not missing a beat. She leaned forward with her elbows tucked in her lap and explained, "There are many things about the story of the adulterous woman that you have to understand." She held out her hand

and counted them on her fingers as she made each point. "First of all, the Pharisees were trying to trap Jesus. Secondly, the Law can't save by itself, and God knew that when He gave it. Third, the grace that Jesus showed the woman did not *contradict* the Law; it *fulfilled* it. And fourth; well, I guess the fourth thing kind of ties the first three all together."

Dave folded his arms across his chest with an obvious look of confusion on his face as Angie clarified.

"The Pharisees knew the Law; even though the Law says that both the man *and* the woman were to be put to death. They also knew that Jesus' reply, whether it be to go ahead and stone the woman or to let her go, would condemn Him in a way."

Angie shifted her weight and leaned her elbow on the chair's armrest before continuing.

"You see, Jews at the time, were under Roman rule, and they were not allowed to put anyone to death themselves. So if Jesus had said, 'Yeah, go ahead and kill her', then He would have been declared a traitor to Rome, which was a death sentence. Even though this was eventually one of the reasons the Jews gave for warranting Jesus' death, at this particular moment, He knew that it wasn't yet His time.

"Now, if He had said, 'No, don't kill her,' then the Pharisees would have accused Him as a traitor to God. Remember, Jesus wasn't alone with the Pharisees and the woman; He had been teaching in the temple to a crowd of people when they burst in. The Pharisees had Him in a perfect trap in front of many witnesses. He would either be known as a traitor to Caesar, and be put to death, or a traitor to God, and no one would follow Him anymore. They *had* Him; or so they thought."

Angie gave Dave a quick smile and then went on with excitement in her voice as she spoke.

"Now, remember that Jesus *was* and *is* God; if He was contradicting God, then He was contradicting *Himself*. And as Jesus said, 'A house divided against itself cannot stand.' He knew the Law better than the Pharisees, and He knew *why* the Law was given.

"The Law was given to convict people of their sins; it was given to show how their sins lead to death. But the Law was not given to *save*; no man can be saved by the Law, because every man sins."

"Wait a minute; what about all those people who were killed because of God's Law, then?" Dave cut in. "Were they damned to Hell because they didn't have time to offer a sacrifice before they died? I mean, were they just, like, *used* by God as an example?"

Angie took a deep breath and sighed. She looked up at the ceiling for a moment, then back at Dave as she replied, "Well, the Bible says that Jesus' death atoned for *all* sins; past, present, and future. So I believe that if the people who were killed for committing a sin before His time believed in God and worshiped Him, then yes, they were ultimately saved."

Dave quietly nodded his head, apparently satisfied with Angie's response.

"I just love what Jesus said; I can just *see* the shock on the faces of the Pharisees!" Angie said with a twinkle in her eye. " 'Let he who has no sin cast the first stone'. Do you know where that phrase comes from?"

Dave shook his head, replying, "No, I don't."

"In the Law," Angie explained, "the one or ones who were witnesses to the act that called for death were to cast the first stones at the guilty, and then everyone else would join in. Now, the Greek word for 'sin' that Jesus used here is actually defined as 'the *exact* same sin'. He *knew* that the woman's accusers were being hypocrites, because they had done this same act of sin themselves; the sin of lust.

"One by one, the accusers all left. Jesus asks the woman, 'Has anyone condemned you?,' and she says, 'No'. Then Jesus says, 'Neither do I.'"

Angie sat straight up in her chair and then said, "Jesus had *every right* to pick up some stones and kill that woman. He said, 'Let he who has no sin cast the first stone,' and Jesus *had* no sin. But did He kill her? No. Because Jesus 'came not into the world to condemn it, but to save it.'"

Angie paused for a few seconds to let that sink in before continuing.

"You see, Dave; it's only by grace that we are saved. And as I said before, the Law and grace *compliment* each other, not the opposite. The Law reveals to us how desperately we are in need of a Savior; it causes us to cry out in repentance of our sins. Our Savior, Jesus Christ, hears us, forgives us, and tells us to quit sinning.

"We know that only God Himself, the Lord Jesus, could ever substitute our sins by His blood; blood that had no sin until it was given for ours. In the Old Testament, a spotless lamb was offered as a sacrifice to atone for people's sins; but that was only a substitute until the *real* 'spotless lamb' was crucified."

Angie leaned back in her chair and paused a moment before asking Dave, "Does that answer your question?"

Dave shrugged as he looked down at the carpet.

"Yeah, I suppose so."

Dave's reluctant response didn't convince Angie. She assumed that there was an underlying issue that Dave wasn't revealing. She had been trained; and trained well; to observe her patient's body language and tone of voice, thereby assessing whether or not the patient was lying, holding back something, or other things of that nature.

"There's something that you're not telling me, Dave." Angie bluntly declared in a sweet, comforting tone. "What is it?"

Dave rubbed the back of his neck in slow, circular patterns while continuing his gaze at the carpet. After about ten seconds of silence, he quietly said, "I...I've asked God a

*million* times to forgive me for all the crap that I've done…"
Dave gradually lifted his head up and looked Angie directly
in her light blue eyes. "But I don't *feel* forgiven. It's like…I
read the story about the woman, and how Jesus just *instantly*
forgave her; I wish it were that easy."

Dave sighed deeply and wiped his palms on the sides of
his faded blue jeans. As Angie scribbled something down in
her notepad, he continued.

"I don't feel any peace within at all. A lot of the time, all
I can do is remember all the pain that I caused for my family,
and how unchristian-like I acted around all of my friends.

"And it makes me *sick*, cause I know that Jesus *died* so
that my sins could be forgiven and everything, and here I
am, wondering if it's true. But…" Dave leaned to the side
with his chin propped up under his fist. "There's really no
other way to say it: I *don't feel* forgiven."

Angie breathed in deeply through her nostrils and then
cleared her throat.

"Maybe you're *not*," she responded.

That obviously got Dave's attention. He snapped his head
up at Angie as his arm fell down in his lap. He furrowed his
brow down, looking quite upset with Angie, almost *angry*
with her, as he scowled and said, "What do you mean?"

Angie's response clearly wasn't to Dave's liking. She
had predicted as such, but it didn't keep her from saying
what she had just said. Angie sat straight up, arms laying on
her chair's armrest as she answered Dave's question with a
question of her own.

"Do you know of the parable that Jesus told about the
unforgiving debtor?"

"Yeah," Dave replied, his body still rigid as a steel pole
as he leaned forward slightly on the futon. "I…well, I *think*
I do; is that the one where the guy forgives two different
people of their debts, and one of them loves the guy more
because he owed him more of a debt?"

"No," Angie declared as she stood up and turned towards her bookshelf. She retrieved the red-leather Bible from the second shelf from the bottom and sat back down. Re-crossing her legs, she flipped to the New Testament and began scanning the pages. After just a few seconds, she lifted her head and smiled.

"Aha, here it is."

Angie read out loud Matthew chapter eighteen, verses twenty-one to thirty-two. She stopped there and handed the Bible over to Dave, asking him to read the next three verses. Dave reached for the Bible, cleared his throat and read,

" 'Shouldn't you have had mercy on your fellow servant just as I had on you?' In anger his master turned him over to the jailers to be tortured, until he should pay back all that he owed.

"This is how my heavenly Father will treat each of you unless you forgive your brother from your heart."

Dave stared down at the Bible, as if he had missed something. He shrugged his shoulders at Angie with a confused expression on his face and asked, "I'm not quite sure of what this has to do with me?"

Angie took the Bible from Dave and sat back in her chair. She looked at Dave in silence for a few seconds, then answered him.

"Jesus said, 'If you forgive men when they sin against you, your heavenly Father will also forgive you. But if you do not forgive men their sins, your Father *will not* forgive your sins."

"Still," Dave replied, shaking his head, annoyance plainly apparent in his voice. "I don't see what that has to do with me."

Angie pursed her lips, not because she was angry with Dave, but because she felt sorry for him. She sighed, and then said, "In His parable, Jesus said that the man was handed over to be tortured until he paid back what he owed. He also said that this is what God would do to anyone who didn't forgive his brother. That's kind of like a parable within a parable; God doesn't put everyone who chooses not to forgive in a *literal* prison, and they aren't always tortured by the devices that might come to mind…but they *are* in a prison, and they *are* being tortured."

Dave squinted at Angie as she raised her eyebrows at him, looking Dave directly in his eyes.

"So, what are you saying?" he asked. "That I haven't forgiven someone, and *that's* the reason that I don't feel forgiven?"

Angie thought about mentioning the thoughts that Dave had expressed before, but decided against it.

"Well," she said, cocking her head to the side just a little. "What do you think? *Is* there someone in your life that you are harboring resentment towards?"

Dave's eyes shot up to the ceiling in a moment of thought. He stuck out his bottom lip and looked back at Angie as he responded, "No."

"That was pretty quick," Angie said with a chuckle. "Think about that again, and give it some real thought. Is there *anyone* that has wronged you in a way that you haven't completely forgiven?"

Dave sighed loudly, reiterating the fact that Angie was aggravating him by her questions. But still, he respected her, and so he did as she asked. He leaned forward with his elbows on his knees and cracked his knuckles. Then there was nothing but silence in the room for a good minute or two.

Although Angie wasn't speaking in words, her soul was speaking to the Lord.

*'Lord God, convict Dave, open his eyes. That is, if I am right about this. Either way, Lord; guide this conversation, as You always do. In the name of Jesus, Amen.'*

Dave looked up and sat back, his arms folded against his chest.

"The only person that I can think of is…"

He paused and bit his lip, his eyes trailing away at nothing in particular.

"Is *who*?" Angie asked in her firm yet gentle voice.

Dave swallowed a lump and replied, his eyes still distant.

"My dad."

Angie nodded slowly and exhaled through her nostrils. Joyce had told her a little bit about Pete; how he had abandoned Jon and Dave at a young age, how he had been unfaithful to Joyce, and about his addiction to alcohol.

"What is it about your father that-?"

"What *isn't* it about him?!" Dave interrupted with an anger in his voice that surprised Angie. "I mean…I don't even know where to begin! He…he…" Dave stammered, his hands held out with his palms up, as if he were holding an invisible two-by-four. "For starters, he *beat* my Mom."

Joyce hadn't told Angie that. She wrote in her notepad as Dave continued.

"He was never around for anything; even before he left; the only real memory I have of him is lying on the couch in a sweat suit and yelling for me and Jon to shut the hell up. Other kids had dads to play catch with, to, you know, talk about girls with…I mean, I had to teach myself to shave. I had to teach myself practically *everything* that a Dad's suppose to do. Well, I had Jon, of course; but an older brother is just that, an older brother. He's not a dad."

Angie nodded sympathetically at Dave. He had finished talking, and was breathing heavy with a mixed look of confusion and hurt on his face. Angie supposed that Dave had been holding these feelings about his father in for quite some time; so long, perhaps, that he may have not noticed that they were there.

"Your dad did a terrible thing," Angie responded softly after a few seconds had passed by. Dave nodded in agreement. "There's no denying that what he did; the way he treated you guys, was wrong. But have you forgiven him?"

"Forgiven him?" Dave repeated, seemingly appalled that Angie would dare ask such a thing. "How do you forgive someone like that? Someone who hits your Mom, and, and, leaves you in the dust as if you weren't even there?"

Dave scowled at Angie as he leaned towards her and said, "It's easy to sit where you're sitting. It's easy to say, 'This is what the Bible says,' and 'This is what you should do.' And honestly, I see where you're going with this, and you're probably right."

Dave settled back in the futon with a look of exasperation on his face. He put his hands behind his head and looked up at the ceiling as he said, "But there's a whole different world between *saying* things and *doing* them." His eyes locked with Angie's as he finished with, "And I can't forgive him."

"You can't forgive him," Angie asked softly, "or you *won't* forgive him?"

Dave threw his hands in the air and turned his head sharply to the side. Quickly looking back at Angie, he exclaimed in frustration, "Why *should* I? For one thing, he doesn't deserve it; and I know what you're going to say, that I don't deserve forgiveness, either. But hey, when *I* do something wrong, at least I *ask* to be forgiven; I ask God *and* the person whom I've offended. He...he hasn't so much as *spoken* to me in, what, over fourteen years now? Let alone ask me or Mom or my brother for forgiveness! How can I forgive someone if they don't even ask for it?"

Angie breathed in deeply through her nostrils and then back out. Resting her chin on her fisted hand, she asked Dave, "What if King Herod had gotten his way, and Jesus had died as a baby?"

Dave looked at her silently with utter confusion on his face. Seeing that she obviously needed to expand on her question, Angie added, "What I mean is, that's all that we would have needed so that our souls would be saved, right? That God would give His Son to take away our sins. So why did Jesus live to be over thirty years old?"

Angie was trying to lead up to the point she was trying to make, but Dave's response stopped her in her tracks. He raised a single eyebrow at her and slowly said, "No; if Jesus had been killed as an infant, that would have meant that He wasn't God's Son."

Angie cocked her head in surprise as she frowned. She was sure that Dave was wrong.

"What makes you say that?" she asked in a nearly condescending tone.

"Because," Dave explained, "of what the Old Testament says about the Messiah. I mean, there are so many, but what comes to mind are things like, 'He will be a prophet greater than Moses,' and in Isaiah it says that He would be 'despised and rejected by men; we would esteem Him not,' uh…'He would be pierced for our transgressions, He would be oppressed and afflicted.'"

Dave shook his head at Angie and said, "I don't think that a baby could be considered as oppressed, and certainly not a *prophet*! And that's not to mention all the other prophecies about casting lots for His clothes, and Him being betrayed by a close friend.

"Other than reading about what Jesus did and said in the gospels, the main reason that I believe Jesus is the Son of God is because He fulfilled each and every prophesy about Him. So like I said, if Jesus had died as a baby, then He couldn't have been God's Son."

Angie smiled widely as she slowly shook her head in amazement.

"You're absolutely right," she said. "I can't believe that I've never thought of it like that; but you are absolutely right!"

Dave's blushed a little as he looked down at the carpet. Angie made a note in her pad, silently thanked the Lord for humbling her, and then continued.

"What I meant, Dave, was that Jesus is not only our Lord and Savior, but He is also a role model for us. I was going to say that He lived that long so He could truly understand what being a human is like, experiencing all our trials, triumphs and temptations, and overcoming them in His perfect way.

"I still think that's true, but now that you've shed some light on it, I see that it isn't the *only* reason."

Angie winked at Dave as they smiled at each other.

"But going back to regarding Jesus as a role model," Angie said as she brushed a fuzzy off from her black dress, "did you know that not *once* in the Bible does anyone ever ask Jesus to forgive them?"

"What?" Dave said in disbelief. "No?" He said "No" as a half-question, half-declarative statement.

Angie hadn't believed it at first, either. Her pastor had mentioned it briefly in a sermon one day, and Angie hadn't heard another word of that sermon, because she had been too busy flipping through her Bible in the pew. She continued her search at home right after the service, and found that her pastor had been right.

"It's true," she said confidently, affirming her statement by nodding her head.

Dave squinted his eyes as he turned his gaze to the side. Angie could tell that his mind was racing, just as hers had been on that day in church. After a few seconds Dave looked at her, with his eyes still squinting, and asked, "What about the guy on the cross? And Peter? Didn't Peter ask Jesus to forgive him after He had risen from the dead?"

Angie bent down and picked up the Bible that she had laid by her feet. Handing it over to Dave, she challenged, "You tell me."

Dave gave Angie a questioning look, as if he was studying her, then lowered his head and opened up the Bible. Dave quickly turned to Luke, the only gospel that records a conversation between Jesus and the criminal. Angie saw that he had found the spot, and she asked him to read it aloud.

"One of the criminals who hung there hurled insults at him: 'Aren't you the Christ? Save yourself and us!'

"But the other criminal rebuked him. 'Don't you fear God,' he said, 'since you are under the same sentence? We are punished justly, for we are getting what our deeds deserve. But this man has done nothing wrong.'

"Then he said, 'Jesus, remember me when you come into your kingdom.'

"Jesus answered him, 'I tell you the truth, today you will be with me in paradise.'"

Dave stared unblinkingly at the Bible, his eyes going left to right. He was obviously re-reading the passage.

"The criminal didn't..." Angie sighed deeply and looked up in thought. "He didn't *blatantly* ask Jesus to forgive him; but he recognized Him as God, and Jesus forgave him because of his faith. Many times in the Bible Jesus says something like, 'Your faith has healed you.'"

Dave looked up at her with his mouth half-opened, confusion apparent on his countenance.

"But...doesn't it say in the Bible that we must *ask* for our sins to be forgiven?"

"Yes," Angie answered, "it does."

Dave shook his head and lifted his shoulders up as he said, "Well then...how was the criminal saved? He never said that he was sorry for what he did; this is confusing the crap out of me. Why?..." Dave slumped back on the futon in frustration. "I just don't get it."

"You really think that he wasn't sorry for what he did?" Angie asked with raised eyebrows. "Listen carefully to what he said: 'We are punished justly, for we are getting what our deeds deserve.' He knew that what he did was wrong."

Angie leaned towards Dave, almost falling out of her chair. She spoke quickly now with excitement as the Holy Spirit led her.

"Compare the two criminals: one mocked Christ, and we know that he was mocking Him, because Luke describes him as hurling insults, by saying, 'C'mon, aren't You God? Then come down from the cross and take us down, too!'

"But the other criminal doesn't. He says, 'Hey, we're up here for a good reason, but this guy hasn't done anything wrong!' He doesn't ask Jesus to save his life, that is, to save his *body* from death. He knows that his crime deserved death, and he doesn't plead for a pardon of that sort. What he *does* do is make a plea for his soul; he asks Jesus to 'remember him when He comes into His kingdom'.

"So I'd say it's pretty safe to say that this guy believed that Christ was who He said He was, yes?"

"Yeah. But that doesn't really answer my question. I think it's Paul who writes that 'even demons believe in God, and they shudder.'"

"Actually, it's James," Angie corrected. "But you're right; even Satan himself knows that there is only one true God. Does that mean that Satan is saved?"

Dave emphatically shook his head no.

"Of course not," Angie agreed. "James says, 'Show me your faith without deeds, and I will show you my faith by what I do.' He also says that 'Faith without deeds is dead'."

"Yeah," Dave said impatiently, wondering if Angie was ever going to answer his original question.

"So what does that mean?" Angie paused slightly before answering her own question. "It means that if you *truly* believe in God, then you will do your best to do as He commands. Like you said, demons believe in God, but they don't *follow* Him; they follow Satan.

"You have to bring what the Bible says together, instead of looking at it only one piece here and there; and I admit, that can be hard to do. But it is even *more* difficult if you don't. I've found myself so confused over one passage that it almost drove me insane!" Angie admitted with a chuckle. Her expression became serious as she added, "But that's not the way God intended it. He wants you to know all that you can about Him; and the best way to do that is to study the entire Bible."

"I definitely agree," Dave said, "And I've been doing that. But..." He shook his head slowly from side to side, and then said, "It seems like...it was so much *easier* when I *didn't* know all this stuff; it's like the more I know, the more confused I am. I mean...why is that? If God wants us to know Him, which I *know* that He does, why is it so hard? So...impossible at times?"

Angie smiled warmly at Dave as she asked, "Do you know more of God than you did, say, five years ago?"

"Oh yeah," Dave responded. "A lot more."

Still keeping her smile, the counselor asked, "And if it had been easy...if it had been easy to learn of the great, almighty, all-knowing, all-powerful Creator of all existence, do you *really* think that our simple minds would have no problem with this?"

Dave produced a slight grin and answered, "No."

"Keep seeking the Lord," Angie said, "and you will not fail. Paul says to 'never tire in doing good, for in due season we will reap a harvest if we faint not.'

"And Dave, it is good to seek the Lord. Don't quit, and never think that you have Him all figured out. He won't leave you in frustration; you might, in fact, you *will* get frustrated; we all do. But God won't *leave* you there. He will bring things together for you in His own perfect timing. Just know that He is perfect, that His Word is perfect; it's *we* who are limited, not He."

Dave nodded in apparent agreement as the two sat in silence for a few moments.

"I know that," Dave said as he sat straight up on the futon. "And I really try to keep myself aware of the fact that even though things might not make sense to me, God doesn't mess up or make mistakes, or do anything wrong at all. But I really feel like things are hidden sometimes; like you have to be, like, a seasoned Biblical scholar before you can put two and two together."

Dave's eyes stared vacantly towards the rug as he continued on in a soft voice.

"I mean, it just seems like there are so many 'ho-hum Christians' out there who think that because they believe that Jesus Christ died for their sins, then they're saved, and they can go and do whatever they want.

"And I hear it all the time, like on the radio, preachers who I really respect saying things like, 'Just ask Jesus in your heart, and you'll be saved.' When in actuality, there's so much more that you have to do."

"Like what?" Angie asked as she scribbled some notes down.

Dave shot her a surprised look, as if Angie had just stepped into the room and had not heard all that was said in the past twenty minutes.

"Like *what*?" Dave echoed, his upper body flinching back as if a strong wind was pushing against him. "Like repenting from your sin, uh, reading the Bible to know more about God, *demonstrating* your belief by what you do and how you live…" He furrowed his brow and squinted as he asked, "Was that some sort of a trick question or something?"

"No," Angie replied as she arched her eyebrows, "it wasn't a trick question, and you answered it perfectly." She smiled as she took a deep breath and exhaled it with a sigh. "These 'ho-hum Christians' are like the criminal on the cross that told Jesus to go ahead and save Himself, if He really was

God, and then save him as well. These people aren't really Christians, because they just want to *use* Christ to save their souls from Hell while at the same time not ever changing their lives around.

"However, someone who truly asks Jesus to come into their hearts is *certainly* saved, and you'll be able to differentiate a believer in Christ from a non-believer by what they do. A Christian will be a person who does what you said just now: someone who repents from sin, who seeks after God by reading His Word, who uses his or her talents for the glory of God and follows His teachings, such as feeding the poor and sharing their belief with others."

After a quick thought, Angie went on.

"Now, what I said before about it not being recorded in the Bible that anyone asked Jesus to forgive them: I don't want you to think that it's okay not to admit that you've sinned to God and ask for forgiveness. That's just not Biblical. In Jesus' model prayer to the Lord, He said, 'Forgive us our sins, as we forgive those that sin against us.' At the time, I was just trying to say that, as Jesus did, we are to forgive people for what they've done to us, regardless of whether or not they actually ask us to. God forgives you because of your faith in Jesus' death and resurrection; His sacrifice is sufficient to take away all our sins, and make us right with God. But we are to do what the Bible says to do, and that is admit that we are sinners, and by the life of Jesus within us, turn from our ways and sin no more.

"Now," Angie said as she reclined slightly in her chair, a wide smile stretched across her face, "after all that, here we are again, right where we started!" Her face grew somber as she looked Dave in the eyes and said, "Simply put, Dave, it's the risen Christ within us Who empowers us and convicts us to do what we should. Could you forgive someone like your father without Christ, who has shown you what forgiveness is? Could I? No, Dave, I don't think that we could."

Angie leaned forward and gently placed her hand on Dave's knee as she grinned at him and said, "But Dave, we *have* Christ inside; we *are* forgiven!"

She didn't have to say anything else; stubborn old Dave finally got the point. He closed his eyes while his chin up to his bottom lip began to quiver. He rocked slowly back and forth on the futon, nodding his head in rhythm with his body.

"I forgive you, Dad," he said out loud as tears came flowing down. His mouth stretched wide open, barely showing his teeth; it seemed to Angie that it revealed the faintest of smiles. "I forgive you, I forgive you, I forgive you," he repeated as Angie kneeled on the carpet and embraced him with a thankful smile.

*November 22ⁿᵈ, 2001-*
*"The devil has his sights on you; keep going; you're not out of the range of his guns. Keep going, my Christian pilgrim; keep going!!!"*
                    -'Life Like a Journey' (the retelling of
                    John Bunyan's classic, Pilgrim's Progress
                    by Duane Priset)

*Lord, guide my thoughts,*
*And guard them as well.*
*Save me from destruction,*
*From the pits of Hell.*
*The glory of Heaven*
*May I always see;*
*Lord, set my mind*
*And my heart on Thee.*

# 32.

I remember sitting in my den at home, reading through Dave's journals, and coming across the above entry. I kept on thinking, *'There's* something *about this'*, but I couldn't quite figure out what it was. I read it over and over again, getting the feeling that I was missing something important.

At the time, I was creating a crude outline for this book. I spent hours in the den, praying for God to guide me as I went through each and every passage in Dave's three journals. When I saw something that I felt could be used, I'd write the date down in my notes, and then continue on. It was normally a very simple process; very time consuming, yes, but simple. Something unusual happened on this particular occurrence; it was as if I couldn't write "November 22nd, 2001" in my notepad, but I couldn't pass it by, either.

It was obvious that the quote from Priset's book and Dave's poem had some sort of connection to each other - that I was sure of. What the connection was, though, seemed puzzling to me. After reading it for the fifth time, I couldn't grasp any correlation. I was about to just skip over it and go on, but I couldn't. It was like I *had* to figure out what Dave was trying to say.

So I decided to paraphrase the quote in my own words. I flipped to a blank sheet of paper in my notepad, read Priset's quote again, thought a while, and then wrote:

"Satan wants to get you, and you're not out of harm's way. Don't give up and don't relax; keep journeying towards the Lord."

I compared my paraphrased version of the quote with the quote itself, and was satisfied that they were pretty much in agreement with each other.

Then I read Dave's poem again. Why had he written it directly under that quote?

After mulling it over for a good twenty minutes, I began thinking that I was trying to make something out of something that was nothing. I could usually tell right away whether or not a certain entry might be useful for this book, and most of the time I'd even know how I could use it. But what Dave had written on the twenty-second was perplexing to me; not only was I unsure of how I would ever use it in the book, I was unsure of what the heck it meant - if anything! Still, I *knew* that I just couldn't overlook it and continue on to Dave's next entry.

I bowed my head and earnestly asked the Lord to solve the puzzle. After a few moments of silence, I opened my eyes and re-read the quote and the poem, truly believing with all my heart that the answer would be revealed, that all of a sudden I would go, 'Aha! So *that's* what it means!' The only thing that happened was my frustration level increased, and I found myself as confused as ever.

I pushed my chair back from the large wooden desk in disgust and walked out of my den.

Anne had been called in to perform an emergency operation on a mutt that had eaten a bellyful of rat poison. It was almost suppertime, and she was still not home. So I decided to have dinner ready for when she got back. I went to the kitchen and opened the cupboards above the sink, scanning the shelves for something that was easy to make.

As I was deciding over some Hamburger Helper or some fettuccini Alfredo, a verse suddenly popped into my mind: 'Now we see but a poor reflection as in a mirror...'

I thought, 'Hmm; that's weird. Where did *that* come from?'

I shrugged it off and reached for the box of Hamburger Helper. As I was reading the cooking instructions, the verse came back in my mind. I sat the box down on the countertop as the verse repeated itself over and over in my head.

I knew where it came from - First Corinthians, chapter thirteen. The famous 'love' chapter. As I thought about it, it then became clear to me *why* it had come to my mind.

I hurried upstairs to my bedroom and picked up my Bible from the lampstand. I turned to the first letter of Paul to the church at Corinth and read all thirteen verses of the thirteenth chapter. I then re-read the twelfth verse, the beginning of which was the one that had "just popped into my head."

'Now we see but a poor reflection as in a mirror; then we shall see face to face. Now I know in part; then I shall know fully, even as I am fully known.'

It hit me like a ton of bricks.

With the Bible grasped firmly in hand, I flew down the stairs and ran into my den. Too excited to sit down, I loomed over Dave's journal, which was still opened to the same page on my desk.

I read again what he had written, and it became awesomely clear to me.

'It's so simple!' I thought as I shook my head with a grin on my face. 'How could I have not realized it before?'

Months later, though, when I began to write this chapter, I soon recognized how complex it all was. That's why it had befuddled me at first; it should be easy enough for even a child to understand; yet, if you really think about it, you discover that incorporated into this supposed "simplicity" is an unfathomable world of wisdom that no human mind could ever produce.

Don't get me wrong; I'm *not* saying that Dave was more than human. I feel the need to clarify that fact, because I heard a eulogy once where a woman pastor (I won't say her name) actually implied that the deceased was an angel. It was very weird and uncomfortable, to say the least.

I will try to put this as simply as I can: I learned something that day that I just described to you; something that I will take with me forever. God has everything planned out for you; *you*, the person that is holding this book in his or her hands. Follow the Lord, dear reader; lean not to your own understanding, and take time to marvel in the wondrous beauty of the life that you have placed in God's hands.

"I just need to get out of the house," Dave said casually, though I sensed that something was amiss. He seemed unable to look me in the eyes, as his own eyes darted around from one spot on the floor to another.

I had graduated from college three months earlier, after four long and grueling years of studying and tests. It had been worth it, though, because the college from which I received my degree was one of the best and most recognized in the state of Pennsylvania for teachers. Before I had even graduated, I received offers for teaching high school literature from five different districts. After much prayer and deliberation, I had accepted the offer from Pennington High, which is in Pennington, PA, a short ten-mile drive away from home.

At first I was going to live with Mom and Dave until Anne and I got married, which would be in less than two years. We decided that it would be best if she finished college before we got married; although neither one of us wanted to wait that long, we knew that it would be better for her if we did so.

My plans changed, though, just a few days before graduation. One of my best friends whom I had met at college asked me if I'd like to find an apartment with him. His name is Jeremy Court, and we had lived on the same floor in our dorm for the last two years of college. Jeremy and I got along perfectly; we liked the New York Yankees, were die-hard Steelers fans, loved to golf, watch basketball, play poker, and shared an enjoyment for numerous other activities. He was a very smart, funny, down-to-earth guy.

I reminded Jeremy that Anne and I would be purchasing a house before our marriage, and he said that was perfect. Jeremy was going to be working for his father as an accountant for the law firm that his dad ran; for his first year on the job, he would be stationed at a branch that was just outside of Pennington. After his first year, Jeremy said that his dad planned to move him to the main firm, which was located in New York City. Jeremy thought that it would be perfect. We'd live together for a year; then he'd move out of state, and I'd move into the house that Anne and I would live in after we were married. We'd have one year to enjoy our friendship before not seeing each other for possibly a very long time. I agreed, and we found an apartment that was more like a townhouse, having an upstairs/downstairs, two bedrooms, and two bathrooms. It was located almost exactly inbetween Pennington and Fairmount, where Jeremy's office was.

Dave had visited frequently after we moved in. He slept over a few nights on the couch downstairs, and he and Jeremy had almost instantly taken a liking to each other.

"So…what do you think?" Dave asked as we stood in the small kitchen of the townhouse.

I closed the refrigerator door and handed him one of the sodas in my hand. After taking a long swig, I wiped some moisture from my forehead, trying to give myself some time to think.

Dave had been helping me situate all of my belongings. For the past three weeks, they had been stored in large cardboard boxes. I had been too busy (or too lazy) to put all my dishes, clothes, and other personal belongings in their proper places. I thought that it would be more or less an easy task; I just didn't realize how much stuff I had until I began going through the boxes. Dave had dropped by as I was rummaging through the many items, and I was glad that he did. If he hadn't helped me, what took us two and a half hours would have taken me forever!

I shrugged and responded, "I don't see a problem with that. Of course, I'd have to ask Jeremy."

"Yeah, that's cool,." Dave said with an excited grin on his face. He opened his soda and gulped down nearly the whole can.

"You'd have to sleep downstairs, you know."

Dave nodded as he slurped down the rest of the soda. After a loud and long belch, he threw the can in the garbage and said, "There's plenty of room down there for my books, and the sofa is really comfortable. I won't bother you guys when I get home at night, and I'll just go out the door down there when I want to have a cigarette."

I nodded slowly as I took a sip of soda. The only real objection that I had to Dave moving in had come as soon as he had asked. That was, what about Mom? She would be so lonely with no one in the house, and I knew that she wouldn't admit to it - especially if she felt that Dave would be happier if he moved in with me.

So I threw in the 'I'd have to ask Jeremy' kind of as my ace in the hole. I knew that Jeremy would have no problem with Dave moving in; not only did he like Dave a lot, he would like the fact that we'd have less rent to pay each month. I would talk with Mom about it, and if I saw that she was hurt by Dave wanting to leave her alone, I'd tell Dave that Jeremy, for some reason or another, didn't want Dave moving in. I didn't feel right about the possibility of having to lie to my brother, but I felt even worse about Mom being all alone.

A few days after Dave had made his request, I stopped by to visit Mom, knowing that my brother was at work. We sat down in the living room, she on the couch and me on a reclining chair across from her. After a couple of minutes of casual talk, I got right down to the point.

Leaning back in the chair, I asked, "Did Dave tell you that he wants to move in with me?"

"Yes," Mom answered as she sat her cup of tea on the white coffee table in front of the sofa. "We had a talk about that. So, he asked you?"

I couldn't sense whether or not Mom liked the idea. Like I said before, I knew that she wouldn't come out and say it if she didn't want Dave to leave, so I had to keep a close eye on her body language.

"Yeah, a couple of days ago. What do you think about it?"

She smiled at me, and without a hint of phoniness in her voice replied, "I think it'd be neat for you guys to live together! You always got along so well, and he really looks up to you. I think it'd be good for Davey to get out of the house for a while. It'll give him a chance to do things on his own, like washing his own clothes and cooking his own dinners. Although I *love* doing those kinds of things for him, it's probably about time that he learned to do them for himself."

I squinted my eyes a little, wondering if this was all an act.

"Are you sure? I mean, you'll be all by yourself. You'll be lonely, won't you?"

Mom lifted up her hand with her palm facing me, then flicked it down, as if she were spiking a volleyball over the net.

"Are you kidding me? I want what's best for my boy; if he's happy, then I am, too."

I leaned forward with my elbows on my knees and said, "Ma, I know that you mean that; but have you really thought about this? You'll be coming home to an empty house every day; you'll have no one to talk to, no one to eat dinner with..."

"Davey was hardly ever home when I was anyway, Jon," Mom said with a smile. "It won't be much different. Besides, you know how your Aunt Sheila calls me all the time. She'll keep me company; don't worry about me. I love the fact that you're concerned about me; but honestly, honey, there's no reason to be.

"And to tell you the truth, I think that your brother moving in with you might be an answer to my prayers."

That caught me by surprise. I raised my eyebrows and asked, "What do you mean?"

Mom took a sip from her tea and then set it back down. As she looked back up at me, I saw that her smile had vanished. Mom had 'smile wrinkles' on her face, the by-product of smiling and laughing all the time. You could only see the wrinkles when she frowned.

I could tell by the long pause that Mom was trying to think of how to put what she was about to say. After a few moments she cleared her throat and then said, "I think there's something wrong with Davey. I don't know *what*, and, of course, he won't tell me...but I can tell that he's hurting."

I listened with great concern as Mom went on.

"A few weeks ago, I was getting ready to go to work. I woke up around five, took a shower, and as I went into the kitchen to warm up some hot water for my tea, I saw that the front door was open.

"At first, I thought that someone had broken into the house, and I was about to run downstairs and see if Davey was alright. But the garage light was on, so I opened the screen door to peek my head around the corner, and I saw Dave kneeling on the ground outside with his back to me.

"I said, 'Davey? Are you alright?' And without moving a muscle he said, 'I'm praying, Mom.'

"I thought that it was weird for him to be outside so early in the morning, kneeling down on the wet grass."

I furrowed my eyebrows and nodded as Mom continued.

"I was in here, in front of the heater, when I heard Dave come in. He had opened the door down to the basement when I called out for him to come see me. At first he just stayed where he was and said, 'I'm tired, Mom; what do you want?' I told him to just come here for a minute, I wanted to see him.

"So he came into the room, and right away I could tell that he had been crying. Even though he wouldn't look at me, I saw that his eyes were all misty and his face was red. I got up and asked him what was wrong, and he told me that he just couldn't sleep. I asked him if he had been crying, and he just nodded his head.

"I asked him again what was wrong, and he just shrugged and said he didn't know. I said, 'Well, you *must* know, Davey.' But he just stood there and didn't say a word."

"What do you think it is?" I asked.

"I don't know, honey. I know that he has trouble sleeping; sometimes when I'm going to work, I see his light on in his room through the downstairs window. And this is at six in the morning. I wonder if he sleeps at all some nights."

"Huh. He's never dropped any hints at all about what it might be?"

Mom slowly shook her head with a look of despondency on her face.

"What makes you think that Dave'd be better off if he lived with me?"

"Because I've been praying about it," Mom replied, as the smile I so love to see returned to her face. "I basically told God, '*You* know what it is, and *You* know what he needs.' And I've asked Him to take care of it. When Davey asked me how I'd feel if he asked you to let him move in with you, I somehow *knew* that this was God's answer to my prayers."

I returned Mom's smile, agreeing with her that she was right. I didn't know *why* she was right, but there was Someone inside me telling me that she was.

We talked on for a little while, and before I left, I wrote a note to Dave saying that he could move in whenever. As I was lying in bed that night, I couldn't get my Mom and our discussion out of my mind. She was such a tiny, frail-looking person; but on the inside she had the strength of a lion. Strength that is faith and trust in God.

I smiled as I thought about how loving and kind she was, how she truly wanted the best for Dave over what her own needs might be. I thanked the Lord for my dear mother, and thanked Him again for being so strong in her.

*September 8th, 2003-*

*Will the Lord set His watchmen at the posts only during the daylight? No! If there is evil during the day, how much more is there at night!*

*Evil lurks in the shadows, and by the cover of darkness it thrives. But take comfort; the Lord posts His children as watchmen in the night. They overlook the city and its surroundings. They hear steps approaching and shine their light upon the danger that seeks destruction.*

*Rest easy, those who sleep during the night, for the Lord never slumbers, and His people are protected by constant guard.*

# 33.

Dave moved into the *Crossroads* apartment complex with Jeremy and me in the winter of 2002. The townhouses that we lived in were incorporated into U-shaped structures, with the front doors facing the parking lot, and doors in the back leading out into an open field where children played after school. During the winter, they would build snow forts and get into snowball fights. When summer came along, the kids played kickball and tossed around footballs and baseballs in the wide-open space.

My brother lived in the downstairs section of our townhouse, which consisted of a room twice the size of the bedrooms in which Jeremy and I stayed. We had been using the area as a living room before Dave moved in. Jeremy's big screen TV, a small refrigerator, an electronic dartboard, and a long sofa had accommodated us quite well. We'd watch games and have a few beers, shoot some darts with a couple of buddies; basically, it was "hang out" for Jeremy and me.

After Dave came to live with us, the only thing that stayed down there was the sofa. We brought everything else upstairs on the first floor, where there was ample room. Dave brought with him two bookcases filled with books, his art supplies, writing materials, and a large oak dresser drawer that we had shared as kids. His art supplies alone nearly filled half the room, and his books never stayed on their shelves.

Every time that I went downstairs, it seemed messier than the time before. Books upon books would be strewn across the floor, so much so that at times it was nearly impossible to see the light brown carpet. Dave had made a makeshift table on which he did his artwork; two sawhorses and a large slab of plywood laying across them. Primitive, yes, but it worked. His wood-burning tools, including the wood itself, paint supplies, canvases, sketchpads, charcoal pencils, markers, and modeling clay (just to name a few items) were literally littered about the entire room. I had no idea how Dave could live in such a cluttered area, much less get any work done! But he did.

From time to time, Dave would show me - and sometimes Jeremy - a painting he had done, a wood-burning, or a poem he had written. It was never an issue of pride for Dave; it was actually the exact opposite. No matter how beautiful something that my brother produced might have been, he always seemed unsure about it. There would be a flaw in one of his paintings that only he could see, a sentence that he thought could have been worded better in his poems. I gave Dave my honest opinion in whatever he showed me, whether it was good or bad. I think that he respected me for that.

In the back corner of the downstairs room, there was a small staircase that led up into the back door of the townhouse. This was convenient for Dave in two ways. He did most of his wood-burnings kneeling on the cement steps, with a fan behind him blowing the wisps of smoke into the air outside. Also, he could go out for a cigarette without having to go out the front door, which creaked loudly every time it opened, due to a desperate need for oil on its hinges. Jeremy was a sound sleeper; I, on the other hand, would wake up to a mouse fart. For the first few days that Dave lived with us, he'd come through the front door after work at around one in the morning, and I'd wake up nearly every time to the long screech of the hinges. I finally asked him to enter through the back, and never again was I woken up by my brother at such an early hour in the morning - that is, aside from that one cold winter's night. It caused the eeriest of chills to come upon me when Dave first fully explained to me what had happened, and does so still to this very day...

It was three o' clock in the morning, and Dave couldn't sleep.

He had gotten home from work at midnight, which was early for him. Following his routine, Dave had read a chapter from the New Testament as soon as he had taken off his work clothes and then wrote a few paragraphs in his journal. After that, he had finished drawing the outline for his next painting - a wolf standing on top of an overhanging cliff, looking down at a herd of sheep.

Dave finished his outline after an hour of work, and then relaxed on the sofa with C.S. Lewis' *The Screwtape Letters*. He turned off the light a little after two a.m. and closed his eyes, tired and ready for sleep.

But sleep would not come. Dave tossed and turned on the couch. Usually, that couch was so comfortable to him that he fell asleep minutes after the lights went out. There was an uneasiness churning in his stomach that particular night, but Dave couldn't figure out why.

Finally, after about an hour, Dave said in his mind:

*'What is it, God? What do you want?'*

Only then, did Dave remember that he hadn't said his nightly prayers. Dave made it a custom to ask the Lord to be with him and to guide him throughout the day when he awoke. At night, he would thank Him and lift up people's names and ask that God took care of each person's needs.

Since Dave did this faithfully every "morning" and every "night" (I put them in quotations, because Dave's mornings were technically nights, and vice versa), he was astonished that he had almost gone to sleep and forgotten about them this time.

Dave threw his blanket off and knelt in front of the couch with his elbows on the cushions. My brother didn't take praying lightly; he took it as it is, or rather, how it *should* be taken – as direct communication with the Lord Almighty. His prayers weren't a simple, 'God, you're great, uh, thank You and forgive me for my sins Amen.'

No, Dave was passionate about talking with the Lord; he *loved* it...*they* loved it, I should say.

When he was finished, Dave sat in silence with his head bowed, listening for that still, small voice. (As Dave wrote in his journal, 'The voice that comes not in through your ears, but out from your heart'). After just a few seconds, Dave got the distinct feeling that someone he had prayed for was in trouble. He began going over their names in his mind.

*'Mom?...Jon?...Susie?...Jeremy?...Uncle Stan?...'*

The list was long, and it took Dave several minutes to name each person. When he had finished, he had no idea of who was in danger, but he still had a very strong feeling that *someone* was.

Dave waited in silence again, but the voice would not reveal the name. Finally, he picked his head up and looked towards the tiny slender window that sat just under the ceiling of his downstairs room. From Dave's vantage point on his knees, he saw the moonlit sky with stars twinkling in the backdrop.

"Tell me, Lord," he said out loud. "If there really is someone who's suffering, or needs help; just *tell* me."

The room was dead silent for a few seconds, and then Dave heard something. It was very faint at first, and he couldn't tell just what it was. All that Dave knew was that the noise was coming from outside, and it was getting closer.

Dave stretched his neck towards the window and squinted his eyes. Every three seconds or so, he heard a *crunch* sound from an unknown source. It got closer and closer, and suddenly Dave realized what it was - someone was walking ever so slowly through the snow, seemingly very close to the back of the townhouses.

Dave glanced down at his alarm clock, and the red glow-in-the-dark numbers told him that it was almost four in the morning.

'*What is this person doing, creeping around at this hour?*' Dave thought. He knelt on the sofa, facing the window with his eyes barely peeking above the top of the couch.

*Crunch...crunch...*

Dave's eyes opened wide, as he saw a pair of legs standing before the window. Although the moon was bright, all he could see was the dark black shape of the person's legs from just below the knees and down.

Before Dave could even wonder what the heck was going on, the figure squatted down low. Dave gasped as he quickly ducked down and lay with his back pressed as tightly against the back of the couch as possible.

Dave froze in fear when a small circular bright light appeared on the wall in front of him. It slowly went about the room and then disappeared after about ten seconds.

*Crunch...crunch...*

Dave was barely breathing now, still wide-eyed as ever. The next sound he heard caused his heart to beat so loudly that he thought it would burst - the knob of the backdoor slowly turned from right to left.

Panic surged through his body like a tidal wave; had he locked the door? Dave couldn't remember whether or not he had, and he knew locking the backdoor was something that he didn't always do.

The doorknob twisted one last time, but the backdoor did not open. Dave closed his eyes and took in a deep breath, realizing only then that he hadn't breathed for the past five seconds or so.

*Crunch...crunch...*

Dave did not move an inch. His eyes stared at the wall where a flashlight had broken through the darkness not half a minute ago. It was all so weird, and it had come and gone so fast that Dave wondered if it had ever really happened. But then he heard the *crunch* of the footsteps again, and even though they had now passed by his door, Dave was still frozen in place like a petrified piece of wood.

After a few moments, the initial shock began to wear off, and Dave's thought process was reactivated.

'What should I do? Wake up Jon? Call the police?'

Before he could answer himself, Dave heard his neighbor's backdoor squeak open and shut with just the slightest thud. Whoever had tried to enter his house had now just entered into the townhouse next door.

The voice inside of Dave was telling him to do something that contradicted the very fabric of his being. All he wanted to do was lay on the sofa and pretend that none of this was happening...but the voice, no matter how small it was, overpowered all of Dave's reason and fear.

*'Okay God,'* Dave thought as he jumped off the sofa, *'let's do it.'*

His eyes were adjusted to the dark, so Dave easily made his way over to the back corner of his room. He quickly lifted the slab of plywood from its resting place on the sawhorses and set it on the carpet. Then Dave picked up one of the sawhorses and hoisted it towards the backdoor. He slipped his sneakers on his feet, unlocked the door, and walked out into the cold night, carrying the heavy sawhorse in his arms.

I sprang up in my bed. The blood-curdling scream that had awoken me still pierced through the air; it was Dave.

I threw off my sheets and ran to the door as Dave's scream faded into silence. As I opened my bedroom door, I saw Jeremy coming towards me down the hall. The scream had been so loud that it had even woken up the world's soundest sleeper!

"What the hell was that?" Jeremy asked as he followed me down the stairs.

"I don't know," I said, as I tied the cotton belt of my navy blue bathrobe in a knot, "but it sounded like Dave."

We ran down to Dave's room, and I felt a rush of cold air hit me right away.

"The door's open," Jeremy said, obviously baffled.

I turned on the light and looked around, but Dave was nowhere in the room. With no time to go upstairs to slip on some shoes, I ran outside in my bare feet. I was surprised to find Jeremy right behind me, barefoot as well, as we stood in the five inches of snow, looking around for any sign of Dave. Jeremy seemed just as concerned for my brother as I was, and I truly appreciated that.

I looked over to my right and saw that our neighbor's backdoor was slightly ajar.

"Dave?" I called out weakly and I took a step towards the door. My heart was beating a mile a minute.

"Jon?" I heard Dave call out frantically from inside. "Jon! Come in here, quick!"

I ran to the door and rushed inside, nearly falling down the steps that led into the neighbor's basement room. It was too dark to see Dave, but I saw the beam of a flashlight that was lying on the carpet, pointing its light towards the front corner of the room.

Before either of us could say anything, I heard the thumping of someone rushing down the stairs, and a worried voice called out, "What in the world is going on? Who's down there?"

A light came on, and my jaw dropped as I saw my brother pinning down a tall, burly man with a sawhorse. The man was not moving; he seemed to be knocked out cold.

"I'm Dave Sullah, your next door neighbor!" Dave shouted the words rapidly, as Jeremy and I took some slow steps towards my brother, still in shock as to what we were seeing. "I saw this guy try to break into my house, and then he broke into yours, so I ran in and knocked him down before he could do anything! Call the police, and do it quick; I think he's starting to wake up!"

Our neighbor, a tall, balding man in his forties, slowly came down the steps to where Jeremy and I stood over Dave.

"Who are *you*?" he asked us, clearly puzzled what he was seeing.

"I'm his brother," I said, nodding down at Dave, "and this is my roommate, Jeremy. We ran over here when we heard the scream."

The man seemed to think that we were pulling a fast one on him. He scowled and said, "Don't move; none of ya. I'll be right back." He hurried back up the stairs and came down just a few seconds later, talking to the police on a cordless phone.

"The cops'll be here any minute now," the man said as he folded his arms across his chest, still holding the phone in one of his hands. "Tell me exactly what happened," he insisted, squinting his tired-looking eyes down at Dave.

Before Dave could respond, a plump woman with curly brown hair cautiously came down into the basement room.

"George?" she said, putting her hands on her husband's shoulders, as she stood behind him. "What's happening? Who are all these people?"

A young boy, no older than ten, came running down the stairs in his Scooby-Doo pajamas and stood next to his mother.

"It's okay, Nancy," George said, never taking his eyes off the four of us. "Take the boy back up to his room. Wait upstairs for the police; they'll be here shortly."

Nancy gave her husband a worried look and then glanced at the four strangers in her house, particularly at the one lying unconscious on the floor.

"Are you sure?" she asked, almost in a whisper.

Sensing his wife's nervousness, George responded, "Everything's alright, dear. These boys are our neighbors. Just go upstairs, and wait for the police."

After a final puzzled gaze at the four of us, Nancy put her hand on her child's back as she led him up the stairs.

George watched as his wife disappeared up the staircase and then asked Dave, "Alright, son; *please* tell me just what the hell is going on."

Dave took a deep breath as he looked up at George. A bit more calmly now, he explained.

"I was in my room, which is downstairs the next door over. All of a sudden, I heard someone walking through the snow outside. I thought it was weird, so I ducked down behind my couch. The next thing I know, I see a flashlight shining all around the room. Then I heard the knob of my backdoor jingling, like someone was trying to get in."

We all gathered around Dave in a small semi-circle as he continued.

"My door was locked, so he couldn't get in," he said, nodding down at the man pinned under him. "But then I heard him go on to your door, and I heard the door open and shut."

George stood motionless, his eyes growing wider and wider as Dave went on. It seemed as if our neighbor was just then realizing what was happening.

"So, I decided that I couldn't just sit there when I knew that someone had just broken into your house. I had this sawhorse in my room, so I grabbed it and went to your back door. I didn't even know what I was doing," Dave chuckled nervously, "but I just threw open your door and screamed as loud as I could; I guess it was the adrenaline. All I could see was the flashlight he was holding, so I ran as fast as I could towards it and literally *smashed* this guy into the wall."

George nodded his head slowly, looking at a dent in the wall to his left. He said, "I don't know what to - ", but was cut off as the large man with long dirty-blonde hair came to. At first he quickly snapped his head from left to right. Then, realizing where he was and what had happened, he began screaming obscenities and struggling to get up.

Immediately, Jeremy and I fell down on the man, and George ran over by his feet to stop him from kicking.

"Get off me, you little piece of *(bleep)*!" the man shouted. "I'll *(bleeping)* kill you! Let me go!"

Although Jeremy wasn't quite as big as the man who had broken into George's place, he was much stronger than Dave and me, and lucky for us, was a former wrestler at Lincoln High School. Jeremy swept the sawhorse away with one hand, and then administered a chokehold on the man that was certainly illegal for high school wrestling. The man gasped for air, and his kicking and screaming subsided.

After the police arrived and took the man away in handcuffs, we sat around at George's dinner table. Dave told an older cop that had seemed to have had his fair share of donuts what had happened while Nancy, still in her pink bathrobe, poured us some coffee. Their son, Hank, sat next to George and casually ate his Cheerios, as if this sort of thing happened all the time.

The fifty-something policeman gulped down the rest of his coffee and sighed.

"Well," he said, "I guess I got everything I need. I'll go down to the station and make my report, and we'll give you a call if we need to."

He pushed his chair out and was about to stand up, but before he did he raised an eyebrow at George and said softly,

"You know, we hardly see this kind of thing 'round here. There're robberies every now and then, but I can't remember the last time that someone was caught and apprehended in the act."

The policeman glanced quickly over at Hank, who seemed more interested in his cereal than what the old man was saying. The cop leaned towards George, and in an even lower voice than before, said, "But usually when you catch a robber in the act, you find a knapsack or a garbage bag on him; you know, somethin' to carry away all his stolen merchandise. All we found on this guy was a twelve-inch blade. What I'm sayin' is, I don't think that this fella was here to rob ya. Get me?"

George opened his mouth to respond, but nothing came out. He then cleared his throat and was able to muster enough strength to say, "Yes sir."

George ran his hand through his son's light brown hair and stared at the boy lovingly.

"Alright, then," the old gentleman said as he got up and put his policeman's hat back on over his gray, thinning hair. "Ma'am, thank you for the coffee. You make sure to lock all your doors now, ya hear?"

"Will do," George replied as he stood up to show the man out. "Thank you so much."

Before he left the dining room area, the policeman outstretched his hand towards Dave. As they shook hands, the man smiled and said, "You're a brave young man. You might be a knucklehead," he laughed, "but you're a *brave* knucklehead!"

November 4<sup>th</sup>, 2002-

*I remember doing a wood burning art for a lady at
Mom's school. Mom said that the lady wanted to pay me
for it, but I wasn't going to accept her money. On the back
of the wood I wrote,'* Our Lord once said, "Freely you have
received, freely you shall give." Please accept this as a gift,
and may God bless you.'

*It moved the woman to tears, as it did me just now.
Why? Because it was God's words that prompted me to do
what God wanted done - it felt right; it feels right. That's
what I want!! I want to prove to others God's love, as
He continuously proves it to me. I want to live in perfect
harmony with God's plan for my life. I want to do what I
cannot do on my own, I want to do what only God can do;
and I have faith that tells me that it will be done. Lord,
Lord: may Your will be done. In Jesus' name,*
    *Amen.*

# 34.

George and Nancy insisted that we come over to their
place for dinner that evening. Dave had the day off,
and I got out of work around four. Jeremy couldn't make it,
though, because he would be at the office until nine or so.

Nancy had asked Dave what his favorite food was, and
Dave had replied with a smile, "I *love* fried chicken!"

Nancy told us to come hungry; she would have enough fried chicken to feed a small army waiting for us. When George let us into their townhouse at a little after five that evening, we saw that Nancy had not been joking! Their long dining room table was set up as if royalty were visiting the Anderson homestead. Fine china gleamed on top of the white tablecloth, accompanied with what looked like new sets of sterling silverware. Wine glasses were placed in front of every seat but one, and on the table sat a huge platter of fried chicken, along with serving bowls of mashed potatoes, corn, applesauce, and gravy.

George invited us to sit down as Nancy came in through the kitchen with a bottle of red wine.

"Are ya hungry, guys?" she asked with a large smile.

"I know I am," Dave replied as we sat next to each other, "but I don't know if you cooked enough food for us!" he said kiddingly. "This is like a Thanksgiving dinner or something!"

"It *is* a Thanksgiving dinner," Nancy said, as she carefully poured some wine into George's glass. "Would you boys like some wine?"

We both said that we would, and Nancy filled our glasses as little Hank came running into the dining room. He sat down across from us and held a fork and a knife in his hands while licking his lips.

George smiled at his son and looked at us and said, "Hank's been excited about this all day; chicken's his favorite food, too."

Nancy started with Dave and began filling our plates with food. The moment that the breast of fried chicken touched Hank's plate, the boy's eyes widened as he picked it up and began devouring it.

"Go on, boys," Nancy said as she took her seat. "Eat up."

I don't think that Dave or I had ever eaten a dinner without first saying grace. We didn't eat dinner together much anymore, like we did when we were kids; but when we did, we always said a prayer. It felt weird as I picked up my fork and dipped it into the heaping pile of mashed potatoes on my plate. As I slowly brought it to my mouth, Dave spoke up.

"Would you mind if I prayed before we eat?"

I sat motionless, with the fork inches from my mouth. *What is he doing?* I thought. *You don't impose your traditions on your hosts like that!*

All eyes went to George, except for Hank, who was shoveling food into his mouth. George set his piece of chicken down, and after a moment replied, "Well, you are our guests, so, if you wanna pray, go ahead and pray."

You didn't have to be a genius to detect mockery in George's voice. Obviously, prayer was not his cup of tea. That didn't faze Dave, though. He just bowed his head, and everyone at the table followed suit. Of course, Nancy had to tell Hank to put his food down and bow his head, but the young lad complied with no complaint.

As I closed my eyes and folded my hands, Dave began.

"Dear Lord, heavenly Father: We thank you for this meal, and we ask you to bless it to our bodies. Bless the hands that made it, and bless us to do Your work. In Jesus' name, Amen."

All at the table added their own "Amen," even George, though he said it very softly.

"Thank you," I was surprised to hear Nancy say, "it's been a while since we've said prayers at this table." She gave George a long stare, but he pretended not to notice.

As we ate, Nancy asked us what we did, if we had girlfriends, and other things to get to know us better. Then Hank talked about playing dodge ball in gym class and how there was this one kid who threw the ball sidearm so hard that no one could catch it to get him out. George stayed mysteriously quiet, though, as he ate his meal, staring down at the middle of the dining table, as if lost in another world. He didn't say a word until he had finished his glass of wine. He sat the empty glass down and picked at some food lodged in-between his teeth. After filling his glass with some more wine, he leaned back in his seat and looked at Dave and asked, "So, are you a religious person?"

Nancy quickly glanced at George and then to Dave. By the look on her face, I could tell that she was hoping that George hadn't offended Dave; or maybe, hoping that he wasn't *about* to.

Dave wiped his mouth with his cloth napkin and nonchalantly responded, "I believe in Jesus Christ."

George leaned forward with his elbows on the table, and, after a dramatic pause said, "Now, I've always wondered why anyone would worship a man who's been dead for over two thousand years."

"George!" Nancy nearly shouted, as she crumpled her eyebrows down, "these are our *guests*. I can't believe that you're being so rude!"

George calmly lifted his hand to Nancy, as if he were holding her back. "I'm not trying to be rude," he said, shaking his nearly bald head as he looked at my brother. "Am I being rude, Dave?"

George asked the question sincerely. It didn't seem as if he were trying to degrade Dave in any way.

After taking a sip of wine, Dave shook his head and replied, "No, I don't think that you're being rude; I think that you're being ignorant, but not rude."

Oh boy! I thought. Here we go; they're going to throw punches!

I cleared my throat loudly as a subtle warning to Dave to watch his tongue. It was very uncomfortable. All of a sudden; I felt my heart flutter and my armpits became warm with perspiration. Even young Hank seemed to sense the tension in the room. He stopped chowing down his chicken and sat dead still. Only his eyes darted from his father and then back to Dave.

"Oh really?" George said in a condescending tone. He grinned smugly as he asked, "And just how am I being ignorant?"

Without hesitation, Dave replied, "Ignorance is not knowing the truth; and the truth is that Jesus Christ died for our sins. Believing in Him is the only way to get to Heaven."

"That's ridiculous," George countered, beginning to speak faster than a kid who had just eaten a pound of sugar. "First of all, it's preposterous for you to call me ignorant when you say that you believe in something as crazy as that. To say that 'Jesus is God', it-it-it..." George began to stammer with his palms held up in the air. If the situation wasn't so serious, I just might have been unable to control myself from laughing. "It just defies all logic! If Jesus was God, then what you're saying is God killed God! Come on! Just how does that make sense?"

Seemingly indifferent to the rising level of hostility in George's tone, Dave smiled and replied, "You want the short version or the long version?"

George folded his arms across his chest and shrugged his shoulders.

"Give me whatever version you think could prove your theory."

Although Nancy didn't say a word, and wasn't looking at either Dave or her husband, I could tell that she was hanging on every word that was said. Her eyes focused intently on her empty plate before her, as if mesmerized by it. But it wasn't as if she was staring off into space. While George leaned back confidently in his chair, I saw Nancy close her eyes, just for a few moments. I thought, *Is she praying?* She opened her eyes and wiped a breadcrumb off her pudgy cheek as Dave answered, "Okay, first of all, this isn't a theory; but if you'd like to call it that for now, that's fine."

The authority in Dave's voice shocked me. My brother had always been probably the most timid, most shy person I knew. I had never heard him speak like this before.

"The best place to start is in the beginning, and you don't have to be a Christian to know this verse: 'In the beginning God created the Heavens and the Earth.' God made the moon, the stars, the sun, the Earth, and then He made us. God said, 'Let Us make man in Our image, and let Us give him dominion over all the birds, over the fish, over the reptiles, and even over the Earth itself.'"

Dave stopped there and looked at George with his eyebrows raised, as if he had just made a point. George obviously didn't catch it, and truthfully, neither did I.

"So?" George said, obviously confused.

"In that very statement," Dave explained, "God gave man authority over the Earth that He had created. He basically said, 'Here's paradise; it's all yours.' God didn't say, 'Let man rule over Earth, and I will rule over man.' If He did, then we would all be robots, pleasing God because we *had to* and not because we *want to.*

"And look at what we did with this paradise," Dave continued, his eyes ever fixated on George. "We ruined it by sin. God gave man a choice as to who to follow - Him or the devil. God told Adam and Eve not to eat the apple, Satan told them to go ahead and eat from it, and the rest is history."

"Hold on, you're getting way off the subject here," George interjected as he scratched the top of his scalp. "What does all this have to do with Jesus?"

"It has *everything* to do with him," Dave replied softly. "I think it was the apostle Paul who said something like, 'Through one man sin entered into the world, and through one man the world was saved from sin.' Jesus was with God in the beginning; God didn't say, 'I will' do this, He said, 'Let *Us*' do this.

"But God couldn't *make* man do whatever He wanted him to do, namely, refrain from sin. He gave us our own free will, which led to us sinning, which made God banish us from His presence. Adam and Eve had to leave the Garden of Eden after they sinned because God is holy, and - "

"Yeah, well, if God is God, and He knew what would happen anyway, why would He do that?" George interrupted. "Why would He make a plan that would ultimately fail? Couldn't He have found a better way to do things?"

"His plan didn't fail," Dave responded confidently. "He knew what would happen from beginning to end. That's where the man we know as Jesus came into play. Since God gave man authority on Earth, and man subsequently handed that authority over to Satan, only man could regain humankind back to God and His intended purpose for man.

"In the Old Testament, spotless lambs were sacrificed as a sin offering for the people. But that was only a prelude to Jesus' death; it was symbolic. Jesus never sinned, and, because of that, He was worthy in God's eyes to *become* sin for us."

"Yeah, I've heard that a thousand times," George said, rolling his eyes, "and every time I do, it becomes more and more preposterous to me. Seriously; you Christians..." George paused as he shook his head, seemingly feeling sorry for the people of our faith. "There's no other way to say this, and I know what you're going to think of me; but, it's like you go around *flaunting* your inanity! Have you ever really *thought* about how ridiculous that sounds?"

George's upper body did a little dance as he looked up at the ceiling and in a mocking tone said, "Ooh, Jesus Christ died for me because He loves me so, and all you have to do is believe in that and then you'll go to Heaven when you die!" George's phony smile disappeared as he looked at Dave and said, "Nonsense!"

That did it for me. I felt a rage burn within, and I was either unwilling or unable to keep it from spewing out of my mouth.

"It's one thing to not believe in my Savior, but it's a whole other thing to *mock* Him!" I said, as I felt my face tingle warmly, most assuredly turning red. "If you don't want to believe in the only way for your soul to be saved, then fine; but have some respect!"

Dave put his hand on my shoulder and gently pushed me back into my seat. I hadn't noticed it, but I was a good half-foot up from the chair, leaning my entire upper body over the table towards George.

Nancy spread her plump arms out, much like how a referee at a football game would signal a missed field goal.

"Please, please!" she said with concern showing on her round face. "This was supposed to be a happy time! George, apologize! Now!"

"It's okay, Mrs. Anderson," Dave began. But once again, George interrupted him.

"No, it's *not* okay," he said softly, looking down at the table. He then picked his head up and looked me right in the eye. "You're absolutely right; what I just did was uncalled for. I'm sorry.

"Hank," he said with a forced smile as he looked at his son, "why don't you go play your video games?"

The young boy grinned, showing his pearly whites. He rushed out of his seat, but before he pushed his chair in he paused and asked, "Wait a second; what about dessert?"

"We'll have dessert later," George answered. "Mom'll call you when we're ready."

After Hank had disappeared into the living room, George sighed deeply through his nostrils and then said, "I greatly appreciate what you boys did for us," George said sincerely, "and again, I'm sorry for offending you. But...there's a reason why I feel the way I do about...about Jesus."

Tears began to brew in Nancy's eyes, as she looked knowingly at her husband. After a moment of silence, he continued.

"In 1995, Nancy gave birth to our first son." George's lip began to quiver, and he had to swallow a lump in his throat before going on. "We named him Edward."

Nancy reached for George's hand, and he grasped it tightly on the table, as she soothingly massaged his hand with her thumb.

"Nancy was, *is*, I suppose, a Baptist, and she was doing her best to persuade me to go to church with her. After we had Edward, the persuasions turned into an ultimatum: either set an example for our son by going to church and raising him to be a Baptist, or sign the divorce papers."

George gave his wife a slight smile and then turned his attention back to Dave and me.

"So I went to church. At first, I was just going to make Nancy happy. I never believed in God, or an afterlife; to me, it was just something that gave people hope, and I saw nothing wrong with that.

"But after a while, I started to listen to what the minister was saying about Jesus, and I actually almost believed it, too. It was during an altar call on Easter Morning, 1996, when it was proven to me indefinitely that God, at least, *Jesus'* God, does not exist."

George's misty eyes trailed away, far past where Dave and I were sitting.

"What happened?" Dave asked delicately, obviously sensing that whatever it was, it had hurt George deeply.

George's eyelids fluttered rapidly for a couple of seconds, and he took his free hand to wipe away a tear that had trickled down his cheek.

"The minister, he...I have to admit, he gave a very moving speech about Jesus Christ; how He died for us, and rose for us, and loves us beyond our own comprehension.

And at the end, he invited anyone who had not asked Jesus into their hearts to come up to the altar and give their lives to Him. He said that it was not something that he normally did, but he felt the 'Holy Spirit' telling him to do so.

"Well, when I stood up from the pew, I don't know who was more surprised - Nancy, or me! I started walking down the aisle, thinking to myself, 'I can't believe that I am doing this!' But it felt right; I felt *good* about it…I know now that it was all psychosomatic or whatnot…

"So I was on my knees, and there were a couple of other people at the altar there with me. The priest was telling us to repeat what he said, and, um…"

George's voice became very strained as he went on. Nancy bowed her head and began to cry softly with her eyes closed.

"During the middle of it, I heard my wife *scream* - this, this, *blood-curdling* shriek. I knew right away that it was Nancy. So I, um…I turned around and saw a group of people huddling around, and…"

Dave and I sat motionless as George broke down crying. Although it lasted for only ten seconds or so, it seemed like an eternity. George wiped his face dry and glanced over to the living room where Hank was sitting Indian-style in front of the television, transfixed by the glowing screen.

After blowing his nose on a dinner napkin, George continued, his voice even weaker now after crying.

"Edward was dead. My little boy, just ten months old… dead. The doctors found a button lodged in his esophagus. How or when it got there, we don't know. But it suffocated him…he couldn't scream, he couldn't breathe…he died there in that church."

I slowly shook my head, stunned. George looked back and forth at Dave and me with misty eyes and a red face as he asked, "Now *why* would God do that? Why, when I was ready to ask Jesus in my heart, would He interrupt that by killing my son?"

I don't think that either of us was prepared to answer that, but George didn't give us a chance to, anyway.

"Nancy and I, we separated soon after that. It took us many long, hard months, but our love eventually brought us back together." He gave his wife a warm smile, and she returned it with one of her own. George's smile disappeared, however, as he turned back towards us and said, "You see, I was blaming Nancy for Edward's death, when the whole time I *should have* been blaming God. How could you argue that, I'd really like to know?" George brought the question up again: "Why would 'God' kill my little boy when I was about to receive His 'Son' into my heart?"

I opened my mouth to say something, but nothing came out. After just a slight pause, Dave spoke in a soft, gentle voice, "I'm so…*so* sorry, Mr. Anderson. That's just an awful thing, and I won't try to pretend that I know why God would allow that to happen, because I don't. But if it's any consolation, I believe that Edward is with the Lord in Heaven right now."

George solemnly nodded his head; it seemed like he appreciated that, but it had no other effect on him. Dave stood up, moved his chair over to the corner of the table, and sat down, right next to George.

"I'm not trying to downplay your tragedy, but sometimes God does things that make no sense to us. And I can certainly understand why you feel the way that you do. But I can say this with absolute confidence: there *is* a God, and Jesus Christ *is* His Son."

Dave said that with assertiveness, while looking deep into George's eyes. After a moment, he sighed and then went on.

"I was born in a Christian family, so all my life I grew up thinking that Jesus was God, and that believing in Him would get me into Heaven. But a while back, I started thinking, you know, 'What if I'm wrong? What if this belief was just inherited because my family believes it?' So I started really…

*checking out*, I guess is the best way to put it, Jesus and Christianity, with an open, objective mind. I really studied what Jesus said and did, and...I don't know; it just all came together in such a way that it would put it to shame if I tried to describe it. Sounds like a cop-out, doesn't it?"

Dave grinned, and George mustered up a weak smile, as well.

"But it's true. So...you don't believe that Jesus is God?"

"No," George answered immediately, shaking his head.

"Would you *want* to know if you were wrong?"

George just stared at Dave for a couple of seconds, not saying anything or even moving at all, for that matter.

"Really think about that," Dave said earnestly. "I mean, we're talking about eternity here. That's a long, long time!"

I could almost see the wheels churning in George's head, as he thought with his eyes fixed on the tablecloth. After a few seconds, he lifted his head and looked at Dave and replied, "Well, yes, I guess I would; but I doubt that you could prove that to me."

"You're right," Dave said, nodding his head in agreement. "I *can't* prove that to you. If one man could prove to you that Jesus is the Lord, then I suppose another man could come around and prove to you that He *isn't*. The only way to know for sure is to ask God Himself. Just pray to Him, something like, 'I want to know if Jesus really is Who He says He is, and if He is, I need *You* to show me.'

"I *know* that He is, because God showed me, in *so* many ways. The Bible says, 'Seek and you shall find,' and there is no lie in God's Word. God doesn't want you to be unsure of Him; He *loves* you, and He wants you to love Him back."

"I don't know," George responded. "I feel like God's given up on me." After catching himself, he quickly added, "That is, if there *is* a God."

"No," Dave answered immediately with a warm smile on his face, "that's not true. God hasn't given up on you.

God is God because He's patient, long-suffering, and full of love. Giving up is a human trait; not one shared with God. If He gave up on people, I would have been lost a long time ago! No; He loves you, George…and I say that with absolute certainty."

I looked over at Nancy, and she was beaming. She rubbed her husband's back, quietly affirming Dave's statement. What George said next amazed me; although his tone was quiet and timid, his request seemed louder than a scream:

"Maybe…*you* could pray for me?"

A smile stretched across Dave's face as he replied, "I already have."

An obvious look of confusion showed on George's countenance, so Dave explained.

"Last night; or actually, early this morning, I was praying down in my room. I can't explain it, but I felt that someone that I had just prayed for was in deep trouble. So I started repeating everyone's name, hoping that when I said the right one, I would know who was in trouble. After about twenty minutes, I thought that I had gone through my whole list of people, but I didn't know who it was that was in some sort of trouble. I thought that maybe I was just whacko or something…but still, I *knew* that someone in my prayers was in danger. I was looking outside my window, asking God to just let me know, when all of a sudden I heard that guy walking around outside. He was being so quiet that I never would have woken up if I had been sleeping.

"Later on, I had a chance to think about it, and I realized that I had forgotten to re-name some names that I had prayed for when I was trying to figure out who was in trouble; President Bush, our military men and women…*and*, my neighbors." Dave said with a smile. "I always pray in Jesus' name, so I believe that if Jesus isn't God, then God doesn't hear me. He heard me, Mr. Anderson, because Jesus *is* God.

I didn't even have to mention your name, although now that I know it, I will."

George stuck out his hairy arm, and he and Dave shook hands. With a smile of appreciation on his face, George said, "You have given me a lot to think about, Dave. Consequently, since we have gotten to know each other a little, when you talk to Him, don't call me 'Mr. Anderson;' call me 'George.'"

Dave understood, and he returned the smile.

*March 9th, 2003-*

*Do I suffer in vain? Do I fight alone? Where, oh God, is Your presence? Shall You leave me by my lonesome, or worse yet, with the company of Satan himself? Who shall win this battle? Certainly not I; but You have left me. Where is my strength, my decency, my perseverance?*

*Have I shunned You, Lord? Have You deserted me for my trespasses? Truthfully, if this is so, then I am no more. I am lost to the devil, and he will have his way with me. Weak and battered, I throw myself at Your mercy; do not cause me to sin! Precious Lord and Savior, Jesus, You are all that is good inside of me. Without You I am cursed to myself. Shall You leave me now when I need You most?*

*No true God would do such a thing, and neither will my Lord. I believe that this is true, yet I am unsure. Reveal Yourself in me! Hide no longer! Clean my messy room, and set things in order.*

*This is it. I can stand it no longer. Lord, I need You. If You are not here for me now, then You never were.*

*Will my questions go unanswered before You? Where is Your voice? Mine tires. Has Yours as well? I feel alone; are my feelings justified, or am I speaking foolishly? Who hears me? Who cares? Isolation...dark, lonesome isolation. Lord, do not leave me here.*

*Forgive me. Cleanse me, heal me, and send me out again with Your love, Your guidance, and Your blessing. In Jesus' name, Amen.*

# 34.

Desperation. What an ugly word that is! We've all been there before, and when we pass by that time in our lives, we seldom look back on it. That's our problem; we tend to forget about our days in the valley and focus all of our attention on our mountaintop experiences.

Don't get me wrong; being on the top is great, but it's not meant to last. Not on this Earth, at least.

We read about Jesus' transfiguration in the gospels of Matthew, Mark, and Luke. I'm sure that you know the story, but let's take a closer look. In Mark, chapter nine, verse two, we read:

'After six days Jesus took Peter, James and Jon with him and led them up a high mountain, where they were all alone. There he was transfigured before them.'

A high mountain; not a soft, grassy little hill. It was steep.

When Dave and I were in our early teens, Mom took us to visit the battlefields of Gettysburg. Our favorite spot was a place called "Devil's Den." I believe it is at the foot of Little Round Top, and it's a small piece of land filled with large rocks. Dave, ever the adventurer, decided to climb the largest slab of granite in the Den. It was around fifteen to twenty feet high, and sat almost perfectly straight up into the air. There were cracks all about the face of the giant rock that my brother used to hoist himself up, inch by inch.

It took a lot of struggling, and even more worried exclamations from my mother, but Dave finally reached the top. He looked down at me with a triumphant smile, hands on his hips, and bet me that I couldn't reach the top as fast as he had.

Not to be outdone by my little brother, I wiped some sweat from my palms and stepped up to the rock. "Go ahead," I said confidently, "Time me."

I made it up the first few feet without a hitch; then things started to get tough. I couldn't find a foothold, and my scrawny arms started to shake under the weight of my body. The hot sun seemed to melt my forehead, causing beads of sweat to sting my eyes. With all the strength that I could muster, I pulled up and stretched my hand out, finding a small crevasse to grab a hold of. By the time that I had reached the halfway point, I had already exerted so much energy that I was sure there was no way for me to reach the top. My limbs were numb, my head was pounding, and I had to take unusually large gasps of air to satisfy my lungs.

I paused for a moment, contemplating how much it might hurt if I let go and fell to the ground. But I knew that if I did that, Dave would gloat for days. So I considered quitting as not an option, and became determined to reach the top. The whole way up, I scraped my knees against the jagged points of the rock. My fingers felt as if they would break off at any moment. Finally, I pulled myself up on top of the rock and stood. My knees no longer hurt; sure, I had ripped holes in my jeans, and my knees were bleeding, but I didn't feel the pain. My fingers were still numb, but that didn't bother me. I was still laboring for breath, but each breath of air was taken in satisfaction, not strife.

Why? Because I had reached my goal; the top. I didn't give up, even though every fiber of my being told me to so.

Now, the rock that the disciples climbed was no mere twenty feet, and they weren't climbing it simply to prove anything to their younger brother. It was a very tall mountain, and they climbed it because they were following Jesus. I'm sure that there were times that they wanted to quit. I'm sure that their muscles ached, and their lips became dry and cracked. Maybe they asked Jesus to let them sit down and relax for a while; maybe Jesus complied, maybe He just kept on walking. Whatever the case, Jesus led them, and they followed.

And what happened when they reached the top? They experienced the most holy, the most awesome sight that they had ever witnessed up to that day.

*March 10th, 2003-*

*Where was my mind, that I would speak to You in such a manner? Who am I, Lord, to doubt You? How patient You are with me, even when I was so close to blasphemy!*

*You cleansed my dirty lips by starting with my heart. You assured me when I was completely distraught. You poured Your love throughout my soul when all there was was sin. You destroyed the lust of my flesh and created peace within.*

*Oh, may I spend the remainder of my days praising Your holy name! May I forever remember Your complete control over all, Your complete knowledge over all, and Your complete love for all!*

*You are the Lord; yet You choose to love me. I am ready, Lord, to do Your work. To do it with joy, and to do it through pain, if necessary.*

*Your rebuke stings my heart, and I will recall upon its sting should I begin to question You ever again. May I praise You forever! May I glorify Your name!*

*Sing, Heaven! Rejoice, Earth! Let us magnify the Lord!*

*Lord Jesus, how I love You, and how humbling it is to know that You, as Lord, love me, a fool. Cleanse my heart from sin, open my eyes to righteousness, fill my mind with wisdom, and forever remind me of how great a privilege it is to praise the Lord Almighty!!!*

# 35.

Mark 9:5:
'Peter said to Jesus, "Rabbi, it is good for us to be here. Let us put up three shelters- one for you, one for Moses and one for Elijah."'

Peter just experienced a fearful yet wonderful sight, and he did not want to leave.

So it is for you and I. The Lord just revealed to us a revelation. We just were in combat with Satan and overcame him by the power and grace of God. We climbed over an obstacle instead of avoiding it, and now we stand on top. And we do not want to leave.

I remember standing on that rock with Dave at Devil's Den. We surveyed the picturesque area: a massive hill of budding trees to our left, behind us an open field lined with canons in the distance, remnants of the great battle that took place a century and a half ago. To our right stood a monument of a Union general, standing tall with the bayonet of his rifle raised high in the air.

The smile would not fade from my face; I didn't think it ever would. Standing on that rock, overlooking the majesty of nature and history surrounding me, caused my heart to overflow with joy. There was something in the air that day, as I stood tall on the rock, and I took it all in. If it had been up to me, I might still be there.

*April 11ᵗʰ, 2002-*

*Humble me, Lord, so that I don't fall.*

*What greatness You have done through me! You make Yourself known to others, and they see You in me. Those that know enough say, 'Praise God,' but the ones who don't know You yet say, 'I never knew you were so smart, Dave.'*

*Lord, let them know! Let them know where these words come from! May they see the inadequacies of a foolish man, and also the strength of the wisdom from God within!*

*You see it, Lord; you see how a part of me longs for recognition and reverence when none should be allotted to me, but only to You. When my lips speak, they say 'All glory to God,' yet my heart still longs for some respect from others. Forgive me, Lord, forgive me. How could I be a trusted servant when I wish to rob some of the glory due to You and have it for myself? Cleanse my wicked heart, Lord Jesus, and save me from my lustful nature.*

*Lord, watch over my family. Keep them safe in Your love, and draw us nearer to You every hour of our lives. Lord Jesus, reign. In Jesus' name I pray,*

*Amen.*

# 35.

'Humble me, Lord, so that I don't fall'.
A man that walks with his head bowed doesn't trip over his own two feet. A man that walks in arrogance with

his head held high can't see the trap laid out before him, and so he falls right into it.

I know that these last three short chapters have, in a way, taken us away from Dave's story for a short while. Perhaps it's because we're nearing the end, and I know that I'll soon be sent through a torrid of emotions. But in all honesty, these three small chapters are what Dave's life was all about: earnestly seeking the Lord, His will, and doing so in the humblest of fashion.

Sure, Dave's cry to God on March 9th was certainly less than admirable; and Dave would be the first to admit that. In fact, he did. In one of his entries, Dave wrote: *What if God had said, "Have you considered my servant, David?" Would I be up to the task? No. I would not be able to put myself in Job's shoes. I thank God that He gives me only what I can handle. But what can't I handle when I put my trust in the Lord? I see that my faith has room for improvement. Lord, fill me. 'I have belief; help my unbelief!'*

What does seeking after God have to do with these last few chapters?

Dave felt abandoned. Abandoned by the very God Whom he asked for help. Even though Dave was hurt, he still went to God. He knew that there was nowhere else to go.

The very next day, something happened. Exactly what that was, I don't know, but Dave, I'm sure, never forgot it. He sang to the Lord a beautiful song of praise; I can just *see* the smile on Dave's face as he wrote it down! The Lord, I'm sure, was smiling right back at him.

God was working in Dave's life; some things I know about, many others, I do not. Instead of accepting all the credit, my brother gave it to the Lord. That's not something an "outstanding" Christian should do; it's something that *every* Christian should do. And Dave didn't try to hide things from God; he admitted his sin, and asked the Lord to forgive him. I never once saw Dave seeking any praise for himself, but apparently, he felt the urge within. So he did the right thing, and prayed about it.

God will lead you places where you do not really want to go. He will test you to see if seeking Him is priority "numero uno" in your life. Don't ever give up. There are steep climbs, mountaintop moments, harsh descents, and valley wanderings in our lives, just to name a few. Always know that God's intentions are pure, holy, and ordained by His love for you and me. Follow Him. Seek Him. Talk to Him, and know that He is listening. Keep an ear open to His gentle voice, and a sharp eye looking for Him in your everyday life. Many times He's right there in front of us; but we're just too busy to see.

I'll end this chapter with an amusing yet appropriate story.

So, Dave and I were on top of the giant rock. We flexed our muscles and smiled widely as Mom snapped some pictures from below. As we were basking in the glow of our successful climb, Mom called out, as if in an afterthought, "Now how are you guys going to get down?"

I sat there stunned. I hadn't even thought about that. Out of the corner of my eye, I saw Dave turn towards me; his slack-jawed expression revealing that he hadn't the faintest idea, either.

Very cautiously, I inched my way over to the edge and peered down. Mom was looking up with her hand over her forehead, shadowing the sun from her eyes. It was way too far to jump.

I got on my knees and turned around, so that my back was facing the side that Dave and I had climbed up. The other sides of the rock were at a ninety degree angle to the ground, just about as straight up as you could get, and impossible to climb up or down. I blindly stuck one foot out over the ledge, hoping to find a spot where I could rest my body weight and start to climb down.

"Jonny, you be careful! That doesn't look safe!" Mom pleaded worriedly.

She was right; it wasn't safe. Try as I might, I just couldn't find an accessible route down the rock. I stood back up, wiped off some small bits of granite that had stuck to my palms, and racked my brain for a solution. Nothing came to mind.

After a few minutes had passed, I was beginning to panic. I thought that Dave and I were going to have to bite the bullet and jump all the way down, possibly breaking every bone in our bodies.

"What are we gonna do?" Dave asked with a hint of humor in his voice.

"I don't know."

Just then, a tour group appeared from the large hill. There was a man in full Union attire, leading about ten people over to where Mom stood in the middle of Devil's Den. Mom frantically waved at him, and as he and the group approached her, the man looked up to where Dave and I were standing.

The short, stocky man shook his head, as he shielded his eyes and said with a chuckle, "Those your boys up there, ma'am?"

"Yes," Mom answered, staring up at us with a slight grin on her face. "They got *up* the rock alright, but there appears to be a problem as to how they'll get down."

It was humiliating. Dave and I sat down, as laughter sprinkled about the tour group. They pointed fingers and took pictures, finding humor in the situation at the expense of our shame.

Luckily for us, the tour guide had a walkie-talkie, and he used it to call his headquarters, which was a small cabin just a mile away. After relating the amusing situation to the person on the other end, the guide called out to us, "Don't worry, guys. Just sit tight, someone's comin' down with a ladder."

After what seemed like an hour later, a man walked into Devil's Den carrying an extendable aluminum ladder over his shoulder. He, too, had a good laugh before securing the foot of the ladder near the rock and holding it in place as I climbed down it, followed by Dave.

The small group roared with applause and more humiliating laughter when we finally touched ground.

*May 19th, 2003-*

    *Most Christians have friends who are not.*
    *We love them more than ourselves.*
    *Their anguished souls will burn and rot,*
    *forever in Hell in their cells.*

    *Can you look at your friend in the face*
    *without a tear in your eye?*
    *Can you hide that you know the place*
    *of where he will go when he dies?*

    *Can you see your friend in Hell?*
    *The worms are eating his skin.*
    *His sore body begins to swell-*
    *it's because of the fire within.*

    *He is tormented and full of fear*
    *as he falls deeper into the Abyss.*
    *Can you say without a tear,*
    *"Oh well; nobody's fault but his"?*

    *Who put your friend into your life?*
    *Who called you to be 'light and salt?'*
    *How could you say to yourself in your mind,*
    *"It is all my friend's own fault"?*

    *What have you ever done to earn*
    *the salvation that God freely gives?*
    *Why shouldn't your soul forever burn*
    *for the sins in the life that you've lived?*

*How can you look at your wicked friend*
*and think he's beyond God's reach?*
*Your torn soul- didn't He mend?*
*Your black heart- didn't He bleach?*

*Christians, please, start with a prayer,*
*ask God to save your friend.*
*To lead him away from the devil's lair,*
*and into God's loving arms be sent.*

*Pray that God does whatever it takes,*
*that He uses you in any way.*
*That He saves your friend for His name's sake.*
*It is your duty, dear Christian: PRAY!*

*Jim. Ben. Scott. Jeremy. Sarah. Jeff. Kelly. Jaime. Jill.*
*Bobby. Jen. Mike. Tom. Cathy. Elaine, her family. George.*
*Anthony. Jeff S. Mary. Everyone. Lord, there are so many;*
*Thy will be done.*

# 36.

My brother was adamant about prayer. Why? Because he knew that it works! Not always in the ways that we expect it to, and certainly not always to our immediate liking; but Christian, how good it is to know that when you speak to the Lord Almighty, He hears you! And our God isn't limited, like we are, in understanding. When you pray, *know* that God is listening, and *know* that He will answer in His own perfect timing, and in His own perfect way.

A week before Christmas 2002, a severe ice storm ravaged its way through much of Pennsylvania. For two and a half days we were without electricity, because the power lines were either frozen or had snapped in half. The good thing was that we all got a much-needed break from work; the bad thing, obviously, was that we had no electricity!

We passed away the daylight hours by playing board games and tidying up the townhouse. At night, we lit candles and talked around the dining room table before hitting the sack.

It was on the second night that Dave and Jeremy had a conversation that I, (and I hope Jeremy as well), will never forget.

The three of us were sitting at the dining room table with two large, round candles burning in the middle, creating just enough light so that we could see each other.

Dinner, for the second day in a row, had consisted of peanut butter and jelly sandwiches, potato chips, and a box of dried prunes that would have probably remained unopened forever, had it not been for the fact that almost everything inside the refrigerator had gone bad.

The massive candles burned brightly. I leaned back in my chair. I was thinking to myself that prunes weren't so bad after all - then chalked that thought up to coming from a delusional, food-depraved mind!

Jeremy sighed deeply and pushed the box of prunes away in disgust. "I don't know how much longer I can take this," he said, slowly shaking his head. "I mean, Jesus Christ; how long does it take to fix a power line?"

Dave cleared his throat and leaned forward with his elbows on the table. "Hey, uh...you remember when we agreed that we'd let each other know if one of us does something that irritates or annoys us?"

The three of us had sat down and had a pow-wow a few days after Dave moved in. We all decided that we would lay our own personal pet peeves on the table right then and there.

For instance, Jeremy hated it when dishes weren't sprayed down before they were placed in the dishwasher. It irked me when nobody changed the garbage, and just let it fill up, and overflow, with trash. Dave didn't have much to say at the time, but we had all agreed that if something ever came up, it would be better for that person to voice his opinion, rather than keeping it to himself.

"Yeah," Jeremy replied, cocking his head to the side with a puzzled look on his face. He obviously had no idea of what Dave was about to say; I, on the other hand, knew for sure.

"Well, it's just...when you say 'Jesus Christ' in that way, it kind of bothers me."

Jeremy nodded his head respectfully and said, "That's right; you're a Christian. I'm sorry, man. I didn't mean anything by it."

"Oh, I know. And I don't want to seem, like...I don't know, *ultra-religious man* or anything, and I know that there're a lot of people who say His name like that, but...I don't know, it just bugs me."

"No, that's cool; I totally understand," Jeremy said sincerely. Jeremy paused for a moment and shot me an inquisitive glance before looking back at Dave. "Can I ask you a question?"

"Sure," Dave replied with a detectable amount of enthusiasm in his voice.

"First off, let me say that I totally respect people's differing views on religion."

Dave nodded and sipped from his glass of warm Gatorade.

Jeremy looked from Dave to me, then back at Dave as he asked, "But how can you say that Christianity is *the* religion?" He raised his shoulders and held his hands palms up in the air. "I mean, it's your viewpoint that all these people, like Buddhists or Muslims or what-have-you, who think they are worshiping God are actually going to Hell because they chose the wrong religion?"

After only the slightest pause, Dave arched his eyebrows and responded firmly, "Yes."

Jeremy smiled, a bit smugly, as he said, "Well I just don't believe that. It makes no sense, *whatsoever*."

"How so?"

"How so?" Jeremy echoed my brother, seemingly surprised that he would even ask such a question. "Where do I begin?" he asked, his voice suddenly becoming on the verge of hostility. "First off, why would God care if people called Him by different names; whether it be Jesus, Buddha or Vishnu?"

Jeremy's eyes focused directly into Dave's as he leaned towards my brother.

"Well," Dave began, seemingly unaffected by Jeremy's cutting stare, "Jesus, Buddha, and Vishnu are three completely different- I don't want to call them 'Gods,' because two of them aren't - let's just say they're completely different. There are gods of this world, who are fake gods, then there's the true God. That's the difference. I believe that people who worship Buddha, or the countless gods of Hinduism, are in fact worshiping gods created by men, inspired by Satan."

"That's interesting," Jeremy replied, a mix of condescension and sarcasm easily detectable in his tone. "So, you think that *any* other religion besides Christianity was inspired by Satan, even though these religions practice the worship of God, and verify the difference between good and evil while striving for the good?"

"I strongly disagree with you about the other religions striving for good. Is it good to go around decapitating people if they don't conform to your beliefs? Is it good to institute terrorism for your voice to be heard?"

"Alright, well-"

"No, wait; let me finish." Dave held up his hand, as if he were holding Jeremy back. One of the candles began to flicker as a moment of silence filled the darkened room. "It says in the Bible that some people will abandon the faith and begin to follow the teachings of demonic spirits. It's one of Satan's M.O.'s to try and copy God; to, uh, I don't know...to mock Him might be a better way to say it.

"Just to name a few examples, Satan will use the anti-Christ to lead people to him, just as Jesus led people to God. The anti-Christ will perform pseudo-miracles and will create a false sense of peace before his true intentions are revealed.

"Also, it says in the Bible that God marks His people by some sort of a mark on their foreheads or something, I can't remember exactly what. But Satan will also mark his people on their foreheads or their hands with his own mark, a demonic one.

"He tries to copy God."

"Where are you going with this?" Jeremy asked, confused.

Dave raised his eyebrows and answered, "Look at some of the other religions. Buddhism, for example. They pray to the East, as Jews prayed towards Jerusalem. They believe in Allah, and Mohammed as his prophet; a comparison that needs no explanation. Uh, let's see...they believe that you must make a pilgrimage to Mecca, like the Jews visiting Jerusalem for the feasts of the Tabernacles, Passover, and Unleavened Bread."

"Hold up," Jeremy said as he shook his head with a slight grin, "you think that just because some practices of Buddhism are similar to Judaism that it means that Buddhism was inspired by Satan?"

After only a second's pause, Jeremy answered himself. "No, no. Come on, man!" he said, leaning forward with the smile still on his face. "If it's so bad to copy Judaism, then why are you a Christian?"

Dave cocked his head and squinted his eyes as he asked, "What do you mean by that?"

At this point, I really had to go to the bathroom- I mean, I *really* had to go! But I felt like it would be rude to get up and leave, even for just a minute. To me, it would seem like I didn't care about the discussion. Even though I wasn't putting in my two cents, I was there, and I did care. Besides, after listening to my brother speak with Mr. Anderson, I knew that this is where Dave shined. So, I silently crossed my legs and let him do all the talking.

Jeremy was no simple-minded adversary. He was Jewish, and knew much, not only about Judaism, but also about Christianity and some other major religions as well. We had talked about faith before, during college, but never to the extent of which he and Dave were speaking now.

"Alright...where do I begin?" Jeremy looked up towards the ceiling with prolonged anticipatory effect. After a few seconds, he looked back at Dave and said, "Jews sacrificed a lamb without blemish as atonement for their sins. What was Jesus called after His death? The 'lamb without blemish.'"

It looked as if Jeremy was prepared to go on, but Dave didn't let him. As Jeremy's mouth was half-opened, Dave interjected, "That's not 'copying' Judaism; that's *fulfilling* it. Jesus *was* the spotless Lamb, because He never sinned, and yet He was killed for our sins. The sacrifice of the lamb was merely a foreshadowing of God sending His Son to die for us on the cross. Do you really think that God would let us into Heaven, because we killed a sheep?"

I think that was meant to be a rhetorical question, because of the way that Dave asked it, but Jeremy responded to it anyway. "No, I don't. And that's one of the reasons that the Bible doesn't make sense. And don't think that I'm trying to tear down your religion, because this pertains to my religion, as well.

"In the Tanakh, or what you call The Old Testament, it says that God told the high priests to sacrifice the spotless lamb for their people once a year."

Dave nodded his head, and Jeremy lifted his shoulders up a couple of inches in the air as he asked, "Well then, if Jesus was a once-for-all sacrifice for sins, then why did they have to do that?"

"Jesus *is* the once and for all sacrifice for sins," Dave responded, "but not everybody is saved. You have to believe that your sins, gone unforgiven, would punish you to eternity in Hell. You also have to believe that because Jesus died for you, your sins are forgiven because of His sacrifice and your faith.

"The people that partook in the sacrifice of the lamb realized that they were sinners, and that their sins needed to be forgiven. Since Jesus had not yet died on the cross, their sacrifice was to be a lamb without blemish. Their faith and obedience to God in this respect earned them eternal life."

Jeremy sat still for a few moments, very slowly nodding his head as he looked off to the side at nothing in particular. I could tell that although he had never thought of it in that way, he still wasn't persuaded.

"Let me ask you this," he said, turning his attention back on Dave. "It's obvious that you're passionate about your beliefs; but how do you know that you're right? I mean, your brother and I knew this kid in college who was a Buddhist, and he was just as sure in his faith as you seem to be. He thought that since Jon was a Christian, and I'm Jewish, that we're both going to Hell. What makes him wrong and you right?"

I sat back in my chair as Dave thought about how to answer that. I remembered the kid that Jeremy spoke of well. His name was Shon Ridjou, and he had been on the same floor as us in our senior year. Shon had adamantly tried to persuade Jeremy and me to convert to Buddhism on several occasions. Although we shared different faiths, the three of us had become close friends.

"I...it's really hard to answer that," Dave replied after a couple of seconds. "I just *know*; I can't explain it."

"You have faith," Jeremy suggested, not as a question but as a statement.

"Yeah. I know that Jesus died for me, and truly believing in Him is the only way into Heaven. If you think about it, why would traveling to Mecca be enough for God to accept you into His presence?"

"*That's* a good question!" Jeremy said as he sat straight up, pointing a finger at Dave. Then he asked a question of his own. "Why would killing a lamb be enough for God to accept you into His presence?"

Dave sat absolutely still as Jeremy paused a few seconds. A grin reappeared on his face before he answered himself by quoting Dave, "It's their faith and obedience to God that earns them eternal life."

*January 19th, 2003-*

*Losing the battle, winning the war.*

*It looked desperate from the Union's point of view. What had started as a sure and short victory for them had turned into a long, arduous war, and they were on the losing end.*

*Two years after the initial bombshells over Fort Sumter had exploded, the Rebels had invaded Union territory and were marching towards their epicenter, Washington, DC. The odds were against the North. Lee's army of Rebels were determined - even when the Southern troops were vastly outnumbered, they still found a way to send the Union boys running.*

*But Lincoln would not give up. He would not let his beloved country stay divided. He continued to send his countrymen to their deaths, knowing that it was for an honorable cause. Many battles were lost. The enemy was growing stronger with confidence. But Lincoln, nor his men, would relent.*

*The Union did not give up.*

*Then came Gettysburg, the turning point of the war. A great and costly battle was won by the Union, and the Confederacy, albeit over time, lost the war during those three historical days.*

*Remember that. Remember that you will lose some battles, whether they be as conversations with an unbeliever or struggles with a particular sin. Whatever it is, keep battling for the good that is your faith in Jesus Christ, your love for God, your devotion to praising Him, your desiret to know Him, and your desire to willfully die to self, so that He may live.*

*Battles will be lost, but the war will be won. Whose side are you on?*

*Praise and glory to God the Father, in the name of Christ Jesus, Amen.*

# 37.

Dave was clearly rattled. He stared blankly at the table. Jeremy leaned back in his chair, assuming a pose of quiet boastfulness, crossed his arms, and smirked at my brother. The candles flickered silently in the darkened room. No one spoke for what seemed like a long time.

Jeremy finally broke the silence.

"You see? You've gotta keep an open mind about things sometimes. It just doesn't make sense to say that there are people all over the world who worship who they believe is God, and that they're going to Hell because they picked the wrong one." Jeremy spat out the latter part of that statement with a notable amount of disgust. "I mean, some of those people have never even *heard* of Jesus; how do you explain that?"

"Well," Dave started slowly, seemingly trying to buy some time as he repositioned himself in his chair, "I don't know for sure. I believe that people will be held accountable for what information came their way. Like, for instance, if someone grew up in the jungle or something, like in a tribe, and they never heard of Jesus or God, then..." Dave squinted up at the ceiling. His voice trailed off. After just a few seconds, he shook his head and turned his attention back to Jeremy. "You know what? I can't really answer that. I'd like to say that people who never heard of Jesus while they lived on Earth would be given some sort of a chance in the afterlife, and who knows, that might be true, but...I just don't know. I *do* know that we're called to proclaim our faith to all nations; but if we don't, and someone dies without accepting Jesus into their lives, because we failed to obey God's commandment, then who's to blame? Them or us?"

Dave shook his head slowly, lost in thought by his own question. A troubled expression appeared in his dark brown eyes, and his face turned a few shades whiter.

"Alright then." Jeremy's voice cut through the silence. He leaned forward with his elbows on the table, challenging Dave. "How about this? There are many, *many* people out there who do outstanding, charitable things for deprived, homeless, sick people - the list goes on and on. Take for example Mahatma Ghandi; are you telling me that he's in Hell, despite the countless amount of good that he did for the world?"

"I don't feel comfortable saying that *anybody's* in Hell; whether it be Ghandi or Hitler," Dave responded firmly. "That's not up to me. What I can say is what I believe; and that's if you don't believe in Jesus, and you don't accept Him into your heart, which is your life, then yes, you're going to Hell."

Jeremy snorted disapprovingly and then said, "So Ghandi's in Hell? A man that did more for his country than anyone before him, and probably anyone after him?"

"I'm not saying that Ghandi's in Hell, I'm-"

"Yes you are!" Jeremy interrupted. A slight grin grew on his face as he held his hands out in the air. "Ghandi wasn't a Christian, and you believe that non-Christians go to Hell. That's what you're saying!"

Jeremy's outburst seemed to fuel a fire that was burning inside Dave. My brother's eyes opened wide as he spat out, "You want me to say it? Fine, I'll say it: I believe that Ghandi, if he truly never converted to Christianity, is in Hell."

Jeremy sat back with his arms folded across his chest. He slowly nodded his head, as if Dave had just ruined his argument for Christianity with that statement.

"I don't *like* saying that," Dave continued, " and I am not in control of what does or does not happen. That's up to God alone. I'm just saying what I believe based on what I know."

Dave sighed deeply and reclined a little in his chair. He took a few seconds to calm down a bit, and then went on in a cool, composed tone.

"I do know that Ghandi was given the chance to become a Christian. He was a very learned man, and religion was certainly not something that he was ignorant about. In fact, he once said, 'I like their Christ; I don't like their Christians.'

"Did Ghandi have a chance? Yes. Did he believe in Christ?" Dave shrugged his shoulders. "It doesn't seem like it, but who knows for sure? Ghandi had more of a chance than many people do to accept Christ as their Savior. If he didn't, than that's that."

After a short pause, Dave went on.

"It doesn't matter how much good you do; we aren't saved by what we do, we're saved by what we believe. Sure, if you truly believe in Jesus, than you're going to do some really good things; but those things are a by-product of your faith in Him, not the means of your salvation.

"Let me put it to you this way," Dave said, cracking his knuckles, as he paused for a moment in thought. "Let's say I come up to you and I punch you in the face really hard."

Jeremy raised his eyebrows as he gave my brother a questioning look.

"Don't worry," Dave said with a chuckle, "this is just an example."

"Good," Jeremy responded with a laugh of his own. "I mean, I know we're getting into a heated discussion; but we are still friends, right?"

"Yes," Dave said with a smile, "we are still friends.

"So anyway, for *example*, I punch you in the face, and your cheek swells and it's all bruised and stuff. But then I turn around and do something nice for you; let's say I do your laundry or something. Does that 'nice thing' rule out the pain that I caused you when I punched you in the face?"

"No, no, no," Jeremy said quickly, shaking his head back and forth. "I see where you're going here, and it has *nothing* to do with what I'm talking about."

"Nothing, huh?" Dave asked in an almost condescending tone.

"Nope; you're using an example that's on a much smaller scope than what I'm talking about."

"Hmmm; that's funny; I see a direct correlation between the two. Am I wrong?"

Dave turned to me as he asked that. I agreed with my brother, but I also was annoyed by his all of a sudden pompous attitude. I decided to stay as impartial as I could by saying, "You're both right in a way. Dave's example *is* on a much smaller scale than what you're talking about," I said, looking at Jeremy, "but I do see what he's trying to say."

"No, no, that's...that's apples and oranges," Jeremy responded with a shake of his head.

"Okay, then let me put it like this," Dave said, looking straight into Jeremy's eyes as he spoke. "So, you're God."

"I'm God?" Jeremy cut in with a wide smile on his face.

His attempt at humor didn't please Dave. With a straight face, he said, "Come on; I'm trying to be serious here."

"Okay," Jeremy said as his smile slightly faded away. "I'm sorry; go on."

Dave cleared his throat, and then continued. "Let's *say* that you're God. You're perfect, you're holy, you're every-thing that's good...and you detest sin. You can't stand sin, and you can't allow it to stand around you."

Jeremy nodded, seemingly in approval.

"But you've got a dilemma; you created people who you absolutely love and adore, but sinning is sometimes all they do. You want to forgive them, so that they will be with you forever after they die, but you can't just pretend like they never did anything wrong, and you can't say, 'Well, they did some good things; I'll just forget about all the bad.'

"No; there has to be a punishment for their sins, something that will take away all the wicked things that they ever did. But what could that punishment be? Should you have them go to a certain town at a certain time in their lives? Should you have them offer up an animal as a sacrifice? No. You know that the only acceptable punishment for their sins is the sacrifice of someone who is pure and holy, without blame. That would be the only thing in your eyes that could remove your creations' sins from your mind forever: knowing that a perfect and righteous substitute was given for the sins of your creation, so that they could live with you for eternity."

Dave took a deep breath and took a quick sip of Gatorade before continuing. He spoke concisely and with confidence, never taking his eyes off of Jeremy.

"But who is perfect? Who is completely holy and righteous? God is. So if you're God, and you want to save your people, what do you do? You send yourself in the form of a man, so that you can die for your creation.

"And that's what God did. He sent Jesus to lead people to Him, and He had Jesus die so that we would be with Him forever. He was the perfect sacrifice.

"Now, imagine that you gave your perfect Son to the world, to teach, to die, and to be resurrected...and there were many people who didn't accept your gift. Not only did they not accept it, but they mocked it, and some even killed others because they had accepted it. What do you do with those people? Do you say, 'Oh, well. Hey, at least you believed in *a* God, that's good enough for me, come on into Heaven.?'"

Dave paused for a few seconds, looking deep into Jeremy's eyes. Jeremy's grin had disappeared completely, and he had a very somber expression plastered on his face.

"No. There's only one true God, and He provided one way to get to Him, and that's by accepting Jesus Christ as your Lord. If you could get into Heaven by any other means, then Jesus died for nothing."

*February 2nd, 2004-*

*Take joy in the fact that you are saved by faith in Christ Jesu,s and know that you will spend eternity with God the Father in Heaven. Take joy in that. But by the true meaning of the words "take joy" in it, we must not just take and not give. If you truly understand and find joy in your salvation, you will want to spread this joy, not keep it all to yourself.*

*Giving what the Holy Spirit supplies to you never relinquishes what you have of Him. It is a well that will never go dry. In fact, the more that you give, the more that you have. That's an aspect of this joy - because you see the joy being passed onto others, the joy grows and grows. Be happy that you are saved, and be even happier when God pours the living water into you and onto others.*

# 38.

Jeremy looked down at the table in a moment of thought, then cautiously lifted his eyes up to Dave. "Yeah, but... that makes sense only if you believe that Jesus was Who He said He was."

"Who do *you* think Jesus was?" Dave asked, with no more than a second's delay.

Jeremy sat dead still for a few moments, staring at the wall as his eyes glazed over. "My ex-girlfriend's mom was a Christian," he said slowly. He continued looking at the wall, as if there was a projection screen showing his past that only he could see. "Megan, um...."

Jeremy shook his head slowly; his voice trailed off. His face took on the likeness of a rock as he stared straight ahead. He had only spoken of Megan once or twice before, and he hadn't said much more than she was his first real love. Jeremy had quickly switched topics both times that her name was brought up, so I knew that he wasn't exactly comfortable talking about her.

Dave nodded his head, nonverbally encouraging him to continue. In a dry, monotone voice, Jeremy said, "Her mom had cancer...they didn't know about it until it had pretty much completely ravaged through her body. I was over there one day when some guy, someone from her church, came over to the house.

"He sat down with us and told Megan's mom that all she had to do was believe, and the cancer would go away. He was very emphatic about it; he said that the only reason why she was still sick was because she didn't have enough faith that she would overcome the cancer.

"He reminded her of all the stories of how Jesus healed the sick; I remember he quoted something from the Bible, something that Jesus said, like, 'Go now, your faith has healed you.'

"He had Megan and her mom convinced that if they just put their trust in Jesus, He would cure her. I knew it was all a bunch of bull, but I didn't say anything ... I wish now that I had. But at the time, it gave them comfort, and I could see the good in that.

"Well, Megan's mom only got worse, just like the doctors said she would. I never saw that guy again, but Megan told me that he came over every now and then, and he'd keep on saying the same thing - just believe that you'll get better, and you will.

"Megan soon started acting different; everything was 'Jesus this' and 'Jesus that.' She said that Jesus was going to heal her mom, and that everything would soon be better, if she held fast to faith. She was so confident about it that she almost convinced me as well.

"It didn't happen; Megan's mom died not a month after that man visited the house. Megan, well ... Megan was beyond grief. She had truly believed that her mom would be better soon, that Jesus was actually going to save her..."

Jeremy pursed his lips in anger and shook his head. His eyes glistened with impending tears as he began to speak again, this time with a weak, crackling voice.

"There was *nothing* that I could do to console her! She was just eighteen years old, her mom was dead, her father had left them years ago; she had no other family around, and the God that she worshiped either doesn't exist or doesn't care!"

Dave forlornly gazed at Jeremy without saying a word, or hardly moving at all, for that matter. He knew that he was letting out a lot of pain, and that sometimes all that you should do is listen.

"She...she barely talked at all, I knew that she wasn't eating...she wasn't herself at all. I mean, her mom had just died; obviously that's going to affect someone; but for Megan, it was more than that. She had put all that she had in Jesus; all her faith, all her trust, all her prayers...and when her mom died, it all came falling down right on top of her. Her faith in Jesus *crushed* her."

This was all unchartered territory for me. Jeremy had kept this all to himself for at least as long as I had known him, and why he was coming out with it now befuddled me. But he wasn't done yet.

"She was all alone in that house, and I stayed with her for a while. My mom and dad offered to let her stay at our house, but Megan wouldn't leave...she just laid on her mom's bed all day long, the bed that she died in."

Jeremy swallowed a large lump in his throat, and as a solitary tear trickled down his cheek, he said, "Megan died there, too. I found her, laying in the fetal position, her body lifeless and cold. She slit her wrists, and ..."

Jeremy put his hand over his face. His body shook uncontrollably. Dave gave me a quick glance, his eyes telling me that I should go over to my friend. Before I could get up, though, Jeremy wiped his face and stared at Dave as he said, "The way I see it, Megan's misconstrued faith in Jesus is what killed her."

He gave Dave an icy stare, as if it was all my brother's fault for what had happened.

"In a way," Dave said softly, his voice barely audible despite the surrounding silence, "you're absolutely right."

*January 4th, 2004-*

*I didn't want to go to church tonight, but deep down I knew that I should. How easily do we turn from our only true comfort and help in our greatest times of need! Why that is, I'm not entirely certain. It could be thought that in our lowest times Satan's attacks are more hurtful to us, and his greatest attack is to keep us from God.*

*Despite my own feelings, I prayed to God and said, "Your will be done."*

*At first, Dad wasn't going to be able to make it to church because he was in Wyoming County, so Mom said it was up to me what to do. I suggested that we just go to dinner and skip church.*

*When we got to the restaurant, Dad called and said he would be able to meet us for church, so after dinner Mom and I went. As He so often does, God didn't let what I wanted to happen actually happen. He sent me to church and spoke clearly to me.*

*You see, I had been struggling with my faith in Christ. For whatever the reason, I kept on thinking, "What if Jesus isn't really the Son of God?" For at least three or four days, these thoughts came into my head and sickened me.*

*I began reading as much as I could about Jesus and His claims in an attempt to further prove to myself what I was certain of, but still had some doubts about.*

*At church tonight, Pastor Henry Tumaso spoke to me, and I knew that God was speaking through him. He gave, as he always does, a wonderful message about God, and at the end he prayed. He asked God that if there were people out there struggling with things, whether they be physical, spiritual, or whatever; he asked that they give their problems over to God. Pastor Henry spoke much more eloquently and passionately than I could try to retell- but the message I will never forget.*

*I said, "God, take my struggle, it is in Your hands," and I trusted in God to do so. Immediately, faith in Jesus overwhelmed me, and I was assured without a shadow of a doubt that He is the world's Savior, the Son of God.*

*It was then that I realized that I had been trying to conjure up this faith on my own. But only God can give this to you, and only when you trust in Him and put it in His hands will your problems be solved. I must never trust myself, nor rely on myself, for I will only bring me down.*

*Praise God forever and always!*

*Amen.*

# 39.

Dave's response startled me. I thought that maybe he was trying too hard to sympathize with Jeremy. I felt the need to speak up, so I did.

"What do you mean by that?" I asked. Jeremy seemed to be as confused as I was. He squinted his eyes at my brother, as if he was trying to figure out what kind of a hand Dave was holding in a poker game.

"First of all - I'm sorry for what happened to Megan and her mom," Dave said in a tender, sincere voice. He paused before going on, while staring at Jeremy with sorrowful eyes. "And what I mean by that," he said, shooting me a quick glance, "is that Megan's faith in Jesus...it seemingly *was* misconstrued."

A painful expression came over my brother's face, as if he had just bitten into a sour apple. "I understand if you don't want to talk about this," he said in an apologetic tone.

Jeremy furrowed his eyebrows down and shrugged his shoulders. "I don't mind at all," he said, a little too quickly, as if Dave were ridiculous for even thinking such a thing.

Dave cleared his throat as he edged forward in his chair. After what seemed like a quick thought, he returned his gaze from the table back to Jeremy and said, "You can have faith in Jesus, but you can't think that He's going to do everything that you want Him to. It is true about Jesus saying things like, 'Your faith has healed you' - but that only happened because He wanted it to."

"So you're saying that Jesus didn't want to heal Meg's mom?" Jeremy cut in sharply. "He wanted her to rot away on that bed and die of cancer? That's what you're saying."

His last sentence was not in question form; it was a clear-cut statement.

Dave sighed deeply through his nostrils, exhaled, and then responded, "I don't understand a lot of what God does; do you?"

Jeremy straightened up in his chair. It seemed like Dave's question had caught him off guard. He paused long enough to swallow some spit, then said, "Well, I understand that if Jesus really is God, He let someone who believed in Him die a terrible death, and then, if that wasn't enough, He let an eighteen year old girl slice her own wrists, as her blood soaked her mother's bed."

Dave shook his head in frustration. He rubbed his tired-looking eyes and looked down at the table. After a few seconds of very uncomfortable silence, his head popped up, and he asked Jeremy, "So, what you're saying is that if Jesus is God, then He would never have let that happen, right?"

"Yes," Jeremy replied confidently.

Dave seemed to study Jeremy's face as he asked, "So God would never let people that believed in Him suffer?"

Jeremy's face produced a blank expression as he sat dead still. He knew enough about the Bible to know that that just wasn't true. He knew enough about history, about his own life, to know that that wasn't true. He opened his mouth; and although I could almost see the wheels churning in his head, searching for a response, nothing came out.

Dave didn't wait for a reply; he knew that Jeremy's silence was enough.

"Faith in Jesus," he said in a quiet voice, "is the best thing that ever happened to me. But it's not all rosy gardens and pretty butterflies; excuse the analogy, that's all I could think of. There are a lot of dark places in my life that I've been through that I would never wish anyone to walk through.

"And there's been times when I thought God didn't love me anymore; you know, I'd think that there's no way a loving God would let me experience things that I have. But I've figured out that it's an awesome thing to trust in God; to know that where I am is where He wants me to be. It's not always where I want to be, believe me!" Dave gave Jeremy a wide grin, his eyes not appearing so tired any longer. "But where I would like to be isn't always what's best for me, so I've learned to pray in Jesus' name that His will be done in my life, and I try my best to remember that whatever comes to me has been preordained by God."

*November 19ᵗʰ, 2003-*

*If a man were drowning, would you wait until he reaches out to you until you pulled him to safety? Or would you dive into the water and pull him from his doom? Many who are drowning don't even know it. And if they don't know that they are in danger, they won't reach for help. Christian, give them the help that you know they need. By God, reach out and save the dead.*

# 40.

A warm sensation came over my heart, and I couldn't help but smile. Although I couldn't see Him, I knew that Jesus was in the room.

Jeremy's eyes were staring off to the side; he seemed to be taking in everything that Dave was saying. Not necessarily agreeing with it, but taking it in, nonetheless. When we had talked theology before, Jeremy always seemed to have the upper hand. He could counteract any point I would make with one of his own; this was the first time that I had ever seen him stumped.

My stomach gurgled, reminding me that I had to use the bathroom. I told myself I'd have to wait; this was much more important.

Dave allowed Jeremy some time to think, not saying a word. After a short while, Jeremy sighed and then said, "It's good that you have your faith, man. But...I don't know; it's just...it's just not for me, I guess."

Dave placed his hands on the table, nonchalantly touching the side of his glass of Gatorade as he said, "You never really answered my question from before - who do you think Jesus is?"

Jeremy sat back and stared up at the dark ceiling for a few seconds. Looking back at Dave, he answered, "I think that He was a man with a messed up perception of His own identity. He was, I have to admit, a genius of some sort; but that doesn't make Him God."

"No," Dave agreed, "it certainly doesn't. But tell me why you think He's *not* God."

"Several reasons," Jeremy replied instantly, but then he had to think for a few seconds before he gave them. "For one, if God was going to send Himself to the world as a man to die for us, I think that He would've said something about it in the Tanakh. And I know what you're going to say, because your brother and I have talked about this. I know that there are passages that some think point to Jesus, but they're all taken out of context."

"Like what?"

"There're a lot of them. Give me an example from the Tanakh that Christians say is a prophecy about Christ."

"Oh, there *are* a lot!" Dave said with a grin. The smile not fading from his face, he replied, "There's a passage in the Psalms that's perfect, but I can't quote it word-for-word. Let me go get my Bible quick, okay?"

"Sure," Jeremy agreed.

While Dave ran downstairs to retrieve his Bible, I took the opportunity to use the bathroom. By the time I had returned and placed one of the candles I had taken back on the table, Dave was just sitting down. He opened his Bible, the red cover torn and the pages tattered, and read:

"'All who see me mock me; they hurl insults, shaking their heads: "He trusts in the Lord; let the Lord rescue him."

"'Yet you brought me out of the womb; you made me trust in you even at my mother's breast. From birth I was cast upon you; from my mother's womb you have been my God. Do not be far from me, for trouble is near and there is no one to help.

"'Many bulls surround me; strong bulls of Bashan encircle me. Roaring lions tearing their prey open their mouths wide against me. I am poured out like water, and all my bones are out of joint. My heart has turned to wax; it has melted within me. My strength is dried up like a potsherd, and my tongue sticks to the roof of my mouth; you lay me in the dust of death.

"'Dogs have surrounded me; a band of evil men has encircled me, they have pierced my hands and my feet.

"'I can count all my bones; people stare and gloat over me. They divide my garments among them and casts lots for my clothing.'"

Dave sat the Bible on the table and said, "That's an amazing prophecy of Jesus on the cross."

Jeremy disagreed. "No, what that is David writing about his own situation. It has some similarities to Jesus, if you believe that what the Bible says is true."

"Hmmm," Dave said, almost with a chuckle. "Some would say there are some very *striking* similarities." He glanced over what he had just read and then began to list them. "Let's see; they mocked Jesus and hurled insults at Him, and they said, 'Let Your God rescue You.' He was poured out like water; His death was a prelude to the baptism of the Holy Spirit. His bones on the cross were in all probability pulled out of joint when they stretched His arms to nail Him on the cross. Jesus' tongue stuck to His mouth in thirst. 'Dogs' surrounded Him, enjoying His death on the cross. His hands and feet were pierced, and His clothes were gambled for by the Roman soldiers.

"I mean, come on! How could you ignore all that?"

"That's just one instance," Jeremy replied. "Give me another."

"Okay," Dave said optimistically. He flipped through his Bible until he found what he was looking for. "This one's from Isaiah: 'Who has believed our message and to whom has the arm of the Lord been revealed? He grew up before him like a tender shoot, and like a root out of dry ground. He had no beauty or majesty to attract us to him.

"'He was despised and rejected by men, a man of sorrows, and familiar with suffering. Like the one from whom men hide their faces he was despised, and we esteemed him not.'"

Dave glanced up at Jeremy, possibly to see if he was paying close attention. He was.

"'Surely he took up our infirmities and carried our sorrows, yet we considered him stricken by God, smitten by him, and afflicted. But he was pierced for our transgressions, he was crushed for our iniquities; the punishment that brought us peace was upon him, and by his wounds we are healed.'"

Dave paused there, purposefully, I'm sure, and cleared his throat before finishing.

"'We all, like sheep, have gone astray, each of us has turned to his own way; and the Lord has laid on him the iniquity of us all.

"'He was oppressed and afflicted, yet he did not open his mouth; he was led like a lamb to the slaughter, and as a sheep before her shearers is silent, so he did not open his mouth.

"'He was assigned a grave with the wicked, and with the rich in his death, though he had done no violence, nor was any deceit in his mouth.

"'Yet it was the Lord's will to crush him and to cause him to suffer, and though the Lord makes his life a guilt offering, he will see his offspring and prolong his days, and the will of the Lord will prosper in his hand.'"

Dave set the Bible back on the table and stared at Jeremy, waiting for a response.

"That can't be straight from the Torah," Jeremy finally said slowly. "I mean...they must have changed some words around to make it seem convincing."

"Why don't you look it up? I'm sure you'll find the exact same passage."

"Well, I don't actually own the Tanakh, but my parents do." Jeremy explained. "Next time I'm over there, though, I'll look it up."

"Good," Dave responded. "I'll write down some passages for you to look up, and then maybe we can talk again."

All of a sudden, the electricity came back on. The television blared in the living room, as most of the lights in the townhouse lightened the rooms.

"Oh, yes!" Jeremy exclaimed, raising his hands in the air in triumph. "Finally, we can watch some TV!"

*November 19ᵗʰ, 2003-*

*If the place is prepared for me, then the way to that place must be prepared for me as well.*

*Can I simply stumble upon my mansion without traveling the path that leads to it? Certainly not! If I believe that I have a place in Heaven, then I must also believe that there is only one path leading to it.*

*I in no way constructed my palace, and I in no way set out my own path before me. Only if I had been to my destination beforehand could I have traced my steps from it to my starting point, thereby leading myself home. This is not the case.*

*So I must trust that my Lord is guiding me up the path that He has ordained for me to walk; never alone, but always with Him. This requires faith. Not faith in myself, but faith in what is unseen, yet what is known by me to be there.*

*Knowing that the Lord graciously made but one road for me to follow, although I don't deserve it, how could I say, "I will go here, and I will do that," without first consulting Him and asking and trusting Him to lead me where I go?*

*Men say, "free will", but honestly, it is not a will that we keep, but one that we give away. Your free will is to do what you want; but ultimately it comes down to this: have you willed your life to follow God, or have you chosen to follow Satan? You give your will to one or the other; like your life, it is not yours to keep.*

*So if I say, "It is in God's hands," not only with my lips but also in my heart, then is my life not the Lord's property,*

*and no longer my own? What a load off my shoulders!
What a burden off my back! For if my life was my own, and
my flesh ruled over it, I would be indulging myself in sinful
pleasures along with the rest of the world. And if the Spirit
wasn't made alive in me, there would be no confrontations
between It and my flesh.*

*But oh, how the battles rage within at times! I want so
much to allow myself something that I know is wrong, and
if it were up to me, I would have caved in long ago. But
Jesus Christ has possession of my very being; not that He
took it by force, but because I gave it to Him. His is the
conviction that tells me "No"; it is He who is in constant
war with my flesh - and although at times I am in despair, I
know that Jesus my God will overcome.*

*I must trust in Him to do so, I must ask Him to do so,
and I must believe that He will. If my heart doesn't trust in
the power of the Lord, then I have never known Him, and
He is not in me.*

*Not that He will always do what I ask of Him; because
of my limited knowledge, I sometimes ask for the very
things that He knows will do me harm. But this I know: He
will battle away the evilness, He will lead me to our Father,
the Lord Almighty, and He will do so as long as I continue
to trust in Him.*

*I pray for this faith- it is not something that I could
provide on my own. Faith, like my mansion and like the
path, is a free gift given by God to anyone who asks for it.*

# 41.

Wednesdays were Dave's only days off from work.
He'd work six days a week at the restaurant, putting

in around fifty hours on average. This kept him very busy and usually quite exhausted, but it allowed him to pay rent every month, while storing some extra money in the bank.

Wednesdays were the teen nights at our church. Dave would head out every night at about a quarter to seven and return home a little after ten. There were between five to ten teens who would show up every Wednesday on a regular basis, and every now and then, some would bring a friend or two with them.

My brother cherished the hours he spent with the teen group. There seemed to be an anticipatory spark of excitement in his eyes almost every night before he left the townhouse to go to church. He loved talking about Jesus, and I think he found his greatest joy in sharing his faith with receptive teenagers. Maybe that was because when Dave himself was a teen, at least for a part of his teenaged years, he had strayed from God and caused some calamity to fall upon his life. He wanted to make sure that didn't happen to anyone else, and he knew that the only way was to have an ongoing and constructive relationship with Jesus Christ.

The Youth Group meetings usually lasted for around two hours, and then Dave and Pastor Stan would sit around and discuss the plan for the following week. Sometimes they would take the group to hear a Christian band play, or they'd plan out a camping trip or a nature hike through the woods. It was a good way to get some new members coming in, while still focusing on our Lord.

In May of 2003, Dave, Pastor Stan, and four of the teens went to a weekend retreat called Koinonia. It was held for three days, twice every year, and involved Christians from all around coming together and sharing testimonies, listening to speakers, and fellowshipping with one another. Dave got Mom to go as well, and had asked if I'd like to go, but I told him that I was too busy with everything going on. There were wedding arrangements yet to be made at the time, and I was still going through a lot of paperwork for the house that Anne and I would be purchasing.

Koinonia is Greek for "the gathering," and that's what it was, a gathering of Christians. One of the teens from the Youth Group, a spunky, plump blonde named Mary Janson, had been to a previous Koinonian retreat, and she had told Pastor Stan about how great it was. He and Dave talked with her about it, and they then decided that it would be a good idea to take the Youth Group there, along with anyone else who might want to go.

At the end of February, they signed up for the May weekend, and it was all that Dave talked about for a good month. He was clearly excited about it; every day, he was like a young child on Christmas Eve. But when the first of May rolled around, and the weekend was ten short days away, Dave began to have a change of attitude.

Instead of walking around with a smile on his face and a bounce in his step, Dave began to worry about things. He stopped talking about the weekend, and how he wished it were here already and started instead to vocalize his doubts to me.

Before Dave went to work one night, he sat down in the living room with me while I was watching the television and told me that he was quite nervous about the weekend...

Dave looked at me with tired eyes and said, "I think I may have jumped into this Koinonia thing without thinking about it that much."

I turned the volume down with the remote and asked, "What do you mean?"

Dave shrugged and looked away, trying to downplay his nervousness. "I don't know, it's just...I don't know the people that're gonna be there, and you know how uncomfortable I am with strangers."

"Well, Mom'll be there, and Pastor Stan, and kids from the Youth Group."

"Yeah, but..." Dave winced a little, as if he were in pain. "You just don't understand. You're an extrovert, I'm an introvert. You're good in crowds, and you can make conversation with people you don't know. I just can't do that. I'm at my best alone in my room; that's where I'm most comfortable. And at this weekend, I know that I'll be expected to meet new people, and...I know it may sound weird to you, but I'm just feeling really uneasy about the whole thing."

"There's no reason for that," I said assuredly. "Despite what you think, you're actually very good with people. I've seen you in action. Once you get over your shyness, you really click with people quite well."

"Well, there's more than that," he said, folding his arms across his chest.

"Like what?"

"Like the fact that I know almost nothing that's suppose to happen. It's like a big surprise or something, and I don't know if I like that. I tried to ask Mary Janson a little more about exactly what goes on during the weekend, but she just smiled and said, 'Oh, it'll be a lot of fun and you'll meet some great people.' What kind of an answer is that, you know? Why is everything so secretive?"

I knew one of the "secrets," or surprises, that would happen to Dave at Koinonia. Since Mary Janson had sponsored Dave and the rest for the May weekend, it had been up to her to contact family and friends of Dave, Mom, Pastor Stan, and the other four teens that would be attending. Mary had asked me to write a personal letter to my Mom and brother. She asked that it be heartfelt and encouraging; possibly describing how dear they were to me. The letters would be collected, Mary explained, and passed out to them on the second night. Since it was to be a surprise, I wasn't to tell them about the letters.

I sighed and then smiled at Dave and said, "You worry too much, bro. You told me that it was Christians coming together to learn about God, right?"

Dave slowly nodded his head.

"And you and Pastor Stan prayed about it before you decided to go?"

Dave answered weakly, "Yeah."

"So?" I said, shrugging my shoulders as I lifted my hands in the air, palms up. "Why're you so worried?"

After a long pause, Dave breathed in through his nostrils and let out a heavy sigh. With a faint smile on his face, he said, "I don't know." He nodded his head at me in appreciation and before he got up from the sofa said, "Thanks."

As I turned up the volume for Sportscenter, I barely heard my brother whistling a familiar tune as he walked out the door.

*September 1ˢᵗ, 2003-*

*Some say that real men don't cry; that they hide their emotions. Well, the best Man that I know is Jesus Christ. He felt no shame in crying; He did not hide His emotions. Neither will I.*

# 42.

Mom loves to reminisce about Dave. She could (and has!) go on for hours and hours, and those listening never seem disinterested in the least bit. My little brother was surely one-of-a-kind. His cleverness, his humor, his laughter, his nature of servant-hood...there are just so many reasons that I miss him terribly.

One of the stories that Mom told me about Dave happened during their Koinonian weekend, spent in a camping place near the woods, just outside of town. There were Army-style bunks in two separated buildings; one for the men and one for the women. Then there were two other larger buildings; one was used as a large classroom of sorts, the other a cafeteria. The place was snuggled nicely just outside a large wooded area and had a pond nearby where you could feed the ducks in the spring.

The weekend, in Mom's own words, "was just completely awesome." She said that she didn't get much sleep - the beds were uncomfortable and people snored loudly - but her lack of sleep didn't take away from her enjoyment of the three days.

When they first got there at five in the afternoon on Friday, they were split up into several small groups. Five or six sat at different tables in the classroom building, with one member of Koinonia attending their table. They met their table mates and introduced themselves to the rest of the group the first night; then they got right into what Koinonia was all about.

There were six speakers, two for each day, and each one gave a short sermon. Then each individual table would converse with each other about the talk, and maybe share some personal testimonies that pertained to the topic of the speech.

They sang some songs, each table made a skit to perform in front of everybody, and they drew posters after each sermon. Mom said that it was a really fun, genuine learning experience.

The person in charge made it so most people at each table didn't know the others with whom they sat, so Mom wasn't at Dave's table. But from time to time, she'd look to where he was seating to see how he was doing, and was pleased to see him eagerly interacting with the "strangers" at his table.

On Saturday night, each table went into a different section of one of the four buildings and shared their own personal testimonies with one another. Mom told her group how Dave's contentious teenaged years brought her closer to the Lord. She said it was difficult for her to share, but the group came together and supported her with hugs, attentive ears, and some tears of their own.

There was a man in Mom's group who related well with her testimony. His name was Kevin Foley, and I would later call him Dad. He, too, had dealt with a prodigal son, and had gone through much of what Mom had. Mom said that they had connected the very first day, but that just brought them even closer together.

By Sunday's church service, Mom said that they were all one big family. One of the songs that they sang that afternoon while together in the spacious classroom said it best:

*"We're no longer strangers....*
*We're sisters....*
*Brothers...*
*Friends."*

Throughout the three days and nights, different participants were asked ahead of time to say prayers before meals and share Bible verses with the group in-between speakers. When Mom told me about what happened on the Sunday afternoon before they left, I asked her to write it down for me in her own words...

"It was just after lunch, and we were returning to the building where the speakers had all given their sermons. As we filed back into the room, I saw that the tables had been removed, and there was a large circle of chairs in the otherwise vacant room. We were asked to take a seat, and Frank (the rector of the Koinonian weekend) walked into the middle of the circle.

"He said that we were nearing the end of our weekend, and told us how grateful he was that the Lord had provided such an awesome experience for him and for us, as well. Frank said that we would be going to the cafeteria one last time shortly (where unbeknownst to us, we would be greeted by at least a hundred Koinonian members who had traveled as far as from Atlanta, Georgia to sing us a song and meet us with a hug). But first, he indicated, he had asked Dave Sullah to share with the group a verse from the Bible.

"Frank stepped away from the center as Davey stood up. I could tell that he was nervous; he cleared his throat and tapped a foot, as he stared down at his open Bible and said,

'I'm just gonna stand here; it's a little out of my comfort zone to stand in the middle of everybody with all eyes on me.'

"Kevin, who was sitting next to me, said with a smile in his deep, cheerful voice, 'Let go and let God.'

"Davey just shrugged his shoulders, said, 'Well,' and without hesitation, walked out into the middle of the circle. Everybody applauded! I was so proud of my boy that even though I wasn't speaking, I felt a tightness in my throat and was instantly choked up. Kevin looked at me with that bright smile of his, saw the tears in my eyes, and reached for my hand. We held hands tightly as Davey spoke. He was obviously still nervous; he'd look around the circle of people from time to time, but never held eye contact with anyone for more than a second. He'd slowly turn around as he spoke, seemingly off balance. Although it was clear that Davey was uncomfortable, he spoke calmly and with assurance, in his soothing deep voice. Despite his awkward body language, he made a speech that touched me, and I'm sure others as well, right down to the very core of our hearts. I'm almost positive that I remember it word-for-word:

"Frank asked me last night before bed to share with you guys a verse or verses from the Bible; anything that I wanted to. Well, I pretty much ransacked my Bible here, looking for the perfect verses to read, but I couldn't really find one that I could commit to. After a while I thought that I'd just pick any old one out, since they're all pretty good.'

"Some people chuckled, and that brought about a smile on Davey's face.

"But then I remembered that I hadn't started out my search as I should have; in prayer. So I closed my eyes and said, "God, You know what I want to say, and You know where it is in my Bible. Find it for me, Lord."

"I remember listening to the radio once, and the pastor said something like, "The Holy Spirit will remind you of verses in the Bible when you need to hear them, but He can only remind you of them if you have read them once before."

"Davey paused as mumbles of agreement passed through the circle.

" 'I'm glad that I have a Bible, and that I read it. It's a privilege; not a burden, or a cumbersome chore that we do to please God.'

"Scattered 'Amens' were called out. Davey's poise by now was not as 'gawky' as it had been at the start. He stood straight up now, and stopped dancing around in a tiny semi-circle.

" 'Well, this is what God brought me to, right after my prayer to Him. It's from Paul's letter to the Philippians.'

"Davey paused and swallowed a lump in his throat, then began reading.

" 'I thank my God every time I remember you. In all my prayers for all of you, I always pray with joy because of your partnership in the gospel from the first day until now, being confident of this, that he who has begun a good work in you will carry it on to completion until the day of Christ Jesus.'

"I thought that maybe Davey was done, because he stopped there and kept his head down. He wasn't done, I found out; he was fighting back the tears. In a strained voice, he continued after a few seconds.

" 'It is right for me to feel this way about all of you, since I have you in my heart; for whether I am in chains or defending and confirming the gospel, all of you share in God's grace with me. God can testify how I long for all of you with the affection of Christ Jesus.'

"Davey composed himself and finished off strongly.

" 'And this is my prayer: that your love may abound more and more in knowledge and depth of insight, so that you may be able to discern what is best and may be pure and blameless until the day of Christ, filled with the fruit of righteousness that comes through Jesus Christ-to the glory and praise of God.'

"Davey shut his Bible while probably all of the thirty-plus people sitting in the circle said 'Amen' enthusiastically.

"Davey held his Bible under his arm as he said, 'There's been so much I wanted to say to you all that I couldn't quite put into words. Then when Frank asked me to share a verse with you, I knew it was God giving me a way to tell you how I feel, and how much you all mean to me. I know that we just met; but it's like I've known you, especially you guys from my table, for my whole life. And I know that we'll have eternity with our Lord to get to know each other better.'

"Again the room was filled with 'Amens,' and it was at this time that Davey lost the fight with his tears. He opened his mouth to say something, but as he did, the tears that had been creeping up on him during his speech poured out of his eyes like a waterfall. He didn't cover his face with his hand; he just stood there in the middle of the circle and wept in front of everyone. I wanted to run to him and give him a bear hug, and I probably would have if Kevin hadn't been holding my hand so firmly. All I could do was cover my mouth with my free hand and cry as the room became dead silent.

"Davey wiped the tears from his reddened face and looked around at the thirty or more pairs of eyes, all focused intently on him. I don't think anyone in that room, not even the men, returned Davey's glance without a tear or two in their own eyes.

"Droplets continued to fall down my baby's cheeks as he said in a tense voice, 'And truthfully, I wasn't going to show up for this weekend. I was gonna make up some lame excuse, because I was real nervous about it and everything. But something wouldn't let me do that; something inside of me was telling me that I had to go. It was the will of God.'

"A fresh stream of tears flowed down his face as he continued.

" 'My favorite verse in the entire Bible is Psalm 46:10 - "Be still, and know that I am God." And that's exactly what we have to do; stop fighting against Him, relax, and know and trust that He's got everything under control. He will work things out in a way we can't even imagine, if we only give Him the right to do so.'

"Davey sighed and looked around at everyone, a large smile appearing on his face.

" 'I'm so glad that I met all of you. I'm not good at opening up with people; especially people I don't know; but you made me feel so comfortable, and I was able to share things that I've been holding in for a long time. You didn't look down on me like I thought you would; you offered me supportive words and shared my tears with me. I am forever grateful for you, and forever grateful to God for allowing me the pleasure of meeting you all. Thank you.'

"As Davey started back to his seat, everyone in the large circle stood and applauded. An older gentleman with a grisly salt and pepper beard that was sitting next to Davey grabbed him, and they embraced as everyone continued to clap. Kevin rubbed my back, and the tears in my eyes made it almost impossible to see."

*May 5ᵗʰ, 2003-*

*You say, "Where is God in all of this?" and you fight
and fight to see it, yet it remains a mystery, your unanswered question reverberating throughout your mind and
your heart. But still, you don't give up. Never do you say,
"There is no God," although at drastic moments you
contemplate the possibility.*

*Faith takes you places where intellect has never been.
You trudge on. You pray. You cry. When comfort is needed,
it is supplied. When you cry out, your voice is heard. Your
soul mutters incomprehensible emotions and words that
flow directly to the Father of all creation.*

*Then you are able to step back from your problems
and bask in the glow of the peace that surpasses all understanding. The walls are caving in, but all is well. You are
neck-deep in rising water, but you are not concerned.
Snarling dogs are charging towards you, but fear is
nowhere to be found.*

*Then you say, "My Lord, my God...You have been here
all along." You realize that nothing can touch you, because
you have already been touched by the loving Hand of the
Lord Jesus Christ.*

*Worries are temporary, pain is fleeting, trials come and
go; yes, eventually they do go! But forever is the Lord. He
has overcome, and forever is He with you.*

# 43

By the age of twenty, Dave had been through some traumatic experiences: he saw his father for the last time at the tender age of five, he lost his best friend in a plane crash, he battled drugs and the addiction that they once had over him, and he parted ways with Susie, the one-and-only love that Dave ever found on this Earth.

Dave was a strong young man, but he was sensitive, as well. He would hardly ever tell me about his pain, but he did write about it. There are numerous entries in Dave's journal pertaining to Susie; all of them heartfelt and sincere. He hid it so well that before reading them, I had no idea of how much of an impact Susie had on his life and left on his heart.

Here is one of the many examples:

*January 2nd, 2002-*

*In a letter to me, she wrote that she loved me with all of her heart forever. It's been almost a year since we last spoke, and I wonder if her words still hold true. I miss that love; I know, though, that I abused it, and our separation is entirely my fault.*

*Spending New Year's alone emphasizes your loneliness greatly. But I must assume that it's for the best that we parted. I pray her to find a nice Christian man who*
*will strengthen her walk with the Lord, who will love her second to God alone. I pray for that, but deep down I don't want to see her with another man. Selfish, yes; but honest.*

*Let it be, Lord; Thy will, let it be.*

*There comes a time when you realize that it's time to move on. They say to forget the past and look forward to the future. In some cases, that's wise counsel. But I will never forget you, my Button. You hold a place in my heart that can not and will not be forgotten. I will move on by the grace of*

*God, yes; but you are a part of me that I can not go anywhere
without.*

*May God bless you in all things. May He be your first
and dearest love, and may you reap the benefits of your
desire for Him.*

*I pray you have a happy life, and if that calls for a love to
call your own, then may God grant you this man and may He
be with the both of you forever in all things. You deserve to be
happy, and I pray to God that you find this happiness in Him.
He loves you, and He will give you all good things in accordance to His will, so far as you love Him first and ask!*

*The Lord be with you always, dear love, Amen.*

Dave lost many things, but one thing he never lost was
his faith in God. He prized his relationship with the Lord
above all else - above the love of this Earth, above the hurt
and pain, above the emotional and physical scars that test-
ings bring about - for Dave, God stayed on top where He
belongs.

Dave was able to endure all that he went through, because
he knew that God was with him. Despite all his problems (or
maybe because of all his problems), my brother only grew
closer to the Lord.

I love how F.B. Meyer put it:

"If in an unknown country, I am informed that I must pass
through a valley where the sun is hidden, or over a stony bit
of road, to reach my abiding place- when I come to it, each
moment of shadow or jolt of the carriage tells me that I am
on the right road."

I am personally facing some difficult situations as I write
this now. Yesterday I had a conference with the parents of a
sixteen-year-old boy who is in my class. I told them that I
would have to fail their son, unless he put some extra-effort
into his grades. I said that he was quite an intelligent lad, but
he was just as equally lazy as he was smart.

They proceeded to threaten me, saying that I'd better not do that, that they knew some people in high places. I kind of smiled and said, "Well I know God, and I bet He's in a little higher of a place than your friends."

As soon as I said it, I knew I shouldn't have. Not that it wasn't true; just that for some reason mentioning God in classrooms is now considered to be a horrible offense. They stormed out of the meeting, loudly vocalizing their disgust, and assuring me that I would be without a job by the end of the week.

Our beloved dog, Aslan, ran away a week ago, and hasn't come back yet. Anne and I scoured the neighborhood for hours, and then spent about the same amount of time going door to door, asking if anyone had seen our golden retriever.

I am becoming somewhat of an insomniac. I get up for work at five, get home at four, do schoolwork for a while, eat dinner, then type this on the computer, sometimes until the wee hours of the morning. Case in point, it's three thirty a.m. right now. I have to be at work in less than three hours, and I don't even know if I still have a job.

But all of that pales in comparison to the status of my heart. It feels like it's being ripped apart in all different directions. Lately, for seemingly no particular reason, I just start bawling. Whether it be as I type, in bed with Anne, or during a lunch break at school, I find myself unable to stop the tears from falling. I knew that I missed Dave; but until I started writing this, I had no idea of *how much* I miss him.

And it's not only having to recall the bad memories - those are mostly already done, though the most wretched memory I have of Dave won't come until pretty close to the end - it's going through my brother's life without actually having him here with me that's killing me inside. Oh, I know that we will meet again - but I want him here now!! I miss you, little brother...so very much.

Anne has been a constant comforter and encourager, and without her I may very well have given up long ago. By the grace of God, this book will someday be completed, and she will have just as much to do with that accomplishment as I.

As much as I appreciate and adore my wife, I know that without God I would not be able to go on. He fills me in places where she cannot. The Lord supplies me with strength that none other can. I trust in Him, and Him alone, to do what I simply cannot.

That's why I'm here in front of the computer at close to four in the morning. Knowing that since I put it in His Hands, God has it in control; that's what keeps me going.

What else matters?

*September 2nd, 2003-*

    *Father...Sovereign and loving Lord God:*

    *Did my mind ever doubt You? Did my lips ever question Your ways? Was my heart ever estranged from Your love?*

    *Where has that man gone, who felt isolated and unloved by the Lord? He has vanished, and I wonder if I had ever known him. Surely he was a fool - a hardhearted man who thought that he had been mistreated, who thought that he knew better than the Lord! That man is no more, and he is not welcome to return.*

    *In the midst of dire difficulties, when I was sure that I had been deserted and forgotten, You, Lord, have proven Yourself once again. How enduring is Your patience with me! How everlasting is Your love! You have not forgotten me, nor have You abandoned me, though I was sure that You had.*

    *My sea of troubles were sure to overcome me; yet, instead, Your love overcame all.*

    *"Where is my Father?" I cried out. "Where is my Lord?" And I went about searching, as if You were hiding Yourself from me. You can't find the Lord unless He presents Himself, and Lord, I have found You.*

    *With love that I don't know about, You have loved me forever. You show it to me in ways that I can understand, yet I know I can't fully comprehend.*

    *I cried out against You - You, Who has no fault! But still, You did not leave me, nor scorn me. You did what only God can do, and that is to reveal Your all-powerful love by a gentle reproach. You chastised me; You humbled me, but in such a loving manner.*

*Not only that, but You blessed me even further. You gave me a man and told me, "This is your father." I now have an earthly representative of my Father in Heaven. What love my Lord gives me is exemplified by him. He has known me for only a short while, but treats me as his own. How can I explain it? I will try, but it will not give him the justice he deserves.*

*He comes home from a hard day's work, and immediately greets me with a smile and asks how I am doing. He enthusiastically talks with me about the Bible, and although he knows so much more than I about It, he never makes me feel stupid as he answers my many questions with ease and wisdom. When I need some help, he drops what he's doing, no matter how engrossed in it he is, and happily gives me a hand. We get in many discussions, and although sometimes our views differ, he doesn't get angry. Even when the argument becomes heated, and neither he nor I can come to an agreement, the gentleness in his eyes never sways.*

*I could go on, and if I did, this journal would soon be full. What it all comes down to is this: I feel loved. I see love in his face, in his eyes, in his actions, and in his words. How priceless is this love! How freely he gives it!*

*My father loves me much; but it's only a small percentage of the love that my Lord has for me. How truly great is this love! It is beyond measure- far, far beyond any measure possible.*

*Thank You, Lord, for my dad. He is yet another example of Your great love for me. Bless him, and bless my mom; above all else, may Your name be blessed. You are the giver of all good gifts- You gave Your Son, and You continue to give Yourself to us.*

*All that is love, all that is kindness, all that is joy and patience, meekness and understanding, faith and hope: they all come from You, oh Lord, and forever we are thankful.*

# 44.

I like the way that Dave described the man whom I eventually called "Dad." He didn't say that he was tall with rugged good looks, a deep voice, greyish black hair, and a friendly smile. He didn't use Dad's external features to describe him; he described him by who he was on the inside.

Dave once wrote:

'When you hear a man speak on the radio, you envision what he might look like. If you ever meet the man, more often than not you see that your vision of him was way off. But when you read the words that a man has written, and if that man has written from his heart, you see that man more clearly than your eyes could ever see him. You see his heart.'

That's the reason I have stayed away, as much as possible, from giving Dave's physical attributes. I want you to see him, yes; but I want you to look past his body and into his heart. I hope that I am successful in doing so.

I didn't know what to think when Mom told me that she was going to get married; it was a complete shock.

She had had a few "boyfriends" in the past, but none that she ever could get that close to. After she turned fifty, she stopped dating altogether, and I was sure that Mom would never find a man to love. I think she was pretty sure about that as well.

We moved out of Crossroads when our lease expired in May. Jeremy moved to New York City, and Dave moved back home with Mom. I had bought a house for Anne and me, and I moved in there myself until we were wed.

Dave was the first to tell me about Mom's new friend. His name was Kevin, and they had met at the Koinonian weekend. Dave said that Kevin stopped by the house every now and then, and he and Mom watched TV and went out to eat sometimes. I was sure that they were just friends, though; Mom was too old to date!

I first met him one night in early June. Mom, Kevin, Dave, and I met up at an Italian restaurant that Kevin liked. As soon as I saw them together, I knew right away that they were more than just friends.

As I walked into the restaurant, I saw the three of them sitting down at a booth in the corner. As he saw me approaching, Kevin immediately stood up and walked over to greet me. He smiled, shook my hand, and said that I looked just like all the pictures that Mom had shown him.

We went over to the booth and sat down. Kevin took Mom's small, fragile hand in his as he sat next to her. She flashed him a wide smile and looked deep into his eyes.

Dave had told me a little about this guy. He said that he was a farmer/engineer who had horses and acres of land full of hay, and was also a professor at South Mesa Community College. He said that Kevin was one of those guys who seemingly knew the answer to any question that you could throw at him. He was extremely intelligent,

extremely humble, and extremely nice. I was sure that something was wrong with him. Maybe Dave nor Mom could see it, but I was sure that I would.

We began talking after the waitress took our orders, and I found Kevin to be a great conversationalist. Not only was his voice deep and soothing to listen to (which was eerily just like Dave's), but he was able to talk with me like he had known me forever. There were no awkward pauses, nothing he said struck a bad chord with me; in fact, it was just the opposite. He was funny, down-to-earth, and a real smart guy-just like Dave said.

I noticed the way that Kevin and Mom looked at each other, how Mom's face seemed radiant and young, how he gently massaged her shoulder after the meal...they were certainly more than friends. And despite the fact that for some reason I had wanted to find some sort of a fault in Kevin, I almost right away found myself liking him instead.

After we indulged in some very tasty Tiramisu, Mom smiled at Kevin as she said, "Would now be a good time?"

Kevin returned her smile and responded, "If you think so, honey."

Mom looked at me and then at Dave, absolutely beaming with happiness. She reached into her purse and retrieved a shiny diamond ring from inside. She simply held it up with pride and said, "Kevin asked me to marry him, and I said yes."

A sound like screeching brakes seemed to explode in my mind as I sat there, bewildered. I hardly even knew this guy, and he was going to marry my mother? Shouldn't she have first consulted me before she made her decision?

"What do you think?" she asked, a wide smile still stretched across her face.

I had to admit to myself that she looked happy, and that Kevin seemed to be a nice enough guy; but she really wouldn't have liked to have heard what I really thought. All I was thinking was,

'It's too soon. You shouldn't jump into marriage like this so fast. How long have you known this man? Three months?'

Dave seemed to think otherwise.

"I knew it!" he said as he stretched over to hug Mom and then shake Kevin's hand. "Congratulations! That's awesome!" There was no hint of deceit in his voice or in his smile; Dave was just as happy about this as Mom and Kevin were.

I couldn't just sit there and not say anything, so I mustered up a smile and said, "Wow, this is a shocker!" I sort of chuckled as I said, "Congratulations; both of you."

"When are you getting married?" Dave asked with joyful enthusiasm.

"We decided there's no reason to wait; you know, Kevin and I aren't getting any younger. So, we'll have a small ceremony at the church in August."

"August?" I repeated, almost choking on the coffee I had ordered after dessert. "Of *this* year?"

Kevin bowed his head a little and started to nervously play around with an empty plastic creamer cup that lay on the table before him. My tone of voice clearly showed my disapproval; and although I felt bad as Kevin's countenance went from cheerful to disheartened, there was no way for me to take it back.

Mom patted Kevin's hand, noting his tenseness, and responded, "This isn't something that we decided on a whim, if that's what you're thinking. We've both prayed long and hard about it, and we know that this is something that God wants us to do." She smiled warmly, as she looked at Kevin and said softly, "We love each other. I've finally found the man that God has made for me, and I'm not going to wait any longer to be with him."

Maybe it was the way that they tenderly looked at each other, maybe it was the conviction in Mom's voice - for whatever the reason, I knew that she was right, and that I had been wrong to question her.

"I'm sorry, Mom, I didn't mean for it to sound like that." I stood up and leaned down to hug her, and she reached her arms around my neck in a welcoming embrace. I then gave Kevin a grin as he timidly looked up at me. I held out my hand, and he shook it and returned my smile.

*October 3rd, 2003-*
    *I closed my eyes*
    *with the word "Dad" on my mind;*
    *what I saw was a dark, dreary place.*
    *The trees were all dead,*
    *the land was dark gray,*
    *the sky a violent space.*

    *But I sat for a while*
    *with my eyes still closed;*
    *I don't quite understand why.*
    *I wanted to leave,*
    *I wanted to go,*
    *I wanted to run and hide.*

    *But the place was mine*
    *and it was meant for me;*
    *I couldn't just leave me there.*
    *Still I cursed the death,*
    *the hollow logs,*
    *the putrid stench in the air.*

    *I hated the place,*
    *and wished it were gone;*
    *yet I knew it would never depart.*
    *Not from my eyes,*
    *not from my mind,*
    *and certainly not from my heart.*

*With my eyes still closed,*
*I saw something wonderful occur;*
*a bright light came from afar!*
*It gave the trees leaves,*
*the parched ground grass,*
*the sky now filled with stars!*

*A beautiful place*
*sprang from my desolate land;*
*so rich and full of love!*
*Now the word "Dad"*
*brings joy to my heart,*
*thanks be to my Father above.*

# 45.

God gave poets the ability to put things in a way none other could. To me, their skill is unfathomable. If you think it's easy to write poetry, either you're a remarkable poet, or you've never tried.

I've tried once or twice; each attempt was disastrous.

It's so frustrating when you want to say something important to someone, but you can't because your emotions tower over your lack of words, and anything that you tried to say would do your feelings no justice. That's why we buy Hallmark cards instead of writing them ourselves; someone else has written the words that you couldn't, although they seem to come from your very own heart.

In the above poem, my brother captured my feelings on the name "Dad" in a way that I would never have been able to express on my own.

Just a few weeks after Mom and Kevin were married, Dave began calling him Dad. Mom had talked with both Dave and Kevin privately about the matter beforehand. Basically, Dave thought of Kevin as his father, and Kevin thought of Dave as his son. And although I had had my reservations about Kevin at first, he had proven me wrong, and I secretly longed to call him Dad as well - actually, half of me wanted to refer to him as Dad, and half of me hated the name so much that I didn't want to give it to someone that I so loved.

Over time, I saw that not only was Kevin's love for Mom genuine and lavish, but that he was altogether a model Christian man. Sure, he had his faults...at least, I'm sure that they were there *somewhere*.

I wish that my brother were here right now; he'd do a much better job at explaining this man to you. Since it's only me in front of the computer, I will have to borrow the words from another. As a matter of fact, it's from a Hallmark card:

*William Franklin writes, "If he's wealthy and prominent, and you stand in awe of him, call him 'father'. If he sits in shirt sleeves and suspenders at a ballgame and picnic, call him 'Pop'. If he wheels the baby carriage and carries bundles meekly, call him 'Papa' (with the accent on the first syllable). If he belongs to a literary circle and writes cultured papers, call him 'Papa' (with the accent on the last syllable). If, however, he makes a pal of you when you're good, and is too wise to let you pull the wool over his loving eyes when you're not; if, moreover, you're quite sure no other fellow you know has quite so fine a father, you may call him 'Dad'."*
*-Peter S. Seymour, "A Father's Love"*

This is the account of how I came to call Kevin my Dad...

"*Fore!!* Gosh *darn* it!"

I couldn't help but laugh to myself as Dave stared angrily at his errant tee shot. He was usually so calm and collected; but for some reason, my brother became so animated whenever he golfed. If he hit a good shot, he'd beam with pride, a huge satisfied grin on his face. If, however, he hit a bad one...

"Man, I can't believe it!" Dave said as he turned around to face me. I quickly washed the grin off my face, as he stared at me with his eyebrows furrowed and a disgusted look. "As soon as I think I fixed whatever's wrong with my drive, I go and hit one that ends up on the wrong fairway!"

"You just gotta relax," I said, as I stepped up to the tee and bent down to set up my ball. "You're rushing your back swing and taking your eyes off the ball. Nice and smooth, man...nice and smooth."

"Yeah, nice and smooth," Dave responded mockingly, seemingly a little annoyed with my attempt to offer some advice.

I shook off his remark and took a practice swing. I always envisioned my shot before I actually hit the ball. It was a tip I had heard from the Golf Channel, and it seemed to do the trick.

The hole was a dogleg left, which was good for me, because I had a natural hook. I took one last look at the fairway, then stood still as I concentrated on my golf ball. After a few seconds, I brought back my driver and *smack*! The ball sailed through the air, appeared to pause for a second, then dropped nicely right in the middle of the fairway.

"Nice shot," Dave said softly as we walked towards our golf cart.

"Thanks."

It was a gorgeous summer day. Not a cloud in the brilliant blue sky, the sun smiling warmly down upon us. Ever since school let out, I had taken every opportunity I had to come to Clear Springs Country Club and get in a round of golf. Dave, though, could only go on Wednesdays, since he worked every other day of the week. Since he worked all the time, and had only one day a week to do miscellaneous chores such as paying bills, getting a haircut, or whatever, golf was an outlet to relieve stress for Dave. And some days, Dave was more stressed out than others.

"What time is it?" he asked as we drove the cart towards his ball, which had landed in the rough by the previous hole's fairway.

I glanced at my watch and replied, "Three-thirty. Don't worry; you have plenty of time before Youth Group starts."

He just huffed and rolled his eyes while he stepping out of the cart and walking towards his ball. Making sure no one was on the last hole's fairway, he grabbed an iron from his golf bag and stood behind the ball. It was half-hidden in the moderately long rough, and there was a tall evergreen tree ten yards in front of him, obscuring the straight path to the green.

"Great," he said to himself, "what am I supposed to do?"

I got out of the cart and stood beside him. Folding my arms across my chest, I said, "Well...you can try to hit over the tree, or you can lay-up so you'd be a pitching wedge away from the green."

Dave shook his head, never taking his stare off the green, some hundred or so yards away, and retorted, "Watch out - I'm just gonna hit it."

I stepped off to the side as my brother took a couple of practice swings, sending chunks of grass flying through the air. Then he slowly set his club behind the ball, drew back wildly, and hit the ball as hard as you could from the lie that it was in. It flew through the evergreen, causing some needles to float softly to the grass, and landed with a thud in a bunker that sat around thirty yards in front of the green.

Dave arched his back and looked straight up in the air, his reddening face about to explode in anger.

"Hey," I said, trying to calm him down, "at least you got it through!"

"Yeah, I got it through," Dave snapped as he stomped towards the cart. "And right into the freakin' bunker!"

He slammed the club in his bag and slumped in the passenger side of the cart. I sat next to him and said, "C'mon, man; you really gotta relax."

"Relax?!" Dave blurted, as he shrugged and held his hands up in the air. "Oh, yeah, relax! Sure, no problem."

"What is it?" I asked, turning sideways, to let him know he had my full attention. Something was getting under Dave's skin; and it wasn't just golf.

He sat there in silence, biting down on the corner of his mouth, nervously glancing around in different directions. After a few seconds, he answered; his eyes were getting teary, and he wouldn't look me in the face

"I don't know...it's just a bunch of stuff. A bunch of little stuff, I guess, that wouldn't seem like much, unless you added them all together." He sighed and shook his head, his watery eyes still dancing about at nothing in particular. "I can't even really explain it."

"Well, try," I said with concern.

He sighed again, this one heavier than before, and began tapping his fingers against his knee. "Oh man...where do I begin? I just don't feel like myself lately. I don't know if it's 'cause I'm living back home with Mom and Dad...it's just, I don't know...it's like I have no idea what I'm supposed to be doing or where I'm going. I feel like I'm just wasting away... doing nothing with what I've been given."

I opened my mouth to interject, but Dave cut me short. "Let me finish. My friends always ask me to hang out, and I can't, 'cause most of them do drugs and drink. They used to really like me...but now I think they think that I don't like them, which isn't true at all. I mean, they all know that I'm a Christian and everything, and some of them are, too...at least, they say they are. So I guess they understand me not wanting to be around that stuff. But it's weird at work now; a couple of 'em don't even talk to me anymore, and the ones that do just do it out of courtesy.

"And *then* there's the girls," Dave went on without pausing except to catch his breath. "I'm not trying to be arrogant here, but it's like almost every girl at work has either had a crush on me or still does. All my buddies are like, 'Why don't you go for her?', you know? But...and I've wanted to, believe me, some of these girls are really hot! But none of 'em are Christians. It's like the first thing I ask them if I get the feeling that they're flirting with me or whatever; but they treat it like it's a turn-off to them. I don't know, it's like I'm meant to be alone, and I know it...but I wish I wasn't.

"It's everything," Dave concluded as he stared sadly towards the fairway. "It's that and more. I just don't know why I'm here, and...I really wonder if I'm doing anything right at all."

Dave turned his head to the side and sat motionless, except for the slight tapping of his left foot. It certainly wasn't everyday that my brother opened up to me; or anybody, for that matter. So I thought hard about what to say before I replied.

The wind picked up just then and blew my visor I was wearing over the front of the cart and onto the grass. Without hesitation, my brother jumped out of the cart and grabbed my visor before it could blow away. He returned to his seat and handed it to me, saying, "Here ya go."

As I took the visor, the wind blew again; this time it was as though God was whispering to me. At that instant, I knew exactly what to say. "You have no idea, Dave. Sometimes the smallest things you do could have the greatest impact on others." I met my brother's confused glance with assuredness in my eyes. "What I mean is, just by professing your faith and living it out, you're doing all that God asks you to.

You gave your life to Him; don't worry about where it takes you, or wonder if you're doing enough. God has your life, and He certainly won't waste it.

"If people know you're a Christian, they'll watch you, believe me. They'll want to see if you're different from everyone else. Don't worry about what your friends think of you or how girls react to you; pray that they'll see the Truth inside of you, that Jesus Christ is real. Their souls are more important than friendship and lust."

As Dave silently took that all in, I smiled at him and said, "To give you a little example, what happened a minute ago fits perfectly in with this. When my visor flew off my head, you were out there getting it for me before I could move a muscle. Now that might not seem like much to you, but for me it proves that you're the type of person I know you are - thoughtful, unselfish, caring. Little things, like getting my visor for me, are the things that you do all the time. They might seem like nothing to you, but others notice and appreciate them more than you'll probably ever know."

Dave cleared his throat and said, "Alright. Let's finish this hole before the group behind catches up. If I remember right, your ball's in the middle of the fairway and mine's in the middle of the sand!"

He smiled as he said it; his former disturbed mood seemingly had been washed away. My brother didn't take praise well, but as we drove up to the ball, he smacked me on the shoulder and said, "Thanks, man. I really needed that."

As I stepped up to my ball with a nine iron in my hand, Dave said from the cart, "Oh yeah, I almost forgot; Dad said that he's got a nice rug that would go well in your living room if you want it."

"Dad"...the word sounded so weird coming from my brother's mouth. I couldn't believe that he was calling Kevin "Dad," and at the same time, I couldn't believe that I was still calling him "Kevin."

I longed to call him Dad. He sure acted like one. He helped Dave and me move out of our apartment; we didn't ask him - he volunteered gladly. Kevin let us pile everything into one of his horse trailers, which saved us numerous trips back and forth. He loaded and unloaded all of the heavy furniture and boxes into the house I had purchased and did the same for Dave, who moved back into his old room downstairs. But the room didn't look the same. Kevin, unbeknownst to Dave, had completely redone his room as a welcoming back. The walls were newly painted, the floor fitted with carpet, the small window replaced with a newer, cleaner one. The cobwebs, which at one point had flourished in the room, were gone. Kevin even made Dave a workbench for his wood burnings and set it in the basement's hallway.

He did even more than that for me. The house that I had bought was a fixer-upper, but the problem was I had no idea of how to fix it. After Kevin saw it, his eyes gleamed with the opportunity to help. "Don't worry about it," he said. "I'll come over tomorrow and do what I can."

Boy, did he! He polished down the hardwood floors (which took over five hours), while making enjoyable conversation with me at the same time. Later he stained them a healthy maroon color; they looked brand new! Over the next month, Kevin came over to scrape the walls and paint them, fixed broken cupboards, installed a washer and dryer, fixed a leak in the sub-pump, and gave me his pushing lawnmower, just to name a few things.

It wasn't just all that he did for me; it was the *way* that he did it. Never once did he complain or seem bothered by the work. He was always eager to help, always met me with a firm handshake and a smile, and always seemed more concerned about my living conditions than he was about his own rest and relaxation.

There was no falsehood in the man; not even an ounce of insincerity. He had no ulterior motives for all that he did for me; he did it because he loved me.

I stood behind my golf ball, pretending to stare at the green as I sheepishly asked, "When did you start calling him 'Dad'?" I already knew the answer to my question, but I was not ready to come out and ask what I really wanted to just yet.

"I don't know...couple a weeks after the wedding."

They had had a small ceremony at our church. Mom wore a bright red dress and a beautiful, glowing smile. Kevin asked Dave and I to be groomsmen, and we accepted. Aunt Sheila sang a touching song with her awesomely glorious voice before they said their "I do's," and I noticed that Dave was fighting back some tears. I, however, never was much of a fighter. Tears streamed down my cheeks as I saw how happy my mother was that day.

I glanced over at Dave as he asked me inquisitively, "Why do you ask?"

I looked back out towards the green and replied, "Well... was it hard for you? Isn't it awkward at all?"

After a few seconds of silence, I looked at Dave sitting in the cart. His legs were over the side with his feet on the grass facing me, his head bowed in contemplation. He cleared his throat and kept his stare at the grass at first as he answered me. "No, not really. After a while, it was hard for me *not* to call him Dad. I mean...he's my Dad, ya know?"

I met Dave's eyes as he looked up at me and nodded my head in agreement.

From that day on, Kevin was no longer Kevin to me. He was Dad.

*August 29ᵗʰ, 2003-*

*Ask for any and all good things with absolute faith that
you will receive them so long as they are in accordance
with God's great will.*

*As a child, I wrote to "Santa" about what I wanted
for Christmas presents. To my delight on Christmas Day, I
unwrapped many a gift that I had asked for. How did this
come about? Because I asked for it! If I had not made my
wishes known to "Santa," I would have received toys that I
did not like and clothes that I would not wear.*

*God, of course, is much different than Santa. He knows
what we want and what we need far better than we do. But
in accordance to God's Word, we first must ask. I wonder
upon how many gifts the Lord has wrapped for me that
went unopened, because I never asked Him to hand them
over to me. Our God is a gracious God - He has the power
and the will to give us good things, but He has the mind
that we would ask Him for these gifts before we receive
them. That's not to say that He might at times give us things
that we haven't specifically asked for - but why leave that to
chance?*

*Lord, give me a life devoted in humility to You! May
Thy perfect will be done in my life. Give me the awesome
responsibility and pleasure of glorifying Your Name.
Give me an endless amount of faith. Give me a beautiful
Christian woman to marry and to spend the rest of my life
with. Give me enough money to pay the bills and support
the needy. Give me vast wisdom and the correct usage of
it in my life. Discourage me from the call of evil, and may
all blackness within disappear in the brightness of Jesus*

*Christ. Give me great memory in Your sound doctrine,*
*all sixty-six books, and every word within. May I display*
*Christ in my thoughts, words, and actions to the highest*
*degree possible. May I be an example and representative*
*of Christ to my friends, family, and co-workers. By Your*
*grace may they see the Truth and become devout followers*
*of You, the true and living God, Creator of the heavens and*
*the earth. May my mind be solid in Your Word, and may*
*my heart beat only for Thee, oh Lord. Be it Your will, Lord*
*God, may all this and more come to me. To the glory of*
*Your Name, in Christ Jesus I ask of it,*
   *Amen.*

# 46.

Sometimes God gives us what we want, sometimes He doesn't. But it's only out of His love for us that He sometimes withholds things. It's easy to get mad at Him when we don't receive what we want; but we must remember His love and His wisdom, and how they far surpass our own.

I prayed that I wouldn't lose my job, and I didn't. The parents of one of my students that I mentioned before threatened to pull their kid out of my school if I wasn't fired. They said that I was teaching religion, not English Literature, but my district superintendent disagreed. Their boy is still in my class, and he is still failing it. I've added him and his parents to my prayers.

Aslan showed up at the house not three days ago, panting and all scratched up. Anne found him waiting by the porch while I was in school. She said that he was dehydrated, and it looked like he had gotten into a scuffle with another animal, but he would be alright. She took him down to her workplace and tested him for rabies, but the results came back negative. It's such a joy to have Aslan back; he might be a dumb old dog, but I really did miss him!

Sleep, however, still seems to be eluding me. I'm not exactly sure why, but I know it has something to do with writing about Dave. I toss and turn so much at night now, that I've been sleeping on the couch as to not keep Anne up all night.

Late one night I told God, "This has to stop! If I don't get any sleep, then I'll just stop writing!"

I gave God an ultimatum! Sure, I said it out of frustration and fatigue, but at the time I meant it. Did I fall asleep right after that? No; in fact, I was kept awake until only a few hours before the sun rose. So did I stop writing? Obviously not, though it was my intention to.

That is, until...

It had been weeks since I wrote. I told myself that I was just taking a little break - hey, I deserved it, right?

I was getting good sleep, and was able to be in my own bed again with Anne. I was feeling healthier and more alert, especially in the mornings, and didn't have a care in the world. I didn't notice it at first, but that was the problem: I didn't care. I didn't care about my promise to God, that I would write this story every day until its completion. I didn't care that I was taking a break from doing God's work. All I cared about was that I was happy, I was getting sleep, I was finally relaxing...I .

One afternoon after school, I came home and threw my jacket on the sofa. As I fell onto the couch, Aslan came running up to me, begging me to scratch him behind the ears. "How was your day, Dummy?" I asked him, as I reached forward with a smile on my face. He shook my hand with his paw, Aslan's one and only trick, and gave me a sharp *bark* in response to my question. That meant that he probably had to go outside, but I was too tired at the moment to let him out. Instead, I scratched his ears while his tongue hung down from his mouth. His round, playful eyes were searching, and it seemed that he was wondering if he would get yelled at if he tried to jump up there with me.

"Don't even think about it," I said in a mock stern voice.

Seemingly ashamed that he had even dared to think about jumping on the couch, Aslan bowed his head and rested it on my lap. I sat there and petted him, a quiet feeling of peace resulting from this simple action. As I scratched Aslan's thin, golden-brown fur, I all of a sudden thought about Dave's poem which he had written for me so long ago, "Man's Best Friend." Thoughts started coming into my head; I had no idea if I was controlling them, or if it was Someone else:

*'Man's best friend will come to greet you, even if you have been away for a long time. He won't abandon you, even if you abandon him...'*

*Have I abandoned God? What is that supposed to mean?*

*'I will never leave you nor forsake you'...so why have you left Me?*

I stared with confused wonder at Aslan, as if he had asked me the questions, as if he would answer them for me. He only lifted his head from my lap and barked, then trotted towards the door while keeping his head turned toward me.

I tried to get up and let Aslan out, but something was keeping me on the couch. It was as if a ton of invisible bricks were keeping me firmly anchored down. I couldn't move; well, I'm sure I could have, but I wouldn't. All I could do was answer the voice with a question of my own:

*'Whaddya mean, why have I left You?'*

Silence...more silence...I bowed my head, pretending that I didn't hear Aslan barking.

*'Lord, if that was You, tell me...how have I left You?'*

Silence...

*You know.*

I had been sitting still for so long - I almost jumped when I heard it. I wanted to look at the clock to see how much time had actually gone by, but dared not open my eyes, in fear that I would lose the connection.

*'What do I know? Why can't You just tell me?!'*

Silence. I sat there with my head bowed for quite a while, but the voice never came back. Disappointed and a little angry, I got up and let the dog run out the back door into our fenced-in lawn. I watched him go to his favorite tree, a big sycamore in the middle of the yard, and do his business. After that, he ran to the far corner of the wooden fence and began barking at the Peterson's dog, a black toy poodle named Wuffy.

"Aslan." I said it forcibly yet controlled at first. "Aslan!" The dog wouldn't stop barking, and it was getting loud and annoying. "ASLAN!" He turned his head toward me for just a second, then continued back to his bothersome, high-pitched discussion with Wuffy.

"Oh, that's it," I muttered angrily under my breath, as I opened the back door and marched towards the corner of the yard where Aslan stood rigid as a pole. He saw me coming when I was halfway there, but gave me no sign of concern. That only annoyed me more than I already was.

My feet pounding the dirt below, I came up to Aslan and gave him a *smack* on the rear. He whimpered in shock and maybe a little bit of pain, then looked at me as if saying, 'What the heck was that for? What'd I do? I'm just being a dog!'

It all hit me at once. It came flooding in like a tidal wave of insight, fighting its way through a tiny crack of an opening that led to my brain.

*'Yeah, Aslan, you're right; you're just being a dog. And God knows I'm just being a human. 'Cept He isn't going to*

*smack me in the butt out of anger; He's going to deal with me out of love.*

'*Lord, forgive me; I know that I should be writing, and I have no excuse not to. Thank You for being such a merciful Father, and forgive me for being merciless, even though it was only towards Aslan.*

'*I want to rededicate myself to doing what You asked me to do after Dave died, no matter how hard it might be. Please Lord, be with me, and I won't be afraid.*

'*Thank You, Father. Amen.*'

I opened my eyes, and saw a pair of big brown, watery eyes staring sheepishly at me. I kneeled on the dirt and patted the ground before me. Wearily yet obediently, Aslan slowly came and sat down in front of me. His head was hanging low, as if he expected another smack.

"Oh, Aslan!" I said, inching closer and then wrapping my arms around his sizeable neck. "I'm sorry, Buddy. I'm sorry, I shouldn't've hit ya. But you can't bark that loud anymore, okay?"

Aslan panted happily, as he placed his paw on my shoulder and licked my face.

We were best friends again.

*July 13th, 2004-*
  *One of my most cherished memories is giving the*
*speech at Jon's wedding. As God has given me that moment*
*in time, so too has He placed it in my heart, so that I can*
*recall upon the joy that it brought me in times of depres-*
*sion, and that joy is everlasting, as it is from God; and He*
*by it has caused my soul to smile.*

# 47.

It was a beautiful summer day when I was wed to my love. The air outside was warm, but there was a nice breeze that kept it comfortable. Birds sang sweetly as they flew about the cloudless sky, announcing to the world the joy I felt.

Two of my proudest moments happened on that day the first was when I said "I do," the second was when Dave gave the toast at the reception...

I was a nervous wreck before the ceremony, pacing through the small room in the back of the church while we all waited for the announcement that Anne was ready. Dave was there with me, and he cracked a few jokes to help lighten the mood.

When I saw Anne slowly walking down the aisle, I almost passed out. I felt my heart tighten up, and my head swam with uncertainty. She finally made it down the aisle, her father sat down after extending me his hand, and then Anne reached out and grabbed my hand firmly. Everything went perfectly after that. It was right, her hand in mine. My nerves finally calmed, I relaxed for the rest of the ceremony and enjoyed it. This was the woman that I'd be spending the rest of my life with; I wouldn't want it any other way.

I'll never forget her smile when Anne's pastor, Pastor Roy Donovan, said the words, "You may now kiss the bride." She looked at me, her pretty, round face covered with pure joy, and mine reflecting the same. We kissed for an eternity. Not that the kiss itself was that long, but our lips are still locked to this day, ever since that moment in the church.

We ran down the aisle and into the warm sunshine, bird-seed tossed at us from all angles. After mingling with the crowd for half an hour, we, the groomsmen, and the brides-maids got into two minivans and were escorted to Anne's mother's house. That short ten minute drive turned into nearly half an hour, as we drove around the streets honking the horns and yelling out the windows.

We arrived at the small but elegant ranch house, situated nicely by a picturesque pond and small fountain in the back yard, and there we posed for the wedding pictures. After that, we celebrated by opening some bottles of champagne and downing them quickly in the warm summer heat.

After taking about a million pictures and striking a thou-sand poses, it was time to go party at the reception hall. Again, what should have been a short trip turned into a much longer one, as the vans wove through the streets of Groton, the small town where Anne had grown up. I don't think anyone minded, though; we were all having fun, hooting and hollering, as the pedestrians smiled and waved back.

Everyone was waiting for us when we got to the recep-tion hall, which was in actuality Groton Town Hall. They allowed it to be used for weddings and formal gatherings. It was spacious, easily accommodating the two hundred people, the tables, a small dance floor, and a bar.

The DJ that I hired to do the music, a man in his mid-thirties with a bald spot in the center of his head and his long, brown hair tied into a ponytail in the back, introduced us two-by-two. We walked down the center of the Hall, and the applause from the crowd erupted each time a pair was called. There was a long table with a red tablecloth draped over it at the far end of the room where the wedding party was seated. After everyone else had sat, the DJ called for everyone to stand as Anne and I were introduced "for the first time as Mr. and Mrs. Jonathon Sullah."

After the whistles and "hoo-hoo-hoo's!" and applause had quieted, the DJ introduced himself as Cliff Riff - a name that I was sure he had made up when I first spoke with him - and told everyone to ask him if they wanted a particular song to be played. He then came to our table, lifted his partially shaded glasses from his eyes, and whispered to Dave, "What's your name again?"

"Dave. Dave Sullah."

Cliff brought the microphone back up to his mouth and faced the crowd as he said, "Now it's time for the best man to give his toast. Ladies and gentlemen, let's hear it for David Sullah!"

Dave took the microphone as Cliff walked away, clapping himself as he did so. I looked up at my brother, who was now standing, looking quite uncomfortable in his fancy tux and new haircut. He waited for the applause to die down, then brought the microphone up to his lips, his baritone voice booming through the large speakers on both sides of the room: "I, uh...I have to, I mean, *you'll* have to forgive me; I'm a little nervous right now."

"No - really?" It was good old Uncle Stan, providing some humor. I couldn't see exactly where he was, but I knew his unmistakable voice.

That got Dave to smile, and some people around started to chuckle. He took a deep breath, produced a few sheets of lined paper from his inside pocket, and held them up in his somewhat shaky hand to enable him to read and look at his audience from time to time. He did a jittery dance as he spoke, slowly shifting his weight from left to right in three or four second intervals.

"Jonathon Sullah is an excellent guy. During high school he was always the smartest person in his class. He's also the most gifted athlete that Auburn High School has ever seen. He carried the baseball team to three sectional titles, and the basketball team won all its games only when Jon was on the court for the full forty minutes. He also excels in football and golf - whatever sport Jon plays, he's always the top athlete on the field."

I remember sitting there, a little embarrassed, thinking, *'Man, Dave; you're laying it on kinda thick, aren't you?'*

He was far from done.

"Jon has a great sense of humor and has always been very popular. He has many friends who enjoy his presence, because he's fun to be around. I think it's pretty safe to say that people envy Jon - they want his good looks, his charm, and his intelligence. They probably wish, even if it were only for a day, that they could be just like him."

I could feel my face turning red. *'C'mon, Dave; this is a little too much!'*

"Jon is also very humble; probably the most humble guy in the whole world, so he would never tell you these things about himself. That's just yet another of his many good traits."

Dave paused there and drew out a prolonged sigh. He set the papers down on the table and looked around the audience as he said, "You know, something was left out here, and that's how unselfish Jon is. To give you a quick example, he calls me the other day, and we got to talking about the wedding, and he asked me how my speech was coming."

A few light chuckles sounded sparsely around as Dave smiled and said, "Some of you know where I'm going with this." After a slight pause, he continued.

"And I told him, 'To tell you the truth, I got a middle and an end, but I'm having some trouble coming up with a beginning.' Jon said, 'Dave, don't even worry about it.'

Dave picked up the papers and held them up for everybody to see. "My brother took time out of his busy schedule - "

He couldn't finish the sentence - the room exploded with laughter. I shook my head and bit down on my lip, a smile on my face that felt like it stretched from ear to ear. People were clapping, slapping their knees, and wiping tears from their eyes.

After about ten seconds or so, the roar began to lighten, and Dave chuckled as he said, "I don't even have to finish the punch line; you're already laughing!"

A few more seconds passed by. Dave humbly lowered his head and accepted the crowd's response with a cheerful grin. Then he brought the microphone back up to his mouth and said, "And he wrote this for me."

More laughter - it was almost deafening. Anne's Uncle William, a large man who was seating near the front, nearly fell out of his chair. Mom was holding her stomach, laughing hysterically as she leaned back in her seat. Dad had taken his glasses off and was wiping his eyes with a napkin. I looked over at my groomsmen and saw Gary, a friend from college, hit the table so hard while he was laughing that his beer spilled all over.

Dave brought the papers back down, so he could start reading from them again. He no longer danced nervously as he spoke, and his tone changed from playful to serious as he said, "When Jon asked me to be his best man, we were golfing at Hickory Ridge."

The room became silent again, the last of the laughter finally dying down.

"At the tenth tee he asked me, 'How'd you like to be my best man for the wedding?' Now, I already had a preconception that he was going to ask me this. You see, my mother..."

He looked at Mom, sitting directly in front of us. Dave shook his head slightly and said with a grin, "I love you Mom, but you can't keep a secret."

The room laughed again, not as much as before, but-well, it really would be hard to duplicate that volume again. I read Mom's lips saying, "I'm sorry!," her voice drowned out by the audience.

"That's okay." Dave winked at her, letting Mom know that it wasn't a big deal.

"Jon must have told her about his decision before he asked me, because just about every time I talked to her, she'd say, 'Did Jon say anything to you about the wedding?'

"I knew by the happiness in her voice what she was hinting at. At first, I thought that Jon was going to ask me to be in his wedding party, but after the thirtieth time that Ma asked me that, I began to think that maybe Jon wanted me to be his best man. I thought about how cool that would be, but it never really hit me until he asked me himself on the golf course.

"I figure that he picked that particular moment to ask me, because he felt bad for me. Now, anyone that's ever been golfing with me knows that I should just stick with Putt-Putt; sometimes the divot goes farther than my ball, and I easily get agitated."

I nodded my head emphatically as laughter spread throughout the room.

"Well, by the tenth tee, Jon was beating me by like a hundred strokes, and I was just slightly angry."

Dave paused for a few moments, then lifted his head and scanned the crowd as he said, "But you should have seen the pride on my face after he asked me! All of my agitation disappeared." He dropped his head back down, keeping his eyes mostly on the paper as he read. "After a minute, the lump in my throat receded and I said, 'I'd be honored.'"

Dave looked right at me, a serious expression on his face and with glistening eyes as he said, "I *am* honored."

I felt that lump in my throat myself as Dave continued to speak. His eyes were now away from me, back to the paper and the audience...but for a good time that he read, his eyes at that moment were all that I saw.

"You see, as a little kid, Jon always took care of me. He never shunned me in front of his friends, as too many older brothers do. He did the exact opposite - he *made sure* that I was included when they played, even though I was younger and probably very annoying. And Jon's friends also accepted me. Even as a kid I could tell whether or not I was wanted. Jon picks his friends out well..."

Dave turned towards my groomsmen as he completed the sentence, "...and they were just as good to me as he was."

I looked around and saw a drastic change in the people at the reception. They were pretty much all sitting perfectly still, looking at my brother, tears in many eyes, but not from laughter.

"For a brother, I could not ask for more than what God gave me in Jon. He was a role model for me growing up, and continues to be so to this day. He is, in all seriousness, an exceptional guy who makes sacrifices to ensure the happiness of others. I want to thank him for all that he's done for me - the things that I know about..." Again Dave looked me directly in the eyes; this time mine were more watery than his. "And the things that he did for me behind the curtain."

Dave paused again and turned his attention back towards his audience. In a strained voice, he said, "I know that it must have been extremely hard for him... but he has been for me a brother, a father, and a friend."

He almost broke down. His bottom lip began to quiver, and he opened his mouth to speak, but failed. Dave covered his mouth with his hand as he stared down at the papers. I couldn't look at him, because if I did, I was sure to cry. But no one else in the room seemed to mind - I saw hardly any face that was dry or at least fighting against the tears.

Dave finally took a deep breath and swallowed, regaining his composure. "I've also got to know Anne a little, and the more that I get to know about her, the more I understand why Jon wants her for a wife. Obviously, she is very pretty-"

The reception hall filled with laughter again. Dave shook his head with a smile, which was good to see, and said, "You didn't let me finish!" The laughter died down again, and he continued. "But, *more importantly than that,* she is kind-hearted and fun to be around. They are a good pairing."

Some women throughout the room sighed, "Awww!", and, "How sweet!"

"When my Mom and Dad got married, they used a verse from Ecclesiastes as their theme, which I think is an appropriate theme for every wedding: 'A cord of three strands is not quickly broken.' Keeping that in mind, let's raise our glasses."

Everyone raised what they had; whether it be wine, champagne, beer, or water, as Dave set the papers down and looked at Anne and me. With his glass of wine tipped towards us, he toasted, "To Jon and Anne - May your love for God and your love for each other bond in such a way that it will last from now and into eternity. Amen."

"Amen!" The crowd repeated in unison. We all sipped our glasses, though I was so emotional that I nearly missed my mouth and poured my drink down my shirt.

I stood up to hug Dave, as deafening applause resounded throughout the room. I wanted to say something; I wanted to tell him how great a speech that was, how it really hit me in the core of my heart - but I was unable to say a word. All I could do was slap his back and embrace him tighter than I ever had.

I sat back down as Anne reached over me and gave Dave a hug. "Thank you," she said.

Dave put one hand on my shoulder and kept his other arm around Anne as he replied, "Thank *you*."

People were still clapping as Dave sat, and I heard my groomsmen saying, "That was great, Dave!" "Best toast I ever heard- hands down!" "Wow, man...wow!"

Cliff Riff came over and took the mike from Dave. As he turned and started walking towards the crowd he said, "I've been to a lot of weddings, and heard a lot of toasts; that was without a doubt one of the best ones I've ever heard. That... was awesome!"

Dave took it all in his humble fashion. He smiled brightly with his head bowed at the table, softly saying, "Thank you," to all the compliments thrown his way.

It was the main topic of discussion throughout the night - family members, friends, Anne's family, people I didn't quite know, all came up to me and said things like, "What a wonderful toast!" "I never knew Dave could write like that!" "Your brother could be a professional speech writer!"

But my favorite one was: "You must be so proud of your brother!"

I was. I am. I always will be.

*April 15th, 2003-*

*Farewells have their highest capacity for emotion
when no words are spoken. The friend who is departing
looks into the eyes of the friend whom he is leaving behind,
and there is a connection; one that is far more powerful
than words could say. All the good times they shared, all
the fun they had, the disputes they got in and overcame- all
the laughs, as well as the tears, are non-verbally remembered in that stare.*

*And as they embrace, their Christian hearts remind
them that this is not a goodbye; it is more like a "see you
later." And as peace flows from heart to heart, it is one to
the other, "I leave you now knowing full well that we will
meet again..." only then that they can break away from one
another, their misty eyes saying*

# 48.

My heart stopped the first time that I read what Dave
wrote on April fifteenth. In fact, the world stopped.
I was instantly taken back to that hot summer day out in
the woods...images began to flash through my mind: Dave,
kneeling down, concern on his face...*flash!*...the bloody
deer...*flash!*...Aslan's barking waking me from my shock...
*flash!*...looking into my brother's eyes as he died...

I sat there on my computer chair and wept a few
moments after reading, what I consider to be, the prophetic

entry of April fifteenth. There had been something in my last moment on Earth with my brother that I couldn't quite describe; it had been eating away at my heart. I was missing something, something important, but I couldn't quite put my finger on it.

It is my concrete belief that God inspired Dave to write what he did; not for Dave to understand, but for me. Finally, after reading it, I felt what I saw in my brother's eyes, I knew what I had felt in his embrace. My mind and my heart met at the crossroads, and I continued to bawl in praise and thanksgiving to my dear Lord and Savior, Jesus Christ.

Physically, I was sitting alone in my den; spiritually, I was in a heavenly chorus not of this realm...and my brother was there, too, singing right along with me.

---

I picked up the telephone to call home; it's funny how the place where you grew up is always called "home," no matter if you live there still or not.

"Hello?"

"Hey Ma."

"Hi Jonny! How's it going?"

"Good, pretty good. Hey; what're you doing right now?"

"Oh, not much, really. I just got back from my walk - what a gorgeous day it is outside! Uh, Dad's down in the basement trying to fix that old vacuum cleaner, and Davey just went out in the woods with his camera. Why? What's going on?"

A smile grew on my face as I responded, "Anne and I were thinking about coming over; we got a little surprise to show you."

"What is it?" Mom asked with childlike curiosity.

"You'll see."

"Oh, c'mon! Not even a hint?"

"You'll just have to wait. We'll be over in twenty minutes; do you think Dave'll be back by then?"

"I'm not sure. You know your brother - he could be out there for hours."

"Well, if he comes back before we get there, make sure he sticks around. And let Dad know we're coming, okay?"

"Okay. Eewww, I *love* surprises!" She gasped, then asked, "Is Anne pregnant?"

"No," I said, chuckling, "not yet, Ma. Soon, but not yet. See you in a bit."

"Okay. Drive safely! Love you!"

"Love you too."

I hung up the phone as Anne came into the kitchen, holding our little surprise in her arms. "Isn't he just too cute?" she said, smiling down at the little ball of golden fur she was cradling. She held the puppy as if it were a baby, lovingly looking into his half-closed eyes. Anne had helped deliver a litter of Golden Retrievers the week before, and the owner had asked if she would like one of the pups. Since we had been talking about getting a dog for a while, Anne immediately accepted. Even though I had wanted a Black Labrador, I wasn't upset in the least bit when she brought home Aslan; he *was* "just too cute"!

I walked over to Anne and crouched a little, so that I was eye-to-eye with our little puppy. I spoke baby talk to him; something that I'd never do with anyone but Anne around. "Hey there, wittle dawgy! You wanna go fo' a wide? You do, don't ya?" I scratched the top of his head with just one finger; Aslan was still too tiny for me to use my whole hand.

Anne set him carefully on the ground, as if he were a breakable vase, and said, "C'mon Aslan, let's go see your Grandma and Grandpa!" Looking at the small puppy as he cautiously took a few steps across the kitchen floor, it seemed preposterous that we had named him "Aslan", after the great lion from C.S. Lewis' The Chronicles of Narnia.

Mom had read the series to Dave and me when we were kids, and it seemed like the perfect name for our Golden Retriever. Well, he'd have to grow into it, but in time he'd resemble that lion.

Anne went upstairs to change into some khaki shorts and a T-shirt that Mom and Dad had bought for her on their honeymoon to Jamaica while I strapped a collar on Aslan. He hated the collar. Whenever we put it on him, he'd scratch at it with his hind legs and try to bite at it with his tiny, yet sharp, teeth. Little Aslan fought with that collar as if it were his mortal enemy until Anne came back into the kitchen.

"You ready?"

"Yeah," she said, putting her long blonde hair into a ponytail. "Your car or mine?"

"Let's take yours," I responded while clipping a leash to Aslan's collar.

"Okay. Just make sure he wets before you put him in; I don't want any messes in my car."

Fifteen minutes and one mess later, we arrived at the little yellow ranch house and parked in front of the garage. Anne hurriedly rushed inside for some paper towels, fearing that the small spot Aslan had left in her back seat might leave a stain.

I lifted Aslan out of Anne's red Sunfire and carried him to the grass on the side of the house, wanting to make sure that he would leave no further messes anywhere. The grass wasn't too long, but Aslan still had to lift his paws higher than usual as he slowly walked around. He lifted his head and sniffed around, then planted his tiny pink nose in the grass by a small pine tree that Dad had planted near the middle of the back lawn. Aslan lifted his leg, a little unsteadily, then let out a small squirt of urine.

"Good boy!" I congratulated him emphatically and bent down and rubbed his head. He closed his eyes and accepted my praise with his head held high, as if he had just accomplished a remarkable feat.

We walked slowly back towards the house, deterred at times because of Aslan's infatuation with the wind as it gently blew through the grass. He'd crouch low to the ground, wait a few seconds, and then pounce at the invisible disturbance that made the grass flow in different directions.

It was a near-perfect day, so I had no objections to staying outside for a while. It was warm, but not hot; comfortable, not sweltering. A few puffy clouds, which looked like the artwork of God, floated lazily in the otherwise bright blue sky. Birds sang their incomprehensible sweet songs and children were laughing somewhere across the street. Did I say it was a near-perfect day? No, it was perfect!

Anne hadn't come out of the house yet to clean her backseat, which didn't surprise me. She and Mom had more than likely struck up a conversation. Anne and Mom both loved to talk. They could get into a conversation about nothing that lasted forever.

I thought it would be good to go in there now and give Anne a chance to soak up the mess Aslan had left; it really was just a small spot, maybe a little larger than a half-dollar, but I knew that if Anne couldn't get it to come out, it'd somehow be all my fault.

"C'mon, Aslan, let's go inside!" I said with enthusiasm. He started trotting after me through the lawn, and I picked him up and carried him into the side door of the garage. I walked through the front door and, just as I had figured, Anne and Mom were talking by the kitchen sink. When Mom saw me come in, she immediately turned towards me. Her eyes widened, and her smile grew even larger when she saw Aslan.

"Ooooh, a puppy!" she exclaimed as I set him on the linoleum floor. Aslan started sniffing the floor, cautiously checking out his new surroundings. Mom gave me a hug and then bent over to pick up Aslan.

"Be careful," Anne warned. "He gets excited pretty easily, and he'll mess all over you."

Mom didn't seem to care; I'm not sure if she had even heard her. She snuggled Aslan close to her cheek. He turned and licked her face. "Oh! He's adorable!"

I went into the cupboard and grabbed some paper towels. "Do you want to clean it up," I asked Anne, "or should I?"

"Oh my gosh, I almost forgot!" She grabbed the roll of towels and said to Mom, "I'll be right back. Aslan peed in my car."

"Honey!" Mom called out as Anne went outside. "Come see what our boy brought over!"

"I'm coming," Dad answered back from downstairs. I heard some heavy footsteps coming up the stairs, then Dad appeared in the kitchen. He was wearing some old jeans and an even older t-shirt, which at one point had been white but was now completely covered in grease; some spots were fresh, some were old and crusted on. "Oh, what've we got here?" Dad said with a large grin on his face. Mom held Aslan up proudly, and Dad petted his tiny head. After lavishing some attention on Aslan, Dad stepped up to me and gave me a firm handshake. His hands were so rough and calloused, but his presence was so warm and inviting. "Is he a purebred?"

"Yeah," I nodded, "one-hundred percent Golden Retriever. Anne delivered a litter about a week ago, and we got Aslan for free."

"You named him Aslan?" Mom asked, still smiling, as Anne came back inside.

"Yup. You know where that comes from, right?"

"Of course! The Chronicles of Narnia; I used to read that to you and Davey when you were little."

"Hey Anne," Dad said, giving her a hug. At six foot-two, Dad had to bend down to hug Anne, but he was use to having to do that with Mom.

"Where's Dave? Still in the woods?"

"I think so," Dad answered. "He's making another collage."

"Have you seen your brother's artwork lately?" Mom asked, obviously quite impressed by her tone of voice and the expression on her face. I shook my head no. "Oh, you ought to, Jon. Your brother is becoming quite the artist."

I leaned forward towards Aslan with a huge smile covering my face. "You wanna go for a walk?" I asked with great enthusiasm in my voice. Immediately, Aslan began to struggle to try to get out of Mom's firm hold. She let him to the floor, and he joyfully leapt up to just below my waist and jumped again several times. I grabbed the leash that was still around his neck and said, "I'm gonna go look for Dave; you want to come, Anne?"

After a moment's thought, she answered, "Sure."

"We'll be right back," I said as Aslan bounded out the door.

"Okay," Dad called back. "Have fun!"

Our back lawn stretched out for acres, and for the most part, it was all wooded. My Grandpa Sullah had owned the land before giving it over to Mom. He had cut some paths through the woods before he moved South, so that Mom could take her walks through them. Dave and I had also used the woods a lot while we were growing up. We played hide-and-seek when we were kids, and then the game graduated to squirt-gun wars and pretend battles when we were teens. Some of our friends would come over, and we'd start out on different ends of the woods; Dave and his buddies were the Rebels, and my friends and I were the Yanks. We'd spend hours sneaking through the paths with sticks, held like rifles, in our hands, creeping up on each other as best we could and yelling, "BAM! You're dead!"

Mom didn't like us running through the woods at first; she was afraid that some trigger-happy hunter might mistake us for a deer. But Grandpa had posted signs all around, warning that this was private property, and hunting wasn't allowed. So Mom let us and the other kids go in the woods, only if we wore some bright clothing, which made our war games a lot more difficult - but it eased Mom's worries.

There was only one path in which to enter the woods, and then the path branched out in several places, creating a maze-like environment. Aslan was leading the way, sniffing the many trees and leaving his mark on one every twenty feet or so. His small tail wagged with excitement, going a mile a minute, as if it were battery powered. After about five minutes of walking Anne asked, "Do you think we should just yell out Dave's name? I don't think we'll ever find him if we don't."

"Naw," I said, shaking my head. "Aslan will find him, won't cha, buddy?" He looked back at me with his tongue hanging down; apparently Aslan already knew his name. As if in response to my question, he yelped a short, high-pitched bark and then turned around and kept trotting down the path.

Anne reached out and took my hand as we followed Aslan. He came to a fallen tree that was too big for him to cross, so we had to backtrack a little. On the way, a chipmunk that was sitting in the middle of an intersecting path sparked Aslan's curiosity. He crouched low and barked, but the chipmunk didn't seem intimidated. So Aslan decided to run after it, but he was held back a little by my lack of speed. The chipmunk easily made his escape up a nearby tree and calmly stared at Aslan as he barked at it.

By now, we were at the edge of our property. About twenty yards ahead of us, the woods cleared and gave way to an old cornfield. Our neighbor down the street, Joe Eldredder, had owned and farmed the land for forty years. He was too old to do so now, and the ten acres of land would go unused until he could find a buyer for it.

"Well, this is the end of the line," I said, bending down to pick up Aslan. He looked tired from all the walking, and I liked to hold him, anyway. He licked my cheek a few times before Anne said, "Ewww, gross! Don't let him do that!"

I smiled and turned my head away from Aslan, so that he'd stop licking me. As I looked out towards the farmland, something caught my attention. I strained my neck towards it and squinted, trying to get a better angle through all the tree limbs.

There was something out there.

The cornfield hadn't been planted or harvested for years, but nature had done its best to keep the corn growing. There were stalks sprouting in miscellaneous spots around the field; most of them were either dead or dying, due to the lack of rain and upkeep by a farmer. They weren't in rows like most cornfields; there was no pattern to where the stalks grew, just nature's own.

"What're you looking at?" Anne asked, as she came beside me and stared out to where I was looking.

I squinted my eyes and took a few steps forward...there seemed to be a...what was it?

"Here," I said, not taking my eyes off the lump-like object lying too far in the distance to make out. "Take Aslan." I slowly broke out of the trees and stepped in the field. The dry dirt was harder than I'd thought it'd be, almost like clay. I heard Anne following behind me.

The tallest cornstalk in the field was only about shoulder-height, so I could easily see over all of them. I pushed past one every five feet or so, making my way towards the middle of the field when - it moved. It wasn't just a pile of rocks or dirt; it was alive.

I was moving faster towards it now, my heart thumping with curiosity and fear. Whatever it was, it was hurt. It had moved ever so slightly, then became still again.

"Jon!" Anne called out behind me. "What's going on?"

Before I could answer her, Dave popped up a few yards away from the thing, waving his arms in the air. He had been hidden from my sight behind a few stalks, whereas whatever he was standing next to was, for the most part, in clear sight.

"Shhh!" he said, putting a finger under his nose.

I turned around and looked at Anne with a confounded expression on my face. Her eyebrows were furrowed, her mouth half-opened; she was just as confused as I was. Aslan didn't seem concerned. He sat comfortably in Anne's arms, the glare from the sun causing his tiny brown eyes to squint.

I stopped walking and softly asked, "What's going on?" I shrugged my shoulders and held my palms up, just in case my brother couldn't hear me.

Dave motioned for us to come over.

He was standing with his hands on his hips; his eyes now fixated on...it looked like a big brown ball of fur. He was wearing a Yankees cap and had his Nexion wide-angled camera strapped around his neck. Dave stood motionless over whatever he was staring at for a few moments, then crouched down next to it.

Anne caught up to me, and we walked together. When we came within fifteen yards of Dave, I finally figured out what had attracted my attention. It was a deer, lying on the ground with his back to me. His head rested on the side, one set of antlers digging into the dirt.

I came within five feet of it and stopped. I had never seen a deer so close before; it seemed gigantic. His horns boasted twelve ivory points, strong and majestic in form. The deer's eyes were half-closed, his nostrils flaring in and out. There was a pool of crimson seething out from the side that he was lying on, merging with the dusty ground and turning it maroon.

"It's shot," Dave said softly, staring at the helpless deer. "I can't tell how bad, though. Whaddya think, Anne?" He looked up at my wife, his eyes wide, caring and hopeful.

"Oh, I don't know...there's probably nothing that we can do for it. Poor guy..."

Dave looked back at the deer, disappointment clearly evident on his face. He reached out to touch it, and Anne said, "I wouldn't get too close, Dave. Animals are unpredictable, especially when they're wounded."

Dave shook his head, his melancholy expression never changing. "I've been with him for at least half an hour now; he knows I ain't here to hurt him." He stood halfway up and loomed over the deer, resting his hands for a moment on his knees. After a deep sigh, he said, "Well, maybe if we can see how bad you're hurt..." He slowly reached down and gently touched the deer's underbelly.

"Dave, what're you-"

I was cutoff in mid-sentence when the deer suddenly kicked his front legs in the air and turned himself so that he was slightly sitting up. In one swift motion, he cocked his head away from Dave and then thrust his antlers into my brother's exposed side. The deer jerked his head back to the right; his antlers were dug so deeply into Dave's side that he was nearly picked off the ground. The buck then bowed its formidable head, ripping his antlers from Dave's rib section, and shot up from the ground and ran across the farmland towards the woods.

My brother fell face-first to the ground, an expression of shock and horror cemented on his face.

For a few seconds that were an eternity, I could not move. I couldn't blink, I couldn't breathe...my mind had completely shut down. I stood there and stared at Dave, but it was like

I was staring past him. I saw him twitching on the ground, but it wasn't real. I recalled seeing a deer tearing into his flesh just a few seconds ago, but that never really happened. I heard Anne's screams, and saw as she fell down by Dave, but that was just my imagination.

Anne was on her knees, frantically calling out Dave's name, turning him over so that he was now facing upward. She spun around towards me, her eyes bulging, face red, eyes watering. She screamed something, but no words came out of her mouth.

*What's going on? When did I fall asleep? I don't like this dream...I want to wake up.*

"Rrrruufffff! Ruurrrr! Ruff-ruff!"

I looked down and saw Aslan staring up at me. His leash hung limply from his collar.

*Aslan? Anne? Why aren't you holding onto Aslan?*

"Rurrrr! Rur-ruf-rruuuuurrr-ruf!"

*Man, it's hot out here!*

"Gggrrrruffffff!"

*What do you want, boy? You wanna play? Well, let's.....*

*Anne? Dave? Oh, no...no, no, dear God, no...*

*This is real.*

"Dave?" I said it so feebly that it was barely audible.

Anne had her hands pressed against Dave's side; they had turned dark purple. Dave was squirming on the ground, his mouth stretched open and his eyes wide with pain. I fell down on my knees beside Anne, the initial shock now wearing off. My brother had been gored by a deer. Its antlers had ripped open the flesh over his rib cage, and had pulled out some innards along with it as it withdrew. Dave's side was mangled...he was struggling very hard to breathe...he had already lost a massive amount of blood, and the flow wasn't stopping...his eyes were becoming vacant...he was going to die.

"No!" I screamed out in response to my own thought. Anne looked at me with a mixture of surprise and confusion on her face. "Go get Dad!" I shouted at her. She didn't move, just kept staring at me. "*Go! Run!*"

Anne took one last look at Dave, then hurried off towards the woods.

I placed my hands where Anne's had been, applying some pressure to Dave's wound. Dark, warm blood oozed through my fingers.

*What do I do? WhatdoIdowhatdoIdowhatdoIdo? Dear Lord, don't take him!*

"Dave? Dave, can you hear me?" His eyes stared lazily towards the sky above. He had stopped squirming; his face showed hardly any emotion at all. His elbows rested on the dirt, and his hands looked like claws, raised motionless in the air. "Dave! You're gonna be alright, do you hear me?"

He didn't respond, didn't move an inch. His breathing had become more labored, and soon I heard a gargling sound every time he tried to breathe. All of a sudden, his upper body began to convulse, and his face went from pale to red to a faint blue color. "Dave!!" Tears started flowing like a waterfall down my cheek. "Dave! You have to breathe! You have to!"

He threw back his head and coughed up a large puddle of blood that rolled down his lips and ran down the side of his neck. After that, his wheezing became extremely intense; he was fighting for air, but not getting it.

"Oh God," I said aloud through my tears, staring up at the cloudless sky. "Heal my brother, in Jesus' precious name, heal him! Don't let him die...oh God!"

I took my hands away from Dave's side and buried my head on his stomach. I wailed loud, grief-stricken, helpless cries until my throat was sore.

Suddenly, I felt a hand on my shoulder. I picked my head up and saw my brother, straining to sit up as he looked at me.

I instantly cradled his head with my left arm and as gently as possible brought his head up from the dirt. His head was shaking, as if he was freezing cold, but his eyes stayed fixated on mine.

"Dave..." It was all I could say.

His hand went from my shoulder to around my neck, and with surprising strength, he pulled me close. His chin rested on my shoulder, and he slung his other arm around my neck. I threw my other arm around him, held him as tight as I dared, which proved to be not tight enough for Dave. I was worried that I'd hurt him even more, but he apparently didn't care. He pulled me into a vise-like grip for a few seconds; then his strength gave way. His body suddenly turned into a wet noodle, and I was sure that he was gone.

I kept him close to me, not wanting to know that he was dead. I refused to pull away and look at his lifeless face. I would stay there forever if I had to.

I closed my eyes and bowed my head towards the ground, resting my chin on my brother's back.

*Dave, Dave...why did you have to take pictures today? Why did you go into the woods? Why did you have to see that stupid deer? If you had just stayed inside today, we'd all be together in the living room, playing with Aslan. You shouldn't be here...this isn't right.*

Then I heard it; Dave was wheezing again. He wasn't dead!

With newfound hope, I pulled back from Dave and slowly let him back down a little, still cradling him with my arms behind his neck and back. I held his head a few feet from the ground, as new tears began exploding from my eyes - he wasn't going to make it. I knew it. I didn't want to know it, but I did. Dave had lost more blood than I ever thought was in a human body, his eyes had almost completely rolled up in his head, and blood was now trickling out of his mouth like a water fountain.

I mustered up all the composure that I possibly could and held Dave straight up in my arms, so that we were face to face. I swallowed a huge lump and tried to speak, but I couldn't. All I wanted to do was tell my brother I loved him, I wanted to tell him how unfair this was, how much he meant to me. I couldn't. Any words that I could have come up with would have done no justice to my true feelings.

I just lost it. My whole body went weak, and I had to let Dave down on his back. My arms just couldn't hold him anymore. I fell over on my side and wept so hard my face started to hurt. My cheek was buried in a mixture of blood and dirt when I heard a "Hhhhuucccch!" I opened my eyes without moving anything else. Then I heard it again: "Hhhucch!" It was Dave, making a noise like he was coughing up a hairball.

I slowly lifted my head and wiped some dirt from my eyes. Dave made the noise again, and I got to my knees by his side and looked down at him.

*Was that...? No; I must have imagined it. Wait- there it is again! Yes...I can't believe it!*

Dave was smiling - or at least, making his best attempt to. The corners of his mouth twitched up, shakily, but it was clear to me that he was trying to smile. I put my hand under his head, so that he could look at me without straining his neck.

For a moment, we just stared at each other, and although I could hardly believe it, a smile had grown on my face as well.

After a few seconds, Dave slowly nodded his head. His wheezing started up again, louder and scarier than before. I bit my bottom lip when I saw the tears form in his eyes. I knew that he was in tremendous pain; but all he did was smile and nod his head, as if everything was alright.

He closed his eyes, his lips trembling, as tears flowed down his face and into the blood that had soaked up around his neck.

"Dave..." I said through gasps of catching my breath, as I cried uncontrollably. *"Dave, I love you! I..."*

Dave's eyes popped open and stared at me. I couldn't describe it...there was something in them. Something that made me feel warm...something that made me feel like my brother wasn't dying in my arms.

He reached out his hand, and I grabbed it. It was shaking, along with the rest of his body...but I hardly noticed. All I noticed was Dave's eyes. They were telling me something... something I couldn't quite comprehend. Those big brown eyes; they were so peaceful, so unafraid, so filled with love...

The faint smile disappeared from his face. His wheezing subsided; his eyes lost the message they were trying to send to me.

Dave was dead.

*January 8th, 2003-*
  *In life, where everything happens for a reason, it's tough sometimes to make sense of it all. Lord, help me. Be with me always. In Jesus' name, Amen.*

# 49.

"...if not, then we could ask Pastor Stan. Maybe he should do it, anyway."

I had only caught the last half of Mom's sentence. The last twenty-four hours of my life seemed more like twenty years. I had gotten no sleep, and was zoning in and out of reality.

Coffee. That's right, there was a mug of coffee sitting before me on Mom and Dad's dining room table. I took a sip, hoping that it would perk me up a little.

"I'm sorry, Ma," I said, shaking my head slightly. "What'd you say?"

Mom smiled at me sympathetically from across the table and said softly, "We don't have to talk about it now, if you don't want to. Dad said that maybe he should do most of the arrangements himself."

"No, I'm...I'm fine," I lied. "I just didn't hear you."

She laid her pen down on top of the blue spiral notebook that was opened in front of her and leaned towards me. "The eulogy. I know I can't do it, it'd be...too hard." For obvious reasons, just thinking about it made Mom's bottom lip tremble and caused her throat to tighten up so badly that she could barely talk. She cleared her throat and put her hand to her chest. She was still wearing the same clothes that she had on yesterday; a faded purple cotton t-shirt and a pair of old blue jeans. But as her hand went to her chest, I noticed that she had strapped a necklace around her neck. It was a shiny, golden heart with *Mom* stenciled in the center, a gift from Dave last Mother's Day.

Mom certainly wasn't the only one surrounding herself with memories of Dave...

Our family came over the moment that they heard the news. First Aunt Sheila, then Uncle Frank, Aunt Harriet, Bernie and Uncle Stan. We all tried to console each other, but for the most part all we could do was cry and hug for a long period of time.

Pastor Stan had come over in the evening, and said many prayers for us all. He had tried to keep his composure, but looked just about as distraught as anyone else. It was obvious that he loved Dave.

Everyone left Mom and Dad's just before midnight, except Anne and I. We decided that we'd stay and sleep on the couch. After an hour of restless tossing and turning, I got up and poured myself a drink of water.

Everything around me was the same as it had always been: the lights in the kitchen came on when I turned the switch, water flowed nicely from the faucet, the refrigerator hummed...but I didn't want it to be like that. My brother had just died. Why are things working like they normally did? My world had completely changed; nothing should work right now. Nothing should be as it is. Nothing.

I sat the empty glass in the sink and took a deep breath.

Dave...he wasn't here. He never would be again. We'd unknowingly played our last game of golf together just the week before. I'd never talk with him again about sports, about theology, about girls, about anything. He'd never be an uncle to my kids, he'd never give me another of his trade-mark horribly wrapped presents, I'd never hear his laugh, see his face, give him a hug.

It wasn't fair! It wasn't right! How could God take away someone like my brother? A kind, caring, thoughtful man in his prime, devoted to the Lord, and filled with so much promise and talent? He had made a mistake; that was it. God, You really messed up.

I sighed and bowed my head as I leaned up against the sink counter.

*Lord...*

Lord what? 'Lord, are You there?' 'Lord, were You asleep when that deer took away Dave's life?' 'Lord, are You *really* in control?'

No. My thoughts scared me. Of course God was there, He surely hadn't fallen asleep, and yes, He is in control. But...

*Lord God, You know my thoughts. You know how desper-ately I need You right now. I...I just don't have the words. Jesus, be my intercessor. I can't speak.*

I stood still with my head bowed, the room completely silent except for the refrigerator's humming. Time passed by - five minutes, half an hour, I don't know.

Nothing changed. I was still heart-broken, still dumb-founded as to why God had allowed Dave to die, still trying to fight the fact that he was indeed gone.

I opened my eyes. The linoleum floor was blurry due to my tears. I wiped my eyes and ran my hands through my hair. I wanted to sleep. I wanted to be unconscious for as long as possible. I couldn't go back to the foldout couch and expect to rest; all I'd do was lay there and think about Dave. What if I went down to his room? Maybe sleeping in his bed would give me some comfort, or perhaps it would allow me to cry myself to sleep.

I went through the kitchen and slowly opened the down-stairs door. The hinges creaked every time it was opened, and I didn't want to wake up Anne. I wanted to be alone.

I walked down the carpeted steps and came to Dave's door. Maybe he was in there. Maybe I'd open the door and see him sleeping on the bed. Maybe this was all a nightmare; yes, that was it! Just like in the movies, Dave's death was all a bad dream! Of course! Dave can't be dead, there's no way...

I opened the door and peeked inside. The lights were off. Maybe...maybe if I didn't turn them on, then it was still possible that Dave was really in there. Maybe I could go back upstairs and pretend that all was well. Maybe...

Jon - what're you thinking? Turn them on.

I slowly slid my hand against the wall and found the light switch. I flicked it up, and the lamp in the corner of the small room came on. I sighed deeply, somewhat because my hope was gone, somewhat because I felt like a fool. No Dave, of course.

I stepped inside and shut the door. The room was a mess - just as Dave had left it. Books and papers were scattered all about the floor, and his small walk-in closet was overflowing with dirty clothes and art supplies. I cautiously made my way to the bed and sat down.

One of the walls was covered with photographs: family pictures, pictures of nature and animals, photos of Dave with Susie. Some artwork that he had done was also pinned up on the wall: two collages on poster board, both filled with awe-inspiring photos of the woods, sunsets or sunrises, and with every season of the year utilized in each. Three wood-burnings that my brother had done were hung near the corner of the wall: one of Jesus holding a baby in his arms and smiling down at him, another of the empty tomb, the sun rising in the background, which Dave had entitled "The Son Rises," written in beautiful calligraphy at the top. The last was a close-up of Jesus' dejected-looking face, deep scars and blood trickling down, wearing His crown of thorns. Calvary Hill was in the backdrop with three crosses standing on top, and in the hill Dave had written, "The punishment that brought us peace was upon Him, and by His wounds we are healed." (from Isaiah).

At my feet by the bed laid about a half-dozen books, all with bookmarks sticking out from the ruffled pages. Books by Frank Perreti, Max Lucado, Charles Stanley, C.S. Lewis, a daily devotional by Charles Spurgeon, and the most worn-looking book of them all, Dave's NIV translation of the Bible.

A painting of Jesus hugging a man as he enters Heaven hung over Dave's bed, and there were many handwritten verses from the Bible tacked up all around it:

"When pride comes, then comes disgrace, but with humility comes wisdom." –(Proverbs 11:2)

"So then, each of us will give an account of himself to God." (Romans 14:12)

"Blessed are the poor in spirit, for theirs is the kingdom of Heaven." (Matthew 5:3)

Two identical wooden bookcases, both about four feet tall and three feet wide, sat across from Dave's bed where his TV used to be. They were packed full of Christian literature, fiction and non-fiction alike. On top of one of the bookcases was a painting Dave had done of the United States' flag, looking as if it were gently blowing in the wind. Over the flag in big, black paint he had wrote "America Bless God".

After looking around Dave's room, I noticed how quiet it was. Too quiet. Quiet enough to hear my thoughts, to concentrate on my feelings. I ran my hand through my hair; then tugged on it a little. I felt an anger burning in my heart as I gritted my teeth. The anger rose- I felt its heat rising up through my esophagus. It stopped just below my jaw, which was tightly clenched...then burst forth from my mouth.

I screamed through my teeth; it wasn't loud enough to wake up anybody, but its unbridled rage certainly scared me. It was filled with angst; helplessness, hurt, confusion, sorrow and bitterness, all entwined verbally as simply, "Errrrrahhhhhhhhh!"

I was breathing heavily, exhaling through my nostrils, still gripping onto some strands of hair on my brow. I felt like any second I would go crazy, but I couldn't help it. I almost didn't even care.

*This isn't you; you're not acting like yourself. Calm down.*

I took a few deep breaths and sighed. I released my grip on my hair and covered my eyes with my hand as I leaned forward on Dave's bed, my elbow resting on my knee.

A shiver ran through my body - what was that? What had just happened? I had been utterly consumed by anger, hate even. My eyes popped open wide and my entire being went limp as I discovered Who that hate was against.

"Lord God," I said aloud with my eyes now closed, moisture immediately protruding from my lids. "Forgive me. Lord, I am a terrible man...You are so good..."

My mind was saying it, but my heart wasn't believing it. Something was wrong...

*'Tell them to leave.'*

What? My heart raced, pounding as fast as the fluttering of a butterfly's wings inside my chest.

*'You don't want them here; good. Tell them to leave.'*

I paused a moment, not moving a muscle. I knew what the voice meant: there was something in the room besides the silence and me.

"I rebuke you, Satan, in Jesus' name! Get away from me!" I said it with strength and conviction, even though I had never done it before. I had been skeptical, to say the least, about demonic influence up until then, but not anymore. A tingling flush of electricity covered every inch of my flesh, from my hair to my toes, and all at once I was at peace.

I jumped down off the bed and knelt beside it, resting my elbows on the mattress. "Father, Creator of all that is, Maker of my soul, Ruler over the heavens and the earth: Lord, I know that You are here with me, I know that You have never left me, not for one second!" I spoke softly, as tears poured down my cheeks. They were tears of unbridled thanksgiving and love. "Father, I need You so desperately...I don't know what to do, I don't know what to think. I'm scared, Lord. Comfort me, sweet Jesus, Lord God! Fill me with Your wisdom, Your strength...Lord, You have a plan. Live in me and through me, so that Your will is accomplished. I cannot do this...but I know that You can. Lord God, may Your perfect and loving will be done!"

My throat had had it; it could squeeze out no more words. I bowed my forehead on the bed while my shoulders shook as I cried. After a minute, I climbed up on the bed and laid down, my wrist pressed up against my forehead, as if I had just expended all of my energy in a marathon.

There must not be an unending supply of tears in the eye ducts, and after a long time had passed, it seemed as if I had used all of mine for the moment. I rolled over on my side and looked down at the floor. My eyes caught hold of something that I had never seen before - lying amongst my brother's books was a maroon covered journal with three golden crosses on the front, the middle one slightly larger than the other three.

Curious, I reached down and picked it up. I looked at it closely , sitting on his bed. On the cover beneath the crosses, faintly written in Dave's handwriting was:

**Life is neither yesterday nor tomorrow, but only now. When eternity comes, life will be forever. But until then, life is only now - and now should be lived with eternity in mind. Amen.**

I read it over and over - had Dave really written that? Or was he quoting someone? I knew that my brother could write, but that sounded like...

*Sounded like what?* I thought. *Sounded like something too deep, too profound, to come out of your brother's mind? No; that sounded just like Dave... I wonder what else is in here?*

I felt a little bad about it at first, as if I was invading my brother's privacy. Maybe I'd just take a quick look.

I opened to the beginning of the journal. Each entry was dated, each written in Dave's sloppy handwriting. I started reading, and soon found that I was unable to stop.

It wasn't a personal record of what my brother did everyday, like a diary; it was an account of his thoughts, his feelings, his insight into the scriptures, prayers to God... seemingly every emotion, hardship, failure, or triumph that life brought him was unabashedly written down, words of which were filled with the wisdom and faith of a man devoted to the Lord.

Before I knew it, I had reached the end. There were more pages in the journal, but they were all blank, beyond what was written at the top of the page, probably around two-thirds of the way into the journal. I took a deep breath as I saw that there was no more writing after it...it was Dave's last entry.

I paused before I let my eyes read it, not wanting to reach the end, but at the same time desperately wanting to know what my brother's last thoughts were. Maybe he somehow knew that his time was coming, and had written some comforting last words. Words that said goodbye, I love you, and this all happened for a reason.

I held my breath and began reading.

*The wounded butterfly! It all makes sense now! Lord God, You are so wonderful, so amazing! Yes, I understand now...*

*I know that You have used me, and how great a feeling that is! Your work is unimaginably beautiful, and You have incorporated me in it! Oh Lord, praise Your holy name forever! Continue to bless him in every way, may he spread the name of Jesus throughout the land, and may he never tire in doing what You have preordained him to. May he marvel forever at Your greatness...may he see it as I do now. Amen, Lord! You are awesome!*

Huh? That wasn't what I was hoping for. What was "the wounded butterfly" supposed to mean? It certainly made no sense to me.

I closed the journal and set it down next to me on the bed. I glanced over at Dave's digital clock and was surprised to find that it was almost five in the morning. The sun was making its way up over the horizon, and I could hear the birds chirping through the small window that was just below the ceiling.

'Hmmm,' I thought, *'Dave'd probably be going to sleep right around now.'*

I took one last look around the room, then went upstairs to brew some coffee.

"What do you think?" Mom asked, her eyes wide with concern, her eyebrows lifted high. She paused, as if she didn't want to say it, as if she was wondering why she even had to say it. "About Davey's eulogy? I should probably just ask Pastor Stan, right?"

My heart leapt up to my throat, like I was going down a free-fall on some imaginary roller coaster. "No," I said, a little louder than I meant to, "I'm gonna do it. I want to do it."

Mom smiled at me and reached across the table with her palms up. I took her hands as she said, "Good, honey. I'm glad...I think Davey would've liked that."

She talked on about the wake, the funeral, floral arrangements, what to inscribe on Dave's tombstone...

I sat there and mostly just nodded, staring at the table. Ma seemed to have everything under control; well, the planning, at least. Her eyes were glistening and bloodshot, her face was pale, her voice weak and strained. I was sure that she was probably going through what I was going through - a complete lack of sleep, lack of answers, an abundance of questions and anguish.

I couldn't pay much attention to what Mom was saying. There had been something eating at me ever since I said that I'd do Dave's eulogy. Why it popped into my mind then and for what reason, I didn't know. All I knew was that it was there, and it wasn't going away.

Dad came into the dining room and bent over to give Mom a big hug. He stood up straight behind her and gently rubbed her back, tears trickling down from his solemn eyes. Dad had volunteered to break the news to the people who hadn't heard yet. Everyone in the church had learned, thanks to the prayer chain; and, of course, our family already knew about it, but there were others who didn't. I had written down some friends of Dave's that I knew about, and Dad called them and also the restaurant that Dave had worked at. I knew that it was going to be tough, and I could tell by the dejection in Dad's face that he had had a really hard time with it.

"How's everything going?" he asked softly. The ever-present cheerfulness in his voice and on his face was replaced with despondency. I had never seen Dad this way.

Mom looked over her shoulder and answered by giving him a "best-as-you-can-expect-under-the-circumstances" half-hearted smile. "How about you? Did you get a hold of everybody?"

Dad took off his glasses and wiped the tears from his weary eyes. "Yes. I called his work..." He shook his head, and then had to wipe away some fresh tears. "I...it was just awful. The poor lady who answered the phone!"

Dad sat down next to Mom at her beckoning, and she laid her head on his broad shoulder. He slowly began explaining what had happened. Apparently, the young lady who answered the restaurant's telephone had thought that it was some sort of a sick practical joke. She had laughed when Dad said that Dave was dead, and it made him sick to have to repeat it to her, and say that it wasn't a laughing matter. Then the phone went silent for a few seconds. Dad thought that he had lost the connection, but it turned out that the girl was either too shocked or too embarrassed to speak. She had handed the telephone over to her manager without a word, and Dad had to again explain why Dave wouldn't be coming to work ever again.

"How about his friends?" I asked after a few moments of painful silence filled the dining room. "Did you get a hold of them?"

"Most I spoke to personally, yes," Dad replied, still hanging his head a little, as if it weighed a ton. "But for a couple, I had to give the news to their parents and ask them to pass it along. They know where the funeral is, and what time to be there.

"The, uh, the manager seemed like a nice guy. He said that he'd let everyone at work know, and that anyone who wanted the day off to attend the funeral would have it."

Mom wrapped her arm around Dad's back and gently massaged his shoulder, as the silence returned. It was eating away at me, causing my head to swim and my heart to pound so loud that I thought my parents could surely hear it.

Mom wouldn't understand what I wanted to do, but Dad might. "Umm, Dad?"

"Um-hmm?"

"I, uh...I want to get that deer. I want to make sure he's dead."

At first, he just stared at me without saying anything or even moving a muscle. Then he got up, pushed in his chair and said, "I'll get my gun."

Mom looked at me with confusion evident on her face. "It's just something I have to do, Ma."

Dad came back from the bedroom, the keys to his tool shed in hand. "We won't be long," he said. "Will you be okay?"

"Yes," she responded, but a look of concern in her eyes said otherwise. "But do you really need to do this?"

Dad gave me a quick glance and said, "I think so, yes. Don't worry; we'll be careful." He bent down to give Mom a kiss atop her poofy blonde hair.

"Okay," she said warily and followed us to the front door. "Hurry back! I love you!"

"Love you, too," Dad and I answered back in unison.

Dad and Dave had built a small tool shed for all of Dad's farm equipment and other items that he couldn't fit into the basement. They had worked on it together for two months, and although it was small it was still impressive. It was laid perfectly flat on a slab of concrete next to the garage in the back lawn, and not one board was crooked. The shed was nicely painted in a bright cherry red color, and the trim and door were painted white.

Dad opened the door and walked in. I waited outside, my hands in my pockets, trying to seem as casual as possible, while feeling anything but.

He came out of the shed and relocked the door. "You ever shot one of these?" he asked, holding up his twelve-gauge shotgun.

"Yeah, me and my uncles went deer hunting back there all the time," I said, looking out towards the woods.

"Oh yeah, that's right. I remember your mother telling me something about that."

He handed me the gun, and we walked into the woods in silence. There was nothing for either of us to say. We both knew why we wanted to kill that deer, and we also knew how ridiculous it was.

Dad finally broke the silence, as we crossed through the woods and into the old cornfield. "How badly was it hurt?"

"Pretty bad," I said as I surveyed the field. All I saw was broken stalks of corn. "It looked like it was shot through the gut."

"Um...which way did it run?" he asked softly.

I pointed to the woods on the other side of the cornfield and replied, "Out there somewhere. I'm not really sure how far it got."

He held out his hand and looked up towards the darkening sky. "It's starting to sprinkle." As soon as he said that, a rumble of thunder came from overhead.

"Alright, let's be quick," I said, taking hurried steps onto the crusty dirt. Hearing the thunder and realizing that we didn't have much time, seemed to be the motivation that I needed. Before that, I didn't know if I had the strength to set foot on that ground.

I tried to keep my mind clear, as we trekked through the dried up stalks, tried not to think, 'This is where I saw Dave kneeling down' and 'This is where he died.' I pushed the thoughts aside as soon as they came to mind and replaced them with, 'Find the deer and kill it. Find that damn, dirty rotten deer and blow its brains out.'

We passed by the spot where it had all happened, and I tried to pretend that it was just as normal as any other place in the field; except I couldn't hide the fact that the dirt there was saturated in blood. Dad noticed the blood, noticed how I quickly passed by it without a glance, and he didn't say a word. I was glad.

There were faint tracks of the deer's hooves still imprinted on the ground, but they would soon be gone, thanks to the rain that was now falling down quite steadily. I broke into a light jog, feeling a maddening rush flow through my veins that thirsted for the death of that deer.

After jogging about fifty yards or so, I abruptly stopped and squatted down. I heard Dad do the same behind me. I was breathing heavily, due to the anticipation of what I thought I saw. I turned my head around slightly, never taking my eyes off of the still brown hide in the distance. "Is that it?" I whispered, pointing straight ahead.

Dad followed the invisible line my finger created with his eyes, as he inched up right behind me. "It's something," he said after a careful study. "But...it looks too small to be a deer."

"You think it's dead?"

"I can't tell; it's not moving, but it could just be hurt. Let's try to creep up on it just to be sure."

We did just that. Slowly, as quietly as possible, until finally I was able to tell what it was that we were sneaking up on - the back end of the deer that had undoubtedly killed Dave.

I relaxed, took my finger off the trigger, and slung the gun over my shoulder, as Dad and I walked up to it. All that was left of the deer was some fur on its face, a few bones here and there, and its rear end, which was untouched except for about a dozen flies that were swarming around it. Coyotes and bobcats were prominent in the area, and it looked as if they had gotten a good meal the night before. Bones were snapped off and laying several feet from where the deer rested. Its insides were nonexistent, save for some scraps of cartilage and some fat here and there.

I sighed deeply; half of me was relieved that the deer had found its end, the other half was indignant that I wasn't the one who had put it there. As I let out the sigh, a memory from the reel of my life flashed like a motion picture before me:

*The snow was gently falling down as I looked up at Dave, perched snugly near the top of his favorite tree. I heard him say it again, but this time his words hit me like a bolt of lightning.*

"Well, I used to think, 'Why would anyone want to kill a deer?' I'd a been pissed if someone shot them deer that we saw. There was just somethin' about the way they drank from the water - it was like...I don't know, it just gave me a good feeling.

"But then I started thinking about all those deer that run out into the road, and cause accidents and stuff. If someone had shot them deer, then there wouldn't be so many car crashes and people dyin and stuff.

"So I guess it works both ways; sometimes it's good that deer live, and sometimes it's better if they die..."

The deer...it had died, but not until...

I almost didn't want to think it, but I finally allowed my thought to finish itself.

...not until it had served its purpose.

Wait a minute; so not only did God *allow* this to happen, He actually *planned* it? That's what He was telling me by all this, but...but why? It didn't make sense, but at the same time, it had to. I tried and tried, but I just couldn't see it.

I felt a hand rest gently on my shoulder and turned my head around, almost expecting to see Jesus Himself staring back at me. It was Dad, of course; but I was sure that God was using him to comfort me. Just that simple act of care caused the storm raging through my mind to cease. He said softly yet with conviction, "Looks like God has already taken care of it for you." He stared at me knowingly, then added, "And He will take care of everything else, too."

I swallowed a lump in my throat and carefully set the gun down next to the deer, then pulled Dad in tight. I slapped him on the back and said, "I'm so glad you're here, Dad."

A tear trickled down my face, and I repeated with a weak voice, "I'm *so* glad you're here."

The rain started pouring down hard. Thunder cracked loudly overhead, and lightning flashed in zigzag patterns across the dark sky. As Dad and I walked back home, I no longer saw Dave's blood soaked up in the earth. The rain had washed it all away.

*February 12ᵗʰ, 2004-*
    *One that walks with God does not prepare for himself
the hour of his death, but he prepares himself for death in
every hour of his life.*

# 50.

The next day Anne and I drove to Mom and Dad's at ten in the morning. The wake was scheduled for one o' clock, but there was something I wanted to do before going.

We left Aslan in his kennel and took the short trip to the house in my Grand Prix. It was a sunny, humid day; a quiet, peaceful wind blew through the air, and all signs that a storm had passed through the area the day before were non-existent.

After making some obligatory small talk with my parents, I excused myself and went down the stairs to Dave's room. I wanted to read more from his journal; I didn't care if it was the same passage over and over again, I just wanted to read it. It had brought me such comfort the night before, and I knew I was going to need some more of that. Dave's wake was only hours away, and truthfully, I wasn't looking forward to it. I didn't want to hear all the well-meaning but useless sympathy that I knew I would receive...I wanted to be alone with my brother, and the best way for me to get there was by reading his thoughts.

I picked up the journal that I had left on his bed and sat down, looking at the cover for a few moments. It was like a precious jewel to me; sentimentally, there was no price that you could put on it.

I thought about going outside since it was such a nice day, and I knew exactly where to go. As I got up, my attention was brought to the bookcases placed tightly against the wall. The one on the right especially sparked my interest because of the bindings of two leather bound covers. They both had the word "JOURNAL" spelled vertically down the spine, one with black, bold letters, the other was in gold.

I quickly snatched the journals from the bookcase, as if they were about to disappear. A warm sensation filled my heart, and holding the three journals under my armpit, I ran up the steps.

Anne and my parents were somewhere in the living room, out of eyesight as I called out, "I'm going outside for a while."

Mom's voice was mixed with confusion and concern as she answered, "Okay...is everything alright?"

"Yeah," I said, halfway out the door. "Just wanna be by myself for a while."

I walked out to the backyard and looked up at the old oak tree, just as if it were a dear friend. Its numerous weathered branches held in them memories of Dave; there he was as a child, about seven feet from the ground, accepting Jesus in his heart...a little higher up was Dave as a preteen, hiding from a friend in a game of pretend war...halfway up the great oak, teen Dave sulked and fumed, angrily tearing away some bark from the limb...almost all the way to the top, grownup Dave sat peacefully, leaning against the tree, quietly enjoying the serenity that the artwork of God supplied to him.

The suit and dress shirt that I would be wearing to Dave's wake were hung up in the back seat of my car, and I didn't care if the t-shirt I was wearing got ripped or dirty on the climb up. I did, however, had to be careful not to tear my pants. I slid the journals partly down my pants, for lack of a better place to put them, and reached up to grab a limb. I hoisted myself up, planted my feet firmly on the sturdy branch, and continued my ascent until I was two-thirds of the way up the tree.

I sat down on the only branch that, at that height, could accommodate my weight and leaned my back against the shaft of the tree. I slowly took the journals from my pants and gazed around at my surroundings. Perspective changes at higher altitudes; I was seeing the same backyard that I had grown up in, but never from this angle. The woods were no longer just a borderline of the lawn; they stretched out for miles, providing shelter for wildlife and a beautiful view for my eyes. The wind blew through the grass, which was in dire need of mowing, creating the illusion of a sea of green waves.

At thirty feet up, I was above things of which I was normally a part. All of a sudden, our ample back lawn seemed tiny, our already small house seemed smaller, my fancy sports car was nothing more than painted metal; the only thing that was bigger or more impressive from my vantage point was the notion that there was so much more out there that I could not see.

At that moment, I knew why my brother liked sitting in the tree. The view was wonderful, yes; but it wasn't just the view.

I looked down at the three journals in my lap and remembered why I had made the climb. I licked my lips and opened the one with the brown leather cover. It had the same format as the one I had previously read - the date was written down before each entry, and Dave's scribbled writing was barely legible.

My heart became revived as I read his thoughts, his insight, his praise and prayers to God; just like what happened when I had read the first journal. I felt sort of like the man who in Jesus' parable had found a treasure and sold all he had, so that he could buy it for himself. The man found the hidden treasure, hid it again, and then bought the land that the treasure was in. Jesus never said what the man did with that treasure after he owned it; whether he kept it to himself or whether he shared it with others. I sure didn't want to share this treasure - it was meant for me, it was mine alone, something special that was for my heart only, a little piece of Dave that was solely for me.

I was merely three pages into the journal when Dave's words proved me wrong:

*March 15th, 2003-*

*I guess if you're reading this, then that means that I am alive. Sure, my body's dead; but I am bound to my flesh no more. I am truly alive and with Jesus.*

*I have come close to death before, and I know of the frailty of life. Whether it be a premonition or just cautiousness, I feel compelled to say a few words.*

*Mom: my dear, loving Mother...you were given to me by God. How I thank Him for you!*

*You never gave up on me, always loved me, the strength and endurance of your love tested in great measure by my disregard or sometimes even abhorrence of it. I treated you with anger, you returned it with care. I lashed out at you, you took the blows with patience and understanding. I mistreated you, yelled at you, took advantage of you...and you prayed for me. It is impossible for me to accurately thank you; absolutely, completely, 100% impossible - without you, I would be lost. I thank God continuously for you, asking that He blesses you in every way possible, knowing that He can give you far more joy than I could ever dream of. There have been many times in the past when I have said 'I hate you.' Just thinking of that sends a chill up my spine. I said that because I knew it would hurt you; I wanted it to hurt you, God forgive me! I know that you know I never really meant it, but that doesn't excuse it or make me feel any better. Forgive me for my rebelliousness as a child, for my spiteful words, and know this: there is nothing below Heaven that I love more than you. For all the times that I said otherwise, dear Mom: "I LOVE YOU, I LOVE YOU, I LOVE YOU, I LOVE YOU, I LOVE YOU, I LOVE YOU, I LOVE YOU!!!!!!!!!!!!!!!!!*

*I could go on and fill the rest of this journal, but I think you get the point. For as long as I live, I will always prove to you how very dear you are to me; no matter what you need, no matter where you are, I will always be there for you, and you will always be in my heart.*

*Dad: 'Dad....' I love saying that word! I love the fact that you are my Dad! I know the Bible says not to envy, but I envy you so very much. Your faith in God, your wisdom of the Scriptures, your kind-heartedness, your easily approach-ability, your humble attitude that you have while knowing so much! You are a blessing to me, and to our family...a blessing that I can't fully describe, and one that you can't fully comprehend. There are so many things you do, so many things that you have said that have hit me so hard in the heart that my only reaction was to sit completely still and silently thank the Lord. You have helped me to understand the Bible, increased my faith in God...there have been things I learned from you that I passed on to people at work who really needed it, but never would have received it had it not been for you. I know that you will receive your reward in Heaven for things that you had no idea that you did. You earned them, though, because you love the Lord, you obey Him, and it is oh-so obvious that He is working in you. I remember once, and this I will never forget, we were talking about a passage from second Corinthians that was disturbing me greatly. Not only did you correct my misconceptions about the verses, we*

*went on and talked for over an hour - you opened up to me
about some things, and I shared with you also some things
that I had never told anyone else. At the end I said, 'Thanks
for the talk. I'm tired, I should probably get headed to bed.'
Outwardly I'm sure I seemed calm and collected; inwardly,
I could barely contain myself. I went downstairs, shut my
door, flopped face down on my bed and cried for a good long
time. I was so happy, I was so thankful to God for you; you
have no idea of how much you mean to me.*

*Jon: I just sat here for a few minutes trying to think of
what I want to say to you. I realized that there is so much
to say, but so few ways to say them...You are my brother,
and I feel as if there can't be anyone, past or present, who
loves their sibling as much as I love you. I'm quiet, as you
know, and I guess I've never really told you how much I
respect you, cherish you, how proud I am to be called your
brother - but bro, God hears about it all the time! I guess it's
easier to explain it to Him, because He knows what I want
to say and how I really feel without me having to put it into
words. He knows how close to you I feel, He knows all about
that very special place in my heart that glows every time
I think about all you've done for me and Mom. He knows
how important you make me feel, how you always included
me in on games we played while growing up. When I felt
like an outcast, sitting back in the dark corner of life, you
came up and brought me into a place where I felt wanted
and accepted. You were my hero growing up - you were so
cool, and all the kids liked you. I probably would have been
happy enough just to know that your friends knew that I was
your brother...but you obviously weren't satisfied with that.
You let me hang out with you, you included me in with all
the cool things you were doing with all your cool friends;
and that made me feel like a million bucks. I quickly realized
that you, my brother, Mr. Popularity...you actually liked me,
you weren't ashamed of me, you wanted me around! Again,*

*you just made me feel so loved, so worthwhile, and that's not an easy thing to do: take someone who thinks they're garbage and no one likes them and make them feel wanted and extremely happy. But you did it, man, just by loving me despite myself. I will always cherish the time we spent together; yes, even the time I crapped my pants at camp! You were always there for me, always treated me with love, always made me feel like I was the coolest guy in the world. My brother, my dear, dear friend: may God reward you for all that you have done in ways I can't even think of. My heart sees your face all the time; I can't put it any other way...I just really, really love you, Jon.*

My tightly pressed, trembling lips could hold it in no longer. A wail that had been creeping up my throat exploded from my mouth, and I held my hands over my eyes and cried and cried and cried.

After a few minutes, I picked the journal up from my lap and flipped back to the page I had been on. There were more people Dave had written to after me; our aunts and uncles, Bernie, Susie, and a few of his friends.

"Thank You, God," I said out loud as I looked up at some thick white clouds overhead. "I needed that."

A breeze blew by me as I started to climb down the tree. I walked into the house, knowing that there were other people who needed it, too.

*January 12th, 2003-*
*If the whole world knew what I know about God, I*
*suppose one-third would be better off, and two-thirds would*
*be wondering where all their knowledge had gone.*

# 51.

The Disciples United Methodist Church, where Dave and I had spent all our Sunday mornings ever since I could remember, sat on a large hill just on the outskirts of town. It was a quaint old one-storied brick building with a peaked roof and numerous long, up sliding windows on each side. There was a nursery for children in the basement, along with several rooms that were used for Sunday School. The sanctuary consisted of four rows of pews, ten in each one, and steps in the front that led up to a raised platform where Pastor Stan gave his sermons. The floor was newly carpeted, and matching maroon drapes hung to the side of the windows.

Anne and I pulled into the parking lot at a quarter after one; the funeral didn't begin until two, so we figured that there would be plenty of time to get situated before people started coming. I saw by the amount of vehicles already filling the ample parking lot that we were wrong. I had to pull all the way around to the very back of the church by the swing sets to a spot that I had only seen used before at Christmas and Easter; the lot was full, and there were still cars coming in. Henry Vendetti, a long time family friend and member of our church, came out to the lot and started directing cars to park on the old softball field where the kids used to play during Vacation Bible School.

By two o'clock, every pew was filled, and there were people standing or sitting on aluminum foldout chairs in the back. I knew my brother was popular and had many friends and people who cared about him - but still, I wasn't expecting a turnout like this!

My parents, Anne, Bernie, my aunts and uncles, and I all occupied the front pews, as we waited for the chatter to die down. Everyone from church was there, as far as I could tell, including the Youth Group in which my brother assisted. I saw many faces that I hadn't seen in a long time, and some I had never seen before. Apparently, the restaurant where Dave worked had to close for the afternoon, because all its workers wanted to attend the funeral.

Pastor Stan raised up his hands, calling for everyone to stand. He was wearing a black robe with a purple sash, the cross and a flame representing the Holy Spirit embroidered in gold on the sash. We bowed our heads as he opened with a prayer, and stayed standing to sing the opening hymn, "It Is Well With My Soul."

For whatever the reason, singing that song and hearing the whole church sing along with me, made me feel at ease. I realized then that, although my brother had died and I was still deeply in grief, it *was* well with my soul. The Giver of the peace that passes all understanding was in the church, and I smiled as I looked up at the roof with blurry eyes and thanked Him as we sang.

Pastor Stan called for everyone to be seated, his warm, friendly voice heard by all, thanks to the wireless mike he wore. He started by reading First Thessalonians, chapter four, verses thirteen to eighteen. He then went into great detail on those six verses, and truly did a remarkable job at explaining them.

He was an excellent speaker. He'd stroll about the raised section at the front of the church in such a way that you never wanted to take your eyes off of him. You could see the passion for what he was saying on his face and hear it undoubtedly in his words. He knew the Bible so well that he could quote nearly every verse, and knew God so well that he always used the verses in their proper context.

At the end of the service, just before the closing hymn, Pastor Stan surveyed the entire congregation for several quiet moments. He swallowed a lump in his throat, then spoke softly; from where I was seated, I could see some moistness develop in his eyes. "I've been the pastor of this church for fourteen wonderful years. I remember Dave as a child, no more than nine or ten years old. He was always smiling, always just full of life, full of happiness." His voice trailed off, as he stared out towards the back of the church at nothing in particular, with a reminiscent grin stretching on his face. "He would always help out in any way he could, and was so nice and friendly to all the other kids. Dave was someone that you wanted to be around, someone who you wanted as a friend. He was extremely intelligent, humorous, and a very caring young man."

Now it wasn't just those seated in the front who could see the tears in Pastor Stan's eyes; they began to trickle down his cheek, and he didn't bother to wipe them away. They just kept falling down.

"There was a time in Dave's life when he...he turned away from God." He stopped pacing and looked at the carpet for a few seconds, then stood still, and lifted his balding head back up. His voice was growing weaker by the second. "Drugs got a hold of him; *Satan* got a hold of him. It hurt me so much seeing him that way, and hearing about what he was doing with his life. Truly, it was burning a hole in my heart."

He looked up at the ceiling and shook his head a little. "I kept on thinking of the parable Jesus told as recorded by Jon Mark; the one about the talents the man gave to his servants. You all should know this one. Basically, a man went away for a while, entrusting his talents, which were a monetary unit at that time, to his three servants." The pastor began to slowly pace again, and his voice began to strengthen as his zeal for delivering God's message energized him. "And I don't think it's by any coincidence that they were called talents; no, no coincidence at all. What 'talents' mean to us today is exactly what they were symbolizing in Jesus' parable, told two thousand years ago. They are gifts given by God to us; *entrusted* to us by Him, and we are to use those gifts to glorify His Name.

"The wicked servant in the parable, the one who hid his talent until his master returned, ended up having his talent taken away, and he was ultimately cast out 'into the darkness'."

Pastor Stan abruptly stopped in the middle of the long, raised platform and slowly scanned the congregation. He spoke loudly, yet with obvious compassion, emphasizing almost the entire sentence: "We are *to use* our *talents* to *glorify God!*"

He finished scanning the faces in the crowd and took up his pacing again. "I saw all this talent in Dave, and I saw it being misused, or not used at all." He looked at Mom and gave her a warm smile as he said, "And Dave's mother saw it too, and it broke her heart, but God bless her, that saint of a woman never gave up on her boy!" They exchanged smiles for a moment before the pastor directed his attention back towards the congregation. "She prayed, we prayed as a church; she never gave up hope, no matter how hopeless things seemed. And praise the Lord," he said with jubilation, his smiling face turned upwards towards the ceiling, "He answered our prayers!"

A few scattered "Amens!" were called out, and I nodded my head in agreement. My family isn't accustomed to shouting things during a church service, but I can guarantee that we were all saying them in our hearts.

"C.S. Lewis once said something like, 'A slow miracle is no easier to perform than an instant one.' It was a miracle by the hand of God that Dave was released from the strangling hold that drugs had on him. It was a miracle by the hand of God that got him pointed back into the right direction." The pastor's words came speeding out of his mouth like a bullet from a gun. His face became stern, his eyes blazed with assurance, and his half-raised hands clenched tightly at his side; he was, as they say, "on a roll." "It was a miracle by the hand of God that He reached out and found one of His lost sheep!"

"Amen!"

"Amen!"

He slowed his speech and said with conviction, "And that miracle by the hand of God happened because of the faith of His fervent saints. Prayer...is just so important. It is communion with our Father; our Father Who loves us, Who wants so desperately to be the center of our lives, to guide us and lead us to do good works."

Pastor Stan slowly walked up a row of two carpeted steps that were stretched out the length of the platform and stood in front of the small wooden pulpit. He bowed his head in silence for a good minute with his eyes closed, then said softly, "Let us pray."

I let go of Anne's hand so that we could fold our hands as he began, "Lord God, Father of all creation; we bow our heads in worship and praise to You. We thank You for the joy You gave to us in knowing Dave. We thank You for his laughter, his sense of humor, his love that we felt for us. We thank You that he lived a life devoted to You, and how blessed we are because of that!

"Lord, this is a trying time for all of us; it is hard to deal with the loss of someone as special as Dave. We know that he is with You now, in the totality of Your wonderful presence, and we thank You for that. Offer to us, Lord, Your comfort; heal our wounds, Lord, hear our cries. Our loss is great, Lord...fill our void.

"Lord God, I know, *we* know, that David Sullah was a wonderful young man, a creation of Your love. He has touched all of our lives in so many different ways. The magnificent wood burnings that he gave to this church, the Youth Group that he led; the wisdom that he shared with those young men and women astounded me. His care and love for the needy, the hurt, the disadvantaged...Lord, he displayed Your attributes to a dark and dirty world, and we thank You, Heavenly Father, for what You did in and through this young man...this young man, who was oh-so-obviously very close to You; and now, because of that, he is with You forever.

"Lord God, I pray that if there is anyone here today who doesn't yet know You, I pray that they wait no longer to accept their salvation by the blood of Jesus, by His death on the cross, and His ascension into Heaven. Let them know the truth, Lord; may they yearn for it. For no man knows the hour of which You will come for him or her; Lord; may they procrastinate no longer. Fill them with the truth, that we are all sinners, and we need redemption for our sins, and that comes by faith in the Lord Jesus Christ.

"Dear Father, we thank You that Dave was ready. You came for him when no one was expecting it, but praise You, Lord, he was ready.

"We thank You for Your presence today; we thank You for it everyday, and we ask that You be with us forever. Give us strength, Lord, and let us do Your will. In Jesus' name,"

We all repeated, "In Jesus' name,"

"Amen."

"Amen."

Although we had all gathered to remember Dave, the Lord had been the focal point. Although we were all hurt and grieved, God had been given honor and glory.

My brother would have been well pleased as to how his funeral service went.

*April 20th, 2002-*

*Nothing on Earth matters. My family, whom I love: Where would we be without Heaven? My friends, whom I cherish: Where will your end lead you? God calls; throughout our lives, God calls. When His last call comes for you, you will find no excuse for denying His many petitions for you. Jesus; what is this world without Him? Nothing that I want any part of.*

*Come, you lovers of things that perish, and drink the water of eternal life and know the goodness of the Lord! Why wait one more second? Lord, let them feel Your love, and may they answer Your calls.*

# 52.

The line of cars slowly made their way through town, headlights on, crawling through the streets, as if the vehicles themselves were in mourning. Anne and I followed behind Mom and Dad's green Taurus, and the hearse was behind us. Looking out my rearview mirror, I saw no end to the row of cars in succession.

I stared ahead blankly, one hand on the steering wheel, nervously biting the fingernails of my other hand. Anne broke the silence that had lasted since we first entered my car. "Are you okay?"

I gave her a quick glance and almost said what a dumb question that was. No, I wasn't okay; far from it. A creeping, sick anxiety was churning through my stomach; my head had so many thoughts and questions within that I thought it might explode. I took a deep breath and sighed it out, giving me a few seconds to calm down before I responded. "I'm nervous; I'm really, really nervous. I don't know what to say...I thought it would come to me, but it's not. I'm gonna ruin it...I'm gonna let Mom down, I'm gonna let *Dave* down..."

Anne grabbed the hand that I was by now chewing on and held it softly between hers. "You're not going to let *anybody* down. You're going to do great."

Her soft voice was so convincing, as if she had already heard me give the eulogy and had thought it was fantastic. I gave her a weak smile and said, "Thanks, hon. I love you."

She smiled, showing off a row of bright white teeth. "I love you, too." She leaned over and kissed me on the cheek, never letting go of my hand until we reached the cemetery.

---

*This is it.*

I stood behind a small wooden podium, facing a crowd of four hundred eyes, all focused on me. I had imagined this moment a countless number of times throughout the past two days, dreaming about how great of a speech I would make, but never hearing myself say any words.

I had tried to write down what I wanted to say, but each time I tried, I never got past the first sentence. After many failed attempts, I was satisfied in trusting what I was hearing in my mind: *You'll know what to say when the time comes.*

Well, the time was here, and all I could do was stare back at all those eyes focused intently on me. None of them knew I had absolutely no idea what to say. None of them knew how much I wanted to run away from this moment, pretend like it wasn't here, pretend like none of this was actually happening.

They were all sitting on aluminum fold-out chairs, ascending somewhat uphill, so that those in the back could see the nervous, jittery man standing before the podium that the cemetery's caretaker had provided. They had also set up small, portable speakers and had equipped me with a wireless microphone, so everyone in the audience could hear every word.

I wished now that the speakers would fail, a sudden thunderstorm would appear; something, *anything* other than making a fool out of myself and bringing dishonor to my brother by not being prepared for this moment.

Anne, my parents, and my uncles, aunts and cousins all sat in the front, as they did during the funeral service. The only thing that changed, other than being outside in the humid temperature instead of being inside at the church, was that I was not among them. I was up here.

*What am I doing? Why did I say I'd do this? What made me think I could come up with a eulogy at the spur of the moment?*

I slid my hands in my black dress pants, looking down at the grass, trying to come up with something to say, while battling the discouraging thoughts that were slipping into my brain. I had been up there for almost a minute now; the people must be wondering what was going on.

*Just say you're sorry, you can't do this. They'll understand. It's too hard. You're not prepared.*

I lifted my head, ready to say exactly what I had just thought, but stopped before I even opened my mouth. There, in the front row just to my left, was my dad, holding Mom's hand, both with their heads bowed. It was obvious what they were doing, and I immediately realized for whom they were doing it.

I would not let them down; I couldn't. This wasn't for me, I realized, and it wasn't even for them. It was for Dave.

*You're not alone*, a different-sounding voice told me. *You may be standing here by yourself, but you are certainly not alone*

I did what I should have done a long time ago; I closed my eyes and said the only thing that I could think of:

*God, help me.*

He did.

Before I knew it, I had opened my eyes and started saying the first thing that came to mind. After that, the words just came to me, as if Jesus Himself was whispering them into my ears. All I did was say them.

"I want to thank you all for coming here today in honor of my brother, Dave Sullah. For those of you who don't know me, I'm Jon, his older brother."

I took my hands out of my pockets and grabbed the sides of the oak podium. I realized that it was the spot used to set down the paper one was reading from. I also realized that, for whatever the reason, God had chosen for me not to have the speech ready. Maybe it was so that I trusted completely in Him. A grin almost appeared on my face; my confidence in Him was in full effect.

"Dave and I loved to golf."

I had no idea where I was going with this; I just knew that it would somehow all come together. Although a part of me was fighting with what I was saying, telling me that I was going to embarrass myself, telling me that this made no sense, I had already started with that sentence. There was no going back now.

A smile stretched across my face as I recalled one of the funniest moments in my life.

"We were out there at Hunington Ridge Country Club about a year ago, just Dave and me. On, uh..." I tried to keep from chuckling, but I couldn't. I was picturing in my mind what I was about to describe, and I couldn't help but laugh. "Oh, man!" The smile felt so good; it was as if it were plastered on my face as I spoke. I controlled my laughter, but the smile stayed as I continued. "On...I think it was the third tee, Dave's ball ended up in a bunker. It was right in front of the green, probably about ten yards or so away."

I saw Mom smile as she looked at Dad. They had heard this story before.

"So Dave gets in the bunker, takes a few practice swings, and, you know, really takes his time staring at the green and digging his cleats into the sand. It was a really tough shot; he had to hit the ball hard enough to get over the lip of the bunker, but soft enough so that it didn't go past the green.

"Just when he's about to take his swing, the...I don't know what you call it; the refreshment girl? You know, the girl who rides around the course in her own cart that holds sodas and drinks and all? Well, she pulls up and stops her cart next to the green. She sees that Dave's about to hit, so she waits there until he takes his shot.

"So that just adds a great amount of pressure on him. The shot itself was hard enough, but now he's got this cute little blond in the cart watching him."

I shook my head as I chuckled again, vividly remembering everything and picturing it in my mind. "And Dave's trying to act all cool; he sees her watching him, but he pretends like he doesn't even know she's there. He takes another practice swing, stares at the green for like twenty seconds, then gets in his stance before the ball. He wiggles his hips, brings the club back, and swings.

"A huge pile of sand flies up, almost going as far as the green, and Dave's looking straight ahead, eyes focused intently, waiting to see his ball flop down on the green somewhere. After a few seconds, he looks over at me and goes, 'Did you see it?' I just raised my eyebrows and gestured with my eyes down by his feet. Dave looks down and is amazed to find that his ball hadn't moved an inch."

There was a sparse amount of laughter throughout the crowd, but I interrupted it with, "That's not the half of it. So his face gets all red, and he makes a quick glance over to where the girl is sitting in her cart. He muttered something under his breath, something like, 'Why does she have to just sit there and stare at me?' Then he took another practice swing. He stared at the green again, then did his little hip-shuffle, and swung. This time a *huge* amount of sand flew through the air, probably a few bucketfuls, but again, no ball. When he saw the ball, unmoved from its position by his feet, he got *really* mad! He started taking swing after swing, like an angry logger trying to chop down a tree, but still couldn't get that ball out. By now I was rolling on the ground." My laughter made me stop again; I couldn't help it. There were tears coming from my eyes as I went on. "And all I saw were waves and waves of sand flying through the air. There was so much sand going around that I thought there would be none of it left in the trap. *Finally*, after at least ten failed attempts, Dave screams in frustration, I heard his iron striking the ball, and I see the ball fly out of the trap, soar over the green, and land in the woods across the road.

"He looks at me laying on the ground, and I'm laughing so hard my stomach hurt, and he says, 'That's not funny.' But then he starts to laugh, probably cause I'm like a lunatic rolling around on the fairway.

"I hear the refreshment girl's cart starting to come over, so I sit up, still unable to stand, 'cause I was laughing so hard. She stops by us and asks if there's anything we need, and Dave takes a five out of his wallet and hands it to her, saying, 'Yeah, here's five dollars; don't ever tell anybody what you just saw.'"

It was good to hear the people laughing. It was good to see their smiles. I thanked God that I hadn't passed up this opportunity.

"Dave and I were competitive, in a fun way, when it came to golf. But he never beat me...not once."

The smile and the reminiscent stare began to fade from my face, but my eyes stayed watery. Not because of laughter, but because I knew where I was going with all this. I felt it in my heart; it became warm, and started to beat faster, encouraging me to go with it.

I paused and let the laughter die down, and spoke softly and with a solemn expression on my face. "But there was something that Dave was much better at than I am, and it's far more important than golf; he could reach out to people with the message of Jesus Christ in a way that...it just blew my mind.

"I've seen it first hand; his knowledge of biblical doctrine, his passion for relating the gospel to complete strangers and friends...Dave was at his best when he was talking about God; whether it be with a fellow Christian or a non-believer. It's what he loved to do." I scanned the faces of the audience, trying to make contact with as many eyes as possible as I said, "What a way to spend your life! What a wonderful, invaluable way to spend your life!"

"Amens" were called out confidently, in agreement with my statement. Their assuredness brought me fresh tears; it wasn't that I needed their approval of what I had said to believe it myself, but it was good to see that the majority of them believed it themselves.

But not all of them.

I knew that there were probably some people who were listening to me who had no idea about how real Jesus is, and how desperately important it is to know Him as Lord and Savior. A thought occurred to me, and I couldn't help but smile: Even though he was dead, my brother could still bring people to the Lord.

"My brother is in Heaven right now. And that's not simply a hope I have filled my mind with to deal with his loss; false hope never helps. I know that Jesus died for our sins, and Dave knew that, too. I know that He rose from the dead and entered Heaven, allowing everyone who believed in Him to do the same. Dave knew that, too."

I sighed and looked at the ground, preparing myself for what I was about to say. After swallowing a lump in my throat, I looked back at the crowd, tears already glistening in my eyes as I said, "I held my brother in my arms as he died." I bit my bottom lip so hard, it went numb. I thought maybe I wouldn't be able to go on; I would break down crying uncontrollably and say no more.

*No*, I told myself, *this is important. Go on; you have to.*

Drawing back on that memory was obviously painful; I had fought hard, yet unsuccessfully, to keep it from my mind ever since the incident. I walked around with it during the day, trying to keep it shut in a corner closet of my brain. At night, when all was quiet and dark, it came at me in full force, and it was all I could do to keep the haunting memory of my brother's death from playing and replaying in my head.

Something was different now, though. I actually allowed the scene to play; I invited it to. I looked past the blood soaking on his skin and on the ground, past his trembling hand and the wheezing noise coming from his lungs, past the "what-ifs" and "whys" I had been repeatedly asking myself, and right into Dave's big brown eyes.

That's when I saw it; something that I knew was there, but had remained hidden up until this point. There was something about the way that he had looked at me, and now I understood.

*Thank You, God.*

I spoke, wondering for a moment how long I had been standing there in silence. "He couldn't say anything because... because of his injuries, but he looked right at me, stared right into my eyes, like he was trying to tell me something. I don't know if I can explain this." I looked up to the sky and gathered my thoughts for a moment. After a few seconds, I was satisfied and returned my attention to the crowd as I said, "He was telling me he loved me." I let a tear trickle down my cheek without paying it any mind. "He was telling me that it was okay; he was letting me know that this wouldn't be the last time I saw him alive."

Seeing Mom and Dad weep caused me to cry even harder. I weakly cleared my throat and swallowed a large lump. "I'm not crying for Dave; I'm crying for me, because I miss him. And I will miss him every day until we meet again. But that's the thing; the blood of Jesus triumphs over the inevitability of death! We *will* meet again!"

I wiped the tears from my face and stared out at the people in the crowd for a moment. I felt compassion for the unsaved souls who were listening. I felt a burning in my heart, a deep longing for them to accept the Truth, and love and cherish Jesus as their own.

A smile broke out on my face - this is how my brother had felt. This is why he spoke so adamantly about Jesus, this is why he prayed so often, this is why he so hungered and thirsted for God; because he knew Him, and he wanted everyone else to know Him, too.

"And it's all because of Jesus. Because He died for our sins, because He lives in our hearts...it's thanks to Him.

"In a moment, my Mom is going to come up and say a few words, and after that we will invite up anyone else who wants to say something about Dave. Before that, I'd like for us to sit here for a minute or two in silence, and I'd like each one of you to ask yourself this question: Where will I go when I die?"

I scanned the crowd one last time, praying fervently that God would touch some hearts today, and that He'd add some sheep to His flock.

"Dave gave his heart to Jesus, and although he went astray for a while, he eventually became just like the David

from the Bible: A man after God's own heart. His faith in
Jesus turned him into the man that we all know, and I have
nothing but absolute love and respect for that man.

"I, uh...I can't say how much Dave meant to me; that
would be impossible. And I know I haven't done him justice
here..." My voice was becoming very shaky. I took a deep
breath and exhaled it audibly. I was thinking I should say
more about my brother, I should keep talking, but...No, this
was it. I had done my part.

"Thank you all for listening, and thank you for coming
today. And please, do me a favor: Seriously think about that
question. Close your eyes and think. You might not have as
long as you think to make up your mind as to where you'll
spend eternity. Dave passed when no one was expecting it;
but thank the Lord, he was ready!

"Please, close your eyes." I waited a moment and seemingly everyone complied. "Thank you. Now ask yourself:
Where will I go when I die?"

*December 19<sup>th</sup>, 2002-*

*When the storms of life are raging, will we find shelter?*
*If we only look for shelter when the storms hit, will we ever*
*know the calming peace of the Lord?*

# 53.

I sat down next to Anne, and she immediately grabbed my hand, squeezed it, and gave me a kiss on the cheek. I bowed my head along with everyone else and thought about the question I had posed.

Yes; someday, I would be going to Heaven. Someday, everything would be perfect. Someday, there would be no pain, no heartache, no troubles. Until then, I could expect imperfection. Until then, I would be well acquainted with the pain, heartaches, and troubles that this world would bring. Satan's attacks would continue to come. He'll attack me, because he hates God, and God is with me. But that's just the thing: God is with me! Although Satan's onslaughts are too much for me to handle, I can handle anything he throws at me, because the Lord is with me always. He will never leave me, He will not forsake me...Ever.

"Hello, everyone." I snapped my head up, not noticing that Mom had gotten up and was now standing in front of the wooden podium. She looked as pretty as ever, wearing a long black sleeveless dress, her short blonde hair curled in an almost perfect semi-circle atop her head.

Dad reached across Anne and shook my hand, nodding his head with a solemn expression on his face, "well done" glistening in his eyes. I returned his nod with a half-smile and then focused my attention on Mom.

"My name is Joyce Foley, for those of you who don't know me, and I'm Davey's Mom." She bowed her head and sighed deeply, her shoulders beginning to tremble a little.

*God, help her; give her strength!*

After a moment, she lifted her head back up and opened her mouth to speak.

Nothing came out.

She leaned forward with her elbows on the podium, her hands covering her face, and wept.

I wanted to run to her. I wanted to hold her, I wanted to comfort her. I couldn't stand seeing Mom like this; she was so vulnerable.

While I was thinking about what to do, Dad stood up and quickly walked towards her. He reached the podium in less than three seconds and threw his strong arms around her. I stared in awe at the seemingly simple scene; the seemingly simple act of an embrace between two people. But there was much more there then meets the eye. There were two people who utterly loved one another, who shared the same deep sorrow, but could do nothing more than let the other know that they were there, and they could relate as to how the other was feeling.

I loved my Dad more than ever before when I saw that. He *was* there for my Mom, and he would be as long as he lived. I saw it in the way he held her.

A knot developed in my throat as I silently thanked the Lord again for my Dad. He truly was a blessing from God. I realized then why it hadn't felt right for me to go to her, although I had wanted to so badly: That was something Dad was meant for, one of the many reasons God had brought the two together. They were the epitome of how God intended marriage to be- no longer two separate people living their lives individually, but a man and a woman as one, sharing all that they have, think, and feel with each other.

I put my arm around Anne and held her close.

Mom sniffed and turned her now red face from Dad's chest back towards the crowd in front of her. She held Dad's hand, letting him know that she wanted him to stay up there with her, and managed a smile as she said, "I'm sorry- as you can imagine, I've been quite emotional for the past few days." She took a deep breath and sighed, pausing a moment to make the transition from apology to speech. "I can't tell you how much it means to me to see you all here today. And frankly, I can't tell you how much Davey means to me, either. He was so bright, so charming, so funny...so much a blessing to me, and I'm sure to you all as well."

Dad stood by Mom as she spoke, head bowed slightly, nodding in agreement from time to time. They looked so good together, so right for each other; I couldn't imagine Mom being able to make her speech without him.

She talked about Dave as a kid; how he was so pudgy and full of joy, always laughing and asking for "tutties," which were cookies in Dave's childhood language. She told stories of him growing up; how he always wanted to help, how he was a constant source of humor, even if he was the brunt of the joke. Dave unabashedly showed his emotions, she said, and he had a particular care and love for the underdog.

The smile that had gradually stretched itself on Mom's face suddenly vanished as she said, "I had a...very difficult first marriage. Davey's father was abusive and, well, not much of a father to him or Jon at all. It was the most trying time of my life; I knew that the boys and I would be better off without him, but I kept on giving him one more chance... I really thought that he would change. 'One more chance' turned out to be about a hundred chances before I finally filed for divorce. I was just beside myself; I didn't eat for days on end, and only got a few winks of sleep for the first month or so."

Dad stepped closer to Mom and began to lovingly rub her back. She flashed him a warm smile and then continued. "I was blaming myself for everything. I told myself that I was a bad mother, that my boys would hate me for driving out their dad, that I hadn't tried hard enough to make my marriage work...I know now that it wasn't all my fault, but I am to blame for not marrying a Christian man."

Mom took a deep breath and exhaled, and then spoke in a weak, strained voice, "What got me by those months and years were my boys..." She covered her mouth with her free hand, her eyebrows arched high, and stayed that way for a few seconds; not quite crying, but looking as if she might explode any moment. "They are just...so precious to me, and I love them so much..." Her voice was becoming weaker and more high-pitched with every word she said.

Dad leaned down and whispered something in her ear. She gave him an appreciative smile, wiped some tears from her eyes, and paused for a moment to compose herself before going on. "What I'm trying to say is that God puts people in our lives for a reason. Davey was just a constant source of joy for me during those difficult years; both of my boys were, and they still are.

"Without Davey and Jon, I don't know how I would've survived. I don't have to wonder about that, though, because they were there with me, and they were there with me because God blessed me with them. I thank God every day for my kids, and for all my family. And it sure took me a while, but I can now thank Him for taking Davey. Not that I wanted him gone; I miss him so much already it hurts...but I know that he's home. He's in Heaven. He's home."

The smile that reappeared on her face said it all. She wasn't just saying it to make herself feel better, she was saying it with confidence because she knew that it was true. The knot in my throat was too big to try to swallow it; I just let it sit there as tears trickled down my cheeks.

"The last thing I want to share with you is my last conversation with Davey. He was going in the woods to take some pictures, and he said, 'I'm going outside for a while.' I said, 'Alright; I love you.' And he said, 'Love you, too.'

Mom scanned the audience with a wide smile and said, "That simple conversation is like music to my ears. I didn't know that that was the last time I would talk with my boy." Tears rolled down her cheeks, but she didn't give them any mind. "I didn't know that that was the last time I would see him on this Earth. But I've always made it a point to tell my kids and anyone else that I love them; no matter if they're going to work or leaving for weeks.

"I've heard it so many times, and it breaks my heart, people saying that the last time they spoke with someone who died was in an argument, or they never really told them how they really felt. I have no regrets. Davey knew that I loved him, and I told him that all the time!

"Please, please," she said, shaking her head slowly, "make sure you let your loved ones know how much you love them. And if they already know, tell them anyway. Tell them again and again and again. You never know if it will be the last time on Earth that you speak with them."

She sniffed and wiped her face dry, then whispered something to Dad. He stepped in front of the podium and leaned forward, bending his back a little to speak into the microphone. He was so choked up he could barely talk. "I, uh...I want to say so much that I don't even know where to begin, and I don't even know how to say it." He cleared his throat, looking down at the podium, for the most part, as he spoke. "I consider Dave as my own son, and I did my best to be his father. I will cherish the moments we spent together as if they were a priceless gem; they *are* priceless. I, uh..." He took off his glasses to wipe away some tears, as Mom now took on the role of comforter. She wrapped her arm around his waist and leaned her head on his shoulder. "Dave was a wonderful man; an absolutely, one-of-a-kind, loving, special man. He will be in my heart forever, and I can't wait to be with him again in Heaven."

I knew that he wanted to say more, but he just couldn't. I had never seen Dad so emotional; not even at his and Mom's wedding. He put his glasses back on and looked out at the crowd as he said in a soft, scratchy voice, "We would love for any of you who wants to come up now and say a few words about Dave."

*May 22ⁿᵈ, 2002-*
> *Lord, may others hear this:*
> "So just call on me, brother, (*or sister*), when you need a hand.
> We all need somebody to lean on.
> I just might have a problem that you'd understand.
> We all need somebody to lean on."

> *May I be that person to direct them towards You, O Lord; may they lean on You.*
> "Lean on me when you're not strong
> and I'll be your friend,
> I'll help you carry on
> for it won't be long
> 'Til I'm gonna need
> Somebody to lean on."

# 54.

At first I didn't think anybody was going to step forward. We all sat there in the sweltering heat, no one moving a muscle or making a sound.

I found myself getting a little angry. It seemed disrespectful that they could all just sit in their seats when this was the time to say something, anything, to honor my brother. They were here because they loved him, right? They were here because he had touched their lives, right?

I turned around and glanced about the crowd as if to say, *"Well? C'mon, this is it! What are you waiting for?"*

Aunt Sheila broke the uncomfortable silence and walked up to the podium. I sighed deeply, letting the worry and anger escape from me.

*This will be the icebreaker,* I thought. *After she speaks, others will follow suit.*

They did.

After Aunt Sheila sat down, right away someone else took her place at the podium. A high school friend, a few friends from work, including Dave's manager, Angie Ashbery, Susie, several teenagers from the Youth Group, people from church. They told stories of Dave, how he had impacted their lives, how he had helped them through some struggles, how they so enjoyed having him around. Some tales were humorous, like Aunt Sheila's retelling of the day when Dave had told the hairdresser he wanted a perm (he was only five years old), because that was what Mom had gotten.

Others were more serious, like what the short, plump, freckled girl with stringy red hair shared.

She introduced herself as Becky Reed, a waitress at the restaurant where Dave had worked. She stood behind the podium, with her arms hanging by her sides, her shoulders slumped as if she was holding dumbbells in her hands. She kept her head down for the most part while she spoke, lifting her gaze for only an instant at a time to the crowd, as if she were making sure we were still there.

"I had a conversation with Dave not too long ago that I will never forget," Becky said in a sweet, innocent voice. "We had our break at the same time, and it was nice outside, so we were sitting on the hill by the side of the restaurant.

"Dave was just real easy to talk to. He'd listen to every word I'd say, and it was cool, because it was obvious that he genuinely cared. And he was so smart, too; it seemed like he

always said the right thing, you know...pretty much everything he said made sense.

"So we were sitting outside, and we got to talking; I'm
not really sure about what, but somehow the conversation
came to drugs. I said something like, 'Oh yeah, I heard you
use to be a real pothead,' or something like that. He just
nodded his head and said, 'Yeah,' and it was obvious that he
was ashamed."

Becky sighed audibly and nervously looked up. We were
still there. After the quick glance, she returned her gaze to
the podium, reading from an invisible script in front of her.

"And I knew that he was religious and all, and we'd had
many conversations about Christianity, and he knew that I
was a Christian, too. I started wondering what he might think
of me if he knew I smoked pot. I started thinking, you know,
'Is it wrong to smoke weed?' So I asked him why he had
quit, and he said he quit for a lot of reasons. I asked, 'Well,
like what?' - and he said something like, 'What it boils down
to is I know that God didn't want me using drugs. They were
making me into a person that I knew I wasn't.'

"And that got me real nervous, because I had been
noticing some changes about myself that I couldn't seem to
control. I knew it was because of the weed, but at the same
time I didn't want to know it was because of the weed.

"I was thinking about whether or not I should confide
in Dave about my drug addiction when he looked at me and
said, 'Why do you ask?' And I thought, 'Well, you might as
well just tell him', so I did.

"And I told him, I said, 'Well, did you know that I smoke
pot?' And he said, 'Yeah; well, I had an inkling. I've been
praying for you.'"

Becky's voice began to quaver, and she wiped a tear from
the corner of her eye. After a sniff from her runny nose and a
slight pause to recuperate, she continued. "And I said, 'Why
would you be praying for me?'" Her already high-pitched

voice became even higher towards the end of the sentence, and this time she covered her mouth and stood still for a little while. She then picked her head up, tears cascading down her cheeks, and called out loudly through her tears, "And he said, 'Because the devil's got a hold of you.'"

Becky cleared her throat and sighed deeply, then went on in her normal, pleasantly sweet voice. "It was just the... the *look* on his face, the way he stared at me; I knew he was right, but again, I didn't want to know.

" I said to him, 'No, I'm a Christian. How could the devil have a hold on me?'"

"I'll never forget what he said. He said, 'Every true Christian has something inside him or her, letting them know if they're doing something they shouldn't. We know when we're doing something wrong; whether it's watching pornography, robbing a bank, or doing drugs. If we do what we know we shouldn't, and continue doing it, then we're not listening to the Holy Spirit inside of us, we're listening to Satan, the father of lies. He tells us it's okay; he tells us to go ahead and sin, then he runs to God and accuses us of what we've done.'"

"Then he stared at me for a couple a seconds - not staring at me like he was mad at me, or disappointed - there was nothing but concern in his eyes. He said, 'If we do what the devil wants us to do, then we're letting him into our lives. We're letting him control how we spend the time that we have.'

"I sat there thinking about that, and it dawned on me that I really was spending all my time and most of my money on marijuana. My daily routine consisted of waking up, smoking, watching TV, smoking, going to work, then the minute I got home, I'd smoke some more and zone out listening to music or playing video games.

"We were quiet for a while before Dave told me that God gave me certain gifts, and I should be using them for His glory. He said he could relate to me 'cause he used to smoke all the time, too, and he said he knew it'd be hard to quit the habit; but he also said it'd be much harder on Judgment Day if I didn't. He told me...oh, I could never put it like he did! It was something about standing before God and trying to explain why you spent your life believing in Him, but not obeying what He said. It sent shivers down my spine; it still does."

Becky looked out around the crowd, her long red hair blowing softly in the breeze. Either she had lost her timidity or had forgotten about it. "I decided right then that I'd quit smoking pot. Dave said he'd help me; that he'd pray for me, and anytime I got the urge to smoke he said to call him, day or night, whatever the time. I haven't smoked since that day, and I know, Lord willing, I never will. I feel better about myself, my mind is certainly clearer, and I've never been happier."

She stretched a smile across her face as she surveyed her audience, her moist eyes twinkling in the sunlight. "I'd still be under the influence if it wasn't for Dave. He loved me enough to tell me the truth, and not sugarcoat it in any way. When I told him about me using drugs, I half-expected him to say something like, 'Oh, it's okay. We're all sinners, God understands.' But he didn't. He told me what I needed to hear, even though I didn't really want to hear it.

"Dave taught me a lot; more than I could tell you, even if I could stand up here for the rest of the day. He got me going to church again, and reading my Bible daily. And when I read something that made no sense to me, he was there to explain it. I called him late one night, it was actually about one in the morning, 'cause I was all freaked out about a verse that said we were evil. It took him some time, but he thoroughly explained it to me. He didn't care that I had called him so late, he never got frustrated when he had to explain things to me in layman terms; he really, truly cared about me, and he did whatever he could to impart to me his knowledge of God. He really was wise way beyond his years, and the most compassionate," her voice shook, "kind-hearted guy I have ever met.

"Thank you for listening to me," she said as fresh tears enveloped her eyes. "And thank you, Dave," she added, looking upward at the clouds, "I love you."

*July 27ᵗʰ, 2002-*

*A wounded butterfly crawled into my room today. It limped around on the ground, struggling to move. Its wings were beautifully colored with designs that only it possessed, and were unlike any other butterfly's, but I thought they were of no use. As I attempted to pick it up, it unexpectedly flapped its wings and landed on my shoulder. I looked at it in amazement, not able to do anything else, as it just sat there for a few seconds. Then it flew out my door, and I haven't seen it since. I've got this really weird feeling that I should be realizing something about all this, but I have no idea what.*

# 55.

An hour passed by as quickly as it possibly could under the sweltering sun. Every now and then, a cloud would temporarily provide relief by hiding the sun's rays, but they came few and far between. But the heat didn't seem to deter people from speaking about Dave or listening to the speeches; people kept on walking to the podium, and we all kept on listening.

It had been almost a minute since the last person had spoke, so I figured everyone had said what he or she wanted to. I stood, preparing to thank everyone and invite them all to the post-burial dinner, when I saw a man walking up the center aisle from somewhere near the back of the crowd. I quickly sat back down, as he made his way to the podium.

He was breathing heavily, probably due to the heat and his portly size. Before he began speaking, he wiped his sweaty forehead with a red handkerchief that was tucked into the breast pocket of his black suit. His black hair was shaved close to his head, Marines-style, and beads of sweat appeared from his forehead as quickly as he could dab them away with his kerchief. He swayed slightly as he spoke, as if a strong wind was pushing him from side to side.

"My name is Eddie Bauhmer."

Immediately, the name sounded familiar. Eddie Bauhmer... how do I know this guy? I racked my brain, but couldn't come up with the answer.

His voice boomed over the microphone as he spoke; it was so deep and rich that I doubted Eddie needed a mike at all. "My mother died of cancer when I was only three years old, and my father had a hard time keeping a job, due to his alcoholism. Me and my two sisters frequently moved from town to town, school to school; Dad lost most his jobs as soon as he found them."

Despite his awkward swaying, Eddie was a good speaker. He looked comfortable and relaxed, even though he had the attention of hundreds of people on him. He spoke slowly and clearly and made eye contact with as many people as he could. "We were far from rich, to say the least," he said with a grin that accentuated his double chin. "Me and my sisters only had a few pairs of clothes, and sometimes we had to go without dinner. I've obviously made up for the lack of food from my youth, though!" Eddie laughed as he rubbed his sizeable midsection, which made it okay for us to chuckle as well. I liked this guy, but I still didn't know how he knew Dave. He was getting to that.

"It was tough, bouncing around from one school to the next. I rarely made any friends, and if I did, I knew that sooner or later Dad would get fired, and we'd have to move on to the next town.

"By the time I turned sixteen, I was sick of it," he said with a solemn expression on his tanned, round face. "Dad lost another job, and I thought to myself, 'This is it. I'm going to make a busload of new friends this time.' I was sick and tired of being an outcast because of my ragged clothes and my shyness; yes, no one that knows me believes me, but there *was* a time in my life when I was shy!" A smile stretched across his face as he patted down some sweat that had condensed on his large forehead. Eddie kept the kerchief in his hand and continued. "I went into my new high school that day with a great hope that this would be a fresh start for me. I had it in my head that for whatever the reason, this school would be different from all the others. The kids there would accept me for who I was, and not only would they not make fun of me, they'd invite me to play football with them, they'd introduce me to all the pretty girls, and they'd include me in every cool thing they were doing."

Eddie shook his head and arched his eyebrows as he said, "My high expectations came crashing down on me hard. Because I believed that this time would be different, the kids' teasing hit me harder than it ever had before." He frowned and said, "I was pushed to my limit; I had had enough."

He sighed, wiped the corners of his mouth, and leaned forward while resting his hands on the podium. "I made up my mind quickly and irrationally about what I was going to do about it. My dad had an old thirty-eight snub-nosed pistol that he kept in a shoebox under his bed. I was going to bring it into school the next day, kill whoever happened to be the first one to taunt me, then put the last bullet in my head."

No sound was made for the next few seconds. The stillness of the large crowd seemed to be a sound of its own. Eddie certainly had everyone's attention.

"I walked into school the next morning with Dad's gun in my backpack. I could hardly believe that I was actually going to go through with my plan. I felt a sick, disturbing rush, as I envisioned what I was about to do. I can't say how sick or disturbing it seemed to me at the time..." Eddie shook his head, staring blankly over the crowd. "But my gut wrenches whenever I recall that moment."

He took a deep breath and exhaled loudly. "I went to my locker and unzipped a side pouch where I had stashed the gun. I stood there and stared at all the kids walking by, basically daring them, *wanting* them, to tease me. But no one did.

"The bell rang, so I tossed my backpack in the locker, knowing that the kids wouldn't harass me in front of a teacher. After taking attendance in Homeroom, the bell rang again, and we all filed out to prepare for our first class for the day. Although I had no intention of ever stepping into another classroom, or any room for that matter.

"The moment that I stepped into the hall, I heard some snickering behind me. There were some kids, whispering loudly enough for me to hear and probably doing so intentionally, about how I smelled so bad and making jokes about my messy hair.

"I almost smiled; for the first time in my life; I was glad that I was being made fun of, because for the first time in my life, I was going to get revenge. I knew that I'd have to kill myself afterwards, but I honestly didn't care. I was happy to reach the end of my miserable life."

A strong wind blew through the air, nearly causing me to fall off my chair. I had no idea how close to the edge of my seat I was.

"By the time I reached my locker, a small crowd had gathered around me. They were all either laughing, pointing, or making rude comments about me. I tried to pay no attention to what they were saying, and focused only on getting into my locker and opening fire. It would have been like shooting fish in a barrel.

"But my locker wouldn't open." Eddie paused to swallow a lump in his throat, and tears began to well in his bright blue eyes. "I tried and tried, but I couldn't get it unlocked. It was stuck. All the while, the kids kept on making fun of me, and all I could do was just stand there with my back to them and pretend like I couldn't hear their taunts."

A warm flush enveloped my face as my jaw dropped; I remembered this...I *saw* it happening...I had been laughing along with the crowd, as I leaned against the wall by the drinking fountain. I knew who Eddie Bahmer was.

"I almost gave up and broke down in tears, but I wouldn't allow that to happen. Their barrage of insults only added fuel to the rage that I was feeling, and I went back to trying to get my locker open, never saying a word to anyone or looking at them, but wanting so badly to retrieve the gun and shut them up."

Eddie's bottom lip began to quiver uncontrollably. "Then out of nowhere, Dave comes up to me." His voice was a few octaves higher than normal, and he was struggling to get the words out. "And he smiles at me..." Tears ran down his cheeks, and he paused to gain some composure. "And he talked to me like I was his friend, even though I had never even seen him before. He opened my locker with a hard tug on the handle, and even defended me in front of his peers. The kids obviously respected Dave, because they stopped making fun of me. He walked with me to my first class and told me that the kids who were making fun of me were his friends, but they were idiots." Eddie chuckled as he wiped his eyes dry. His facial expression turned from a grin to dead serious in a flash. He slowly scanned the crowd, seemingly taking in each pair of eyes before saying, "That simple act of kindness prevented the ruination of countless lives, including mine."

I relived that moment with Eddie as he described what had happened. Except I wasn't the poor kid taking abuse from others while contemplating awful thoughts. I was one of the kids laughing at him.

Every inch of my body was frozen in place as if I were a statue. On the outside, at least. Inwardly, my stomach seemed to have sunk below my waistline, and my heart was beating so fast and loud that I was sure Anne could hear it.

*Dear Lord, forgive me!*

"Thank God for Dave," Eddie said. "But saving my life isn't the half of what Dave did for me. By the power and grace of God, he also had a role, a very important one, in saving my soul."

He paused and bowed his head for a moment, gathering his thoughts.

There was something about Eddie; I couldn't quite put my finger on it, but my initial reaction of liking him was only strengthened as he stood before us all and spoke. He was genuine. That was for sure. He wasn't trying to gain any sympathy, he didn't bad-mouth the kids who had teased him...or had laughed at him. There was just something about the guy.

"I ended up staying at Auburn High School, where I had met Dave, for almost six months. One of Dad's longest runs at keeping a job, before he overcame his alcoholism, that is.

"Dave and I became good friends. He was..." Eddie furrowed his brow in contemplation for a moment, then said, "...*is*, with the exception of my wife, the best friend that I have ever had. Even though for the last few months of my stay at Auburn Dave and I...well, he started hanging out with a different crowd, and I saw less and less of him every week; but he still was without a doubt my best friend.

"We exchanged addresses, and promised to write each other and to stay in touch as much as possible. I was moving to Ohio, so telephone calls would be too costly. For a while we wrote to each other once a week, but before long I was sending out ten letters without getting any response back. So I stopped writing him, figuring that he had gotten sick of me or whatever."

Eddie took a deep breath and sighed, dabbing some beads of sweat from the side of face as he did so. "I graduated from high school in South Bend, Illinois, two years after I met Dave. I hadn't heard from him in well over a year, so I decided to give him a call. I wanted to thank him; I had never told Dave, or at that time *anyone*, how he had unknowingly saved my life and the lives of others that day at school. I had saved his number along with his address, so I picked up the phone and dialed, hoping he hadn't moved away.

"To my delight, Dave answered the phone. When I heard his voice, I remember thinking that he was going to think I was weird for calling him after all the time that had passed. I started thinking, 'Why would he want to talk to me? Why would he care?'

"I almost hung up.

"But I couldn't. No matter what, I had to tell him how he had saved me. I had to tell him how important he was to me.

"So I said, 'Hi, Dave. This is Eddie Bahmer. You probably don't remember me too well-' Before I could go any further, he cut me off. He said something like, 'Of course I remember you! Wow, this is awesome; I've been praying for you!'

"He explained that he had written me a few letters lately, but I hadn't gotten them, because I was no longer living at that address. After he received a 'Return To Sender' letter he had written for me, he assumed that either I had moved, or I was mad at him for not staying in contact.

"After I assured Dave that I was in no way angry at him, I asked why was he praying for me. He told me that a good friend of his had died in a plane crash years ago, and he had felt extreme remorse because he had never shared Jesus with his friend. Dave said that God had put it on his heart to speak with me about Him, so after he had tried and failed at contacting me, he prayed about it and trusted in God."

Eddie stood still for a few seconds as a distant look appeared in his eyes. He then looked about the crowd and said softly, "I have learned of that trust since then. When Dave first tried to explain it to me it seemed ...well, farfetched. I thought the idea of there being a God was ridiculous. Why would I be living such a crummy life if there were a God Who loved me? Why had my Mom died? Why was Dad an alcoholic?

"All those thoughts passed through my mind as Dave told me about Jesus. I listened just to be polite, keeping my arguments about the existence of God to myself.

"Dave must have picked up on my unbelief by the way I answered some of his questions. But he wasn't pushy or demanding; at the end of our conversation he said, 'Write me or call me any time. I'll keep praying for you.'

"It wasn't until after I got off the phone with him that I realized I had forgotten the reason I had called. I never told Dave about that day in school; I never thanked him for being my friend or for saving my life."

Eddie sighed and breathed the air out through his nostrils, looking down at the podium for a few seconds. "Dave didn't convert me. Initially. But I found myself thinking about his words a lot over the next few days. His belief in Jesus was emphatic. His faith undeniable. Despite my reservations about Christianity, his words struck a chord with me. Dave was the most kind, caring individual I had ever met. And I could tell by his use of vocabulary and the way he presented his case for Christ, that his intellect had vastly matured over the last two years. But was the good inside of him due to the Lord living in his heart, as Dave had claimed? Or was he just a smart, nice young man deluded by religion?

"It took me a week of brooding over these thoughts until I realized that Dave had sparked an interest in me. I wanted to know if Jesus was real.

"I ended up going to a nearby church the following Sunday. I sat in the back pew and listened, trying to keep an open mind about what I was hearing. I found myself in the same church the next Sunday, and the Sunday after that."

Eddie smiled widely, revealing his pearly white teeth. "If I shared with you the intricacies of all that followed, I'd be up here for a very long time. I became saved. Then my sisters did, too, and finally, my dad.

"Dad, after almost fifteen years of alcoholism, never picked up the bottle again. We moved to Salt Water Springs in Idaho, and for the first time it wasn't because Dad had gotten fired; he had gotten promoted.

"We quickly found a church we liked, and our family went together every Sunday. I found myself drawn towards becoming a missionary; I wanted to share my Jesus with the poor and neglected people of the world. Probably because I could relate to them."

He soaked up some more sweat with his red handkerchief; the thing had to be as damp as a wet paper towel by now. "Our church had a training program in which they'd train you for missionary work, then send you out to a Third World country. I got a job at a potato farm to pay my way, and two years later, I completed my training and was sent to Jakarta, Indonesia."

Eddie arched his eyebrows and said, "And I thought *I* was poor! These people live in mud huts and sleep atop straw on the dirt. Mice and scorpions indoors are as common as the swarms of flies outside. I had been told that this was how it was over there, but it never really hits you until you see it with your own eyes.

"I'm still in Jakarta, and the Lord is certainly doing some great things over there; especially with the children." Eddie smiled, and his eyes stared off at nothing in particular, as if he were seeing the kids in his mind's eye. "The reason I'm here in the States right now is because I met my wife in Jakarta, and she gave birth to our first baby girl five days ago." Some light applause sounded through the crowd, and Eddie beamed. "It's funny- she lived so close to me in Idaho, but I had to literally travel half way around the world to meet her."

His grin faded to a near frown as he said, "When I got home a week ago, I realized that I had been so busy with all I was doing that I had forgotten about Dave and what he did for me." He shook his head, as if he was ashamed, while biting down on his lower lip. "So I called him, what was it? Four days ago, and told him about me and my family becoming Christians, and how I was a missionary, married, and a father. He was ecstatic to hear from me, and kept on saying, 'Praise God! Praise God!'

"I told Dave that it wouldn't have been possible without him, and without hesitation he said, 'No, Eddie; it wouldn't have been possible without God.'

"And he was right, but still..." He looked up at he sky, lost in thought. Turning his attention back to the crowd, he said, "If Dave hadn't unknowingly come to my rescue that day at my locker, would I be here right now? If he hadn't shared Christ with me, would I be saved? Would my sisters, my father? Would I be a missionary in Jakarta, with a beautiful wife and baby girl?"

Eddie let his questions soak in our minds for a while before continuing.

"I wanted to tell Dave about that day so long ago, when he had stopped an awful thing from happening just by being nice. I also wanted to do it face-to-face. So I asked him if I could stop by with pictures of my wife and child, and he said that would be great." He stared down at the podium for a long time. His bottom lip began to tremble, and when he spoke it was with an anguished tone. "I showed up at his house two days ago...and his mother told me that he was dead!"

Eddie's eyes closed abruptly, as if he had just been socked in the face. He turned to the side and wept, his large shoulders heaving rapidly.

I looked over at Mom, and she was crying just as hard.

Eddie controlled himself enough to go on, but tears were still streaming down his face as he said, "When we get to Heaven, I believe there'll be a time for us to tell certain people how very much they impacted our lives, and to thank them properly in ways we just can't do now."

He looked up at the sky, as if he could see Dave up there; as if he was looking right at him. An expression of joy overtook his face as he said, "And I just know that Dave's going to have a line of people a mile long waiting to see him. I'm going to fight my way to the front of that line," he said with determination, "so I can be the first one to tell him, to really tell him, how much I love him, how important he was and is to me." His whole body began to tremble, but his eyes never parted from the sky; the look of determination never left his face. His voice quivered, and his eyes poured out tears as he said, "And then I'm going to walk a mile back to the end of the line, just so I can say 'thank you' again!"

If there had been any dry eyes in the audience up to that point, they were now saturated with tears. My vision became so blurry that I barely made out Eddie as he left the podium and went back to his seat.

I had thought before that there was something about Eddie; something that made me like him, but I couldn't quite put my finger on it. I realized then what it was. He was humble, funny, smart, had a special place in his heart for the poor. He loved God, gave Him all the credit and lived his life for Him.

It became clear to me; he reminded me of Dave.

# Afterword

In the beginning, I told you that I was going to tell you a story that you probably weren't going to believe. Perhaps some of you feel cheated.

That's good; that means that you believe in miracles.

Either that, or they were so subtle that you didn't recognize them. The most obvious one, I think, is Dave's mother, Joyce, recovering from her heart attack. There were other ones; maybe not as spectacular as parting the sea or turning water into wine. But they are miracles nonetheless.

I'm talking about changing the entire course of an individual's life by being a friend to them. Isn't that miraculous? Or is it unbelievable?

How about overcoming the powerful addiction of drugs and alcohol and doing a 180 from living a life of sin to living a life for God? Miraculous? Unbelievable?

How about this: you love God and follow Him closely, reading His Word and having faith in Him; you admit that you're a sinner, and Jesus is your only hope of salvation; you hunger and thirst for Him as if finding Him was your next breath, your next meal dependent on your chasing and finding the Lord. And because of all this, His perfect and loving will is done in your life - something you could never even imagine constructing on your own.

Miraculous? I'd sure say so!

You may never know how much you have impacted a person's life just by living yours as a Christian. The Bible says, "Never tire in doing what is good, for in due season we will reap a harvest if we do not give up."

Sometimes being a Christian is hard. Many times it is. It was meant to be this way. Many times I have cried out, "Lord, Lord! I can't do it! I can't go on!" And you know what He has told me, time after time after time? "That's right, Daniel, you can't go on. You can't do it. That's why I am here."

"With man this is impossible, but with God all things are possible."

I pray that you live your life in love, faith, and fear towards God. And I pray wholeheartedly that this book has allowed you to see Him more clearly.

# Special Thanks

Jesus: You know there is no simple 'Thank You' that I, or anyone, could put into words to say how much You truly mean to me. I think the best way of showing my thanks is by living a life that's pleasing to You. We both know I need help with that; I thank You that I have that help. Thank You for the cross. Thank You for Your love. Thank You for never giving up on Your prodigal son.

Most of the characters in my story I didn't have to make up. Their love and dedication to me are as real as they are amazing. Without them,…well, I don't even want to think about it. Mom: You have dealt with me for twenty-six years now; what's your secret? God knew I needed someone real special for a Mother; someone who could raise three children on her own. Someone who could wake up early every day to pack three lunches, go to work, come home after a long hard day and cook dinner, then spend every possible second with her children so that they knew they were loved. Someone to take her boys to baseball practices and games almost every night of the week, and to buy them ice cream, even though extra money was as rare as a snowless winter in New York. Someone who could take the angry insults hurled at her by her son. Someone who could stand by him while he was addicted to drugs. Someone who would love him no matter what. He gave me you; I thank God every day He did. The treasure you have stored up in Heaven must be its own little world.

Don: My brother, and so much more. You are always looking out for me, always making me feel special. I know me, so I know that's hard to do! You taught me how to play basketball and baseball as a kid, how to love the game and have fun. You also taught me how to golf, but I think you might be withholding some knowledge since I can never beat you! You reared me as a father would, and I know you will make a great one. You taught me so many things, among which what friendship is all about; I am proud to call you my brother and my best friend.

Angie: Little Sis. How does someone younger than me teach me so much? Yet you have. I look back fifteen years ago and see a little girl who I always made fun of. Now I see a beautiful young lady whom I admire so much. I am proud of you, for your dedication to the Lord, and everything you are doing with your life. There are those who show their faith by what they say, and those who show their faith by what they do. You do both. Keep on singing, keep on praising God in your heart and with your voice. You have no idea how many people you will touch. I love you.

Kevin: You have been my Dad for a few years now, and what an indescribable blessing you have been to not only me, but to our entire family. You didn't forcefully take me in, you did it with love and kindness. When I needed help with anything, you were always there. You set your time aside and gave it to me. You're one of the few people I can beat in golf. You are a wonderful source of counsel and wisdom, bringing cheer with you wherever you go. I have learned a lot from you, and am sure to learn a lot more. It is an extreme rarity, almost a paradox, that one man could possess such knowledge and such humility. You have taken the name 'Dad' and made me love it again. For that I am forever thankful.

Thank you to Aunt Beth, for your pumpkin pies and for editing the book. Thanks to Anne, simply for being the person that you are: a kind, warm, fun-loving girl who didn't get mad at me for thinking she was a veterinarian. For Debbie Restivo, for reading the rough draft, for your constant encouragement, and your friendship. To Anna and Mike Tower, for your much needed support. Rob Carter; I wonder if I would have ever published this, had it not been for your contagious enthusiasm. For Uncle Duane- a quiet man filled with godly wisdom, Uncle Dennis and Aunt Sheila- for taking me in, for the summer camping, for the golf clubs and your unwavering kindness, Aunt Sue- as a teenager I could talk to you about things that I couldn't with anybody else, Aunt Cherrie- for taking care of us when Mom was away at work for all those years, Uncle Jim and Aunt Alice-I don't remember everything that you did for us all, but that which I do remember constitutes my undying thanks, Uncle Tom's, Uncle Dick, Aunt Amy, Aunt Leigh and Uncle Chuck- for your hospitality and all the times you fed me at your table, Uncle Ron- even before you married my aunt you treated me better than I deserved. Donald and Ethel (Betty) Ashbery- no words of praise would do you justice. You are the two most loving, unselfish people I have ever met. My fondest memories of you are every moment we ever shared, and I will carry them with me forever. You served me the strongest form of love; unconditional and mixed with rebuke, and our entire family has been blessed to have you both in our lives. Charles and Hilda Cater, through it all you always took care of us. You could have forgotten about your grandkids, but you never did, not for a moment. You have been extremely generous to us all, and gave us more than we deserve. Thank you for your love. All my aunts, all my uncles, all my cousins; anybody who ever had to deal with me, in fact. I love you all.

Printed in the United States
51763LVS00004B/67-306

9 781600 341380